When a man loves a woman

Recovering addict Nick Dorsey finds solace in his regimented life. That is until he meets Shyla Metha. Something about the shy Indian beauty who delivers take-out to his Greenwich Village loft inspires the reclusive writer. And when Shyla reveals her desire to write a book of her own, he agrees to help her. The tale of a young Indian girl growing up against a landscape of brutal choices isn't Nick's usual territory, but something about the story, and the beautiful storyteller, draws him in deep.

Shyla is drawn to Nick, but she never imagines falling for him. Like Nick, Shyla hails from a village, too…a rural village in India. They have nothing in common, yet he makes her feel alive for the first time in her life. She is not ready for their journey to end, but the plans she's made cannot be broken…not even by him. Can they find a way to rewrite the next chapter?

I0679335

Books by MK Schiller

Unwanted Girl

Published by Kensington Publishing Corporation

Unwanted Girl

MK Schiller

LYRICAL PRESS
Kensington Publishing Corp.
www.kensingtonbooks.com

First Electronic Edition: January 2016
eISBN-13: 1978-1-60183-500-0
eISBN-10: -60183-500-0

First Print Edition: January 2016
ISBN-13: 978-1-60183-501-7
ISBN-10: 1-60183-501-9

To Papa for teaching me to enjoy the learning as much as the lesson. You will always be in my heart.

Author's Foreword

My daughter asked me to watch a documentary with her about female gendercide, a subject I had little knowledge on, but I can tell you it haunted me afterward. I was shocked to discover how rampant the problem was even among middle-class families. I wondered if it was possible for a girl who'd had firsthand struggles with this kind of unforgivable violence to have a happily ever after. Then I remembered I was a romance novelist, and I could make it happen…at least in fiction form. I promise that although this book deals with heavy topics, it is at its core a love story, and an optimistic one at that.

For more information on Female Gendercide, please visit http://www.gendercide.org/case_infanticide.html

Acknowledgements

I think every child remembers that one piece of advice a parent gives to you that becomes part of your blood and bones. For me, my papa always said no matter what anyone takes from you, they can never take away your education. He further supported these words by taking me to the library every weekend and encouraging me to check out as many books as I could devour in a week's time. In later years, my mom would always buy me a book at the grocery store, no matter how little we had or how many coupons she had to clip. Occasionally, she turned the other way when a paperback with a shirtless, longhaired muscular man made its way into our cart. "I suppose any reading is good reading," she'd say.

It's fitting that the first people I shared the idea that became Unwanted Girl with were my parents. Actually, I think it's the only book I've written that didn't turn my face a splotchy shade of pink when describing it. My papa was proud of the concept and my mother....well, she was just proud of me in general.

Shortly after I received the contract on this work, they were both hospitalized with major health issues in a land far away from me. In addition, I was struggling with my own depression. I can honestly say it was the darkest time of my life. Had it not been for these thoughtful individuals, this work may not have seen the light of your e-reader.

To my children and husband who held my hand through every ugly cry (and trust me, I have never cried pretty).

To all my relatives, some of which I hadn't spoke to in twenty years, who looked after my parents and me.

To my writers group who encouraged me to write through the emotion and more importantly, to write with it.

To my editor, Corinne DeMaagd and agent, Amanda Leuck, who took a chance on my work, refined my heap of words, and understood the personal pressures I was under.

To all my friends, who somehow made the sun shine even in the darkest times.

To my readers who supported me in every way (and a special thank you to Susan who sent chocolate-covered mangos!).

Most of all to Mommy and Papa for never limiting my world.

All of these people represent my world and I would walk around them in three full circles if I could.

Ultimately, this book is about family. The family you're born to and the ones you pick up along the way.

Chapter 1

Nick Dorsey ran every morning, although he no longer ventured to guess whether he was chasing dreams or fleeing demons. As he exited the brick building on Bleecker to a grim, grayish sky, the promise of another sunless day revealed itself.

His feet pounded the pavement in a stride that ranged from sprint to run to jog, matching the same footpaths as TS Eliot, Faulkner, and Poe. He'd insisted on the Village because it was a literary mecca. Although, these days, it could be argued the high rents favored capitalists over the creatives.

He'd hunted for months with a petite blond realtor until she found a place in his price range. The realtor was intelligent and assertive—during negotiations and sex—two traits Nick valued. In the end, it got him a nice place in the West Village with a working elevator, architectural charm, and original hardwood floors. It got her a fat commission check and about the same number of orgasms. Too bad the only thing he turned on these days was his computer…and that relationship was near terminal.

He rounded Thompson Avenue, passing the bookstore where his latest novel occupied the window. He allowed the smallest flicker of pride before picking up speed. How far he'd come from the poor kid whose life was hand-me-down clothes and secondhand books.

He reached Washington Square Park ready to do a complete loop. Nick's runs used to consist of random thoughts about his characters and plot points. The beauty of being a writer was you could work anywhere anytime. One of the best scenes he'd ever written was during a tax audit. Now, his mind lacked the spark required to conjure creativity. He emerged from the park, slowing his pace until he reached the glass door of The Ole Time Floral shop with its annoying wreath of greenery and bells that signaled his arrival.

"A white rose, please," he said to the florist, who was already reaching into the barrel to retrieve the item.

"You know, dear, its romantic how you buy her a rose every day, but I'm sure she'd be more impressed with a whole bouquet at once."

Nick frowned. "I don't want to impress her. I just want her to know I'm there."

The lady arched a bushy brow, waiting for further explanation, but Nick did not intend to satisfy her unsolicited curiosity. He shoved the money at her and clutched the thorny bud in his hand. She no longer asked if he wanted it wrapped with a sprig of greenery.

He ran an additional mile until he reached the tranquil snow-covered grounds behind an ornate metal gate on Sullivan Street. It looked like a park with its lush landscape of willow trees and benches, but the stone angels, marble pillars, and simple markers jutting from the ground gave away its identity.

He fell to his knees, the crunch of fresh snow against hard earth disturbing the serenity. Nick gulped in the cold desolate air, reading her gravestone for the thousandth time, even though every curl of the fancy lettering chiseled on the surface was already etched into his brain. He'd become a creature of habit, and the repetition of every act provided a strange comfort. He bowed his head, joined his hands together, and begged in silence for forgiveness that would never come.

An hour later, showered and freshly dressed, he walked through the heavy wooden doors of the old church on Grand, the location of his second daily errand. Nick originally chose the ten a.m. timeframe to avoid crowds. It was flawed logic, bordering on reckless naiveté since the term "avoid crowds" was a fool's ambition in this city. Although there weren't any stockbrokers or executives, plenty of actors, singers, and housewives packed the large room. They all chatted amicably while drinking percolated coffee, which Nick, a coffee connoisseur, admitted was the best he'd ever had.

He sat in the uncomfortable metal chair, waiting for the meeting to come to order. When the time came, Nick spoke clearly and honestly.

"I'm Nick Dorsey, and I am a meth addict. It's been eighteen months, two weeks, and three days since my last fix." He talked about his addiction until his three minutes of indulgent introspection were up and his Styrofoam cup runneth empty.

He arrived back at the Bleecker Street loft with all his errands accomplished, but no sense of accomplishment for it. Gaping at his keyboard, a fresh cup of caffeine in his hand and a stifling lack of imagination, he sat down.

Wanting to alleviate the harsh glare of the blank page, he clicked on the keyboard in quick snapping strokes. *The rain fell in thick sheets as if the sky weighed in on Max's decision.*

Shit.

Did he actually start the fucking book with a weather report? The greats—George Orwell, Charles Dickens, or Dr. Seuss were capable of such openings, but Nick Dorsey was not. He hit the backspace, erasing every individual character with a scorning strike. He wondered what other words could describe rain. He walked over to the large bookshelf that spanned an entire wall. As it turned out, Webster's had thirty-two words for precipitation from the descriptive *drencher* to the very simple *wet stuff.*

He slammed the book shut, tired of his pathetic attempts at procrastination.

He didn't mind the timid knock at nine p.m., though. That was a welcome break from the unrelenting flutter of the cursor.

Sandwich girl was here and right on time.

He opened the door, and there she stood as she had almost every night for the past year since he'd discovered the corner deli delivered. The tall, thin girl with raven hair offered a nervous smile. He often speculated on the length of her hair. She always wore it in a tightly coiled bun except for the few loose strands that framed her face.

When her smile widened just right, it would create the slightest dimple on her left cheek. As much as he enjoyed the appearance of the dimple, what struck him the most was her accent. He'd heard all kinds of Asian accents, but never one as lyrical as hers with each simple word drawn out softly, a seductive hum as it left her lips. Her loose trench coat, too mild for this weather, slipped off one shoulder as she inched her knapsack higher on the other.

"Hello," she said cheerfully, handing him the brown paper bag that contained his turkey and Swiss on whole wheat.

"Hiya, Sandwich Girl." It was their usual greeting. No names—the time for civilized introductions had passed long ago.

He fished a twenty from his wallet. She shoved her hand in her pocket searching for change.

"Keep it," he said.

"Thank you. That's very generous."

Why they went through the same motions, he didn't know, except she was polite and unassuming, and he found a certain comfort in the repetition. "Don't mention it."

Her head began shifting downward, but she paused and lifted her gaze to meet his. In the beginning, the shy girl would never look him in the face, throwing the bag at him and taking off before he yelled after her that he had yet to pay. Then she'd slowly shuffle back, her head down, holding out her trembling hand. Now, they held actual conversation between them, and although it lacked any depth, those few minutes became the most enjoyable part of his scheduled day.

"It's getting nicer outside. I think spring will arrive early this year," she said.

"Is that so?" Maybe she believed Nick never went out, and her weather reports were a necessary service to give him insight into the subtle climactic shifts of his own environment. Or maybe she was just making small talk.

"Yes, but it might rain." She dropped her voice as if conveying a secret. "I think it *will* rain actually."

"Will it be a soaker, a mist, or a monsoon?" he asked, happy to apply the seldom-used words to his vernacular. The thesaurus hadn't been a waste of time.

She clutched her jacket around her. "Definitely a drencher. I don't think we have to worry about monsoons on this side of the world."

"Your forecasts have never been accurate…not once."

She bit her lower lip, her expression thoughtful. "Really?"

"Nope. But in case you're right, do you have an umbrella?"

"I don't have far to go."

"Wait here." He set the bag on a console table and grabbed an umbrella from the hall closet. "Take this."

"Oh no, I couldn't."

"You can return it tomorrow." He held it out to her until she gripped her fingers around it.

"Thank you."

"Be safe."

She'd rewarded him with a brilliant, dimple-inducing smile the first time he'd said that, and it became his customary farewell to her in the days that followed. The smile never disappointed.

"Good-night."

"Night," he said, leaning against the doorjamb until the elevator arrived.

A minute later, he strolled to the window and watched her exit onto the street, headed north on Bleecker, her coat flapping around her. He reassured himself it was the comfort of routine along with the quality deli meat he craved. It had nothing to do with the delivery girl. Never mind he opted for Chinese or pizza on Wednesdays and Sundays—her days off. Sure, she was a pretty girl, but definitely not his type. He preferred the kind of women he wrote about...buxom blondes and rambunctious redheads with confident personas and hungry appetites.

This girl was shy, awkward...and for some reason, intriguing. He had no idea why he looked forward to their silly chats, except they made him a little happier. Any ounce of happiness was such a rare occurrence in Nick's life, he seized it gratefully.

Nick started the process of shutting down the computer. He'd eat, work out for a few hours, take a shower, read, and go to bed. The same as he did every night. He hesitated at the customary question of *Do you want to save changes?* There were no changes to save.

He cracked his knuckles and stretched his back. His fingers landed on the keys like a mocking friend, both beckoning and humiliating him in that order. Except now, the words coursed through his hands with great speed and little consideration as the page filled.

Sandwich girl, you are a mystery. A sweet, sad smile that never reaches your big brown eyes. Silky hair tucked and clipped away as if forgotten, save for the few rebellious strands struggling for freedom. Would you welcome my advance or retreat into the shadows? I can see your inexperience, an odd fit, wrapping around you like another coat. But there's something else there, too. A profound strength that exists as if you're a lone soldier, battling your way through a battered life.

Nick highlighted the section and hovered a finger above the delete key. Instead, he labeled the document *Sandwich Girl* and saved it to his hard drive. It wasn't his best work and nothing he could use in a novel, but it meant something to him. It represented the first paragraph he'd managed in almost two years.

* * * *

Shyla Metha watched his window from a darkened corner some distance away. On warmer days, she'd stand in this area for twenty minutes until sufficiently shamed by her lurking. Still, she was drawn to him.

It wasn't just his looks, although she couldn't deny the pull of his broad shoulders, sandy hair that fell somewhere between brown and blond, and dark ocean-colored eyes. The beard was interesting, too, creating an air of mystery around him. Funny, she'd never expected to be attracted to physical characteristics so different from her own, yet she'd developed a dimwitted crush on this boy...man.

He'd been aloof in the beginning, and she was timid, a combination that never mixed, but one day she'd added a comment about the weather, and he had grinned, the rigid stiffness of his posture easing for a few seconds. Although they came from different worlds, they had something in common. Nick Dorsey was lonely and sad…perhaps even broken.

She clutched the black umbrella in her hand. Her time was growing short. She'd be returning home when her student visa expired at the end of the semester. Now was the time for risks! Or rather tomorrow when he ordered another sandwich.

Chapter 2

Dressed in a charcoal suit, Nick entered the fancy fusion restaurant, wondering why he hadn't tried to cancel again. Not that Carrie would accept anymore of his bullshit excuses. He adjusted the noose-like knot of his navy necktie as the maître d' showed him to the table. Carrie sat in the corner booth sporting a bright pink dress and even brighter red hair that rebelled against the sedate opulence of the monochromatic colors surrounding her. Unlike him, she enjoyed dressing up. She crossed her legs, pointing the toe of her red-soled, polished heel toward Nick.

"Do you always have to pick a pretentious restaurant?" he asked before kissing her cheek. He took the seat across from her.

"When it's a tax write-off, I do." She leaned in as if revealing a secret. "The duck here is to die for."

"I won't be dying today," Nick replied.

"You look great, Nick. You've been working out…a lot," she said, reaching across the table to squeeze his bicep. "You have a license for these guns?"

"I'm taking advantage of the gym in my building."

"What's your regimen?"

"I doubled up on my running time. I do reps of one-armed push-ups, sit ups, and chin-ups." He continued on, detailing his nightly ritual, until he noticed her eyes shifting around the room. "Shit, you don't want to hear about this, right?"

"It's interesting, but honestly you lost me somewhere between progressive overload and muscle confusion. Who knew there were so many terms?"

"I do," he snapped. "I'm trying to explain them to you." Nick sucked in a deep breath, wishing he could erase his harsh statement. Carrie was there for him when he needed someone most, and here he was acting like a complete dickhead.

"I'm sorry." He ordered a tumbler of Johnnie Walker Blue from the waiter.

"Nick." She leaned into the table, her voice stern but compassionate at the same time. "It's me, remember? Your best friend?"

"How are you, friend?"

"I'm well." The waiter set down her Chardonnay and Nick's Scotch. Carrie interrupted in the middle of his specials spiel, requesting another moment. "Are you allowed to drink?" she asked, as soon as the waiter departed.

Nick winked, trying to put her at ease, because the line of questioning certainly wasn't doing much for either of them. "I'm twenty-seven years old. I'm pretty sure I've surpassed the legal drinking age in this town."

"You know what I mean."

"I wasn't an alcoholic, Carrie."

Nick searched for the waiter, but he was nowhere in sight. "What did you want to talk about? As I recall, this is a business meeting."

"We can get to that," she replied, waving a hand at the hot bread on the table like a game show hostess, displaying a parting prize.

"Are you trying to con me with carbohydrates?"

"You have to try this bread. You can dip it in this extra fine, extra virgin olive oil or use this French herb butter."

"I prefer my olive oil with a little experience. It should, at the very least, mature to second base."

Carrie laughed much louder than the joke required. "I swear you'll make me bust a button on this dress."

"I'd be a very talented man if I could undress a woman without touching her."

"Indeed," she agreed. "Flirting has always been your..." She paused, searching for the right word.

"Strong suit?" Nick offered.

"Coping mechanism," she retorted.

"Ouch. Well then, I suppose we should get down to business."

"Why the rush? I haven't seen you in a long time, Dorsey. Let's catch up."

"I want to make sure you get your well-earned tax deduction."

She bit her bottom lip, her telltale sign of anxiety. "The publisher wants you to do a book tour."

"No," Nick said with enough bark that the waiter stopped just shy of approaching them and veered off in a different direction.

"Nick—"

"I've never done one, and I'm sure as hell not about to now."

"Not that your sales aren't high, but this could catapult them." She gestured toward his face. "Even though I don't approve of the Duck Dynasty beard, the fact is you're gorgeous."

"Duck Dynasty?" he asked, tilting his chin and running his fingers through the thick growth, mocking offense at her joke. "Are you fucking with me?"

"ZZ Top?"

"Try again," he said, fighting a smirk.

"All right, Brad Pitt circa *Legends of the Fall*, but that's my final offer."

"Sold!" Nick said, clapping his hand on the table. "You're always negotiating, aren't you?"

"I am an agent." She slathered butter on her bread.

He rubbed his chin. "You don't like the beard I've had for over a year now?"

"I miss your face. You have such a nice one. I bet you could sell bibles in Babylonia."

"I have a feeling you're buttering up more than bread."

"I still have eyes, despite not being interested."

"Your disinterest is a fact that I have mourned for a great many years. Along with all the other men in the five boroughs."

Carrie shook a well-manicured finger at him. "You want me to tell them no?"

"Emphatically. Also, while you're at it, inform them there won't be any more books. My character and I have irreconcilable differences. He's giving me the silent treatment."

"You're still blocked?"

"Like an iceberg. The kind that halted the Titanic."

"It happens."

"It's been a long time, Carrie." It felt good to admit things to her, to say his troubles aloud and relieve himself of the secrets, much in the same way he admitted to being an addict now. The last two books he'd given her were trunk books, squirreled away from an earlier time when writing was as natural as breathing. Now his trunk lay open, bare of any contents.

"You've had a lot going on in that time. You're not under contract, and I'll let them know there are no plans for a new book."

"Thank you, Carrie." Her quick agreement meant a great deal. After all, it wasn't only his paycheck they were discussing. "How's Maya?"

"She's good. She misses her Uncle Nick, although Tara's pretty pissed at you right now."

"Why is Tara mad? She should be happy. She got the girl after all."

Carrie shot him a reproachful glance, but her mouth quirked, fighting her grin. "She's still upset about your Christmas present. Who sends a puppy to another person's kid?"

Nick shrugged innocently. "I have a reputation to protect. I'm cool Uncle Nick. Besides, Maya asked for a puppy."

"Maybe next time ask her mom…either mom."

"Are you suggesting I should hold off on the pet snake?"

He expected her to laugh, but her expression was serious. "If you want to do something for her, get your butt to Brooklyn sometime. She misses her Uncle Nick."

"I'm not the most sociable guy right now." He dropped his voice, leaning into the table. "Besides, do you really want a meth addict around your daughter?"

"Are you ready?" the waiter asked, interrupting them once more.

"A few more minutes, please," she said.

He gave them a reproachful glance before heading back toward the kitchen.

"Jesus, Carrie, what does a man have to do to get a meal around you?"

She straightened in her seat, a gesture that fell between intimidation and consideration. "I have a few more things to say. You are in recovery, and she loves you. I won't lie. We were all shocked when it came out, but you were part of our lives when you were using even though we didn't know. I don't throw people I love away even when they make stupid mistakes."

"It's more than a mistake." He slugged back his drink, searching for the courage to confront his internal conflicts. "I was in denial for a long time…longer than you know. But I swear I never used around your family, Carrie."

"I believe you, but that's my point. Why are you ignoring us now when you need your friends the most?"

"Because I'm not in denial anymore." He couldn't explain the shame he felt for the person he was…is.

"You're living like a recluse." She waved her hands dramatically. "I don't even know how that's possible in this city, but you're managing it."

"I don't own enough luggage to pack for the all-expenses paid guilt trip you're taking me on. Now, can we table this and enjoy a steak or whatever fancy fusion name they call it in this place?"

"Watch it, or I'll downgrade that beard to Grizzly Adam status."

Chapter 3

Shyla checked over the notes from her morning classes. Every day was the same. She went to school, learned first world techniques, and mentally applied them to the third world classroom she'd be teaching. She had worked hard, so hard that in this last semester of her senior year, she had a very light load and little schoolwork left to distract her.

She started preparing for work. She twisted her long hair into a tight knot and changed into one of her black T-shirts, the uniform she wore at the deli. Each movement set at a precise pace that came with practice.

"I'm leaving for work," she told her dorm mate, Elaine, who'd had her nose in a book all afternoon.

"Oh, okay," Elaine muttered, running her hands through the purple strand of hair that broke up her natural honey coloring.

"Must be a good book."

"It's the new Keegan Moon." Elaine nodded rapidly as if that simple statement spoke volumes.

Shyla smiled, not because she agreed, but she knew better than to argue with Elaine when it came to her favorite author.

"Do you want to come out with us tonight? Everyone's coming over here, and then we'll probably go to a club or something."

Shyla had gone to a club with Elaine before. She didn't enjoy the experience. Men grabbed her as if they had some claim to her. The other girls fit in with their skimpy outfits and wild laughter. She felt out of place and wondered if the aftermath of her culture shock would ever wear off.

Elaine wiggled her eyebrows suggestively. "Joel will be there, and he's been asking about you."

"Maybe some other night."

She had gone out with Joel three times. He had seemed like a nice boy until he told her he loved Indian literature. Unfortunately, he wasn't referring to the *Bhagavad Gita*, but rather the *Kama Sutra*.

She considered Elaine a friend, but they weren't exactly close. They conversed, but they didn't have much in common. Elaine wanted to talk about television shows, designer outfits, and boys. Shyla didn't have insights, much less contributions, on those subjects. It wasn't Elaine's fault. She'd made many attempts to socialize with Shyla, but Shyla's introverted personality presented barriers. Perhaps she wasn't even capable of forming a true friendship.

* * * *

Her shift at the deli bordered on hectic, keeping her mind focused and free of Nick Dorsey, the man who made her toes curl without her consent. Geet Dhillon bustled around the kitchen, her long braid flopping around her as she floated through the space like a passenger on Aladdin's magic carpet. She'd been like this since her engagement to a successful lawyer.

"He's a nice Indian boy with a bright future," her mother had said. "He will make a fine son-in-law, and they will give me beautiful grandchildren." Her father had beamed. "He's Sikh," her brother, Adesh, had added, perhaps his only criteria in his sister's arranged nuptials. "He's hot," Geet had countered much to her brother's annoyance.

Geet sang as she worked with an infectious, bubbly energy. Shyla's expression faltered as a small pang of sadness took hold of her. The remnants of niggling jealousy followed. She hated the unwelcomed reactions, especially since the Dhillon family embraced her like one of their own.

The deli had once served the area as a thriving Indian restaurant, but the neighborhood changed and a more corporate ethnic eatery opened nearby with cheaper prices. The Dhillons were smart, though. Instead of resigning to their fate, they simply changed the menu.

Now the restaurant sold deli sandwiches and, as it turned out, there was a high demand for such things in a city where people rated convenience on par with quality. The Dhillons still sold Indian fare, too, but it was the simple sandwiches that kept them in business. Mr. Dhillon often spoke of the great American dream and how he'd come to this country with very little. There was pride in his voice when he looked at Adesh, the non-verbal passing of the torch conveyed in the exchange.

Geet turned on the small stereo, slicing through Shyla's thoughts. Bhangra music, a fusion of Punjabi folk and British rock, permeated the space, the fast-paced drums matching the girl's enthusiasm. Adesh raised his eyebrows at Shyla. Music, in her opinion, was the greatest barrier breaker that existed. Her body moved to it, responding to his unasked question. He grabbed Shyla's arm and spun her around while the Dhillon family clapped for them. She moved her hips and managed to shake her shoulders in the demure, feminine way that portrayed the subtle intricacies of Indian dance and the sexiness of Bollywood. For some reason, her shyness didn't surface with the Dhillon family. It was easy to dance with Adesh. They had clear harmony, even though they lacked chemistry.

He moved her toward a quiet corner. "I can always marry you and then you can stay," Adesh said as if the absurd idea added weight to his argument.

"You're going to marry a Hindu village girl? And a Gujarati? What will your Punjabi parents say?" she joked, although such mixed marriages were now commonplace. Still, it seemed odd when considering he insisted his sister marry a fellow Sikh.

"They'll ask the one question we Punjabis ask. Can she dance? And the answer is yes."

Shyla laughed, spinning away from him. "I'm sorry, Adesh, but I have to decline. My family has plans for me."

"You know, we can just run away together. Every happy ending begins with a good song and dance number," he said with an impish grin.

The abrupt halt of the music drew their attention. A uniformed officer walked through the door, a frown on his face.

"Is there a problem, sir?" Mr. Dhillon asked.

"We've had a complaint about the music."

The deli was empty of customers, and the radio wasn't loud, but the neighboring businesses always had issues, even though the bar across the street blared music several octaves louder.

"Our most humble apologies, policeman sir. We will keep it down," Adesh said, his voice in a high-pitched imitation of the stereotypical Indian accent. His handsome face transformed into a sour expression that bordered on a scowl. Mr. Dhillon winced.

"Be sure you do." The officer walked away but stopped and turned back once more, his gaze lingering on Mr. Dhillon's head covering.

"This is a turban," Adesh said slowly, pointing to his father's head. He held up his hands in a signal of surrender. "No need to freak, officer. We are Sikh. We come from Punjab, which is in India. India is not in Pakistan or the Middle East."

"That's enough," Mr. Dhillon admonished his son.

"I am aware of that," the officer replied. "Keep the music down and make it easier for all of us, please."

Adesh went to open his mouth, but his father clasped a hand on his son's shoulder in warning. Shyla gripped the edge of the stone countertop, silently praying for the officer's swift departure.

"Why do you incite, son?" Mrs. Dhillon asked when the officer left.

"Because they have no right to judge us. There are two kinds of people in this country. The ones who think we're lovable people because they've watched *Slumdog Millionaire* and those who believe we are terrorists because of our skin color and turbans."

"I didn't bring you here for a better life to watch you throw it away with your hostility. That's not who we are. You insult our crowns with your disrespect," Mr. Dhillon said.

Although Shyla was Hindu and not Sikh, she knew enough to understand the turban represented the Sikh identity and the commitment to their faith. It wasn't a piece of cloth, but rather their own self-crowning and desire to live like their guru who fought for equality and peace. In recent years, the turban had falsely transformed into a symbol of terrorism. Funny how meanings could be misconstrued. The Hindus had considered the swastika a visual image for good luck long before Hitler shifted the design for his own purposes.

Shyla headed toward the kitchen. The previous jovial mood had dissolved into thin air. She organized the next day's deli platter orders, trying to ignore Adesh's hostile voice.

It wasn't long before he found her. "My dad's always on my ass," he said, moving to stand beside her. "Can you believe that bullshit?"

"The officer was doing his job. He has to respond to every complaint."

His frown turned to a glare. Clearly, he had sought her out in search of an ally, and she'd failed him yet again.

"I understand why—" she began, but his bitter laugh cut her sentence short.

"You understand nothing, gullible girl. I guess it's true what they say. You can take the girl from the village, but you can never wash the village off the girl."

The order slips fell from her shaking hand. She'd had it. Her anger required a great deal of fuel, but Adesh had sparked it like a lit match tossed into a keg of kerosene.

She lowered her voice, but her words came with clipped clarity. "You think because I wasn't born here I can't understand racism? You think it's hard to live here because people judge you once in a while? That kind of thing exists everywhere, even at home. In fact, it's worse there. You know why? Because there we all look the same, and yet we're still judged on our language, religion, caste, and the money in our bank accounts, so don't you tell me I don't understand."

His clenched jaw loosened. He placed his hand on her shoulder, his expression contrite. "I'm sorry. I'm fucking tired of explaining I'm not a Muslim. I feel like wearing a badge that says *I am not a terrorist*."

"Most Muslims aren't either, you idiot. I hope you take a few minutes to analyze the irony of your own statement."

His lips pinched in a tight grimace, and the air thickened around them, making the ringing phone sound like a warning siren. She'd never spoken to him this way, but in the heat of the moment, she didn't care. He was a good person…hotheaded and misguided, but good. She liked him, but sometimes she wanted to slap the unnatural scowl from his face. That expression didn't fit him. He was the boy who took heavy groceries from her, made funny jokes, and spontaneously danced with her.

Luckily, Geet's voice rang out, slicing through the tension. "Number five for 15C on The West Oracle Tower."

"Excuse me, that's my order," Shyla said, marching past him.

He grasped her arm. "We're not done with this conversation."

"I have nothing else to say to you. Let go of me."

He withdrew his hold. She rushed away, but his eyes continued to follow her while she made the sandwiches and bid goodnight to the Dhillons.

Gripping the handle of the umbrella tightly, she marched toward her destination, grounding out each step with determination. Even though the cold wind whipped around her, she burned hot. Still, she found a sweet vindication in the argument with Adesh. She'd bitten her tongue so many times that her voice was always thick around him.

Adrenaline coursed through her, creating a newfound courage as she repeated her mantra once more. "Now is the time for risks."

Chapter 4

He opened the door wearing a Yankees T-shirt, faded blue jeans ripped at the knees, and a charming smile.

"Hello," he said, leaning his tall muscular body against the doorframe.

"Hi," she greeted, handing him the paper bag and his umbrella. "Thank you for lending me this."

"You were wrong…again," he said.

"Yes, I was." She nodded, matching his playful expression.

"But I'm glad you didn't get stuck in a downpour."

He handed her a bill, and she reached for it the way she always did. She searched her pockets for change, but he held up his hand.

"Keep it."

"Thank you."

"Any predictions for tomorrow?"

"Why ask me? I'm always wrong."

"I've learned if I do the opposite of what you suggest, it works out well."

Her skin prickled as she took in his features. Because of her attraction to Nick, she found it difficult to look at him. She tried holding her gaze at his bare feet, but that didn't work. Tilting her head toward his seductive smirk wasn't a bright idea either. So she let her gaze linger at his broad chest, which wasn't any easier. "I have nothing to report."

"I guess this is the part where I tell you to be safe."

This was when she'd take her leave, and she almost did, her courage peeled away by his presence. "Nick Dorsey." The timid whisper of her voice didn't sound natural.

"That's me."

"I know because your name is on the order slip," she stammered, wincing at her lame attempt at conversation.

He smirked. "Your detective skills are impressive."

She laughed nervously. "Did you know you are my last delivery of the night?"

"I assumed based on the hour."

"I always pack an extra sandwich for myself. I also eat dinner very late."

"That's interesting." He dragged a hand through his thick hair.

"Yes, and I go to school at NYU. My roommate will have people over tonight, and our place will be crowded. It's difficult to think, let alone enjoy a meal in peace."

"Is this going somewhere?"

"Nick Dorsey, it looks like you have a nice, quiet place where one may enjoy a sandwich."

"Are you inviting yourself to dinner?"

"In a way, except I'm bringing my own food." She held up her own brown bag to cement the point. "I was wondering if you'd share your space and perhaps your company?"

He studied her, a look of suspicion crossing his face. Shyla cursed her stupidity and lack of feminine prowess to correctly assess the situation. He wasn't interested. She lowered her gaze and began to turn away, but his foot kicked the door open. "Come in."

He took the second paper bag from her. As he set down the food and put away the umbrella, she took a minute to study his home, still shocked she stood on the other side of the door. The loft was spacious by New York standards with lots of windows, modern charcoal-colored walls, gleaming hardwood floors, and intricate molding. The bookcase captured most of her attention, though, spanning an entire wall with hardcover spines from floor to ceiling. A rolling ladder rested against it.

She began shrugging off her coat. He came behind her, easing it off her shoulders. The polite action caught her off guard. Nick held his hand out for her scarf, but she shook her head, pulling it tighter.

"Would you like something to drink?"

"Yes, Nick Dorsey, I would."

"Why do you keep saying my full name?"

She bit her lip, realizing she didn't have an answer to the question. "I don't know."

"My name is Nick. Call me Nick." He walked over to the glass dining table and pulled out a chair, gesturing for her to sit, but she stood in place.

"For Nicholas?"

"Yes, but I prefer Nick. I don't know your name. I call you Sandwich Girl, but that seems very disrespectful right now."

She held out her hand. "Shyla Metha."

"Shyla," he repeated slowly. He took her hand to shake it, but held on longer than courtesy required. He sucked in a deep breath. As his hold tightened, she imagined him pulling her closer, but instead he pulled free of their connection as if their touch had become uncomfortable for him. How could such a small gesture scream so loudly? Although she felt the sting of his rejection, she also welcomed the idea she wasn't the only one who was nervous.

"What would you like…" He paused, a slow smile tugging at the corners of his mouth before it tightened again. "To drink?"

"What do you have?"

"Water, scotch, and very old scotch."

"What are you having?"

"Scotch."

"I'll have one too, please."

He stared at her for a moment that stretched a few seconds too long for comfort before heading into the open kitchen area.

She took the seat he'd offered. At least in this position she could cover her shaking knees.

"How old are you?" he asked from the kitchen.

"Are you afraid of contributing to the delinquency of a minor?"

He laughed, bringing back a bottle of amber liquid and two small glasses with ice. "I'm sure you're delinquent enough without my contribution."

"What would make you think that?" Did he think she was a loose girl? Then again, her actions weren't exactly characteristic of piety.

His grin put her at ease. "You invited yourself into a stranger's house."

"I've been delivering to you for a year now. You're hardly a stranger." He poured the liquor into each glass and slid one in front of her. "Besides, I have pepper spray in my pocket," she added.

He shook his head before slugging back his drink. "That's wise. Inform a possible attacker of the weapons you're carrying and their location."

Shyla shrugged. "You don't know all my weapons. Just the one, and I can use it as a decoy should you choose to make me feel unsafe."

He frowned, a look of regret flickering on his face. "You're safe with me."

"I believe you."

He shook the ice cubes in his glass. "Shyla is an interesting name. Does it mean something?"

"It's Sanskrit for daughter of the mountain."

"Oh," he said, dismissively. "That's it?"

"It's also the name of a goddess."

"Definitely more appropriate." He spoke barely above a whisper.

A heat crept across her neck. She took a large gulp of her drink to cool herself.

Big mistake.

The butterflies circling her belly burst into flames once the liquor hit. Her eyes watered, and her insides burned. She sputtered and coughed, placing her palm against her mouth for fear a dragon-like spear of fire might shoot free.

"Hey," he said, crouching in front of her. He took the glass from her, setting it on the table. "Are you all right?"

She nodded, swallowing hard, hoping to extinguish the liquor-induced inferno. "I'm sorry."

He brought her a glass of water. Gratefully, she sipped and apologized again.

"It's fine. It could have been worse."

"Worse?" she asked, embarrassed by her actions.

"You could have asked for the old scotch. That would have been a waste."

She widened her eyes until he grinned mischievously. That grin was dangerous, both relaxing and stimulating. "How can you drink that?"

"Straight up and on the rocks. The question is why did you ask for it if you don't like it?"

"I didn't know I wouldn't like it. I thought it would taste like butterscotch."

"Yeah, it's definitely not candy. Back to my original question. How old are you?"

"Twenty-two."

He sighed, looking relived. "You're a very innocent twenty-two."

"You just said I was a delinquent."

He placed a hand on her shaking knee. It stilled immediately. His command over her body was stronger than her own. "I was wrong."

"I guess it's a matter of opinion." She played with the frayed edges of her scarf, deciding scotch would never touch her lips again.

They both ate in silence, lost in their own thoughts. "You always order the turkey," she finally said.

"I'm loyal to what I like." He looked at her food. "What are you having?"

"It's a veggie sandwich—cucumbers, tomatoes, avocado, and green chutney. I'm a vegetarian."

"What are you doing here, Shyla?"

"In your apartment?"

"Yes, but let's go broader. Why are you in New York? You're far from home, aren't you?"

"I'm from India."

"Whereabouts?"

"A rural village in the western part of the country known as Kutch. I'm here on a student visa."

"What's your major? Please don't say it's meteorology because it's definitely not your calling."

She covered her mouth to hide her giggle. "Elementary education, thank you very much. I'll be graduating in a few months and returning to India."

"And you'll be a teacher when you go back?"

"That's the plan."

"Seems like an odd choice."

"Why?"

"We're not exactly shining in that area. Why would you want to attend school in the new world when your own is excelling on every front?"

The question wasn't original. Her answer came easily. "I respectfully disagree. A country that's constantly producing is pretty amazing."

"I hate to break this to you, but we don't produce anything anymore."

"Yes, you do. You produce great ideas, and with great ideas come great thinkers."

Nick let out a low whistle. "I stand corrected."

She pushed aside her half-eaten sandwich. "Do you mind if I look at your books? You have quite a collection."

"Be my guest."

She walked across the space, carrying her glass of water toward his bookshelf. He kept the distance between them and chose to stand against the wall at the opposite side of the room with his arms crossed. On one of the shelves was an old turntable with a stack of neatly laid records. She picked up a strange mask that lay next to it.

"I used to play goalie in this beer league a few years back."

"Is it a competition where you drink beer?"

He chuckled. "We probably would have been better off doing that, but we actually played hockey first and drank beer after."

She ran her fingers against several spines, her excitement growing as she silently read each title. Maybe they had more in common than she'd thought. "You must love to read."

"I do. Luckily, I have an e-reader now, and just in time since I was running out of wall space."

"We like many of the same authors."

"Oh yeah? Who?"

"Swift, Dickens, and Larsson for a start. But I like the modern stuff, too. I love Frank McCourt and Hosseini."

"Me, too," he said, a surprised inflection in his voice.

"You don't have any romances."

Nick chuckled. "Not unless you count my collection of vintage *Penthouse* magazines."

"Huh?"

"Never mind, it was a bad joke. I've never been a fan of romance. I have hard limits on how far my belief will suspend."

"That's a shame. They are my favorites." She sighed, pulling one of the more colorful books off the shelf. The cover featured a striking man in an army jacket with a bikini-clad blonde in his arms. "You have the Keegan Moon novels, I see. It looks like you have the whole set—*The Adventures of Max Montero*." Shyla didn't know why the blonde needed to wear a bikini when Max was dressed head to toe, especially since the backdrop was a snow-capped mountain, but she guessed it had more to do with sales than plot.

"Have you read them?"

"My roommate's a big fan. She lent me the first one."

"What did you think of it?"

She shrugged. "The writing's good, but I didn't care for the characters."

"Why not?"

"They felt one-dimensional. He comes across as a womanizing, self-indulgent fool."

Nick arched his brow, his lips quirking into a grin. "He's got his faults, but I wouldn't describe him that way."

"As bad as he was, though, the heroine was even worse. She seemed stupid and fake…almost vapid. She was always getting herself into trouble and falling into hot water." Encouraged by his amused smile, she continued, "And I refer to hot water in the literal sense. The one I read, the girl was suspended from the ceiling over a pot of boiling water until Max Montero swooped in at the last minute."

"It was acid, and he likes saving beautiful women from danger. What's wrong with that?"

"She could have saved herself, or better yet, not gotten into the situation. And he…well, he could have been nicer to her in general."

"Not every hero comes in a one-size-fits-all package, Shyla. Don't hold back, though. Tell me what you really think."

"Okay, I will. I can appreciate a different kind of hero, but I'd like one with a functioning set of scruples. In the scheme of things, these books don't deserve shelf space with the others. They definitely fall into the dime store drivel category."

"Ouch," Nick said, pouring himself another drink. "I don't think you understand the concept of sarcasm."

She opened and shut her mouth as the realization hit her. "You were joking when you asked me to tell you what I really thought?"

"Yeah, but don't worry about it."

"So, what do you do for a living?" she asked, anxious to change the subject. It was possible she'd accidentally insulted one of his favorite novelists.

"I'm an author."

"Have you written anything I might have read?"

"The dime store drivel you're holding."

Uh oh.

The drivel in question fell from her hand, as did the water. Shattered glass and liquid marred the gleaming floors. She knelt before her mess. "Oh, my God." Her hands hovered above the jagged shards of glass.

He moved swiftly, grabbing a roll of paper towels and covering the space between them in long strides. "Don't," he said, clasping her wrist before she picked up a chunk of glass. "You'll cut yourself." His dark eyes and square jaw captured her attention from the task at hand.

In that moment, she battled with the urge to either pull him closer or push him away.

Instead, she remained frozen. His thumb moved along her wrist. Could he feel her racing pulse?

"Stupid," she muttered.

"Careful. You might be in danger of getting hurt and find yourself in need of rescuing."

Her tummy twisted in reaction to her physical and social clumsiness. To her surprise, he laughed.

"I'm so sorry. I... I... The writing I enjoyed."

"Don't."

"Don't what?"

"Don't take it back. Once words are airborne, they become stale, and you can't breathe them in again. You don't have to apologize."

"I do. It was rude and insensitive."

"It was honest." He threw down some paper towels while she took the book and wiped it against her shirt, holding it as if it was a valuable work of art.

"Look Shyla, I know my work isn't going to change the world, but Max Montero gives people an enjoyable escape for a few hours, and I'm happy to provide that outlet."

She held up the book. "If I had known."

"But you didn't, and I'm glad you didn't. Honesty is a rare and treasured trait for me. Trust me, I've gotten far worse reviews than yours."

His reassurances did nothing to assure her. "The books say Keegan Moon is the author."

"That's my pseudonym."

"Why do you write under an alias?"

He stood, holding his hand out to assist her. He opened a hall closet and retrieved a broom and dustpan. "For a few reasons. My first book was under my real name, and it's very different from the fifteen Max Montero books. My agent figured it would be a good idea to use a penname. Once readers get to know an author, they have certain expectations of their work, and we didn't want to disappoint them." Nick scooped up the glass, walked back to the kitchen, and deposited it in the bin. He returned with fresh water for Shyla, but this time it was in a plastic bottle. "We shouldn't chance it again," he said with a wink.

"That's probably wise."

"Anyway, I decided I liked the other name, and it gives me a bit of anonymity."

"What was your first book about?"

Shyla started clearing the table, but he took over, gesturing for her to sit. She flopped on the dining room chair, playing with her scarf, happy to have something to occupy her hands.

"My grandfather's life."

"Like a biography?"

"Sort of. He didn't relay his whole life story, but he gave me some interesting snippets. I pasted enough together to write the book."

"He must be very special."

"He was," he said in a low voice.

"I'm sorry."

"He had a good life." Nick glanced at a picture on the wall. "He was kind of a bastard….but a loveable one." Nick's blue eyes grew wistful. "He used to have all these grampisms or grumpisms, depending on how you looked at it. He would give me advice, but it always fell a little short of its mark. Like he'd say, 'Nicky, it's true you can be anything you want to be in this country…but for fuck's sake, make sure whatever you choose, you aim for rich.'" Nick's voice had turned gruffer when he quoted his grandfather.

"It sounds like you were close to him."

"He raised me." Nick took the seat across from her again. She forced herself not to stare at his ripped jeans or bare feet. Why was that appealing?

"What happened to your parents?" she asked, folding a paper napkin into a tight square.

"I don't have any," he said without emotion.

"I'm sorry for your loss."

"I don't mean to lead you astray. My parents are very much alive, but their existence has no bearing on mine."

"I understand," she said, although she didn't. She wondered if she should take her leave now that her constant curiosity had ruined the mood.

"You do?"

"Not really."

He sucked in a deep breath. "I was four when my dad left. I've seen him maybe a dozen times since then. All of those visits involved monetary requests...on his part. Another reason I chose an alias."

"That's awful."

A flicker of a frown eased into a dismissive shrug. "It could be worse."

"Your mother?"

"She resented being saddled with a kid. She'd take off for weeks at a time, depositing me with Gramps. The last time was when I was eight. He told her not to come back again." Nick laughed cynically. "The one time she listened to him."

Shyla wanted to find some words of comfort, but nothing came to her. There didn't seem to be much else to say, but Nick didn't appear to need a response. "Wow, this turned into a therapy session, didn't it? Would you believe I never talk about this stuff, or have you already categorized me as a wallowing prick?"

"I would believe you with no doubts. I shouldn't have asked so many personal questions."

"Inquiring about someone's parents isn't a personal question...not usually, but you can ask me anything."

Her heart wrenched for him, but she was grateful for the warmth of his words. "Your grandfather must have been proud of you."

"I finished the book right before he died. He was the first one who read it. He cried. He said it was like his life had a purpose. I've been lucky enough to receive many accolades in my career, but the statement from Gramps, by far, was my greatest moment as a writer."

"I would love to read that book."

Nick strode over to the bookcase. He jumped on the ladder, skipping several rungs, and then leaned his body until the whole structure slid effortlessly to the other side of the long shelf.

She tensed at the carefree, almost reckless way he carried himself. "Be careful."

"I do this all the time."

He reached for a book on the top without looking, and then jumped off. He walked over to her and deposited the small hardcover in her lap. "Here you go."

"You're lending it to me?" She traced the embossed cover that featured a black and white deck of playing cards. She cleared her throat and gripped her fingers on the novel with enough force to cause her knuckles to crack.

"You won't find it in a bookstore anymore. It did well critically, but it was no commercial success. You can keep it."

"I couldn't."

"I insist. I have other copies. Besides, you can't hate my work if you haven't been exposed to all of it."

"Thank you. I can't wait to read this." She held up the small book with a surprisingly steady hand. "*Irish Hold'em?*"

"Yeah, it's a play on Texas Hold'em, my grandfather's favorite game. He was a gambler. He didn't win much, and it's probably the reason we were always broke, but he sure as hell loved the game. He'd take me with him when I was younger."

"To the casino?"

Nick shook his head. "He didn't like casinos. These were underground games. Gramps knew it wasn't the right place for a kid, but he also couldn't resist the lure of a poker table. We'd go to the library first where I could check out all the books I wanted. The kicker was I had to read them the same day. I guess that's where my love for reading started. Because in those hours in smoky pool halls, while old men played cards, I was able to go to a different place and have adventures of my own."

"Is that when you came up with Max Montero?"

"Yeah, I suppose it was," he said, as if realizing it himself. "I had this imaginary friend as a kid. I guess it's not uncommon, but my friend wasn't exactly normal. He drank hard liquor, swore, and had some crazy adventures. Eventually, he developed into Max Montero."

"I've always wondered how writers come up with their ideas."

"I can only speak for my own methods. You know why people like Max? Well, besides present company?"

"Tell me."

"He appeals to everyone. Men enjoy the action-adventure components and his badass personality. Women appreciate a man who's both a voracious lover and a lovable jerk."

"You really think women like that?" she asked, genuinely curious. After all, it was exactly what she disliked about the character.

"Women are compassionate and kind. They have this innate need to fix broken when they see it. And Max Montero is all kinds of broken."

Shyla had a feeling Nick Dorsey was "all kinds of broken" too, but she kept the thought to herself. "I see."

"Anyway, you'll be happy to know Max Montero is done with his kickass life and panty-dropping adventures."

"What? You killed him off?" she gasped.

"No, he has a strong fan base, and readers would hate me if anything untoward happened to him. He's simply going away."

"Why would you stop if the books are successful?"

"It appears my imaginary friend has abandoned me."

Shyla blinked her eyes in confusion.

"He used to talk to me. Shit, that makes me sound crazy."

"You have writer's block?"

"Yes."

"Does it hurt?"

His laugh held little joy. "No, it just feels empty, frustrating, listless… unproductive…lazy. I guess those are the right adjectives."

"Maybe you just need some inspiration," she offered, part statement and question.

"A muse would be welcome." He lifted a brow suggestively.

Shyla inhaled a deep breath, attempting to recover her composure before he managed to crumple it once more. "Where would you ever find one?"

"You seem like a qualified candidate."

She stood and started backing toward the doorway. "I should go."

He stood, but remained rooted in the spot, shoving his hands in pocket. "Did I make you uncomfortable?"

"Not at all. It…it's late. Thank you for this," she said, holding up the book. "I can't wait to start it. And thank you for tonight."

"It's no big deal."

"It is…or at least it was to me."

He helped her with her coat. She took swift steps toward the door, clutching the book against her chest, hoping it would mask the harsh sounds of her beating heart.

"Shyla," he called, leaning against the doorjamb, just as she was once again on the outside of his home. Perhaps the side she belonged on.

She pivoted toward him.

His lips turned up in a tight smile as he dragged a hand across his thick hair. "If I ordered a sandwich tomorrow, would you deliver it?"

There was something endearing in the way he'd asked. Her answer came automatically without any forethought. "Of course, I'm your delivery girl."

"Would you stay and eat with me?" The hope in his voice surprised her.

"If you wish."

"Do you wish?"

She did wish, more than she had wished for anything in a very long time. "I would like that very much."

"I'll see you tomorrow night then." He took out his wallet and handed her another bill.

"You already paid me."

"It's later than usual. Take a cab back to the campus tonight."

"I don't have far to go."

"It's not the distance I'm worried about. I'd rather your pepper spray remain unused."

She swallowed back a tiny lump. "I'll take a cab, but I can pay for it myself."

He opened her palm, placed the bill inside, and closed her fingers around it. "That's not the point." There was something in his stance that deterred her from quarrelling. Not to mention his proximity made the simple task of articulation difficult. She whiffed his intoxicating scent, clean and soapy, yet masculine.

"Thank you."

"Be safe, Shyla."

Chapter 5

Nick's day followed the usual sequence. A morning jog with a stop at the flower shop, followed by a visit to the cemetery, repeating his apologies to a girl who could never answer back. A mid-morning addiction meeting complete with robust coffee and painful stories. He spent the remainder of the day gawking at the damn blinking cursor, mocking him with its slow, shameless dance. Today was different, though. Not in his habits, but definitely in his demeanor. He was excited…to see her again.

He disapproved of his own enthusiasm. He shouldn't like her this much. It was dangerous for him. Her name was appropriate because she was shy, but at the same time opinionated, perhaps even brash. Oh, and she did have goddess-like qualities. She had a sense of humor, and she listened to him with rapt attention. He listened to her, too. In fact, her lyrical voice made his dick jerk, which in turn made him feel like a jerk, but hell, that part of his anatomy had a mind of its own. Interestingly, it had been inactive for a very long time. It was good to know, unlike his career, his dick wasn't dead.

She arrived on time, wearing her large trench coat and an even baggier blue sweater underneath. She certainly didn't dress to impress, which was almost a sin in this city. Yet, she managed to be sexy nonetheless.

"Hello, Shyla," he said, gesturing her inside.

"Nick," she greeted.

She placed the paper bag on the table. Nick helped her with her coat and took her knapsack, and just like the night before, she seemed surprised by his small gesture. His hand twitched slightly, aching to tuck the loose strand of hair behind her ear, but he refrained.

She cupped her hand to her mouth, her grin transforming into a long yawn.

"Tired?"

"Very much so, and it's your fault, Nick Dorsey."

"My fault?"

She reached into the knapsack and pulled out his book. "I read this last night. I stayed up very late, but it was worth it. I loved it."

Nick tried to subdue his grin, but couldn't help it. The fact she liked something of his meant a great deal, especially coming from such a harsh critic.

"I'm glad you enjoyed it." *And relieved, too.*

"It's amazing, Nick."

"Stop swelling my ego." *Among other things.*

"I have to get this out. The fact you can get a girl from rural India to sympathize with an Irish poker player from New Jersey…well, that's pretty special. I think that's what a good book does. It brings us together as people no matter how different we are, because in the end, the human experience connects us."

Nick swallowed as he took in her words. A sense of gratitude filled him, but he wasn't sure why. "I'm humbled by your description."

She handed the hardcover back to him.

He held his hands up. "I told you to keep it."

"I plan to. I was hoping you would autograph it."

"Of course." He walked over to his desk and grabbed a pen. "Would you like something to drink?"

"I bought drinks this time."

He took his time autographing the copy for her. By the time he handed it back, she'd set up the table for them. She handed him his drink.

"Juice boxes? Is this a joke?" The confused look on her face made it quite clear she wasn't joking. "I haven't had one of these since preschool."

"I know it's childish, but I love them. I thought you might like one, too. They actually do taste like candy."

God, she was so fucking innocent. How would she survive in this city? He shook the ridiculous question out of his head as soon as it entered. She *had* survived, and it was a miracle in some ways. Not because she had—naive girl versus the big, bad city wasn't a unique story. That she survived with her innocence intact was the true miracle.

Nick laughed, taking one of the small boxes with its colorful design and tiny straw. She misunderstood his hesitation because she took the straw, freed it from the wrapper, and punctured the tiny dot at the top of the bright yellow box.

"Thank you." He sipped, wincing at the artificial sweetness.

"You're most welcome. He had such an interesting life, your grandfather."

"Yeah, he had some good stories."

MK Schiller

"Enlisting in the Army at a young age and then losing his wife. And the relationship you two had. I can see how you both needed each other. How he influenced you." She walked over to the wood frame hanging in a prominent place in his living room and ran her finger along the border. "These are the cards, right?"

"The only royal flush ever dealt to him. When I graduated college, he gave them to me." Nick deepened his voice, bringing out the Jersey of his Gramp's accent. "He said, 'All I have to give you are these cards I've been carrying in my back pocket for twenty years and some advice. You're smart enough to know there is a sucker at every table, but I hope you'll be wise enough to realize that sometimes it's you. I never was.'"

"Wise words." Her smile widened when she opened the book and read his inscription. "To Shyla, a shining light in a dark world. Love Nick Dorsey." She looked up at him, the dimple deepening with her grin. "It's beautiful. Thank you."

"My pleasure."

"Do you think the world is dark?"

"Sometimes." He didn't want to have this discussion with her. She had an ability to draw out his sorrow in a way that both relieved and surprised him. "But not tonight. I don't want to talk about me anymore. Tell me about you."

"What do you want to know?"

He pulled out a chair for her. "Anything." *Everything.*

"My father is retired. My mother passed away a while ago."

"I'm sorry. That must be difficult."

"It was."

"Any brothers or sisters?" he asked.

"I'm an only child."

"Me, too."

"That's about it."

"I doubt it. Do you like NYU?"

"It's a great school. I'm here on a scholarship."

"Impressive. I graduated from there myself."

"Why didn't you say so yesterday?"

"I didn't want to change the subject. Big surprise, I was an English Lit major."

"How come you didn't move back to New Jersey?"

Nick dropped the needle on the record player, hoping the music would defuse, possibly distract him from making an advance on her. Nick didn't have a trace of an accent so he wondered for a split second how she knew he was a Jersey boy before it dawned on him that she knew a great deal about him from the book.

"I love Jersey, but this city has an ebb and flow that's conducive to writing."

"I get it." She gestured to the turntable with its record spinning on the track. "Who is this?"

Nick tilted his head. "Jimi Hendrix. The song's called "All Along the Watchtower."

She moved her lips, silently repeating the name as if trying to commit it to memory. "Jimi Hendrix, I'll have to remember the name."

He arched a brow. "You've never heard of Jimi Hendrix?"

"No, but I like this."

"I have so much to teach you."

She chewed her sandwich slowly. "Are we friends then?"

Nick hadn't quantified it. To him, friendship was something natural that progressed without definition, but she needed reassurance. "Without a doubt. Why do you like the song?"

"I can feel the words. Do you understand?"

"I follow."

Her voice lowered to a whisper. "This has to be one of the most crowded places you can live. It's exciting, exuberant, and exhausting. It's easy to get lost, in every sense of the word."

"You're right, but it's also one of the few places where a guy like me and a girl like you can break bread and converse. What made you ask to come in last night?"

"You seemed nice. I'm not usually this forward."

"I know." He arched his brow. "It took you a year to talk to me. At least about anything more than the weather."

"You could have talked to me, too. Why didn't you?"

"I'm not really sure."

"We wasted time, didn't we?"

"Not really. I wasn't the same person. I'm glad we stuck to weather reports. Anyway, besides being a teacher, what else?"

"What else what?"

"What else do you dream of?" She lowered her head. He leaned forward. "You can tell me."

"It's silly. You'll laugh."

"Your dreams are safe with me, Shyla." Nick expected her to answer with future forecasts, including marriage outlooks and the number of children she'd have.

"I'd like to write a book."

Nick crushed the juice box in his hand. "You're kidding, right?" he asked with a slight annoyance.

She narrowed her eyes. "Why do you say it like that?"

"Everyone is thinking about writing a book."

She played with the plastic wrapping of her sandwich, smoothing it out against the table. "You must hear it a great deal in your line of work."

"I've heard it three times this week so it's a little under quota, but yeah. What's your book about?"

"It's a love story."

He laughed. "That figures."

"What do you mean?"

"You said it was your favorite."

She narrowed her eyes, her lips pursed. Nick cursed himself...not just for pissing her off, but because her angry look turned him on. "It's not glamorous or even particularly pretty. It's definitely not cliché if that's what you're implying."

"I'm sorry. I can be an assuming ass sometimes."

"It's not a love story in the traditional sense. It touches on some heavy ideas."

"Like what?"

"Female gendercide, for one."

Nick almost choked on his sandwich. "Female gendercide? As in the act of systematically killing female babies?"

"Yes."

"Sounds like a real feel-good kind of book."

"I know you're being sarcastic, but ironically it is."

"What do you know about the subject, Shyla?"

"I've read and heard stories."

"So basically you know nothing."

She shook her head slowly, her long lashes fluttering over her chocolate brown eyes.

"One of the most important rules in writing is to write what you know."

Something he said must have resonated with her, but not in a good way. She stiffened before she leveled her head, squared her shoulders, and met his eyes. "What experiences do you have with the Russian mob, Nick?"

"Excuse me?"

"Well, if I recall correctly, and I think I do, in the Max Montero book I read, he infiltrated the Russian mob. I suspect you have some real world experiences in that area since you're all about"—she paused dramatically, fingers in air quotes—"'write what you know.'"

The girl had gotten him. He bowed slightly, conceding to her argument. "Touché."

"You asked me my dream, and that's one of the big ones. I have this crazy urge to write it. Like if I don't, I'll combust."

Nick understood better than anyone what she described. As a writer, when he came up with a story, it wouldn't leave him alone until he put it to paper. Unfortunately, he had no more stories to tell.

"How did you come up with the idea?"

"I, too, have a character that speaks to me."

Nick fetched a yellow legal pad and his favorite cross-pen from his writing desk. "What's the story?"

"I don't have it all worked out yet."

"Tell me what you have."

"Now?" she asked, looking around the room, as if someone else might answer her question.

"No time like the present."

She yawned again.

"Unless you're too tired," Nick added.

"I'll be fine."

"Would you like coffee?"

"I brought some."

"You brought your own coffee?"

"I always carry it with me."

To his horror, she reached into her knapsack and pulled out a familiar plastic jar. Nick's gut clenched in revolt. He tilted his head, trying to keep his expression stern, but failing. "You insult me by bringing freeze-dried, instant coffee into my house."

"I only need water, and I can make it anywhere. It's convenient."

He picked up the jar and chucked it behind him. It landed perfectly into the trashcan by his writing desk. "It's crap. If there's one thing I can teach you, it's this. Not all coffee is created equal. I'll make you a real cup."

Her mouth gaped, but before she could respond, he took her hand and led her into the kitchen. A part of him regretted the action because he understood her decisions were not based on preference alone. Even though he was no longer part of that class, he would never forget those struggles. Poor recognized poor. He couldn't solve those problems for her, and he doubted she wanted him to, but he could damn well make her a real cup of coffee.

He brewed hot water and grinded fresh beans like a professional barista, explaining each step to her.

"What's this?" she asked, gesturing to the glass mug with a silver lid.

"A French press. I usually use my coffeemaker, so I'm giving it to you. I wanted to show you how to make it."

"Why?"

"Because instant coffee sucks."

The skeptical look on her face melted as the rich aroma of fresh brewed coffee filled the room. "I don't have a coffee grinder."

He opened a top cupboard and took out a silver package. He tossed it to her. "That's already ground." He took out the three spice jars in the cabinet. "Do you like chocolate, cinnamon…nutmeg?"

"Isn't it cream and sugar?"

"Not the way I do it."

"You choose. I should be angry with you for throwing away my coffee."

"Try this, and then tell me how angry you are," he said, handing her a steaming mug. Their fingers touched briefly, making the exchange more awkward.

She blew before taking a sip. Her eyes widened, and she ran her tongue over her full lips. The reaction so subtly demure and downright sexy, it caused Nick's dick to twitch. She opened her mouth, but paused and took another sip as if trying to verify her appreciation.

"Mmmm," she whispered.

"Yep."

"Touché, Nick Dorsey," she said, clinking her mug against his. The best laughter came from the gut and worked its way up. And that was the exact laugh that came from him. One he hadn't heard in a long time.

Seated again at the dining table, half-empty mugs later, Nick waited patiently for her to start. "Shyla, we don't have to do this if you don't want to. I figured I could give you some advice and make up for being an ass."

"The coffee made up for it. It's not that. I haven't told anyone."

"Every single book starts the same way."

"What way is that?"

"With an idea. Sometimes you can have a great idea and a piece of crap book or vice versa. I promise, even if you don't write it, you will feel better for talking it out."

"I'm not sure where to start."

"Chapter one unless there is a prologue."

"No prologue. Here it goes." She took a deep breath and pulled her legs up, encircling her arms around them. "Once upon a time, a very long time ago in a land very far away, there lived a village woman."

"What the hell are you doing?" Nick interrupted.

"Telling you the story."

"Are you writing a fairy tale?"

"No."

"Is that how you would start it?"

"Um...yes."

"Okay, let's try something else. Tell me the story like you're talking to a friend, not as if you're reading it out loud."

"I am talking to a friend."

"Yes, you are."

Nick moved his chair closer to hers. There was still a distance between them, but he caught a whiff of her vanilla scent. It was subtle like her, but even more pleasant than the coffee aroma.

She cleared her throat and began again. He jotted notes while she spoke. Soon though, he put down the pad and propped his head in his hands, listening to her lyrical voice. He wasn't sure if it was the allure of her voice or the interesting story that held his interest—probably both.

"I think you have something," he said when she was done.

"I don't. It's just an idea."

"Why don't you try writing it?"

"I'm not a writer. It comes off bland and emotionless on the paper. I want to do it justice." She yawned again. "I should go. It's late."

He walked her down, put her in a cab, paid the driver, and secured her agreement to come back the following night. He tried to go to bed himself, but sleep would not come. He either tossed and turned or studied the skylight over his bed. The window provided a framed visual of stars lighting the universe. He traced the scar across his abdomen. Finally, he closed his eyes, only to snap them open a few seconds later. The snippet of the tale she'd told replayed like a record set on repeat. She had the right words, but maybe not the adjectives and connectors to drive it home. Finally, at one in the morning, he flipped off the covers and staggered to the writing desk.

Nick cracked his knuckles as he regarded his once friend and now foe—the blinking cursor. But this time, a new energy coursed through him. Before he could give the idea much contemplation, he began typing.

Her story flowed through his fingers as they tapped and whirled on the keyboard in a frantic pace. The connection between his hands and brain lacked any hesitation. The words came effortlessly as they once did. She was the composer, he was the conductor, and the story was the music. It was a rough draft for sure, but he'd filled in the blank spaces and colored her outline. He saved it under his drafts with the working title *Asha's story* by Shyla Metha.

He swallowed, wondering what her reaction would be. Would she appreciate his help? Nick Dorsey had many critics. Perhaps they even outnumbered his admirers. His work experienced both hail and ridicule in some of the most prestigious media outlets by professional editors, passionate readers, and even celebrities, but he'd never been as nervous about a review as right then.

Chapter 6

Asha's story

Nalini Mistry hadn't planned the long hike to the neighboring village to purchase vegetables, but she'd woken with one simple goal—to make her husband happy. The calluses on her feet throbbed with the extra steps she took, but it was worth it, because the farmer would have the cauliflower she needed to make Deval's favorite dish.

Their lives had taken on a dark depression since their only child, Dipesh, died the year before at the tender age of twenty. The image of her sweet boy caused a tear to slide down her weathered face. This would have been the year of the bride search. Now, she would never welcome a daughter-in-law into their home. Instead, Depal and she lived a lonely life, mourning their son and cursing the malaria for taking him away.

As if the melancholy wasn't enough, the burdens of heavy debt created further misery. They had called a doctor when Dipesh fell ill, draining their modest savings. Deval had purchased a new truck in preparation for his son taking over his route. In every village family, there was a passing of the torch where the sons go from beloved child to family provider. This was the time for Dipesh to take over his duties and for Nalini and Depal to enjoy old age. A time to welcome a daughter-in-law into their house and, most of all, grandchildren, more sons to bless their home.

They had always lived in shades of poverty, but before they could manage to purchase nice things on occasion. A new sari for Nalini, a television a few years back, and tobacco for Depal, but now every day was a struggle. As if to cement her fears, she stepped into a pile of mud. Unfortunately, it wasn't mud.

She tried to scrape off the foul-smelling substance from her sandal, but it was no use. The smell followed her, taunting her misfortune. Finally, she walked to the river to wash it off.

The river was high from recent rains. Its long channel flowed through several villages, providing an important fresh water source. Nalini washed the stench from her shoe. A memory of her son playing along these banks flashed through her mind.

Why did you do this to me, God? The emotion of the question crumpled her composure. She wept tears so fat and salty they flowed with the same urgency as the water. Grief was an indulgence she could not afford. At home, she tried to be strong for her husband, but here alone with her solemn thoughts she was able to mourn freely. The pain poured out in her unanswered wails.

Except she wasn't alone.

Another cry merged with hers. The voice, a loud screeching scream, silenced Nalini. She looked to the west and east along the riverbank, but didn't see anything. Then she looked across from her. The invading sounds emerged from a small wooden box caught in the thicket. The kind of container they packed cashews in for export. She took off both sandals, lifted her sari, and waded across the river, trying to keep her skinny legs steadfast against the current.

She ran her fingers along the crude puncture holes at the top of the box. She lifted the lid, saying a silent prayer for its occupant. The sight of the newborn baby nestled inside a dirty blanket wrenched her heart. Nalini carefully lifted the child. Who would do this to a baby?

She lifted the material covering the child and confirmed her suspicions—a baby girl.

An unwanted girl.

Nalini rocked the baby gently and sang to her. The wails softened until the infant quieted completely. Then she carefully gathered water in her palm and cleaned the child as best as she could. She tore off a length of her sari. Carefully, she wrapped the child in it. She watched as the waters carried the dirty blanket downstream.

What shall I do with you, precious one?

Nalini wasn't one to ponder for long. She was a woman of action. The city was even farther than the next village. She'd have to set the baby down to rest along the way. She didn't want to take the wicked box, but leaving the baby on the dirty road was not an option either. She placed the infant back inside and cooed softly to her.

She walked with the child for five kilometers toward the city. The stench of decadence and decay filled her nostrils, signaling she'd arrived. The place struck an unnatural fear in her with its fast traffic, crowded streets, and many dangers. There were beggars, including many children.

One girl who couldn't be more than eight wore a ripped frock and held a baby of her own. Although the infant was real, she carried it like a doll. That's what it was…a prop to garner sympathy and additional coins. She gazed at the box in her arms. Would this baby suffer the same fate? Not if she had anything to do with it. This child would be raised in the suitable hands of someone who loved her.

Nalini asked five pedestrians before an elderly woman pointed her to the local hospital. The formidable building hummed with activity as people moved with frantic speed. Everyone passed her, ignoring her inquiry for help. Some even shoved her. Her kind wasn't welcome. She resembled someone who would more likely clean the hospital than be a prospective patient.

She grabbed a doctor's coat. He pulled away, his harsh look of disdain causing her to wince. "Doctor, sir, I found this baby. I don't know what to do." She spoke in a villager's dialect he didn't understand. His teeth clenched in frustration as he glanced at the baby.

He pointed to a large desk in the corner of the room where a lady mid-yawn handed out badges to a long line of visitors. Shuffling slowly, she took in the huge sign above. Not that it did much good since she couldn't read. By the time she reached the front of the queue, the attendant didn't even bother covering her mouth during the next yawn. Speaking without taking a single breath, Nalini managed to explain how she'd come into possession of the baby. At least the impatient young woman appeared to understand her.

The woman stood up and peered down at the child from behind the counter. "She looks healthy. We don't take non-paying patients."

"But she's not mine. She needs a home."

"We are a hospital, not an orphanage."

The wooden box was getting heavy, and the muscles in her arms burned against its weight. Nalini set it on the counter for fear of dropping it.

"Take it off! It's filthy, and this is a sterile place," the attendant yelled. Nalini complied at once. There was a certain order of respect, and among these people, Nalini belonged on the bottom rung. It was a fact she had accepted all her life, and like all the women before her, never questioned.

"Where is the orphanage, *memsaab?*" Nalini asked, using the proper term of respect for a woman in authority.

The attendant told her the name of another city, but it was much too far for Nalini to walk, and she couldn't afford cab fare.

"That's too great a distance. What do I do?"

The attendant sighed, a look of scorn taking over her pretty features. "Take her to the police station then."

After securing directions, Nalini carried the crate another kilometer in the crowded streets until she reached the station. Here, amongst all the harsh glares of men, she felt even more out of place than in the hospital.

Thankfully, the officer who approached spoke her local dialect. His face shifted between the baby and her as she went through the story once more.

He held up his hands to quiet the mocking laughter of his co-workers. "Her parents didn't want her. You should put her back where you found her, Auntie."

Nalini wondered if perhaps there *was* a language barrier. "Officer *saab*, I cannot. She will die."

"She'll die, anyway. The question is do you want her to suffer? Old woman, you are in the wrong place."

She struggled to find the right words to make him understand. "Will you take a report?"

"For what? No one wants her. No one will be looking for her. She is no one's concern."

Nalini patted her chest, as much to calm her raging heartbeat as to make her claim. "She is mine…my concern. What do I do?" she asked for the third time that day.

He dropped his voice, leading her toward the exit. "Salt works well. Put a pinch in the baby's mouth. It takes little time, and there is no pain."

Nalini staggered back, shocked by his words. The barrier between them had nothing to do with language. He continued, as if she needed more clarification. "Listen to reason, old woman. She can suffer her whole life or be at peace in one instant."

She clutched the crate tighter as she exited the building with swift steps, trying to place as much distance from the devilish man's suggestions as she could.

Confused, frustrated, and tired, she journeyed back to her home. The infant must have sensed her emotions because the crying started again. The cries turned to wails until Nalini stopped at the side of a dirt road that led to her village. She gently rocked the baby, trying to nourish her with words when she had no food to offer.

"Do not cry. You are a godsend. There are some girls who are blessed and cursed at the same time, and in many ways they are the luckiest because God gave them the strength to face both sides of life. There was another child once. His father and mother were imprisoned because his ruthless uncle, the king, was told through a prophet the eighth child of the couple would kill him and bring peace to the land. The child survived because his father snuck him from the prison and placed him in a basket on the banks of the river. That child was Lord Krishna."

The child quieted. "Baby, no need to cry. You have to be brave like Lord Krishna."

She looked down at the sleeping infant. *What will I do? There are no village families who would take in a child, especially a girl child.*

Then Nalini thought of the school where she worked. More specifically of the young nun with golden hair and eyes the color of emeralds who taught there. Nalini had never conversed with her. She couldn't since they spoke different languages, but her friendly gestures conveyed the woman was nurturing and sweet. She was a woman of God. Maybe not her Gods…but all paths were pure. Surely, she would help.

* * * *

It was Saturday. A day Sister Sarah reserved for reading. The knock on the door of her small cottage surprised her. She prayed it wasn't another hostile villager threatening her. At the same time, she was in no mood to receive a friendly villager offering gifts of sweets. She feared the former, but was happy to receive the later. Not today, though. Today, she craved solitude. Tomorrow, she'd make the announcement, but today was about coming to terms with her decision to leave her life here.

She let the first set of knocks go unanswered. They were heavy and urgent, signaling Sarah to be extra cautious. Who would have imagined a school could cause such controversy? Villagers either hated or loved it. Some said it wasn't appropriate to have white foreigners teaching their children and possibly converting them, while others were grateful their children had an opportunity for education.

When she heard the woman's voice call, she finally opened the door. Her spine stiffened at the sight of one of the cleaning ladies cradling a wooden box in her arms. Nalini spoke rapidly in her own tongue, not stopping even when Sarah held up her hand. But when she lifted the lid of the box, Sarah's heart wrenched at the sight of the tiny baby with a shock of black hair and large brown eyes.

Sarah, a woman of action herself, set about bathing the baby properly and swaddled her in a clean blanket. She asked her house servant to fetch a translator and a bottle of rice milk. She held the baby, feeding her, while the translator, one of Sarah's brighter students, sat between the two women. Sarah understood some Hindi, but not the Gujarati dialect Nalini spoke. She controlled the raw emotions of anger, shock, and despair as the interpreter translated Nalini's explanation.

MK Schiller

She looked down at the sleeping child, suckling a finger. Such a hard start in life. Sarah counted fingers and toes, surprised by how miraculously healthy the baby appeared. A child who had come into their care, much the way Moses had come to the Pharaoh's daughter along the Nile River after being set afloat by his mother in an effort to save him when the Pharaoh ordered all male Hebrew children should be drowned in the Nile.

Sarah pointed to the box. "Perhaps someone put her in this vessel to save her."

Nalini shook her head slowly. "No one was trying to save her."

"No, look," Sarah said, tapping the lid of the box, clinging to a shred of optimism. She ran her fingers over the small slits over the wooden lid. "Air holes for the child to breathe."

Nalini regarded Sarah as if she were a child herself. Sarah's heart rate increased as the older woman secured the lid back in place and made quick jabbing motions with her hand. Despite the tropical climate, a strong chill ran down her spine as the translator repeated Nalini's explanation. "They placed the baby in this box and punctured it with a knife several times. The wood is soft enough to yield to a knife, but the blade wasn't long enough. The sharp end didn't reach the baby."

Sarah choked back a sob, the idea of such brutality almost causing her to wretch. "Why?"

"Girl," the older woman said in English. That one word spoke volumes.

Girls cost money, especially in the form of dowry. There were stories of parents going bankrupt to marry off their daughters. Contrary, boys brought in money and dowry. Sarah, horrified with the violent description, could no longer hold back her cries. She set the child atop a clean pillow. She wept openly and took Nalini's weathered hand in her own. Nalini appeared surprised by the gesture and tried to withdraw her hand, but Sarah held it tightly.

"What do we do?" Nalini asked once more.

"Pray with me."

Sarah didn't have an answer. The school had strict instructions not to get involved with the local residents. Their job was to educate and make the villager's lives better, but there were directives, and any inappropriate behavior could result in a shut down.

For these reasons, Sarah decided she would not inform her superiors. They would suggest the orphanage some distance away as a place to deposit the child. It seemed the obvious choice, except it was all wrong. Rumors circulated the children were severely mistreated and even sold into prostitution. There was no proof, but Sarah would not risk it—not when it came to this baby.

She couldn't explain it, except that some motherly instinct and responsibility had invaded her body. But what could she do? She was leaving this place, a decision she had prayed on for months. Now, all her certainty dissipated as she looked upon the tiny infant whose mouth curved into the most adorable gassy smile.

"She's beautiful," Sarah whispered.

"That she is," Nalini agreed.

Although both women hailed from different corners of the world with different backgrounds, religion, and life experiences, somehow they communicated without the benefit of a translator or even words. They each bowed their heads.

Sarah prayed to Mary and Jesus and Nalini to Rama and Sita. Both of them hovered their hands over the baby. When the child wrapped her tiny fists around each woman's finger, a powerful surge flooded Sarah's heart.

Sarah lifted her head, meeting Nalini's eyes, knowing what the woman would say before she spoke.

"I will keep her and raise her," Nalini announced with complete conviction. "She will be my daughter. I love her."

"Your husband will allow this?"

"He will not agree. He will show her little kindness, but a mother's love is strong enough to overcome any obstacle."

"I will help you raise her. I will make sure she has a good life," Sarah added. "I will love… I love her, too."

"What shall we name her?" Nalini asked. Typically, a naming ceremony involved family and input from the grandparents, but in this case, Nalini's parents were deceased as was all her family.

"What is the word for hope?"

"Asha," Nalini explained, a genuine smile on her face. "That is a fine and fitting name."

Sarah nodded in agreement, wiping away her tears.

For the first time in Sarah's life, her feet felt steady on the path she'd chosen. Nalini, old and destitute, was in no position to raise a baby. Sarah, a young nun, who was not allowed to interfere, was also in no position to raise a baby. But together, they could both give the child everything she needed, everything they had to give. These two women, who would never associate with each other in any ordinary circumstance, formed more than a pact that day. They formed a connection, a friendship, and through Asha, they became family.

Chapter 7

Nick paced the room, his anxiety increasing with every step, while Shyla perched on his couch, reading his pages. Her brows knitted in stern concentration. One thing was for sure. She read at a snail's pace, resulting in a kind of torture for him.

She put down the final page and wiped the tear before it could fall down her face.

"It's so bad it made you cry?" Nick asked, his voice tense.

"It's so good it made me cry."

Nick expelled a long breath, one he'd been holding in since she'd arrived.

"I'm glad you like it. I wanted to show you a rough example of how you could write it."

"It's as if you were in my head. Yesterday, I gave you a brief description of the plot, but you added the emotion."

"I tried to imagine what it must have been like for two women in that circumstance. I just colored in your outline, that's all. I'm relieved you're not angry."

"Why would I be angry?"

He chuckled. "I didn't want you to think I was trying to steal your story."

"I would never think that. It makes sense that Sister Sarah would make the connection to Moses and Nalini to Krishna. You did some research?"

"A little in terms of the Hindu faith. I'm Catholic, so Moses is who I thought of when you told the story."

Her lips parted slightly, as if his admission surprised her.

Nick cleared his throat. "These are just ideas. I don't want to dampen your creativity."

"What creativity? I have a string of events, but you made it a story. You brought it to fruition."

"Easy Tolstoy. It's one chapter. One chapter does not a book make."

She leaned forward, pulling her legs under her. "I have a proposition for you."

"That's gotta be the scariest sentence in the English language."

"What if we worked on this together?" she asked, arching her brow.

"No."

"Why not?"

"It's your story."

"But you're the writer."

"Shyla, this sounds like literary women's fiction. That's not my genre. In fact, I wouldn't even read a story like this much less collaborate on one. Besides, I don't work well with others."

"I think we work well together. I'll tell you the story, and you write it. Simple."

"It's not simple. It's incredibly complicated."

"Why?" she challenged.

"Well, for one thing, money."

"Money?"

"Yes, if it gets published, how will we divide those profits? The story isn't mine."

"We'll split it. Or you can take it all. I don't care to make money on it."

Nick laughed at her innocence. "You say it now, but I've seen greed firsthand. It changes people. And truthfully, I really don't want to make a profit on this either. I wanted to give you a starting point, that's all."

"If neither of us is interested in making money, then why are we arguing about it?"

She had a point. He sat beside her on the couch. "Look, you can do this by yourself. I have faith in you."

She shook her head. "I can't. I've tried," she said with a defeated frown.

"You can take classes. There are some great professors at NYU. I can recommend a course for you."

"This is my last semester. It's too late."

"You can take online courses when you go home."

She turned toward him. "Nick, don't you understand we can help each other right now?"

"How so?"

"I have a story to write, but I don't possess the skills to do it. You have the skills but no story."

"I'm just blocked right now."

"Yes, but obviously something in this idea spoke to you because you were able to create this," she said, holding up the pages. "Maybe it will give you inspiration to write other things. Maybe Max Montero will start talking to you again."

He tightened his hand around the arm of the couch, not wanting to admit she vocalized his own thoughts. "I know some other authors who write in this genre. They might be willing to work with you. I can talk to them."

She shook her head vehemently. "I don't feel comfortable with strangers."

"I was a stranger, Shyla."

"Yes, but now you're my friend. That took a year of weather conversations to happen. I don't have another year."

She gathered up the pages and stood. "I should go."

"Don't be mad."

"I'm not. I'm sad. Thank you for the pages. I'll cherish them."

Shit.

Nick never had envisioned writing that rough draft would lead to this. She was right. The story had sparked something in him—kick-started his creativity in a way.

He escorted her to the street and hailed a cab.

"I don't want you to pay for my cabs anymore, Nick."

"I worry about you walking home."

"I'll take a cab if it makes you feel better, but I can afford it."

He shoved his hands in his pocket, fighting the urge to argue with her.

"Are you going to stop coming now?" He cursed the pathetic nature of his question, but the time he spent with Shyla was both precious and precarious. He didn't want it to end.

A cab stopped, and he held the door open for her.

Her lips quirked in a half-smile. "Of course not, I'm your delivery girl."

He tilted her chin toward his face. "You know what I mean."

"Nick, I'll invite myself to dinner as long as you let me in." She smiled wider, just enough for the dimple to make an appearance. God, he loved the dimple. "I understand why you don't want to work on this with me, but it doesn't change the fact we're friends." She moved to get in the cab, but paused, her eyes level with his chest. "My time with you is the best time of my day."

He swallowed, replaying the sentence in his head. "Me too, Shyla."

"Be safe, Nick."

* * * *

That night, Nick Dorsey paced so much he could have created a groove in the floor. The girl brought laughter into his quiet, lonely life. He missed her when she was gone. And yes, he was attracted to her, but he was careful to cloak those feelings around her. He craved her friendship most of all.

The next night she showed up complete with juice boxes and sandwiches.

Nick took the food and set it down. Then he led her to the couch. His digital tape recorder lay on the coffee table in front of her.

"I don't understand," she said, studying the device.

He remained standing. "Here are the rules. We do this until one of us no longer wants to. You tell me the story, and we write it together. If I determine it's good enough, I'll share it with my agent. If it's published, you'll get the lion's share of the profits, and I'll take a five percent cut."

"Only five percent?"

"Consider it my editing fee."

"But you're doing more than editing. You're writing it. Surely, you deserve more."

"It's all I want. Those are my rules. Do you have anything to add?"

"It's a very generous offer. One I can't pay you back for. Thank you." The girl didn't understand. She was already paying him back. Or rather, she was bringing him back.

She stood and walked toward him. He staggered back, unprepared when she threw her arms around his neck. She didn't let go, tightening her hug. Nick closed his eyes, took in her scent, and embraced her. He felt the curves of her body under the thick material of her clothes. His own body reacted.

Shit.

He backed away clumsily before she could decipher the non-verbal communication. He took the seat opposite the sofa and placed his notepad over his lap. "Ready?"

"I think so."

He turned on the recorder. She sat with her legs beneath her.

"This is so I can remember without taking notes."

She nodded and leaned down until her mouth was inches from the device.

He laughed. "It'll pick up your voice. You don't have to do that."

She sat back. "Oh, okay."

He punctured the top of the juice box. She did the same with hers. They didn't cement the decision with a contract or a handshake. Instead, they toasted with colorful cardboard boxes.

"Before we start, I wanted to ask if you have a title?"

"Not yet."

"Sometimes it's better to let it come to you as the story unfolds."

She cleared her throat and continued the story. He hung onto her every word, wrapped in the trance of her rich, seductive voice.

Chapter 8

Asha's story

Sarah loved the child as if she were her own flesh and blood. Asha grew up headstrong and compassionate just like the two women who raised her. In the village, it wasn't uncommon for a woman to turn up pregnant and have a child without the other villagers knowing beforehand. So no one questioned Nalini's new baby. Truthfully, the birth of a girl was a rather unremarkable event and often yielded more sympathies than celebrations.

Sister Sarah was disappointed how true Nalini's prediction was. Depal never loved the child and barely accepted her, but he allowed his wife the indulgence of keeping the baby and supported the secret of the child's origins. Sister Sarah helped Asha as much as she could. She swore the translator to secrecy. She allowed Nalini to bring the baby to work where the two women often cooed over her. Sarah spent every free moment with Asha, humming hymns and reading from scripture.

Unbeknownst to anyone, Sarah also had a proclivity for non-secular texts and often read those to Shyla, too. The infant grew surrounded by the sounds of the Gita songs Nalini sang in the morning, the biblical stories Sarah told in the afternoons, and the occasional passage penned by the sisters Brontë.

Sarah, the youngest of eight children, grew up in a strict Catholic home on the outskirts of Manitoba. Her mother planted the seeds of faith and service at an early age. Sarah questioned if being a nun was God's true plan for her, but she acquiesced to her mother's wishes. In truth, she yearned for adventure and the chance to do good works in the world. When the opportunity arose to teach in a third world country, Sarah took it willingly. The plan was to set up the school and stay for a year or two until she was relieved of her duties, but now Sarah knew she'd never leave—not when she had a baby to take care of. Never had she felt so certain she was in the right place. Never had she believed in her mother's dream as she did now.

Both women agreed never to divulge the way the baby came into their lives…not even to the child. They didn't want the girl to feel unwanted. "God has a plan for you, child," Sarah often told baby Asha.

When Asha was sick, Sarah brought her difficult-to-obtain western medications. When Asha needed clothes, Sarah purchased them so Nalini wouldn't have to ask her husband. When the child cried during the day, Sarah rocked her.

At night, Nalini carried the child to her home. In the small hut, she nursed Asha and told her of the great Hindu parables. Ironically, the stories contained very similar morals as Sarah's.

Depal often grumbled about the child, openly calling her a burden, but his wife quieted him. "If she is a burden, then she is my burden," she said to her husband. Depal resented the girl. He was old, his muscles hurt, and the last thing he wanted was another mouth to feed. She stole away what little they had, but his main concern was the cost of the dowry he'd have to pay when she was of marriageable age.

When Asha turned five, she attended the missionary school as a student. The other children made fun of her because of Sister Sarah's special interest, but Asha held her head up high. She felt lucky, proud, and even a little vain the pretty nun favored her.

Nalini agreed to stay later than the other maids. In those hours, she sat on the floor in the corner of the school building running her fingers over her *Mala*, a necklace similar to a Catholic rosary, while Sister Sarah tutored the child in more advanced subjects.

"The girl is fair skinned and beautiful," Nalini remarked with motherly pride.

"The girl is smart and hungry for knowledge," Sister Sarah countered.

Although both women disagreed about Asha's best attributes, clearly each loved her.

Asha spoke English, Gujarthi, Hindi, and the village dialect fluently. Sarah supplemented her education by giving her books to read from both English and Indian authors. Asha didn't mind she had no friends, because in many ways, the characters she read about became her closest companions.

"One day, your brave prince will come, *beta*," Nalini told her daughter, using the endearment for child. "Just as Rama came for Sita when the evil Ravana kidnapped her."

"I don't want a prince to rescue me," the child retorted.

Nalini's startled expression made the girl laugh.

"Every girl wants a prince."

"Not me, Ma. I want to *be* the brave prince."

Her mother snorted, waving a reprimanding finger at her daughter. "*Arey*, silly girl, what nonsense you're talking."

The girl, much too stubborn and headstrong for her own good, refused to denounce her views. "I'm going to be an astronaut like Sally Ride."

"Who?"

"I'll travel to the stars and bring back rocks for you, Ma."

"Why would I want rocks?"

Asha shrugged. "They are from space."

"Have you gone mad? I think there are rocks in your head." Nalini placed her hands on her hips. "Where are you getting such ideas?"

Asha bit her lower lip, unsure if she should answer, but it was clear from her mother's stern expression, an answer wasn't required.

The school building, a modern structure, contained a few tiny alcoves one could sit and go unnoticed. It was in one of these secret places, seven-year-old Asha curled up, hidden, as the two women in her life discussed her future. The little girl knew it was wrong to eavesdrop, but surely, there were exceptions to this. They were discussing her, after all.

It was rare the two women bickered, but on this topic neither refused to yield.

"I have allowed you to educate her, but you are filling her head with dangerous ideas, Sister," Nalini said, mixing her native tongue with the broken English Asha had taught her.

Sister Sarah understood enough. Over the years, the two women had formed some understanding of each other's language. A translator was no longer necessary.

"She can be anything she wants. Why are you limiting her?"

"She cannot. You paved a difficult path for her. Her future is already determined. She will marry and have children. That is the way here, and it is a good way."

Sister Sarah expelled a frustrated sigh. "It seems I believe in her more than you do."

"You know nothing, Sister. You give her hope she has no right to. Your beliefs will cause her great heartache."

Asha didn't understand why they disagreed. If it made her mother happy, she would marry and have children. She could do that and be an astronaut on the side. The solution to the problem didn't seem all that complicated, at least not to the little girl with two braids in her hair who hid in the alcove clutching a worn copy of *The Secret Garden*.

* * * *

Two years passed, but the women never resolved their disagreement. It always simmered in the background, threatening to boil over like the water she heated for her papa's chai each morning.

Asha ran to the school building, her braids flapping behind her. The Hindu festival of Holi, signifying the changing of the seasons, was her favorite holiday. She wanted to show Sister Sarah the pink and orange-colored powder on her dress.

School wasn't in session, but Asha knew Sarah would be in her little house behind the building. She often sat in the garden reading, and that's exactly where Asha found her.

She wasn't alone.

A tall white man sat with her sipping tea. She recognized him from the day before. Sarah had introduced him as a school benefactor. The child's natural curiosity reached new heights yesterday when she'd laid eyes on the man, who was even paler than Sarah with fire-colored hair and eyes the same hue as the river, but much clearer in color. Asha had made him laugh.

"Pleasure to meet you, sir," she had said, borrowing phrases from a book she'd read.

"Your English is impeccable, young lady," he complimented.

"Thank you, sir. So is yours," Asha replied, managing a clumsy curtsey.

He had flashed an amused smile. His straight teeth were blindingly white. "It should be. It's my mother tongue, after all."

Asha's mouth gaped in horror. "You stole your mother's tongue?"

The man had exchanged a look with Sarah before they both burst in laughter.

Today, he wore an expensive linen suit and fancy hat, the kind she'd seen on movie stars. Although Sarah and he spoke English, his voice pronounced words in a clipped, delicate fashion. Asha hid herself behind the shrubbery. She'd never seen Sister Sarah yell. The scene was far too intriguing to let her conscious interfere with the fact she was eavesdropping again, despite Sarah's stern warnings.

"Don't make me feel guilty," Sarah said.

"Is that what you think I'm doing, Sarah? I'm trying to make you see reason. I want to save you from this."

"This is where I belong."

He was quiet for a minute. "She's a pretty girl."

"Beauty fades. Her best feature is her aptitude and intelligence."

"Does it even make a difference here?"

"I believe it does." Sarah pushed a newspaper toward him. "Have you read this?"

"I can't say I have. The local papers don't make my required periodicals list. I doubt there's an abundance of business news in it."

Sarah tapped the paper as if to drive in her words like nails. "Another girl was found in the jungle today. That's six girls in one year, in this region alone."

"This has been going on for centuries. It's culturally ingrained."

Sarah shook her head. "It's an economic problem at its roots. Girls require a large investment, a debt that is never repaid. Boys, on the other hand, allow a family to prosper, bringing in additional income. The problem's actually getting worse. It's an epidemic."

"You can't save all of them," his said, clenching his perfect teeth.

"A wave starts with a single ripple."

"My dear, delusional girl, I'm afraid you're attempting to tame a tsunami. Besides, you've done enough, haven't you? She's alive and healthy."

"She needs me still. I need her, too."

She heard a loud banging on the table as if the man slammed his hand down. "This quest is a fool's endeavor."

"Then I am a fool."

"What does that make me?" His voice was slightly above a whisper, yet it sounded as if he was scolding her. Asha's fists curled. She did not care for this man at all. No one spoke to the good Sister with such disrespect.

"You shouldn't be here," Sarah said.

"I came to deliver a check for your charity, my dear."

"Don't be coy. You came for a different purpose. We shouldn't be alone together."

Asha had never heard a sad laugh in her life. It seemed a contradiction, but that was what the man's laugh sounded like.

"Is it better to be alone apart, love?"

"Don't."

"Who should I be angry at? God or the girl?"

"I hope you're referring to me when you say the girl because I, and I alone, am the one to blame."

"Sarah, you know you belong with me…to me."

She stood up and walked to the far side of the garden. Asha retreated farther into the thick growth that separated Sarah's cottage and the school. When the man approached Sarah, he placed his hand on her shoulder. Even through the obstruction of branches, Asha saw the woman's body shake as the sobs overtook her.

"Why do you even want me anymore? Why?" she screamed, hitting his chest. Although she didn't understand, tears fell from Asha's cheeks, rolling though the brightly colored powder decorating her face.

The man grabbed Sarah's wrists and stilled them. "I'm going home, Sarah. That's what I came to say to you. I'm leaving for London in less than a fortnight. Come with me."

There was a long silence. Asha cupped her hand over her mouth and nose to conceal her sneeze. Sarah said something too low for Asha's ears. Then he was talking again. He talked a great deal…too much. "You don't even allow me the catharsis of hating you with all your damn righteous benevolence."

Asha pushed aside some thicket, and through the opening of the vines, she witnessed a scene so shocking she almost screamed. The man had his hand on Sarah's back and his mouth on hers. The evil man was attempting to pilfer Sarah's breath just as he stole his own mother's tongue. The little girl almost bolted into the clearing, ready to defend Sarah, but her knees gave out when Sarah's hand caressed his cheek.

It dawned on Asha she'd observed a kiss, something she'd read about in fairy tales and theorized were rare, magical events. She'd never witnessed one. Her parents never kissed. They didn't even hug. There were no displays of public affection in the village, at least not between adults.

"I'm going to hell," Sarah said.

"I would chance an eternity in hell, because in you, I have found heaven."

She pushed him away. "Go home, my sweet prince. Take a wife. Make your life. I'll pray for you."

His expression turned cold. "Save your prayers, Sarah. I don't desire or deserve them." He sighed and kissed her once more on the forehead. "I will always love you." His voice had lowered to the volume of defeat, low and grim.

Sarah stood in a rigid stance, watching him walk away. When he was no longer visible, the nun slowly made her way back to the chair, her shoulders slumped unnaturally as she fell into the seat, as if she carried an invisible weight on them.

"I will always love you, too," Sarah said, although he was no longer there to hear it…but Asha did.

Sarah buried her head in her hands. At first, Asha thought she might be praying, but then the sound came, a defeated, angry cry like she'd never heard. Sarah might be cross with the little girl for spying, but Asha had to comfort her. She covered the distance between them until she stood in front of the woman.

"Sister."

Sarah looked up at her. "Naughty girl," Sarah chided. "You know better, young lady."

"I'm sorry."

"You mustn't tell."

"I promise," she said, although the whole secret wasn't clear to her. "Why are you crying, Sister?"

"I am sad."

"Did that man hurt you?"

"No child, I hurt him."

Sarah held her arms out, and even though Asha was too big to sit in her lap, she did. The colorful powder made from spices rubbed off Asha's face onto Sarah's dress. She tried to wipe it away, but the bright stain simply deepened.

Sarah held onto her, and somehow Asha knew not to speak too much. She waited for Sarah's tears to subside. It was apparent the man had caused much damage to Asha's very special friend and teacher.

"One day, I will make him suffer for your tears, Sister," Asha said with great drama and conviction.

"Asha, we don't talk in such ways. Remember, your name means hope. Promise me you will always be the peacekeeper."

Asha nodded, although silently she rationalized there were times when one had to make war to secure peace. And any man who made Sarah cry should be punished severely because, surely, this was a sin of great magnitude.

"I promise, sister," she said to appease Sarah. She tugged on the nun's skirt. "Come to the festival with me, sister. It will make you joyful again. The seasons are changing, and everyone is happy today."

Sarah's mouth curved slightly. After a few more pleading looks from Asha, she finally agreed. Hand in hand, they walked together toward town. Asha fit in with her clothes sprinkled in every possible color of the earth. Sarah looked odd and strange in her long western dress stained with pink powder.

Asha stopped at the temple and bowed before a plaster statue of an elephant-headed man.

"Do you know Ganesha, the Elephant God?" Asha asked Sarah as if she was making an introduction.

"I know of him," Sarah said. "I'm aware of his origin and how he came to have an elephant's head."

Asha sighed, unimpressed. "Everyone knows that story, but did you know that Ganesha is the remover of obstacles?"

"How did he get such a prestigious title, little one?"

Asha smiled with excitement. The chance to teach her brilliant teacher presented a rare opportunity.

"Many stories exist, but there is one which is my most favorite. Shall I tell you?"

"Yes, please," Sarah said, her sadness appearing to lessen.

Asha not only told the story, but she acted it out with gestures and dancing. "Lord Shiva and Goddess Parvathi were a divine couple. They lived with their two divine children, Ganesha and his older brother Karthik. The two brothers were as opposite as the sun and moon. Ganesha was fat with a big belly and an elephant's head." Asha jutted her belly out, which made Sarah laugh. "Unlike his brother, Karthik was a beautiful boy full of strength and energy. The brothers loved each other very much, and they had great love and devotion to their parents, who were the rulers of the universe."

"Rulers of the universe? My, that's a hard act to follow," Sarah said.

"Yes, it is, but both boys were smart and wise. One day, the other Gods began to question which one should take over for Shiva and Parvathi. They had a competition to decide."

"A competition?" Sister Sarah asked.

"Yes, the boy who could go around the world three times and return home first would be the best one.

Karthik, an athlete, immediately mounted his vehicle, the peacock, and rushed off on his voyage. He raced with great speed and grace. Ganesha was slow and fat. His vehicle was a rat."

"A rat?" Sarah asked in surprise.

"Yes, Sister. A rat cannot beat a peacock." The child sliced her hand through the air and shook her head as if to cement her point. "No way."

"Certainly not," Sarah agreed.

Asha smiled, tapping her head three times. "But wisdom is in the brain, not the body, and Ganesha didn't need a vehicle at all. While Karthik flew around the world at lightening fast speeds, Ganesha circled his parents at a very slow pace. Once, twice, three times." The girl demonstrated by walking three lazy circles around Sarah.

"His father asked Ganesha why he wasn't racing and allowing his brother to win. Ganesha explained he had already won. Both parents were confused at first, but not after Ganesha enlightened them."

The storyteller paused for affect, waiting for her audience to demand a conclusion. Sarah didn't disappoint. "Well, don't keep me in suspense, dear. How did he win?"

"He said, 'I'm your son, and to me, you two are my whole world. Why should I go farther to win the contest? Circling you is the same as going around the universe.'"

"From that day on, it was decided Ganesha was indeed the wisest of the brothers. He teaches us any obstacle can be overcome, that solutions aren't always obvious, and to honor your parents above all."

Sarah clapped her hands. "You are a wonderful storyteller, Asha. What a valuable lesson."

"Come, Sister," Asha said, putting her hand in the nun's and leading her to town where the tossing of colors took place. Men and women sprayed colored water on each other while dancing to the beat of a *dholak*, a two-handed drum. Children ran through the crowds with water balloons, carefully surveying the scene for their next targets. Asha heard the villager's whispering about the strange duo of a little girl and the tall white woman. It wasn't the kind of atmosphere in which one would expect to find a Catholic nun.

Then again, Sarah and Asha were both peculiar in their own ways. Neither female was suited for the expectations of propriety set by others.

Chapter 9

Nick's routine didn't change. He jogged every morning, purchased a single white rose, dropped to his knees in front of Jenny's grave, and attended meetings. But the cursor no longer mocked, and the vacant, blank pages rapidly colored themselves in meticulous eleven-point font. The hours between nine and midnight became his time with her. She didn't belong to him, but that time with her did. Nick grew happier as the world shifted, a slow thaw melting away the last of the cold, bathing the dismal skies with precious light. "I brought you a plant," she said, handing him a pot of dirt with a sprig of green sticking out of it. Nick regarded the peculiar object, holding it at an angle.

Shyla laughed and took it from him. "It won't bite. I thought you could use something stimulating."

"That's why I have you."

Nick loved her voice, but perhaps her laugh was even lovelier. *Careful, Dorsey*, he warned himself for the umpteenth time since she'd entered his life. All of his concerns manifested in a millisecond, souring his good mood. *She drinks juice boxes. She's too innocent for you. You're too different. She's leaving soon. You'll fuck her up. Why? Because you're a fuck up, that's why.* He silenced the jerky ping-pong match going on in his head and focused his attention on her.

She set the plant on the table. He helped her with her coat, as was his habit. She no longer acted surprised, but she did always smile gratefully. Today, her jeans were fitted, showing off the perfect curve of her hipbones. Nick allowed himself a few solitary seconds to take her in. Although she wore a simple black T-shirt, her breasts and waist were proportionate to perfection.

She came out with a cup of water and slowly fed the potted foliage. He liked how comfortable she was in his home. It had taken a while to get to this place.

"Thank you for the plant." He made a note to buy more. After all, the surplus of air became dangerously low when she stood too close to him. Anything that expelled oxygen and purified his dirty thoughts would be a necessity at this point.

"You're welcome. Happy spring," she said as if it was a holiday, then Nick realized based on what they wrote, it was a holiday for her.

"Happy Holi, Shyla."

"Thank you, Nick."

He set up their meal and took the chair opposite her. "I'm getting tired of sandwiches."

"We could order a pizza again or Chinese."

Wisps of her hair fell around her face. She pushed them back with annoyance. The gesture both provoked and amused him. In the brief moment, all his previous reservations collapsed like a bad poker hand—folded but not forgotten. "I'd like to ask you out...on a date."

"Oh," she said with hesitation.

He sucked in a deep breath. *Nice going, Dorsey.* The meals they shared were simple, but to Nick, it was the best part of his routine day. He wondered if he had wagered away those hours because his dick wanted in on the conversation.

"I take it you don't want to go out with me?" The man, who would have considered himself a failure if he didn't sleep with a woman on the second date, cursed himself for moving too fast. Truthfully, he wasn't that guy anymore, except when the remnants of the miserable man-whore still rose occasionally...figuratively and literally.

She bit her bottom lip. "It's not that." She took a deep breath. "I assumed we were dating."

Nick repeated her words in his head, a flood of relief and confusion battling to clarify her statement. "You think we're dating?"

She popped a cherry tomato in her mouth. Nick waited patiently for her to chew, all the while annoyed by cherry tomatoes, specifically the time it took to eat one. "Well, yes. We eat together almost every night. Sometimes we talk or write. Last week we watched a movie. Aren't we dating?"

"Technically, I suppose, but I would describe what we are doing as hanging out. I want to take you somewhere nice—a place where they have dim lighting, expensive food, and candles. I want to laugh with you under the stars, maybe slow dance with you, and then take you home and kiss you good-night at your doorstep."

She smiled, a cute lopsided grin, which made Nick's mouth curve in response. "I don't know how to slow dance."

"I have so much to teach you."

She bit her lower lip, her eyes darting to the kitchen. "Do you ever use that room for anything besides brewing gourmet coffee?"

He looked over at the open space that housed a set of matching stainless steel appliances and a one-of-a-kind concrete countertop as if he was noticing it for the first time. "Sure, it's a great place to store chips and cereal."

"Don't you ever cook?"

"I think of that area as a very fancy art installation. I can heat up soup, boil water, and fry some eggs. Unfortunately, that's my entire arsenal of self-made meals."

"What if I made you dinner?"

"That would be very nice."

"Do you like Indian food?"

For a brief moment, Nick considered lying, but it passed quickly. "No."

"You don't like Indian at all?"

"I like the people, especially this one particular girl."

She laughed, shaking her head. "I'll make you something you'll enjoy."

"I would like that."

"I don't work tomorrow. I can come earlier, and we can eat around the same time."

"I can't wait."

"I guess tomorrow night will be our first date then."

He leaned across the table. "Has anyone ever taken you on a date?"

Her posture became rigid before she blurted, "Sure, Elaine set me up with her brother's boyfriend once."

Nick's mouth gaped. "Come again?"

She inhaled a deep breath. "Shucks, I meant to say her boyfriend's brother."

"Yeah, it takes on a much different meaning the other way." He jerked his head around to face her. "Did you just say 'shucks'?"

"Hey, you made me watch the pasta western. They used that word a lot. Did I say it wrong?"

"It's referred to as a spaghetti western, but you did use the word in one of its correct contexts. It's just not something that's used very often, and it sounds strange coming from you."

"Because everyone else would say the other words?"

"What other words?" His lips twitched into a devious grin, and she gave him a look he described as *I know what you're doing, Dorsey.*

"You know…the one you would say."

"You mean shit or fuck?"

"Yes, those words. But shucks is perfect. It combines both of them, yet it's not a swear word."

"Does swearing bother you?"

She raised her eyebrows. "I've lived here almost four years. It doesn't bother me. There's many ways to color a language. People swore in the village, too. I'm trying not to fall into the habit. I will be teaching children in the near future, after all." And with that last sentence, his doubts surfaced again. She would be teaching…in India. She might as well be on the moon.

She nibbled on a slice of cucumber. She always seemed to be picking at food. The girl ate like a bird. He thought about remarking on it, but he knew better. Never comment on a woman's diet or her weight. Rules to live by.

"What are the other meanings for shucks?" she asked.

"It has many definitions. It can be a husk on the outer layer of corn. Or it can mean worthless." She gave him a questioning look so he offered an example, dropping his voice slightly. "Like I don't give a shucks about what we do as long as we do it together." Her face flushed slightly, her smile turning suggestive. Encouraged, he dropped his voice a few octaves more. *Test the water, Dorsey, but don't fucking dive in!* "Or it could mean to discard."

"Discard?"

"As in peel off. For example, she shucked off her black T-shirt in a hurry." His feet dipped into the complicated waters he'd avoided, waters that could heat up to boiling point if they kept creeping down this dangerous path.

"I see. So if I said, do you mind if we don't shuck tonight, that would be a proper use?"

Nick opened his mouth to respond, to try to eat up the words already spilling out into the atmosphere, but she held up her hand, and her lips parted slightly. "But I hope we do shuck one day."

Naughty girl.

He didn't have to worry about diving in. She'd just pushed him. "That's not the right way, but who the hell cares? Words are flexible. They can bend, contort, twist." Ironically, he'd just described many of the same things he wanted to do with her. He stood and stretched. "I was wrong."

"About what?"

"You are not a shy girl."

"What am I?"

"It's probably better I stop trying to define you." No definition...
only discovery.

"I am shy, but not with you. I'm not fragile. I won't wilt."

"I know." He stood up and cleared their plates. "Unfortunately, the
plant you bought me may not be as lucky."

Chapter 10

Shyla took a step back when Nick opened the door the next night. She swallowed hard, blinking her eyes in disbelief. "You shaved."

"Yes, it was time for a change. Do you like it?" he asked, rubbing his square jaw.

Like it? The beard made him look mysterious and rugged, but seeing the naked beauty of his striking face caused her mouth to go dry. He looked much younger....almost boyish, except for the long jagged scar that ran along the left side of his face.

In a way, the imperfection added to Nick Dorsey's attraction, giving him a special brand of menacing mystery she found incredibly sexy, but endearing, too. She wanted nothing more than to run her finger against the wound and wash away the pain. She decided it must be the reason he grew a beard and the reason he was now standing awkwardly so that side of him would be less exposed. The simple act of shaving highlighted his other features, too. His hair looked lighter, similar in both thickness and color to a lion's mane. He wore dark jeans and a blue V-neck sweater, which matched his eyes...dark blue with a midnight quality that made them appear almost black. Shyla allowed herself the indulgence of traveling down the length of his body, taking in his broad shoulders and muscular arms, which stretched the fabric of his garments in an alluring way. If a man could look regal in casual clothes, than that's how Nick looked—aristocratic, almost patrician but with rough edges. The effect of him was so captivating she stumbled, searching for the right words.

"Shyla, are you just going to stare at me?" He rubbed his cheek in a way that made it clear he wasn't fishing for a compliment, but sincerely asking a question. How to answer that? There weren't enough antonyms for dislike to appropriately reply.

"Yes," she said, although it sorely lacked the appropriate depth. She focused on what else she could say, but her tiny sigh must have communicated better than any words because he grinned.

"Are you planning on coming in?" he finally asked.

"Yes." Shyla walked past him, trying not to sniff the air, but her nose betrayed her. His scent, like the rest of him, disarmed her with its mixture of clean, sexy, and masculine.

"Do you want me to show you where the pans are? I actually own a few."

"Please."

"Oh good, I was wondering if you might respond with the word 'yes' all night." His grin turned wicked. "Although, that's not necessarily a bad thing."

He helped her with her jacket.

"The Who?" she asked, pointing to his record player. Nick's vast collection of records almost rivaled his books.

"Very good," he replied.

"'Behind Blue Eyes,'" she said, naming the song. It wasn't exactly a happy song, but Shyla found herself humming along to the melody. She entered the kitchen where he'd set up all the items she requested. She checked the fridge and hugged him when she saw all the brightly colored packages of juice boxes. Some poor child wouldn't get a drink in his lunch because Nick had bought out the store of these particular refreshments.

"I see you did some extra shopping. This wasn't on the list."

"I wanted to stock up on what you liked."

"That's very considerate."

"I'm not sure if you'll find everything else in order."

"Why?"

"Well, an interesting thing happened. I got to the market, and I was zipping through your list until I got to the Garbanzo beans. I wasn't sure if you wanted canned or dried."

"Canned."

He sighed, rubbing the back of his neck. "That figures. I got dried."

She found the packages on the counter and held them up. "I could have used these, but they have to be soaked for at least a day."

"That's not the issue. I can go out and get the right kind of beans. My point is I was going to call you to confirm, but guess what, Shyla?"

"What?"

"I don't have your phone number. I mean, it's my fault, too, since I never asked, but it seems odd to me we never thought to exchange numbers." He pulled out his phone. "What is it?"

She focused her attention on the other items, organizing them. "I don't have one."

His jaw dropped. "How can you not have a cell phone in New York? Or anywhere for that matter?" His question, ripe with more admonishment than curiosity, made her uncomfortable.

"I don't need one."

"What if there's an emergency?"

"I'm either in class, at the dorm, at work, or here. I had a cell once but it was a pay as you go, and I kept forgetting to add minutes to it. If I need to use the phone, I use Elaine's or the one at work. It's not like I have anyone to call."

"What about your dad?"

"We email each other. It's cheaper."

"But what if someone needs to get a hold of you?"

"No one ever does. No one really cares where I am."

He frowned at her statement. She smiled brightly, hoping to reassure him and lighten the mood. She twisted a strand of her hair and secured it behind her ear. "I'll get another phone soon."

"I don't believe you."

"Why not?" she asked, narrowing her eyes.

"Because you can't bluff. You have a tell."

"What do you mean?"

"It's a habit which conveys you are fibbing. Are you fibbing?"

She placed a hand on her hip. "What's my tell?"

"A good card player never reveals someone's tell. I'll keep the information in my back pocket for a rainy day."

"Are you going to get going? I want to start cooking, and I need beans."

"No one should ever utter the phrase, 'I need beans,' but yes, I will go."

"While you're out, maybe you can get a bottle of wine, too?"

Nick raised his eyebrows, an amused grin returning to his face. "You like wine?"

"You don't think I only drink juice boxes, do you?"

"I honestly wasn't sure. What are we having for dinner?"

"Aloo Chaat."

"I need a little more help than that, Shyla."

"Sorry, it's potatoes and chick peas mostly. Also, coconut rice."

"Hmm...I'm not sure what wine goes with vegetables alone."

"How about red? I like red."

"Red it is. I'll be back."

Shyla took her time. Nick's kitchen was clean, but she distracted herself by wiping down every surface. She walked around to each appliance as if silently introducing herself. The untouched quality of them made her a bit giddy. She showered the vegetables in cold water. She began the laborious task of chopping, peeling, and dicing all the items. She didn't mind, though. She loved cooking, although the idea of preparing food for Nick filled her with slight terror.

Nick was taking a long time coming back. Alone in his apartment, her mind raced. Just like the dishes she planned, she wasn't his usual fare. Her movements became less confident, marred by her own self-doubt. She doled out the spices carefully, using smaller quantities than she normally would. Once she had them all laid out, she decided to cut them in half again. Better safe than sorry.

Nick finally returned, depositing a dark bottle and metal cans on the counter.

"What can I do?" he asked. The kitchen was an adequate space but the presence of his tall brawny body made it seem much smaller. Shyla feared the tension from his proximity in this tight spot would be perilous to her safety. She could chop off a finger or burn herself…or worse, she might cause him injury.

"I can do it on my own."

"Seriously, put me to work. I may not possess any culinary skills, but I'm capable of following directions."

"Why don't you watch television or write?"

"We don't have enough material for another chapter."

"Then write something else." She shook her head, wishing she'd thought before she spoke. "Sorry."

"It's okay. I guess I can read."

He walked over to the bookshelf. Shyla let herself enjoy the sight of his broad back and tight butt. He grabbed a volume without even looking. She wondered if all his choices were easy.

"What are you reading?" she asked, depositing the potatoes into boiling water.

"*The Road* by Cormac McCarthy. Have you read this one?"

"No."

"It's depressing but crazy good."

"Will you read it to me?"

Traveling with slow, seductive, masculine grace, his deep voice filtered through the apartment.

"Can you read something else?" she asked after twenty minutes had passed. She decided, although McCarthy was an excellent author, she could not absorb anything sullen tonight.

"Any requests?"

"I was thinking Keegan Moon's, *Max Montero and the Three Wise Women*."

Nick laughed, holding the hardback cover of McCarthy's book over his face. "In the mood for dime store drivel, are we?"

"It's growing on me."

"That's book three. Wouldn't you rather hear book two?"

"I'm on book three. I think I left off on chapter eighteen."

Nick stared at her as if she'd announced McCarthy, himself, was joining them for supper. "You're kidding."

"I decided I'd give it another chance. I still have some issues, but I can see why people like them."

"Shyla, it's not a prerequisite you like my work to be my friend…or anything else. You can always be honest with me."

"I am being honest with you. I don't love it, but I do like it."

Nick looked unconvinced, but he exchanged books and his voice took over again. To hear him read his own work, orally communicating the thoughts once trapped in his head was a privilege. The book was twenty chapters so Nick concluded the story.

"I would tell you I enjoyed it, but I don't think you'll believe me. I will say the heroine, or rather heroines, were a bit batty for my taste."

"Batty? There's a word you don't hear every day. Anyway, I believe you."

"How come?"

"You have a tell, remember?"

"Oh, yes."

"Do you need my help yet?"

"Thank you for the offer, but I want to do this on my own."

"Suits me. I'm going to watch the hockey game. I think the Devils are playing."

To her amusement, Nick was quite vocal when he watched sports. As he watched the game, he fiddled with his phone. She came out of the kitchen, a dishtowel draped over her shoulder. She took a seat next to him on the couch. He put an arm around her and drew her close.

Her heart raced with his spontaneous gesture. She gazed at him wondering if they'd kiss now, but he kept his eyes on the screen, gently running his fingers down her arm, creating a flurry of goose bumps on her flesh. She laid her head against his chest. Despite his trained expression, his heart beat an audible, fast-paced rhythm of its own.

"It's almost ready."

He kissed the top of her head. The tenderness left her speechless for a moment. "It smells delicious. Thank you for doing this."

"My pleasure."

His other hand came around, and he placed a phone in her lap. "Here."

She turned the device over in her hand. "Do you want me to call someone for you?"

He rubbed her shoulders. "It's not my phone. It's yours. I put you on my plan. You don't have to worry about buying minutes anymore. And now, I won't worry about you…as much."

She pulled away, dropping the phone, but Nick's quick reflexes caught it a few inches from the hardwood floor.

"Hey, watch it. I got you a strong protector case, but let's not test it out."

He had lined up the packages on the coffee table, each one adorned with a colorful bitten apple. "I can't accept this."

"Yes. You. Can."

"It's too extravagant," she said, trying to give it back to him.

With one finger, he raised her chin until their eyes made contact. "It's a necessity. And if you don't accept it for yourself, at least do so for me."

"Why?"

"Because someone cares where you are, Shyla. That person is me. Also, I want you to be able to call me if you need something…anything. Do you understand?"

She held the device in her hand, moved by his generosity. Not just the monetary investment, but the weight of his words, spoken with such determination. "Thank you. I don't know what else to say."

"There is nothing else to say. Promise me you'll keep it with you at all times."

"I will. Shall we exchange numbers?"

He took it from her. "I've already set it up. I put my number in there and downloaded some music for you."

"You did?" She peered at the screen while he scrolled through the selections.

"Yeah, the stuff you like—Pink Floyd, Led Zeppelin, The Doors, and of course, Jimi Hendrix. I got you ear buds so you can listen to it whenever you want. We can always add more."

It was all the artists he'd introduced her to—a whole world she didn't know existed. "Will you show me how to access the music and how to call you?"

Nick's loud chuckle rumbled through the space. "Are you sure you're Indian? You seem to have some problems with simple technology."

She laughed, playfully punching his chest. "I suppose I was absent the day they passed out that particular DNA strand to my people."

Nick patiently demonstrated all the fancy features of her new phone, keeping on arm around her the whole time, making it near impossible for her to retain the information. "Dinner's ready," she announced when her breaths became audible.

She found some candles and placed them on the small dining table. Nick lit them and set the table as she brought out the dishes. He poured the wine.

"You can use the fork if you want. I won't judge you," she said when they were finally seated.

He picked up the thin bread. "I'll go traditional." Her stomach tied in knots as she watched him take a bite.

He chewed slowly, giving away no emotion. When he finally swallowed, he smiled. "My compliments to the chief. It's delicious, sweetheart."

Sweetheart? A word she'd heard said to other women all the time. It had never phased her. But him saying it to her…now. A shiver traveled down her spine. Who knew a word could be so powerful?

"I'm happy you like it."

"To our first date," he said, holding up his wine glass. They clinked glasses, and Shyla tipped the liquid back, relishing the aromatic balance of grape and sugar.

"Wow, sailor, take it slow."

"It's very good."

She slid her glass over so he could refill it.

"I'm happy you like it," he replied, mimicking her words. "So, have you thought of a title for the book yet?"

She was quiet for a minute. "*The Choice Less*. What do you think?"

"It sounds interesting, but I'm not sure if it's enough of an attention-grabber. Plus, I don't see how it applies to what we've written."

"It will. It's still early. Let's not talk about the book tonight. I think we need a break from it."

"What would you like to talk about?"

"What are we going to do on our second date?"

His restrained smile widened. "Any suggestions?"

"You pick. I picked this."

"Well, as much I love our intimate setting, I think we should go out. What are some things you like to do in the city?"

She was quiet for a moment, unsure of an appropriate answer. "I haven't done much. I've been to Central Park, and I had tea at the Grand Hotel. I've been to Brooklyn a few times. Mostly, I've stuck to Greenwich."

Nick tilted his head. "This is the greatest city in the world, and you've hardly seen any of it."

Shyla's fears flooded with newfound inadequacy. He was used to worldly women…not women who came from another world. Yet, at the same time, she dared not apologize for who she was. Her lack of experience supported her dedication to being a successful student, diligent employee, and all around responsible girl. Nick, always helpful, eased away her doubts with his next statement. "Perfect. There are so many places I want to take you, and I'm honored to be your guide."

"I couldn't think of a better person."

* * * *

Nick walked Shyla out of the apartment. He kept a firm arm around her for two reasons. First, because he loved touching her. Second, and perhaps more important, the girl was wasted. Nick was having a hard time…literally. She was grabby and giggly and the most fucking adorable drunk he'd ever seen.

Although he'd normally never complain about assertiveness, he didn't feel it was appropriate to take advantage of the situation. He wanted both of them to be active parties in their intimacy. He wondered where all this newfound stamina had come from. Not the stamina to have sex for hours, which had always been a strong suit of his, but the kind of Herculean strength required to hold off fulfilling his gratification. Willpower was a trait he sorely lacked.

The cab pulled up, and he held the door open for her. She stepped in and looked up at him, a pretty pout on her lips.

"Good-night, Nick."

"Scoot over," he said.

She slid to the other side of the cab, her eyes widening along with her smile. "You're coming with me?"

"Don't you remember how the date's supposed to end?"

"Something about my doorstep and a kiss?"

"That's right."

"I can give you one right now," she said, her hands threading through his hair.

He placed a finger against her mouth. "I'm traditional in some things. That's not the way it's going to happen."

He craved her kiss so badly, he would have stolen it in any location, but he held off. It didn't have a damn thing to do with tradition and everything to do with her safety. There was no way she was getting in a cab alone when her faculties weren't operating at full force.

She leaned her head against his shoulder. He kissed her hair. She craned her face, looking into his eyes, her mouth parted invitingly. He grazed her cheek and played with the soft loose curls, which had escaped her bun. As curious as he was about the length of her hair, he liked how she always kept it up. She had a beautiful neck that required exploration. Luckily, Nick was just the kind of man in need of such adventure. He pressed his lips against the dimple at her cheek and traced his finger over her lips. He closed his eyes, his breath climbing slightly as she parted her mouth and sucked his finger. She stopped suddenly, her body tensing. Nick followed her gaze. The cabbie peered into the rearview mirror, slicing right through their moment.

Nick flexed his jaw in irritation as he moved his body so his face covered the full width of the mirror, blocking the cabbie's view of Shyla. "A lot of traffic tonight, buddy?"

"No, the street's empty," the cabbie replied, straightening up.

"Are you going in reverse?" Nick demanded through gritted teeth.

"No," the cabbie replied skeptically.

"Then there's no reason for you to be looking in the rearview. Eyes straight ahead."

The driver grumbled some expletives, but looked ahead. When he imagined her alone with this creep, he clenched his fist. He turned his attention back to Shyla, who had cupped a hand over her mouth, trying to hide her laughter.

Her dorm was a mere two miles from Nick's house. He helped her out of the cab. Then he sent the cabbie on his way. He sure as hell didn't want the man in audience any longer.

"My old stomping grounds," he said, taking a deep breath, inhaling the scent of fresh pizza, stale beer, and young dreams.

"Did you live here?" she asked, stepping onto the staircase. She was still shorter than him, but she didn't have to crane her neck as much this way.

"I couldn't afford to live in the Village." He jerked his head back. "I lived across the tunnel in good old Hoboken."

"That's in New Jersey?"

"Yeah, but we locals just call it Jersey."

She swayed slightly. Nick placed his hands on her hips. Shyla wrapped her arms over his shoulders as the cool March wind blew around them.

"Sometimes I wonder if you really like me," she said, the words smashing together with her slur.

Nick considered her statement, taking a moment to let his fingers twist a loose strand of hair. "You're very drunk right now."

"That doesn't make my statement less valid."

He inhaled her heavenly scent. "I'll be honest with you, Shyla, because I need to say this aloud, but also I doubt you'll remember this conversation. I like you very much. In fact, the large quantity of like I have for you frightens me. I don't want to push you away by moving too fast. You're very young, and I don't want to risk the friendship we've built."

"You're only five years older than me." For some odd reason, she held up her hands and counted down fingers for him. It took her three tries before he helped her, kissing each of her knuckles as she bent them.

"It's more than a number. Experience isn't measured by math."

"We don't have to fit perfectly. I don't have to be right for you. I just want to be here for you."

"Who said you're not right for me?" he asked, surprised at how much her statement hurt him. He didn't ponder on it long, though, because the sky, without any warning, suddenly fell open, dousing them.

"There's that rain you're always talking about," he said, shaking his head.

"Shucks," she murmured.

Nick chuckled, but his laugh died as soon as her lower lip trembled.

"Do...do you not want me?" she asked.

"Want? I don't know what's worse—being near you without holding you or being apart from you." He ran his hands up her arms in a lame attempt to warm her. "We'll talk later when you're sober and...dry. Do you need help getting inside?"

"No, I live right there," she said, pointing to a first floor window. She shivered slightly. Nick tightened his hold on her.

"Wave to me from the window once you're inside." He knew the allure of a drunk girl in a co-ed dorm, and there was no way he was leaving without seeing her safe behind the pane of glass.

"Maybe I'm not savvy enough to figure out what you're saying. I'm not looking for you to take care of me."

Ironically, that's exactly what Nick wanted to do and one of the reasons for his chaotic thoughts. "What are you looking for, Shyla?"

"I want to hang out with you. I want us to keep laughing. I want to go on more dates and make more dinners. I want an experience. I want a memory. Something I can hold onto when I go home. But right now, I want your kiss."

He pushed back the soaked strands of hair on her forehead. He brushed his lips against hers, and then forced himself to back up before he did anything else. Her eyes remained closed with her mouth pursed while sheets of rain fell upon them and pelted the sidewalk in some angry war cry. Nick's heart mimicked a similar sound. "You should go inside before you get sick."

She blinked her eyes, her mouth twisted in a frown before she turned. Dissatisfaction was bad enough, but Shyla's disappointment he could not tolerate. He grabbed her by the waist and spun her toward him. She squeaked as he crushed his lips against hers. Her mouth felt warm and soft despite the cold sheets of rain surrounding them. Her body melted into his. He lifted her off the landing, holding her tight. Shyla moaned against his mouth, her arms wrapping around him. Nick's advance was immediate. His tongue found hers. She tasted spicy and sweet and all things delicious. His hands threaded through her hair until it fell loose around them. He sucked on her lower lip, sliding his tongue across the area. Her breasts heaved against his chest.

He ignored the twitch of his cock and the silent plea it made to pick her up and run back to the loft. To make her moan all night. To taste every inch of her delicious flesh. To possess her body with his. When she shivered, he finally set her down. If not for that shiver, he would never have let her go.

"Better?" he asked, thankful for the sound of the pattering rain that drowned out his deep breaths. It didn't matter, though. The cold made every breath visible as the air swirled between them. It looked as if a cloud of smoke encircled them—or rather connected them—each of her hot, heavy breaths colliding and mingling with his in the chilly night air.

"I don't know. Do it again," she said between pants.

He chuckled and kissed her cheek. "Go inside, my horny girl. Remember to wave." She nodded, but stood there for a moment.

"Shyla—"

Before he could finish, she wrapped her arms around him once more, embracing him. Nick would have found her aggressiveness amusing if there wasn't a war raging between his two heads. "You're going to catch pneumonia," he said as he nipped her ear.

"I'm going to take a hot shower."

"Good idea."

"I'll be thinking of you."

"I'm going to take a cold shower. I'll be trying not to think of you and failing miserably. Inside. Now."

She released him, giggling as she staggered toward the door. He waited under the minuscule covering of the small awning, watching for her.

To his aggravation, she opened the window and stuck her head out. "Tomorrow?"

"Yes."

She searched the empty street. "Shall I call you a cab?"

"You don't even know how to use your phone."

She laughed. "True."

"I'm sure there's one further down the street."

"Take this," she said, holding out an umbrella to him.

"I don't need it."

"Take it. It will make me feel better, and hurry up."

He took the brightly colored umbrella from her, wincing at the sight of what he was sure would be a pattern of flowers once he opened it.

"Good night, Nick."

"Good night, sweetheart. Be safe."

Chapter 11

The Choice Less

Life in the Indian village was a duality of belonging and separatism. There were divisions based on caste and an ancient hierarchal system governing the rules of socializing. In this, there was comfort since you knew your place. In the old days, it would determine your occupation, the people you associated with, the amount of education you could receive, and whom you would marry. Having a clear demarcated path kept you from falling off the road and slamming head first into a ditch. As the village modernized, the concept became more muddled, though its most basic principles held true.

Asha was a peculiar girl. She loved the village and its simple life, but each new book she read whispered of other places and possibilities. In those hours, she found interesting people and lives so different from her own. The brave women who said outlandish things and outlandish women who did brave things became her personal heroes.

Gripping pangs of guilt often pricked at her heart for wanting to leave her home. After all, she had a loving family…well, at least a loving mother. Her father didn't much care for her, and she had attributed this to his ceaseless mourning for a lost son. A brother she'd never known, but clearly, he must have been capable of great things to create an air of grief in their small home, even fourteen years after his death. At times, the sorrow seeped from the walls of their one-room mud house, suffocating the three inhabitants.

Asha's father would mutter about his aching bones and curse the loss of his child. Asha's mother would tear up and offer her daughter a half-hearted smile. Asha tried to make herself smaller, hoping for invisibility, which she managed to achieve frequently. In those times, she would seek refuge in journeying to a new place, and her chosen mode of transport was always contained within the pages of a book.

When she was fifteen, the infectious melancholy manifested itself physically. Asha and Nalini had nursed Depal through many bouts of illness. Even though Depal never showed affection to the child, Asha had a sense of obligation to her father. His well-being was her priority. But this time it was Nalini who fell ill. Her mother rarely complained and refused to acknowledge any pain, so to watch her lay down on the thin mat in the middle of the day caused a sense of foreboding in Asha.

She skipped school to tend to her mother. She took over in the house, making the dinners and doing all of the chores. Her father grumbled tirelessly of how she lacked the skills of her mother. The deepening lines in his face conveyed that his grievances came from a place of fear rather than criticism.

"Asha, bring the water," Nalini ordered. She had always been a tiny woman, but her body took on a new frailty, which frightened her daughter. She watched in horror as her mother coughed and sputtered until blood poured from her mouth.

"You're very sick," Asha cried, wiping the thick, red liquid and trying not wretch.

"My time is near, *beta*."

"No!" Asha screamed, as if the Gods would respond to temper tantrums. "I won't let you go."

Nalini managed a small laugh. "My dear, sweet, beautiful girl, I may die, but I will never be gone from you. I will exist in your life forever. I will be recreated in a better form, and I shall always watch over you."

Asha didn't want to hear about any other life her mother would go to. She wanted her in the present. In this life…her life.

Sister Sarah came on that day. Nalini had been sick for over a week. The arrival of a visitor, especially one as prominent as Sarah, circulated among the town like a wild fire. All of the village women crowded into their small home, offering Sarah tea and sweets from their meager supplies.

"Thank you, but I'm here to take care of Nalini. That is my purpose." Sarah's response was both firm and polite.

"Sister, don't worry about her. That's no work for you. We can watch over her. You're a guest," they all chimed, picking up where the last women left off. Asha wondered why they hadn't visited earlier if they wanted to take care of her mother so badly.

"It is my duty to her."

"Why?" they asked, looking from one to the other, trying to find answers for the strange white woman's behavior.

"She is my friend," Sarah said simply.

Although there had been whispers about the odd relationship between the two women and Sarah's favoring Asha as a teacher's pet, the women reacted with shock. A Catholic nun and a Hindu village woman being friends, sounded like the preamble to a joke.

Nalini coughed then. Sarah's eyes widened. She instructed Asha to cover her mouth immediately. In the seconds that followed, Sarah's typical docile demeanor transformed as she yelled commands in a mixture of several languages. Asha would have translated, but she'd been told to cover her mouth. It didn't matter because the gestures Sarah made were clear.

"Get out of the house," she told the women. "She may have consumption. It's contagious."

She pointed toward the door, and the women fled as if a wild animal were chasing them. Then she gave Asha money and told her to fetch the doctor in the city. Sarah's doctor.

Asha ran until her legs ached before finding a cab. The doctor, a middle-aged woman with short hair, didn't hide her disdain for being summoned to a villager's home. She quickly verified Nalini didn't have consumption, but she did suffer from a serious lung infection.

"She won't survive this," the doctor said, wiping her stethoscope against her sari.

"What if we take her to a hospital? They can do X-rays. Give her medicine," Sarah suggested.

The doctor shook her head. "It's too late, Sister. I can give you pills to make her comfortable, but she will not recover."

In the end, the teenage girl and Catholic nun took care of Nalini, making her as comfortable as possible in her final days. Depal chose to stay with friends, grumbling that it would be improper to stay in the same house with a woman who wasn't family.

"Shall I leave?" Sarah asked. "So you can be with your family?"

Nalini shook her head in a small movement. "I have already told him what I need to. He will take care of Asha. He promised to find a suitable match for her."

"No," Sarah said. "She's too young."

"He will wait a few years, but it has to be soon."

"Nalini, the child is capable of doing great things."

"Do you think getting married and having children is not a great thing?"

Sarah wiped her forehead and sighed, her voice dropping to a whisper. Standing outside, Asha peered at them from the lone window of the house.

"She can see there is more to the world than this place," Sarah said.

"What use is the world to a single village girl? You fill her head with dreams she can never attain."

"That's not true. She's my smartest pupil."

"Her education is a waste. A hobby born of indulgence."

"How can you say that? It is never a waste to educate someone."

"It is if they cannot use it."

Their voices grew louder. Nalini's sounded raspy and Sarah's strained.

"Nalini, we both love her. Tell Depal not to do this. Please. I don't want to fight with you, but we both know he will follow your wishes. You have the power to change her life. You're being cruel."

"You think I don't want the best for her? We both do, but my ideas are truth and yours are lies, like the books you give her to read. She will never achieve the greatness you have in mind, and that is the greatest kind of cruelty."

Asha couldn't stand anymore. To hear the two women she loved bicker about her well-being confused and upset her. Her mother was dying. Why was Sister Sarah being so stubborn at a time like this? Sarah's words came back to her from years before. *You must always be the peacekeeper.*

She scurried back into the house. Nalini's bed lay in the center of the room to make it easier for Sarah to tend to her. Sarah sat cross-legged, hunched over Asha's mother, holding her hand. Although their positions conveyed tenderness, both of them were frustrated.

"Don't fight," Asha said.

"Asha, this is not your concern," Sarah reprimanded. "You must stop eavesdropping."

"It is my concern. You are speaking about me."

"We both want what's best for you," Sarah said.

"My daughter, you will find happiness in this life. The village is where you belong. Being a mother and wife is a woman's natural course," Nalini offered. Sarah looked hurt, but then again, Sarah's words hurt Nalini, too.

"I never said she shouldn't marry," Sarah countered. "Why not let her finish school? She could go to university. I can help her. She can see the world."

"I can do both," Asha said. Her voice wavered slightly, but there was a conviction in her statement that made both women take notice. The girl walked around the two women in three slow circles.

"What are you doing?" Sarah asked, although her shoulders slumped in defeat as if she understood.

Upon completing the third circle, Asha fell to her knees, taking her mother and Sarah's hands in each of hers. "I have been on my trip around the universe. Now I can get married." She gazed at each woman. "Both of you are my world, and by circling you, I have seen everything."

Nalini beamed with triumph. Sarah wiped a tear from her eye but offered Asha a small nod.

* * * *

The months following her mother's death marked a period of great mourning for Asha. The grief stayed with her as if burned into her soul, like a wound that never closed. Because her life changed so rapidly, she couldn't sort out when one time ended and another began.

She returned from school one afternoon to find strangers in her house. Strangers, in their tight-knit community, were rarer than a white tiger in the jungle.

A tall man with dark eyes, a sour-faced older woman, and a young boy with a sweet smile sat on their shabby chairs. The young boy had the face of a cherub and messy hair. She recognized him from school. He was in a lower class. She smiled back, and he waved at her before his mother pinched his arm.

"Asha, make tea," Depal ordered.

Asha gathered the supplies, concentrating on making the least amount of noise possible so she would not miss the conversation.

"She is quite beautiful, Uncle," the man said.

"She looks weak," the sour-faced woman replied. "She won't be able to work on a farm."

"You're mistaken. She can make fine tea and food. She works hard," Depal offered. Upon hearing her father extol her virtues, something he never did, Asha's skin prickled and her hands shook.

She served them tea in clay cups. The man with dark eyes assessed her, his gaze lingering far too long. She felt a small flutter of something unfamiliar in her stomach…a mixture of indigestion, fear, and something else. He was handsome.

"We have issues with this match," the sour-faced woman declared. Obviously, she was the speaker for the group.

"Tell me of your concerns so I may eliminate them," Depal offered.

"There are certain rumors of her birth. If she is not a legitimate child of your village, it will cause problems for our family. She could have bad blood inside her. She could be born of a poor caste, or she may even be… Muslim." The woman's shudder was so exaggerated Asha might have laughed, except her heart beat too wildly for any silly sound.

"Vicious village gossip," Depal said. "She is my daughter. And as your son has said, she is beautiful. In fact, I'd wager she's the most beautiful girl in any village, including yours. She's obedient, as well, and will make a good daughter-in-law for you. She will produce many sons for you."

Asha's body tensed with every word as the confusion gave way to the cold clarity of the situation. He was arranging her marriage already? She dared not speak or state her mind on the matter, for Depal was right. She wasn't a brave or outlandish woman. In the end, she was an obedient girl.

"Hmpf," the lady replied, not satisfied, but she also didn't venture further into buried secrets of the past. Asha had heard the rumors herself. Children had called her a throwaway girl. She'd asked her mother before, but Nalini dismissed it, stating they were jealous.

"Is there anything else? She has many possible suitors," Depal said, crossing his arms in the gruff manner he used when telling a lie.

"As does my Aditi. Our farm is profitable. My son is smart and good-looking. There are many girls in line for his hand. The dowry you offer is insulting."

"It is not up for negotiation. I will not pay any more, nor will I pay anything once she is married. If the offer is not suitable, then I think our business is done."

"No, Uncle, please don't get angry. We will discuss it," the tall man, who must have been Aditi, stated. "I will give you my answer within a week."

Asha risked a glance at him. *He may become my husband.* He had thick dark hair and a pleasant smile, but his lips coiled more than curled. His eyes grew darker with every passing second.

Asha confronted Depal once the visitors had left. "Ma said you would wait."

"Ma is gone, isn't she?" Depal retorted, a new harshness in his voice that had surfaced since Nalini's death.

"I want to finish school at least."

There was a bitter edge in his laugh, causing Asha to wince. "Stupid, selfish girl! You are nothing but a thief in my home, and I will be glad to get rid of you."

"What do you mean, Papa? What did they mean about the rumors?" Depal was quiet for a moment, appearing to regret the words, but Asha made the mistake of prodding on. "I refuse to get married, Papa. Not until I finish school."

He made a motion to slap her. She shut her eyes and braced herself in anticipation, but nothing happened. Instead, he used his words to leave a mark much deeper than any physical injury. "No one is concerned with your wants. Your real parents failed to kill you, and their failure has been my misery. I never wanted you. I've struggled to support you, and now I have to pay to marry you off. Your marriage prospects are slim as it is, but as long as the truth is shielded in whispers, there is a chance. Open your eyes!" he screamed. She complied.

He clasped her hand and dragged her to the other side of the room. There, in the cupboard under Nalini's saris, he picked up an old wooden crate. Asha was surprised by it. The house was small and their possessions slim. How had she never seen it? He grabbed her hand and ran it down the lid so she could feel each puncture hole. Splinters pierced her skin, and she screamed, begging him to stop. When he let her go, she retreated into a far corner. Covering her ears, she sunk to the floor.

"This is what your real parents wanted for you."

He flung the box at her. It hit the wall next to her before shattering on the ground. Asha's tears were warm and heavy as she replayed her father's words. Only he wasn't her father. He was just a man who'd carried a burden for the last fifteen years. She pulled her legs up in the fetal position, rocking back and forth as tears rolled down her face. The splinters in her fingers dug deeper into her skin. Splinters from the now broken box.

Her birthright.

Her casket.

* * * *

Sister Sarah's attempts to comfort the child were met with great obstacles.

"I don't have any parents. No one wanted me," the child cried, her head in Sarah's lap.

Sarah combed though her hair. "That's not true. Your mother loved you."

"I was a second-hand placeholder for her dead son."

Sarah lifted the child's chin and made her look into her eyes. "Nalini was your mother. She saved you. She loved you. She didn't have much to give, but she gave it all to you freely." Sarah told her the story of how Asha had come into their lives. How Nalini had walked many kilometers before bringing her to Sarah. How they both prayed over her, and God gave them the answers.

"Do you think I'm Muslim, Sister?"

"It's possible your parents were. The Muslim village isn't far. But child, it doesn't matter who you were born to. Muslim, Hindu, Christian, or Jew are all paths to the same place. The same sun shines on all roads. It warms my body just as it warms yours. What matters is how you live your life when you walk along your path."

Asha was young, but she realized what a difficult statement it was for Sarah. Not because she didn't believe it, but because she did, despite her vows. "Child, God has a plan for all of us. It's not always clear, but there is a reason you survived. I choose to believe you are a blessing that came to your mother when she needed one the most. And to myself."

"To you?"

"Yes, because when I held you, I felt whole for the first time in my life."

The girl absorbed the woman's words, her sobs weakening. "Why did you hide the truth from me?"

"We didn't do it to deceive you, honey. We did it so you wouldn't feel the loss of what never was. So you'd be happy in your life."

"I will be miserable now."

"This doesn't change anything."

"He's going to marry me off. That changes everything."

Sarah wiped the girl's tears. "Not if I have any say."

Asha laughed, and surprisingly, it took on the same bitter quality as Depal's. "You don't, Sister."

True to her word, Sarah tried to stop the wedding. She even went so far as to offer Depal money not to marry Asha off. Depal, embarrassed and angered by the nun's offer, demanded she leave and never set foot in his house again.

Asha married a month later. Everyone said the union suffered from disproportion. The girl, lacking in both wealth and pure blood, would taint her new family. Asha didn't contemplate her life too much. She didn't have a choice in the matter so why waste time dwelling on it? If she refused marriage, her father would cast her out. If she sought refuge with Sarah, the school would come under scrutiny, and there would finally be a reckoning, which could result in its closure.

She could run away to the city, and then what? Panhandler and prostitute were the occupations available to a girl like her. Why was she fighting the proposition of marrying a handsome man and living in a nice house where she could form her own family? That wasn't just the right choice, but the only one.

In the village, where everyone was divided and united by caste, religion, and economics, she knew of another group. A woman's freedom was tangible, measured by her choices. In this group, there were no choices. They were their own caste, and if they had a name, Asha thought they should call themselves "The Choice Less."

Chapter 12

Nick kept glancing at Shyla as she read the newest pages. "We can always change it. It's just a rough draft," he said.

"I would tweak the paragraph about her depression. She wasn't depressed. She was …stoic."

"I disagree," Nick said. "She accepted her fate, but it would be natural for her to be dejected. She lost her mother, she discovered the shocking secret of her birth, and then she was married off without her consent. She was a victim of her circumstance."

Shyla carefully set the pages on the coffee table and turned to him. "Nick, we are not writing a story about a victim."

"Then what are we doing?"

"Writing a story about a survivor."

"Is it still like that?" They had been careful to keep the story separate from their relationship, but his mind constantly wondered. "You said you based it on women you knew."

"Old stories, but still true in some cases."

"What about you?"

"I don't have to worry about it."

"Why not?"

"I own my choices. I have that luxury."

"That's a right, not a luxury."

"It *should* be a right…but it's not. Not everywhere."

"Then how do you know you'll get to choose?"

She took a deep breath. "I just do. Anyway, speaking of the story, I think we could just edit it a bit."

"You're changing the subject."

"Because I've already answered your question, Nick," she said, the exasperation reflected in her tone.

He sighed, putting his arm around her. He drew her close and kissed her temple. She tilted her head back, giving Nick the prefect angled to trace her lips with his thumb. "We'll tweak it. Do you want to work on it now?"

"We've done enough today. Shall we do something else?" she asked, teasing him with her dimple-creating smile.

"You ask a wicked question."

She arched her brow. "Do you have a wicked answer?"

"Let's go out." Her pout almost did him in, but he refused to yield to it. "It's a nice day. I want to take my girl out on the town."

"I'd like that."

"Good."

The air was crisp, but the wind behaved itself. Nick's fingers twitched when her hair captured the light of the sun.

Armed with light jackets and matching smiles, they walked down Bleecker. They held hands, except when the narrow sidewalks became crowded, then he let her lead, resting his palm against the small of her back. First, they went to an early lunch at the Rothman House, a tiny café with checkered curtains and strong coffee, Nick's favorite place to eat, both for its eclectic and ethnic food choices.

The stout middle-aged waitress immediately scowled at the state of their table and the scattering of tiny crumbs on its polished wooden surface. Her spiky, frosted blond hair with its hot pink tinged tips and her apologetic demeanor slowly etched into the creative part of Nick's brain, which was dusty from lack of use.

"I'll clean it up straight away," she said, marching away before completing the sentence. She rushed back and wiped the crumbs, sprayed the table, and ran the rag over it once more. Then, as if to double check her work, she took a step back and surveyed the surface with a sharp eye. Nick immediately found a place for the woman's unique physical traits and compulsive tendencies in his next novel. *Your name will be Odessa Del Ray*, he thought for no particular reason, except he liked odd names and odder characters.

"Thank you," Shyla said, bringing Nick back to reality.

The waitress finally stopped wiping and took out a pad of paper. "Sorry, it's a pet peeve of mine. I hate messes. What can I get you folks?"

Shyla ordered the grape leaves and lemon rice soup. Nick stuck with his old standby, the good ol' cheeseburger, complete with spicy relish.

"You looked far away just now. What were you thinking of?" Shyla asked when the waitress departed.

"I was writing."

She arched her brows. "In your head?"

"That's where every story begins for me. I'm here with you, and there's no place I'd rather be, but sometimes my mind wanders, and I have to pull it back."

"You're not blocked anymore then?" Her happiness for him was clear in her beaming smile.

He grasped her hand and caressed her palm with his thumb. "I guess the freeze is thawing."

The waitress set down their drinks, eyeing the table carefully before she left. Shyla twirled a straw in her Mango smoothie. "I suppose you are never lonely."

"How so?"

"Because you always have people with you."

Nick frowned, adding a packet of sugar to his coffee. "In a sense, but you're wrong. I am lonely." Or at least he was. "Enough about me. Are you excited about graduating in a few months?"

"Yes. I'll be sad to leave New York, though."

"Have you ever considered staying?" he meant the question nonchalantly, but as soon as he asked, he realized how desperately he wanted the answer.

"I need to go home."

Nick felt a sudden surge of jealousy. He dismissed the ridiculous nature because its aim was not at another man or anything he could compete with, but an entire country, one on the other side of the world.

"How long since you've been home, sweetheart?"

"I haven't. Not since I arrived."

"You must miss it."

"It's funny, I thought I wouldn't, but the place where you're from is like a limb. You take it for granted, complain about it when you get aches or pains, but if you lost it, you'd feel unbalanced. I guess that's the way I feel about India. It's part of me."

"You feel lost?"

"Sometimes." She knitted her brows, and Nick felt a tug of remorse for asking the question. She swallowed and lifted her head, her smile sad. "I don't know why I'm telling you this. I'm sure you can sympathize."

"I can?"

"You must feel the same way about New Jersey."

His laughter bellowed throughout the restaurant with such volume the other diners stopped in mid-conversation to stare at him. He reared his head back, the laugh traveling so deep it became uncontrollable. When he faced her again, she looked confused and…pissed? That made him laugh even harder.

"Something funny?" she asked, crossing her arms.

"I'm sorry. I know you were being serious." He let the last chuckles die down before clearing his throat and regaining his composure. "Don't get me wrong. I'm proud to be born in Jersey, but I would hardly describe it as a missing limb."

She looked away from him out the window. "It's just one way of putting it."

"I'm not as sentimental as you."

"Yes, you are."

"I assure you, I am not."

She leaned into the table, focusing all of her attention on him. "You have playing cards in an archival frame displayed prominently in your home to honor your grandfather's memory. You still have his record player, and you prefer vinyl because you like the natural scratches in the music. You remember not only the plots of books but what you were doing when you read them. And you always root for the New Jersey Devils because they are your home team. Don't tell me you aren't sentimental. I don't purchase that for a moment."

How was it possible she knew him so well? "The phrase is 'I don't buy that' not 'I don't purchase that.'"

"Whatever it is, you are a poor salesman, Nick Dorsey."

"And you are a very astute girl."

The waitress came back with their food. She picked up Shyla's discarded straw wrapper and Nick's sugar packet before leaving them. She eyed the table once more and frowned at the miniscule dots of sugar next to Nick's coffee. The rag made another appearance as she swiped them away. "Pet peeve," she explained once again.

Shyla leaned into the table. "Speaking of sayings, isn't that an odd one, too?"

"What saying, sweetheart?"

"Pet peeve. I wonder what it means."

"You don't know?"

"I can figure it out from context, but it sounds strange, as if you're angry with your dog or something."

Nick grinned, grateful he had an answer for her. "Pet doesn't refer to an animal, but rather something you favor, such as a teacher's pet. And of course peeve comes from the word peevish and signifies an irritation.

It's a recently coined term…probably within the last one hundred years. It literally translates into my favorite annoyance."

"How do you know so much?"

Nick shrugged. "I'm a writer. I know a lot of useless information."

"It's a strange combination of words."

"I suppose it is, but it makes sense. The stuff that pisses us off is as subjective as the things we like." He gestured to the waitress, who was busy scrubbing another table near them. "One person's crumbs are another's chaos."

"What are some of your favorite annoyances, Nick?"

"I have more than my fair share. For one, I get annoyed when people name their pet's people names."

Shyla arched her brow.

Nick continued, "The other day I was jogging and this guy was yelling, 'Nick, hey Nick, get over here now.' I turned, wondering who the hell was calling to me. Turns out it wasn't me he was barking at, but his dog. And the worst part—it wasn't even a strong dog like a Great Dane or a Boxer. Nope, he was talking to a Chihuahua. Can you believe it?"

Shyla giggled, cupping her mouth. "Ironic your pet peeve actually has to do with pets."

"Yeah, I guess it is."

"Anything else on the list?"

"People who talk in the third person."

"I understand what third person is, but what exactly do you mean?"

"Like if I was to say 'Nick's really enjoying his day out with Shyla.'"

"I get it." She rewarded him with a gracious smile.

"I sound like a nut job, don't I? These are dumb examples of the little things that get on my nerves. Do you have any?"

"Any pet peeves?"

Fresh drinks arrived, and Nick wondered if the peculiar waitress would once again wipe their table, but she left after asking them if they wanted anything else. "I can't think of any right now."

"That's good. It means you're a patient person."

After their meal, Nick took her to the corner bakery. It was the kind of place that nourished every sense. The rich, decadent aroma of fresh pastries and bread greeted them. Shyla stopped just inside the door, closed her eyes, and inhaled the air. He watched her, wanting to take her in his arms just then. She treasured simple things. All the things he took for granted.

"I think this is what heaven smells like," she said.

In Nick's opinion, heaven would smell like her, not decadently sweet but temptingly provocative, yet subtle—the scent of coconuts, vanilla, and something decidedly hers alone. They made their way to the long counter where hundreds of frosted bites of blissful goodness lined glass cases, each one a work of art. She took her time, studying them, pointing out their features.

"Nick, look at this one. It has tiny birds on it."

The clerk, who also happened to be the baker, stepped in. The young girl took her time explaining how they molded the bluebirds from fondant. It was obvious the counter girl was proud of the creations and happy someone was taking an interest. Nick ordered coffees and took a seat at one of the small café tables, waiting for Shyla to make a decision. Instead, she asked more questions, which spurred the offer of a tour complete with detailed explanations of the recipes. Normally, this sort of thing would bore Nick out of his skull, but her enthusiasm deterred any objections.

"They're so beautiful, I don't want to eat one," she said.

"If everyone felt that way, this place would go out of business, so pick one or ten," he responded.

"Since we're sharing, you should pick," she suggested.

"Nice try. Pick one already."

She took her time but returned to the table with a large cupcake, decorated with sugar shaped shamrocks and glossy white butter cream frosting. "The girl told me its whisky and Irish cream flavored."

"Nice," Nick said.

He fed her pieces of cake and, being a little sloppy in his technique, gave her an apologetic expression while wiping the frosting from the corner of her mouth.

After they'd had their fill of sugar and caffeine, he took her on his own personal walking tour of the village. He showed her the places once frequented by Mark Twain, Truman Capote, and Edgar Allen Poe. Also, the venues where James Taylor, Bob Dylan, and Jimi Hendrix had performed.

He took her hands and pressed her palms against the brick façade of an old building—one of the oldest structures in the city. His mouth hovered over her ear. "Close your eyes."

She complied, her breath hitched, his hand against hers.

"Do you feel it?" he asked.

"It's almost tangible…like holding history in your hands."

He nipped her ear until she moaned and his erection pressed against her. "Exactly."

They ended at the Old Town Bookstore. Just like in the bakery, Shyla sniffed the air. The place smelled of old paper, binding, and words.

"I changed my mind. This might be the way heaven feels. Or maybe this mixed with the bakery."

"Old books and cupcakes are your version of heaven, huh?"

She nodded. "I can't think of a better image." She swayed to the piped music. Nick caught the question in her expression before she even asked.

"The song is called 'I Can See Clearly Now' by Johnny Nash."

"It feels so…"

"Appropriate."

"Yes."

A look passed between them as they listened to the music. Nick vowed to search for the record and download it to each of their phones. The lyrics and music were in tune to their lives. To whatever they had become.

It was their song.

The loud chatter of other shoppers broke the moment. The voices of two giddy girls carried through the shop.

"I told you they'd have the newest Keegan Moon book here," a tall brunette said.

"I love his books," her blond companion answered.

Nick took Shyla's hand and led her toward the counter area. He pretended to look at the periodicals there. "You could make them very happy," she whispered.

"How?"

"Tell them you'll sign a copy."

"No."

"Why not?"

"Because today is about me and you. Not Keegan Moon. Not Max Montero."

The man behind the counter with a silver lip ring and intricate neck tattoo greeted them, his eyes resting on Shyla a little too long for Nick's liking.

"May I help you find something?" he asked her specifically.

"Do you have any books on poetry?" she asked.

The man cracked a grin, sucking in his lip ring. Nick rolled his eyes.

"You're in the right place," he said, coming from behind the counter. "Who do you like? Frost, Dickenson, Whitman? I'm guessing you're a Sylvia Plath girl?"

"Yes to all, especially Sylvia Plath," she said.

"We have poetry readings on Wednesday nights. Do you write?"

"No," she said, "but I'd love to listen."

"We'll be there," Nick replied in a brusque tone.

"Fine, let me show you the poetry section then."

"I'm very familiar with the layout." As an added gesture to clear up any confusion lip-ring guy might have, Nick put his arm around Shyla and led her toward the back of the store.

"This isn't where the poetry is," she said, studying the shelves. "These books are about tax codes."

Nick smirked. "Yeah, no one ever comes back here."

"So why are we here?"

He placed a hand on each side of her hips and backed her against the wall. He ran his nose down the length of her neck, inhaling her scent. He pressed his mouth against hers. Her body tightened in surprise at first, but soon her fingers threaded through his hair. She drew him closer. His hands moved against the curves of her body. He lifted her, holding her legs around his hips. She moaned as his tongue found hers. She tasted like whisky and cupcakes—he longed to get drunk on her mouth. His hand traveled up until he reached the curve of her breast. Her body responded, welcoming his touch.

As far as Nick was concerned, they were in the poetry section, the architects of their own work.

"Someone's coming," she said, as the sounds of footsteps echoed close. *Yeah, and it's not me.* Nick muttered a few obscenities, setting her down and backing away. He noted the darker shade of her chapped lips. She brushed her hand through his hair again, but in a way meant to smooth it back from the mess she'd created.

Their breaths weren't visible this time, but they were audible, intermingling with each other in the warm air of the dusty bookstore. A potent look of lust passed between them before Nick remembered where they were once more.

The bejeweled bookseller cleared his throat. "This is a bookstore. If you want to make out, don't do it here."

Nick didn't acknowledge him. His eyes stayed on Shyla. "Sorry," Nick called out finally, hoping it would send Mr. Tattooed Piercings away.

"Most sorry," Shyla said, looking sufficiently guilty, her eyebrows drawing together.

She bit her bottom lip, causing Nick to laugh at her worried expression. The clerk muttered as he walked away, ranting about how they should go to 6th avenue if they were looking for a sex shop. "You got us in trouble," he whispered against her ear. "What am I going to do with you?"

"I think the question is what *are* you doing to me?"

"I'm showing you the poetry section." He took her hand and led her to the area closer to the front.

The clerk left them alone, most likely since they were visible and behaving themselves. Shyla pointed to a book on the top shelf. He was tall enough to reach it. Also, there was a step stool, but he didn't suggest either of those things. Instead, he grasped her waist and lifted her. She giggled in surprise.

"Do you like poetry?" she asked, showing him the small leather-bound book with gold lettering—a compilation of love poems.

"No."

"Why not? Does it go against your male tendencies?" she joked, patting him on the chest. He kissed the underside of her wrist.

"I want a beginning, middle, and end to everything. I crave completion. I recognize and respect the medium, but it's never satisfied me."

"Hmm…you read like you eat."

"What do you mean?"

"Everything has to be sandwiched." She tapped the book. "I'm going to buy this for you. It has some of my favorite poets."

"I'll read it based on your recommendation, but I'll buy it myself."

"You haven't let me pay for anything."

"Now *that* is something you can blame on my masculine tendencies."

"I insist on buying it. I think if you gave poetry a chance, you'll really enjoy it."

"Why?"

A solemn look overtook her features. "Sometimes, it's the fragments of feeling that are the most potent. Not the before or after of it all…but the here and now."

Nick could agree. The *here and now* of Shyla was more powerful than anything he'd ever felt.

Chapter 13

They arrived back at Nick's place as the sun set. The day had been a full one, but the night was just beginning. So many hours in the night. But the small voice nagged at Nick, as it usually did, taking all his wicked thoughts and analyzing them with the finite visualization of a microscope. His version of a conscious had grown exponentially, constantly competing with his cock. Neither could be sufficiently suppressed. She had this innocence about her, and the last thing he wanted was to have any part in its destruction.

When he sat on the couch, though, she plopped on his lap. The silent scream of his erection, much louder than his inner voice, took over.

"Careful," he said. "You're not making this easy for me."

They'd limited themselves to make-out sessions most nights. Nick saw her off in a cab, ending his night with an arctic shower. His right hand had never seen so much action.

"No, it's very hard, isn't it?" she said, arching a brow and shifting herself.

"A double entendre? And such a sexy one, too."

She looked away from him. "Nick, you don't have to treat me as if I'm made of glass. I won't shatter."

"I want you like I've never wanted anything else. But, I'm afraid to make love to you." "Make love" wasn't his usual expression. He typically said fuck, but it didn't feel right to him.

"Why?"

"Because it will change us. Complicate things."

"I'm not experienced, but I have done this before."

That surprised him, but it also put him at ease. It would be easier knowing he wouldn't be physically hurting her.

He cupped her chin. "Let me kiss you for a while first. I want to taste you…everywhere."

"As long as you want."

"Then it will be a very long time."

He slid his hands up her body until he reached her hair. Once he released her clip, her locks tumbled down in waves of coconut vanilla scented silk. He grasped her hair and tugged it back. She tilted her head, giving him full access to her neck. Nick sucked her earlobe.

"Yes," she murmured.

He tugged at the hem of her sweater until she raised her arms. He flung it off her, disappointed with the number of buttons on the oxford shirt underneath. He slid her off his lap and laid her down on the couch. He carefully undid each button with shaky fingers, touching his lips to her smooth, warm skin.

Her bra was simple black, no lace or intricate design adorning it. Somehow, the simplicity turned him on even more. Her breasts were beautiful on their own. He unhooked the garment before pushing it up. Nick longed to tell her how exquisite her breasts were in their plump perfection, but he couldn't find the words. He didn't read, write...or recite poetry. So instead of using words, he used actions. He traced his tongue over her nipple, then flicked it, before ending with a kiss. He did this repeatedly to each one until she moaned his name and her fingers tugged his hair.

"Nick, please," she pleaded.

Yes, Nick, please, he said to himself. His kissed her cheek and dropped his head into the crook of her neck. "This is embarrassing."

Her body tightened. "You can't perform?"

His head jerked up, a mixture of anger and surprise colliding inside him. "Of course not." As if to cement the point, he pushed her legs apart, grinding the hard length of his erection against her. "I will fuck you all damn night with plenty of encores."

A soft blush crept up her cheeks. "I'm sorry. I shouldn't have assumed."

"Why did you?"

She cringed, biting her lower lip. "I thought of the worst possible thing you could tell me, and that came to mind."

Despite the intensity of the moment, Nick chuckled. "That's the worst possible thing, sweetheart?"

"Right now, I think it is."

"I don't have a condom. I believe that's the worst possible thing."

"Oh," she said, clearly surprised. "Are you joking?"

"Well, I do somewhere, but they're probably expired. It's been a long time for me."

"So we can't use them."

"I would chance it if you are on birth control? Tell me you are."

She shook her head. "What are we going to do?" She asked with such disappointment it caused Nick to chuckle again. She slapped his chest playfully and continued pouting. "It's not funny."

"And it's not a big deal either. I'll go get some."

"Shall I come with you?"

"Oh you'll come, but not right now."

She giggled against his neck. "You're very naughty sometimes…but I like it."

He kissed her again, softly at first, then with more intensity. "Go," she finally said, pushing on his chest.

Nick stood up and sighed at the sight of her lying on his couch. "Damn condoms."

She closed the fabric of her shirt, obstructing his view. "Don't think of me right now."

"How can I not?"

"Because it's obvious."

Following her gaze, he looked down. The zipper of his jeans jutted out. "Shit, it sure is."

He grabbed his wool coat. The weather didn't call for it, but it covered him more appropriately than the leather jacket.

Nick sprinted to the corner grocery store. He found the condoms first, throwing them into the basket and decided to get lube for her comfort. Then he figured Shyla might like some wine, so he grabbed a bottle of the red she enjoyed. He added a bottle of white, too, in case she wanted something different. He thought maybe she'd like something sweeter. So he added a six-pack of hard lemonade to his red basket as well as a six-pack of beer. As he passed the chrome metal of a freezer case, he caught a glimpse of the scar on his cheek. All his worries manifested at once. He'd done a damn good job convincing himself his hesitation was all about her…and most of it certainly was. The fact was, he hadn't been with a woman in almost two years. Before then, he was rarely with the same woman twice. Now, he relied on the services of his right hand and his imagination to satisfy his libido. They were doing a poor job of it.

What would she think when she saw the rest of the scars littering his body? And what would happen to them after sex? To Nick, a relationship was defined as two parts. BS and AS. Before sex and after sex.

He enjoyed their flirtatious friendship. The quiet hours they spent together every night. He didn't want it to change. Was he really willing to risk it all for an hour…okay, several hours of sex?

He swallowed, glancing down at his right hand once more. Unsolicited, his mind conjured the image of her body squirming beneath him, her soft hair brushing against his skin, and her mesmerizing voice moaning his name.

Fuck yeah, he'd risk it.

Chapter 14

Shyla's bare feet slid along the wooden floor. She picked up an album they'd listened to the other night. She set it on the turntable, placing the needle how he'd taught her. "American Girl," by Tom Petty filtered through the room, the scratchy bits of the record adding to its charm. She could identify with this song. It seemed no matter how big the world, all girls shared similarities.

She walked into his bathroom, her favorite place in Nick's apartment, specifically the large claw-foot bathtub. He'd never used it, opting for the large enclosed shower instead. How could he ignore the gleaming, inviting tub? She ran a finger over the rim. Before she deliberated too much, she inserted the drain and started the hot water.

She'd asked Elaine what might appeal to a western man. Elaine responded in a giddy scream, asking for details, but Shyla had none to offer, and nor was she inclined to talk about Nick. Whatever was happening between them was fragile, and she did not intend to jeopardize it.

In the end, Elaine had given her practical advice. "Shave everything," she had said, and then did an up and down glance at Shyla. "And I do mean everything."

Shyla took her roommate's advice in anticipation of this event. Now that it was here, she wondered if perhaps they'd put so much emphasis on it, they'd both end up disappointed. Her body wasn't model perfect. She was wide in the hips and her waist wasn't flat. She could borrow a cup or two in the bosom department. She wished she'd brought some supplies with her. Lotion or perfume or something to make her more appealing. Elaine always took an overnight bag when she stayed at her boyfriend's place, filling it with all sorts of beauty concoctions, but Shyla didn't bring anything.

Then again, who knew if Nick would want her spending the night? She found his toothpaste and squeezed a small amount on her finger, rubbing it on her teeth. She gargled some mouthwash and grabbed the bar of soap from his shower. It smelled like him—clean, fresh, and masculine.

She lit the candles they'd used during dinner the other night. Easing herself into the tub, she let her mind go blank for a minute. She closed her eyes and pulled her legs against her chest, wrapping her arms around them tightly. Fear and anticipation battled inside her. *Please, let me be what he wants. Let him be what I need.*

Distracted by her mind, she didn't notice when his shadow fell on her.

"I bought you some wine," he said in a husky voice.

"Thank you. I hope you don't mind I decided to take a bath."

"I'll join you."

"Yes…please."

She tilted back the wine, hoping for some bravery. She handed him the empty glass. She wondered if this was right, but she wanted to reveal herself to him—all of her, uncloaked and shameless. She wanted to witness his reaction. She released her legs and lay back in the tub, giving him the full view of her body in the dim light. His intense gaze traveled from her curled toes and slowly inched up her frame until he reached her face. His expression lingered with such hunger it was tangible. His fingers curled tighter around the stem of the glass before he finally set it in a safe corner.

He sat on the edge of the tub. "I regret I'm not a poet because your body is worthy of a sonnet. You're beautiful, baby," he whispered, dipping his fingers in the water, circling them back and forth, creating tiny ripples. He turned his back to her, unbuttoning his shirt with one hand. She knelt, bringing her hands around to work the lower buttons loose. He sought her mouth with his. She began fumbling with his belt. She'd never taken off a man's clothing, but she worked it loose with a dexterity that surprised her. She unbuttoned and unzipped his pants.

He shrugged off his shirt, revealing a detailed ink carving. The large barren tree covered the expanse of his muscular back, its branches twisting and curving over his right bicep until they faded away. She'd never understood why people used their bodies as permanent canvases, but viewing the artistry of his tattoo changed her mind. She flattened her palm against his spine and moved up the intricate tree. The skillful artist incorporated Nick's scars into the artwork, using them to create depth. But she could feel the raised skin, the cuts that never healed.

He took a deep breath, wincing at the contact. "Shyla," he said, reaching for her wrist.

"Please, let me touch you," she pled. She kneaded his muscles. She kissed his shoulders and neck. She repeated the process until his stiff posture relaxed under her care. "You're beautiful, too, Nick," she whispered against his ear.

He grabbed her wrist and kissed the underside before standing up.

Her breath hitched as the last few garments fell. Another tattoo occupied the left side of his chest, right over his heart.

"Why a Celtic cross?" she asked.

He licked the bottom of his lip, causing her belly to flutter. "So I can remember to be a good Irish Catholic boy."

"Do you need reminding?"

His smile bordered on boyish charm and devilish wickedness. "All the time."

She took a deep breath, drinking in the sight of his body. Having leaned against it, she knew his chest was hard, but she'd never seen a man so finely shaped. His broad shoulders and chest with a smattering of golden hair gave way to a chiseled waist with six solid bumps. She'd read about six-packs in romance novels and, at the time, thought it was an ideal born of fiction. How deliciously wrong she'd been.

She paused her visual observations, taking in the appendage between his muscular legs. She'd felt his erection beneath her when she sat on his lap, but to see the solid column at a perfect ninety degree angle created a whole set of worries.

She slid forward. "Come in. The water's perfect."

He got in behind her. She leaned back against his warm, solid chest. The steamy water combined with the heat of their skin shouldn't have elicited a shiver…but it did. He played with her hair and kissed her temple.

"Why are you nervous?" he asked her.

"I don't want to disappoint you."

"It's not possible."

"I don't want you to disappoint me either."

"Okay…no pressure there. You suck at foreplay, sexy girl."

"Foreplay is not my forte."

"Lucky for you, it's mine."

His hands slid down her front, grazing her breasts, causing them to harden. He worked his way down her waist and her hips. They were large hands with a precise, firm touch. Clearly, he was much more skilled than she. Her body flushed, rising to temperatures warmer than the water. Her breath hitched, and her heart began beating to a rapid, unfamiliar tune. She craned her neck to face him.

Nick mastered her body with the same grace as a musician strumming a delicate instrument or a sculptor carving his clay. With each stroke, she unraveled. He leaned forward, running his massive hands down her legs until he pushed them apart. He caressed her inner thighs. All the while, his mouth nibbled on her ear. He wasn't simply touching her body. He was coaxing it awake.

She gasped as his finger penetrated her. It wasn't unpleasant, but definitely unexpected. He eased in and out slowly until the shock gave way to the pleasure...small waves of pleasure building towards a precipice. She squirmed against him. His arm encircled her waist, holding her steady. He added another finger and increased his speed. She called out his name.

"Kiss me," he commanded.

She did. His tongue swiped across her mouth, requesting entrance. She obliged. He added a third finger. She cried out. His thumb rubbed her nub in a slow circle. The buildup gradually grew higher, emerging from the area he touched until she experienced this overwhelming sensation of tingles coursing through every vein and cell she owned.

"Disappointed?"

"Uh...no. I'm appointed."

His laugh turned into a growl. "Out of the tub now."

They didn't speak as they stood. He covered her in a thick soft towel, drying her quickly, before placing another around his hips. Shyla felt safe but wonton. Satisfied but not sated. Timid and bold at the same time. Nick took her hand and helped her from the bath. He put out each candle between his thumb and index fingers. The tone of the singed flames added to the lusty lyrics of their soundtrack.

She'd seen the king-size platform bed with its large, white fluffy down comforter many times. It looked like a cloud in the middle of the room. A small red, square packet lay already open on the nightstand along with a small bottle. Their towels dropped at the same time, landing with a soft thud around their feet. His hands skimmed up her arms. She tilted her head back, staring at his dark blue eyes.

"You tell me if there's anything you don't want or you want to stop."

"I've done this before, Nick."

"Not with me."

He kissed her then, backing her until she fell onto the bed. He leaned his elbows into the mattress, keeping his weight off her, his mouth against the hollow of her throat. His tongue and lips on her neck turned her soft moans into fierce demands.

"Nick." Shyla dug her fingers into his flesh. His kiss became more demanding. She could get lost in his kiss forever, because through this touch she could convey all the things she wanted to say without the barriers of language. She heard the rip of the condom. He spread her, his hard length sheathed. He ran his tip over her entrance several times before pushing into her slowly, watching her with intensity as he deepened their connection. She arched her back, pushing her hips up.

"Don't encourage me. This is hard enough." The strained quality of his voice both surprised and excited her.

His thrusts were gentle at first. She instinctively wrapped her legs around his hips, and his propulsions became more powerful. He covered her face and lips in hungry kisses while he grasped her hip with one hand. Their bodies grew warmer, then burned hot, a sheen of slickness emerging between them. He spoke her name in coarse whispers against her ear.

"This is my version of heaven, Goddess."

She screamed his name with a breathless, raspy voice. Her thighs quivered. The pulsating sensation worked its way through her body just like before. Now, the orgasm wasn't a small wave, but drove into her with fierce force, awakening every cell in her body until she closed her eyes and let it drown her completely. When she opened her eyes, he was looking at her. His expression was raw, primal, and needy.

Nick's thrusts took on more urgency until he said her name once more and collapsed on top of her. Both of their heartbeats bounced audibly, their harsh breaths filling in the silent spaces. He placed his palm on top of hers. She curled her fingers against his.

"You will spend the night with me. I will hold your body against mine...all night, our limbs entwined. Your head will lie over my heart, and you will tell me, not with your words but your hands and mouth, when you are ready for me again. I will make you come as many times as you let me. I will earn all your moans, your bliss, and your gratification. And I will own them."

Although he spoke in low tones, there was a new control and authority in his voice. The change in demeanor claimed her in both body and spirit. She nodded, submitting to him. In those simple words, she knew what he did not.

He was a poet.

Chapter 15

Before Shyla could even step inside the door, Nick picked her up and spun her around, squeezing her so hard she squeaked.

"Sorry," he offered, tilting her chin and kissing her softly.

"Why are you so happy today?"

"I'm always happy to see you."

She walked to the kitchen to fetch water for the plant as she usually did.

"I already watered it, sweetheart."

"Oh," she said, amazed he'd remembered. The plant itself was growing rapidly. "You're going to need to transplant it soon."

"One thing at a time. I have something to show you." He clasped her hips and brought her to the couch. He placed a pile of paper on her lap. She picked up the pages, reading each one.

"I don't understand. What is this?"

He plopped next to her. "It's the next Max Montero novel."

Her heart leapt in excitement. "Max is talking to you again?"

"This is just a rough outline with some character profiles and stuff. But I have a new story in my head."

She was excited for him. Nick never dwelled on his writer's block, but she understood how desperately he wanted to write again. He needed the outlet, just as he needed to work out every day. It wasn't a job, but an integral part of him. "That's wonderful, Nick."

"We'll finish your story first."

"Do you want to work on this instead?"

"I have it all up here," he said, pointing to his head. His grin faded for a moment. "Besides, we have a deadline, don't we?" It was a topic they usually sidestepped. The fact she would be going home soon.

She ignored his statement, scanning the page until her eyes stopped suddenly. "You have an Indian heroine?"

"Yes."

"You based her on me?"

His laugh was dismissive, perhaps even nervous. "What? Just because she's Indian? You aren't the only Indian girl, you know."

She jabbed at his chest. "I am the only Indian girl in your life."

"Correction, you are the only girl in my life."

He cupped her bottom and pulled her onto his lap. The pages fell from her hand.

Shyla reached to pick them up, but his hold wouldn't yield. "Leave them."

He unwrapped her scarf. She lost coherent thought for a moment when his lips moved against her neck. "Tell me about her, Nick."

"She's smart, sexy, funny, and very charming. She sweeps in and steals Max's heart." He punctuated each descriptive word with a slow kiss.

"So sweet."

He fell back on the couch so she was on top of him.

"She also steals the state secrets of a small country." He smacked her ass. "Naughty girl."

She laughed, leaning her forehead against his. "If you're going to make me a villain, I hope you at least give me a very cool, sexy name."

"You have a very cool, sexy name," he replied, rubbing the place he smacked. "Plus, I wouldn't call you a villain. You have your reasons."

"Will you use my real name?"

"Never," he said with such conviction it surprised her. "That name is mine and mine alone. I won't even let Max have it."

"Than what will you call her?"

"Any suggestions?"

"You'll let me pick?" she asked, excited about the possibilities of naming one of his characters.

"I'm willing to listen. You are my muse after all."

She pressed her lips in contemplation, willing her mind to conjure an interesting name. Nick ran his fingers over her lips, making the act of thinking almost impossible. "Natasha," she murmured, before playfully biting his finger.

"Natasha? Really?" He whispered the next words using a Russian accent. "Interesting choice. This character requires an authentic name to match her special gifts."

"What are her gifts?" Shyla asked with hitched breath.

"She's capable of not only bringing a man to his knees, but making him enjoy every increment of his crashing descent."

She grew quiet with his description, her breaths increasing. This type of foreplay was driving her mad. "She sounds intriguing."

"And bonus…she has big breasts."

Shyla laughed, wrapping her legs around his waist. "So she's not based after me."

"She is."

"I don't have huge breasts."

"Oh no? Let me check."

He lifted her T-shirt. Nick cupped her breasts, his thumbs skimming the fabric of her bra right over her nipples.

"What are you doing?"

"I'm writing," he said.

"This is writing?"

He pushed each of her cups aside, freeing her breasts. "Well, actually right now if you want the technical term, I'm plotting the story."

"I think you're plotting my body."

His flicked his tongue over her nipples before answering. "I just want to be accurate about the physical characteristics."

"Is this your version of write what you know?" Her voice wavered as Nick's teeth grazed her nipple.

"I'm fact checking. I wish my muse would let me work in peace."

"I was just thinking you have something else wrong, too."

"What's that, baby?"

"You said she can bring a man to her knees. I have yet to witness any such activity."

"True."

To her shock, he pushed her back into a sitting position and got on his knees before her. She'd said it as a joke, an attempt at flagrant flirtation, trying to keep up with this man who clearly had a grasp on that skill set, but she never expected him to take her literally. He untied her shoes and slipped each one off, followed by her socks. He did her jeans next, sliding them down along with her panties. Nick grabbed each ankle and pressed a kiss on each one. He slowly worked his way up her legs, alternating kisses with each advance. When he got to her thighs, he spread her legs farther apart. Her breath caught in her throat, half gasp and half inhale. He licked her opening.

"What are you doing?" A stupid question since she had an inkling, but the sensations he invoked prevented clearer articulation.

He looked at her, his eyes hooded, his tongue swiping across his lower lip seductively. "I'm going to eat you out." Then he grinned in that charming, wicked way of his. "Has anyone ever done this for you?"

She sucked in another breath before shaking her head.

MK Schiller

He looked pleased, as if it was some sort of triumph on her part…or perhaps his. "I have so much to teach you."

"About sex?"

"About pleasure. Stop moving," he commanded, firming his grip on her thighs.

His tongue pierced her folds, gently at first and then with more fervor. She grabbed the arm of the couch, squeezing it tightly. The sight of Nick's head with its lion's mane of hair bobbing between her legs was an image she wanted to preserve. She wasn't sure what was more shocking. That he was doing this or how much she loved it. He hooked a leg over each of his shoulders and drove deeper still. His tongue flicked her nub and then sucked. He was making love to her with his mouth. She'd read about this, but she'd always associated the act as something disgusting. Nothing he was doing felt disgusting. It was delicious.

She echoed his name between each harsh breath. She struggled to keep from squirming and not close her legs or push herself into his tongue. It was such an exquisite experience, and although he was the instigator, she wondered what possible pleasure he could get. But those thoughts flew in and out of her mind as her body trembled under his expertise. Every muscle tightened before a surge penetrated her, rendering all of her higher functions useless.

He stood up, surveying the outcome of his work. He flopped on the couch next to her and pulled her against him.

Nick kissed her, rolling his tongue against hers. He tasted like his toothpaste, minty and fresh, but there was something else there. Again, Shyla wondered what was more astonishing—that she was tasting herself in his mouth or how much she loved it.

Chapter 16

On the deck of the sightseeing cruise, he stood behind her while she took in the view. She looked so beautiful with dangling earrings and a long silk scarf wrapped around her head, tied at the side. Queen of the gypsies. Owner of his heart.

"I'm enjoying this. Thank you," she said.

He kissed her temple. "This isn't a big deal."

"Not just for today, Nick. For all the days. Thank you for the best days of my life."

Her statement stirred something powerful in him. He wanted to reply in kind. God knows, it was the truth. But something held him back, some conflict spurred by his conscious and need for self-preservation. She didn't know the truth about him, and she never had to. In her eyes, he was the man he wanted to be, and that was enough for him. He was falling for her. The crash would be imminent and painful, but right now they could just take each day…each best day as it came.

A subtle misery foreshadowed every moment they shared, but he was determined to enjoy every sweet increment of his descent.

"You're welcome, Shyla," he said, hating himself for the lame, unemotional response.

The day was warm, but the wind on the harbor felt chilly. He wrapped his coat around her. While she watched the magnificent sculpture of the regal lady rise up from the harbor like a goddess, he watched her.

"I know this is a cliché touristy thing to do, but I love coming here."

"It's perfect. I've been wanting to do this since I first arrived."

"Everything about her is symbolic. The broken shackles at Lady Liberty's feet are meant to denote the breaking away from oppression. The seven rays in her crown represent each continent. Even the twenty-five windows symbolize the rays of heaven shining on the earth."

"It feels surreal in a way. Like you know you're in the presence of something great."

"My great great great grandfather came over here from Ireland on a boat like this." Nick looked around. "Well, people weren't snapping pictures and wearing *I love New York* shirts, but I imagine what you're feeling is the same thing as the old buildings in the Village. It's like you said, holding history in your hands... It's tangible."

"Isn't there a poem?"

"Emma Lazarus wrote the poem to inspire immigrants." He tucked a tendril of hair behind her ear. "Give me your tired, your poor, your huddled masses yearning to breathe free. The wretched refuse of your teeming shore. Send these, the homeless, tempest-tost to me. I lift my lamp beside the golden door!" Nick recited it from memory. "I suppose that's an example of poetry I do enjoy. Although things have changed since those days."

"I don't know about that. When I walk down any street here, I feel like I'm at the center of the world. You can hear about thirty different languages, and people from all over the world of every kind of background share the same space. It makes you feel special and distinct, but like you belong, too."

"I'm glad to see the city hasn't lost its charms."

"I didn't feel that way at first. It took me a long time to get to that place from the lost girl who arrived here four years ago. I was given many warnings before I left home."

"Like what?"

"I was told to make sure people knew I was from India and that I'm Hindu, but I always wondered why I should need to correct other people's judgments. I imagined New York to be a very cold place...both literally and figuratively. And that maybe the people would be cruel because of recent history."

Nick swallowed and spun her around. "And were they?" His jaw clenched at the idea.

She caressed his face. "It's not blatant, but once in a while I hear hushed voices. Even worse is when someone talks down to me because they believe I'm not capable of understanding. But when I look over my years here, those were rare exceptions." She lowered her eyes, watching the water passing them by. "I was mugged my freshman year."

"What?" Nick's heart constricted. He let her go and wrapped his hands around the railing so tight his knuckles whitened.

"I was walking to class and someone lifted my purse right off my arm. He pushed me down so I wouldn't run after him."

"I'll kill him."

She pressed her hand over his heart. "Nick, calm down. That's not the point of the story. I'd gotten cynical and dispirited being so far from home. I found myself looking for the meanness in people, perhaps even creating it. That moment when the mugger stole my purse, I wanted to yell at the sky and beat the ground."

"I don't blame you." All his muscles tensed.

"But what happened next changed me. This man took off running after my attacker, and his wife stayed with me to make sure I was all right. They didn't even know me, but they treated me as if I was a sister or daughter. He didn't get my purse back, but they did take me to the police station to file a report. She gave me some pepper spray and showed me how to use it. They gave me tips about which streets to avoid and how to carry myself so I wouldn't be such an easy target. They bought me coffee and walked me home. I had an epiphany that day. Cruelty can live and breathe in any place, but so can kindness. You'll find either or both depending on how hard you choose to look. There are so many kindnesses that I see every day, which I would have missed because my own bitter heart blinded me to such things."

"That's really beautiful, Shyla, but I still want to kill the bastard who mugged you."

She smiled crookedly, patting him on the chest. "He's a minor footnote in the story. That's not the point."

"What is the moral of the story?"

She paused, considering her words. "We are a result of our experiences, and even darkness nurtures. We can't appreciate what we take for granted."

He sucked in a breath, nodding at how the statement applied to him as well.

He wanted to say something more about that, but the boat docked at their destination—Ellis Island.

* * * *

Shyla looked around, drinking in all the history that encompassed the building. Nick pointed out the interesting architecture and exhibits of the once active gateway that welcomed millions of immigrants to the New World.

"I wish I had a camera. It's amazing."

"You have one," Nick replied, taking the cell phone from her back pocket. He showed her how to use it.

"I keep forgetting how much you can do on this device."

She ended up taking as many photos of Nick as she did the building. He looked so handsome in his knit cap, charcoal grey sweater, dark jeans, and black boots.

"Stop it," he said.

"Why? I'm getting the hang of this," she replied, snapping another photo.

He took the phone from her and held her against his chest while he snapped a picture of both of them with the harbor in the background.

"I want you in all my photos," he said.

They walked down the great hall, listening to the real accounts of people who took the journey through the portal that was Ellis Island. Nick showed her where his ancestor had signed the registry. He insisted on buying her the official guidebook as well as a book of poems written by the very immigrants who came across this threshold. She forced herself not to read it while they had coffee and sandwiches in the small restaurant.

Like all her days with Nick, it was perfect. The two of them were as different as people could be, but despair and desolation sounded the same no matter what the language. Shyla knew they had those traits in common, and in spite of it, or perhaps because of it, they made perfect sense together.

They stopped at a café in Manhattan for "something more substantial" as Nick called it. The weather was enjoyable enough to sit outside.

"Tell me how your mind works," she said, buttering her croissant.

"What do you mean?"

"How do you create a story, for instance?"

"Well, living in this city helps. There's stimulation everywhere." He gestured to the droves of people that walked past them. "I always start with a character and build from there. Max is easy because he's been with me so long, and I based him on my grandfather, myself, and several other men I've met. But when I need something new, I just look around. It's like window shopping."

"I'll never understand that."

"It's not so difficult. I'll show you. Give me a person, any person."

Shyla looked around before subtly jerking her head toward an older man who looked out of place from the crowd of sharp-dressed, hurried people. He walked with a slight limp and scowled at the people rushing past him.

"That's so easy. His name will be Samuel Jenkins. He served in Vietnam maybe. He left a young man with strong aspirations and a ripe future that included a red haired, freckled-faced girl. He came home broken, defeated, and half-dead. While he'd been battling a war, his life escaped him. The girl moved on. His father died. His laughter became hollow. His tears saltier. His bones brittle."

"Sounds very sad."

"It is, until he meets another girl, one that brings sunshine into his dark life."

"How can you create a whole life from merely glancing at a person?"

"I've been doing it for a long time. You gave me someone very easy because he doesn't fit in, but it becomes more difficult when you pick someone ordinary because then you have to find those inner feelings that makes them stand out. Why don't you try?"

Shyla searched the crowd, noticing a man with a business suit, which wasn't unusual except for his lime green tie with a pattern of pink polka dots. He would be easy to draw from. "I pick him."

Nick's smile shifted into a frown. "We should go."

"Why?"

Nick didn't answer. He stood quickly and threw down a few bills before reaching for her hand, leaving their barely finished food. When she turned back, she saw the character she'd picked was leering at them, his footsteps quickening.

"Don't run from me, Dorsey!" Lime green tie screamed.

Nick tightened his grip on Shyla and led her down the street.

"Nick, what's going on?" she asked.

Nick halted, taking a deep breath. He placed a hand on each of her shoulders. "Go home, Shyla. I have to talk to him."

"But—"

"Go home," he said, pushing her away.

"Nick!" The man yelled, rushing toward them.

"What can I do for you, Tim?" His demeanor transformed in that brief moment. His tone, composed and unruffled, seemed very opposite the aggressive man, as if they were having two different conversations.

"I want to punch you again."

"I'll let you if it makes you feel better, but we both know the last time it hurt your fist more than my face." Nick let go of Shyla's hand, turning to the man. "I can't talk to you right now, but if you want to have a real conversation I would like that."

"What I have to say to you will just take a minute. Stop leaving roses on my sister's grave. In fact, stop visiting her all together."

"You can't ask me to do that."

"Haven't you done enough? You really need to mock all of us with your false grief?"

"Tim, just calm down."

"Calm down? What the fuck is wrong with you, Dorsey?" Tim turned his attention to Shyla. "And are you doing the same thing with her? Are you going to introduce her to your sick, twisted life, too?"

Nick grabbed a fistful of Tim's shirt and pushed him against the wall. Tim's eyes widened. Nick was taller and outweighed him. "You don't talk to her."

"You afraid I'll tell her what a sick fucker you really are?"

Shyla gasped as Nick slammed his fist against the brick wall several times.

"I'm sorry," he repeated the words as he let the man go.

Tim straightened his tie and fixed his jacket. "I would expect nothing less from you. You can say you're in recovery, but we both know you'll always be a junkie. You can apologize until the day you die, and it will never be enough." He turned toward Shyla, a warning in his face. "You should keep better company."

Shyla opened her mouth to reply, to object, to defend, but Nick shook his head before she could utter a word. "Don't say anything."

"He can't talk to you like that, Nick."

"Yes, he can."

Tim stalked off the direction he came. Nick walked to the edge of the sidewalk to hail a cab.

"What just happened?" she demanded.

"Go home. I'll take the next cab."

That was a ridiculous idea since they were headed in the same direction. She took his hand in hers, surveying his bloody knuckles. "You're hurt."

He pulled away. "My own fault."

"Let me help you."

"I don't need you."

There was a new cold edge in his voice she'd not expected. In response, she made her voice as calm and collected as she could under the circumstance. "I'm going with you."

Her simple statement must have worked because he didn't argue. He didn't say anything. A cab stopped, and they got in. Everything had happened so quick she couldn't even process it. She held his hand and leaned against his chest, but he didn't embrace her in any way. He looked straight ahead like a statue. He didn't even react to the pain of smashing his fist into a brick wall.

Shyla led him up to his apartment and walked him straight into the bathroom. He sat on the closed toilet lid while she tended to him.

He was quiet, even when she put the antiseptic cream on his raw, bloody knuckles.

"Why don't you ever ask me about the scars?"

She was grateful he was talking, but his voice, distant and cold, made her shiver. "I could see it was a painful subject for you. I figured you would tell me when you were ready."

"There are things about me you don't know."

"I know you are a decent man, Nick. You don't deserve the things he said to you."

"He lost his sister. He blames me. And guess what, Shyla? He's right."

She bandaged him up and followed him to the kitchen. He poured himself a scotch.

"I don't believe that."

"I'm a meth addict," he said without any emotion. He sat on a dining room chair and held his glass out to her as if he was toasting her. She didn't know much about the drug except that people who suffered such addictions were often dangerous. Nick had never made her feel that way, though. He made her feel safe and cherished. Still, she took a step back. She regretted the movement at once when his mouth twisted in a tight, pained smile that held no happiness.

His voice lowered, filling the silent room with a shadowed whisper. "Most people have that reaction. I'm glad you do. It shows me you have a good sense of self preservation."

She swallowed, confused and alarmed by his admission. "I'm just surprised. You don't act the way I think an addict would."

"Well, you don't act the way I think an Indian village girl would. I guess neither of us fit a mold."

"How did you start?"

He paused for a while, and she wondered if he would answer her. Her heart wrenched for him.

"A few years ago when I needed to meet some deadlines for a book. I was careful, though. I made rules for myself and stuck to them, so how could I be a meth head? I smoked at night when I needed extra energy to write. I never emptied my bank account. I didn't get all hyper and nervous." He chuckled cynically. "Hell, I even have perfect teeth, and they're all mine." The words sounded hollow and rehearsed. Yet, there was a raw pain, as if being passive allowed him to get through the story.

"Why do you think you harmed that girl?"

"I didn't just harm her, Shyla. I killed her. Her name was Jenny. She was a fan of mine. She was innocent and sweet...like you. I got her hooked on the stuff."

"Did you love her?"

He shifted his gaze toward his hand as if just realizing he was hurt. "No, and that makes it worse in some ways. I used her like I always used women. She wanted more, but I wasn't interested. She asked if she could smoke with me one night. And I was stupid enough to agree. She changed from a happy girl to a strung out, depressed addict. It happened very fast. She stole from her family. From me. I tried to get her help, which was probably the most moronic of all the ironies in my life, because I, too, was an addict. I just couldn't admit it."

"What happened?"

"What usually happens to addicts. She overdosed and died. That was supposed to be my fate, not hers."

"Are you still addicted?"

"I haven't smoked in a long time, but you're never free of it."

She swallowed, her knees going weak as she replayed his confessions. She placed her hand on his shoulder. "It's not your fault."

"It is my fucking fault, Shyla," he snapped, jerking her hand away. "You know the funniest thing? You would think that dark period would have been my rock bottom, but it wasn't. I gave into my addiction even more after that. I became the definition of a tweaker. I woke up one night in a strange place with two naked girls beside me. I had no idea where I was or what we had done, except judging from the packets of crystal and pipes, I knew we'd had a party. I got on my motorcycle and took off. Thank God I didn't kill anyone else that day, but I did crash into a tree. That's why I have the scars. I checked myself into a clinic after I got out of the hospital. I stayed there for several months. That was over two years ago."

Shyla crossed her arms, bracing herself against his words. "You pulled yourself out of it. You're a different person now."

"That's not the point."

"Then what is?"

"I can change who I am, but I can never change what happened. I killed her, Shyla."

"You didn't kill her."

"I put her in places she would never have gone."

Shyla took his hand and slowly caressed it. She ran her finger down the scar on his cheek. He winced at her touch but didn't pull away. "Listen to me. Did you force her to take drugs?"

"No."

"Right, it was her choice. She made those decisions. When a woman has choices, she also has responsibility and, more importantly, accountability to herself. You weren't innocent in all of it, but you certainly did not cause her death. You said yourself you tried to get her help." She cupped his face in her hands, leveling it so he could see her sincerity. "Nick, her family blames you because it's easier for them than to cope with the loss, but it wasn't your doing. You have to stop thinking that, or you'll never truly heal."

"You are so innocent you only see the good. That's what I wanted you to see in me. That's the side I showed you."

"Don't do that. Don't act like I'm some stupid, naïve girl who doesn't understand how the world works."

Nick took her hand, but it wasn't a sweet gesture. He stood abruptly. He pulled her toward the door. "You need to go."

She yanked her hand away, standing in place, their bodies close enough that she could hear his heartbeat. She swallowed back the lump in her throat. If she started crying, she wouldn't be able to articulate what she needed to say. "Are you asking me to leave for the night, or to never come back?"

He closed his eyes. "Both."

The dam of emotion assaulted her then. Salty tears fell across her face. Her head hurt, her heart pounded, and her body shook.

"You're going to leave in a few months anyway, so this was inevitable. You can finish the book on your own." His voice sounded heavier, as if the air had thickened around them.

"We still have time. I'm not ready to say good-bye. You aren't either."

"I'm ready now. I don't have room for you in my recovery."

"You're saying that because you think you might hurt me. You won't. I'm strong. I would never make those choices. I can help you."

He took her shoulders, gripping her. "You are strong. I have no doubts about that, but I am weak. Please go."

She pulled out the phone in her back pocket. Her hand trembled as she held it out.

"Keep that." He clasped his hand over hers. "I want you to have it in case of an emergency. You can still call me if you really need something."

What she needed was him, but what more could she do to convey the message? She put the phone back in her pocket, not so much because of the emergency part, but because she wanted the photos of them. She wanted the memories.

Chapter 17

The next three days were the longest of Nick's life. They reminded him of those first days of detox, followed by the first somber weeks of sobriety. He went back to his routine, which had altered since Shyla had come into his life. He went to more meetings and talked to his sponsor, which helped. He went to Jenny's grave but didn't bring a rose with him.

Although his body went through the normal motions, the girl who'd brought sunshine into his world owned the majority of his thoughts. He wondered what Shyla was doing. If she was safe. She'd become such a part of his life that he found himself listening for her timid knock on the door. His hands groped the other side of the bed in search of her. He came up with lists of random books and movies she might enjoy and made a mental note to share them with her before he realized that wasn't possible. Nick Dorsey had seen his share of misery, but this pain was new, fresh, and merciless. He told himself it was just as well. It would be worst when she left, but he longed…lusted for the months he'd carelessly tossed away.

On the fourth night, he did hear the familiar knock. He hated how rapidly his heart beat in response. She didn't wait for an invitation. She marched right past him. He glanced at his watch.

"Were you going out?" she asked, watching him button his jacket.

"Why are you here, Shyla?" he answered her question with his.

She set a brown paper sack on the dining table. "I brought you a sandwich."

"I didn't order a sandwich."

"I know how picky you are. I wasn't sure if you'd found another place. I wanted to confirm you were eating well."

He chuckled. "You're worried if I'm eating?"

"It's not funny."

"We talked about this."

"No, Nick, you talked and I listened. But I'm talking now. I finally figured out what my pet peeves are."

Despite trying to remain aloof, his curiosity couldn't be dampened. "What are they?"

"People who have a false sense of failure. People who shut out other people. Oh, and definitely people who back out of their agreements."

She shifted through her messenger bag and took out a stack of papers. "I wrote the next few chapters. I tried to mimic your style. You can read them or not. It doesn't matter. I thought you might want to see how the story progresses."

"Shyla—"

She held up her hand. "I'm going to leave now." Her voice cracked. Nick struggled not to take her in his arms. "I don't know who this guy is you spoke of the other night. I'm sure he existed, but I haven't met him. I met you. The man who became my friend and later my lover. The one who always made me feel comfortable, safe, and special. And I think he must have existed all along, but he was buried under that other guy."

"He didn't exist, or maybe I should say he doesn't."

Her lower lip quivered, and he saw her internal fight to control it. "I care about you, Nick Dorsey, probably too much too soon for my own good. But I'm smart enough to know that whatever is happening with you, only you can fix." She marched over to him and placed her hand on his heart. "If you're looking for redemption, start here."

With that, she walked out the door. He waited for a few minutes to pass until he followed her. He stayed in the shadows until he saw her go into her building and turn on the light. He'd been following her home to confirm she'd made the commute, carefully keeping a large distance behind her. It was a ridiculous idea. After all, she'd been making the walk on her own for years, but he justified his actions when he read the morning paper and saw a random story about a mugging or rape, even though most of those occurrences were nowhere near the vicinity of the Village.

When he came back to his place, he tried to avoid the stack of bright white paper that sat on his table. He walked around it, threw a magazine over it. Out of sight, it wouldn't matter as much. But it did, no matter how many layers covered it.

He unburied the sheets and lifted them to feel for weight. She'd written quite a bit. He scanned the first page, then the second. Eventually, he found himself hunched over on the couch, the pages before him, getting lost in another world. He was thankful she'd done this on her own. He couldn't write this part no matter what. He had difficulty enough reading them, let alone trying to gage those painful feelings.

Pain, Nick thought as he read Shyla's work, was a universal epidemic. It shut people down, tore them apart, but it also built them up again. Most importantly, it had the power to bond. Sometimes, it took understanding someone else's to work through your own. Even fictionalized pain could have that impact.

Chapter 18

The Choice Less

Asha, like most Indians, regarded weddings as a sacred and cherished celebration. Asha and Aditi's wedding was no different. The bride, dressed from head to toe, felt the weight of every layer she wore. There was a tiny sliver of gold in her nose and a million yards of fabric on her body. A *Mangalsutra* around her neck signified she was now a married woman. Although it wasn't large, it felt foreign and cold against her skin. Her hands and feet, decorated with paisley and flowers in intricate henna paste looked strange to her. It was a happy occasion, so she tried to hold her smile in place, but by the end of the long day, it hurt too much. The guests wished her well, but she caught their whispers. Her lack of dowry, her lineage, and her reputation for obstinacy provided fodder for many conversations.

She imagined she might feel different being a married woman, as if her biology would transform once her and Aditi took the four rounds around the holy fire that signified their tie to each other. But she was still the same girl. Maybe those changes would happen now when he claimed the last thing she had to give.

She waited for her husband in the dark room of her new house that contained many rooms on a farm that contained much land. He turned on some music—an act meant to comfort her as well as drown out the noises of what was to commence. In her mother's absence, the village women had taken it upon themselves to educate the fifteen-year-old in the intimate duties required of all brides. Some told jokes, which made Asha laugh. Others frightened her with their stories of not being able to breath and screaming out in pain. In the end, she was more confused than ever. She missed her mother, feeling incomplete and alone without her guidance. She closed her eyes, pulling her legs up to her chest, and leaned her head against her knees.

He sat next to her on the thick mat made of woven straw, their marital bed. She wondered what he was thinking. Truthfully, she wondered who he was. They'd barely conversed, and the few times they did was in the presence of others. Now he was her husband for eternity.

"I wish to speak with you, Asha."

She nodded, unsure if he required her confirmation. Surely, he didn't have to ask for permission.

He continued after the uncomfortable pause. "There were many girls interested in marrying me with larger dowries than your father offered. Enough so we could buy more land and equipment."

Asha wondered if he expected her to apologize for the lack of funds she brought into the marriage.

"I chose you out of all of them. My mother did not approve. People in my own village laughed at my choice, but I didn't listen. I desired you as my bride."

She slowly nodded her head. "Yes, husband."

"I don't ever want to hear you are the source of trouble in our house or you are disrespecting my mother. You will be a perfect wife and prove everyone wrong. Am I clear?"

"Yes, husband," she said again, wondering if this might be the answer to all his questions.

"You will have a good life here. You will work hard and produce many heirs for me."

"Yes, husband."

He appeared satisfied with her docile answers.

"Good." His expression shifted, and his eyes traveled down her body. "Now lay back."

* * * *

Asha had done chores all her life, but never like this. Her mother-in-law woke her before the sun rose and instructed her to feed the animals. She had no idea how to carry out the task. Never having seen them up close, animals frightened her. Aditi left for town without saying good-bye. She didn't mind, though. Her body was still sore from his callous hands and forceful manner.

She cursed the heavy bucket she carried, the handle digging into the creases of her fingers as she staggered across the stretch of land, throwing feed in her path. A goat nudged the back of her knees with such force she fell forward into some mud…only, it wasn't mud. She forced herself not to retch as she washed it off. The sun scorched her skin, causing a thirst she'd never experienced. All the while, her mother-in-law followed her, griping commands and criticizing her every action.

"You are frail. I told Aditi you'd never survive this life. Your parents have spoiled you. He chose with his eyes and not his brain," her mother-in-law mocked when she dropped the bucked.

"You need to move faster," her mother-in-law demanded when she rested her body against a stone pillar. "When I was your age, all the animals were fed by mid morning."

"If your father had paid a decent dowry, we could have hired more workers, but now we have only you. We have nothing," her mother-in-law lamented when she picked the vegetables.

Asha ignored all the comments, her posture demure and accepting. She knew enough to understand you didn't disrespect your elders…ever.

"Mother, I haven't eaten yet. I'll have more energy after lunch."

"Why should we feed you? You haven't even worked enough to earn a decent meal."

It was only when Mukash, Aditi's brother, came home that she found reprieve.

"*Bhabhi*," he said to her.

Asha did a double take when Mukash called her the term for older sister-in-law. "Yes?"

"*Bhabhi*, you're doing it wrong. Let me show you." He took the bucket from her and placed it on the ground. Asha rubbed her arms, trying to get the circulation to work again. The ache settled into her limbs, burning her insides just as the sweltering sun crisped her skin. Mukash ran to the side of a building. When he returned, he had a cart with him. The boy placed the bucket in the rolling cart. "Like this."

Asha wondered why her mother-in-law hadn't shown her the small piece of equipment that would have made her life so much easier. Then again, she most likely had other motives in mind. It didn't take any mental acuteness to realize the woman hated her passionately. She was angry at her son's choice. Of course, she couldn't take it out on him. Asha made the perfect victim for the woman's malice.

"Sister Sarah asked about you," Mukash said, breaking into her thoughts.

"What did you tell her?"

"I told her we'd take care of you. I've always wanted a sister."

She combed through his hair. "I've always wanted a brother."

"She gave me this for you," he said, holding out an envelope. "It's a letter. Don't worry, I didn't read it. I can't."

"Thank you." Asha took it, a fierce cry building inside her when she saw Sarah's neat handwriting.

He scanned the empty field before letting it go. "Hide it, *bhabhi*. My mother will not like it."

Asha nodded, stuffing the envelope into the folds of her sari. "Don't worry, my mother stays in the house in the afternoons. The sun hurts her eyes." Asha made a mental note of the information. Mukash went to his lunch pail and handed her a thermos of water. She drank the lukewarm liquid so fast she almost retched again. Then he held out his half-eaten lunch. She shook her head.

"Take it, *bhabhi*. I'm full."

She took the bread and vegetables he offered, finishing them off with the last of the water. She'd never been so hungry in her life. Finally, when her head felt anchored to her shoulders again, she kissed him on the forehead.

"Thank you, brother."

He beamed proudly at the moniker. "Most welcome, sister."

"Now tell me what you mean you can't read the letter?"

"I can't read at all. The teachers have tried, but I don't understand."

"You can't read Gujarthi, Hindi, or English?"

"All three," he replied, plucking a weed next to him.

"Would you like to learn?"

He shook his head. "I can't learn. That's what the kids at school say. I'm simple."

"I doubt that."

"I don't need it, anyway. Ma would take me out of school except she promised my father before he died. I don't really need to be smart like my brother."

"Why does he need to be smart, and not you?"

"He runs the farm. After him will come his son." He looked up at her. "Your son, and so on. I'll just always be a helper."

Asha looked across the fields, saddened by his acceptance of his fate. This boy's whole life was mapped out as a lackey, and he'd never achieve anything more. Then again, wasn't her life also mapped out? "Mukash, you are already smart."

He gave her a suspicious glance as if she was joking. "What are you talking?"

"You brought me the cart." She crouched and placed a hand on his shoulder. "We can help each other."

"How *bhabhi*?"

"You can teach me about the farm."

His face wrinkled in confusion. "Teach you what?"

"How to feed the animals, do the chores, get the goat to stop kicking me."

Mukash laughed loudly before cupping his hands over his mouth, as if the sound was surprising to him. "The goat's cranky. If you feed him first, it helps."

"See, that's what I mean. Look at what a bright boy you are. I am ignorant when it comes to this," she said, gesturing to the fields. "But I am knowledgeable about other things…like how to read in all three languages. I can teach you."

"Where is the time? I'm at school or working here."

"We can teach each other and learn at the same time."

Asha picked up a stick and wrote the letter *A* on the ground. "That's the letter A."

The days following became routine. Her arms grew muscular, her skin didn't scorch, and she learned to control her hunger and thirst for long periods. She could balance baskets on her head. She laundered all their clothes and prepared the evening meal. The exhaustion set in her bones, but she fought against it. It was the only thing she could fight.

Mukash showed her many ways to make her life easier. No matter how much she accomplished, though, it was never enough to please her mother-in-law, but the woman's berating only lasted two hours in the mornings and at dinner where she invariably found something to complain about. Sometimes Aditi stood up for Asha. Most of the time, he agreed with his mother.

Giving her a sense of purpose, Mukash became the lone bright spot in her routine life.

Sarah wrote her secret notes, asking if she needed anything. Asha never told Sarah of her troubles, but she was sure the nun suspected. Sarah couldn't cure of her being a Choice Less, so Asha kept her burdens locked away. In reality, it could have been worse. Aditi didn't beat her or force himself on her. Then again, she would never refuse him either.

After a few weeks, she did find the courage to ask Sarah for books. And Sarah, being the voracious reader she was, sent them through the metal tin that was Mukash's lunch pail. Sometimes, she'd send fruit or even candy. Asha would always split the sweet treat with her new brother, and they'd work together for a few hours while she taught him the alphabet. The boy had trouble at first, but he caught on, proud of his accomplishments. His mother even commented on his improved grades. Mukash and Asha shared a conspiratorial smile. Then she said the vegetables were too soggy, and it was unfortunate God had blessed her with a daughter-in-law who was incapable of cooking a simple meal.

Asha worked through her chores, getting faster every day, so she could sneak off and enter someone else's world, if only for bits of time. She'd often read to Mukash. The boy would sit and listen with rapt attention, often telling her, although he didn't always understand, those were the best times of his day.

Asha understood, though. The books helped her avoid the melancholy of her life. In the stolen hours she read, she imagined another existence. She was the beautiful but impetuous Elizabeth Bennett, verbally sparing with the dashing Mr. Darcy in Austen's *Pride and Prejudice*. She freed a slave on a harrowing journey down the Mississippi River in Twain's *Huckleberry Finn*. She escaped a prison and set about to avenge those responsible in Dumas's *The Count of Monte Cristo*. Then she read *Jude the Obscure* by Thomas Hardy. She put in a new request in the lunch pail. *No more books like this one.*

Sarah wrote. *I'm sending you every book I own in order, but I will edit my selections from now on. It's acceptable to be miserable. You can ask for help.*

Asha wrote back. *The fruit makes me strong. The books keep me occupied. That is more help than I need and far more than I deserve.*

What did Sarah think she was going to do? Pray for her? Any act of interference on Sarah's part would cause an outrage in the village. There were rules here. You didn't meddle in other people's lives, especially their marriages. And in Asha's mind, she was one of the lucky Choice Less.

Sure, there were women whose husbands treated them like spun gold. But there were other stories. Asha knew them because her mother-in-law always brought them up at dinner. Stories about girls beaten like animals, or worse, murdered because they brought a low dowry into a marriage. Asha was smart enough to recognize those conversations were meant as warnings to her and potential advice for Aditi. Each time her mother-in-law relayed a horrible tale, conveniently cloaked as village gossip, Asha's spine went rigid and a trickle of cold sweat formed on her brow.

One night, Aditi came home early. He looked as if he'd aged five years in one day.

"What's wrong, *beta*?" his mother asked.

"The man I sold the birds to disappeared without paying me."

Asha knew the mistake would cause a great deal of strife in their household. The evening meal that night was especially sullen. No one spoke. Even her mother-in-law didn't comment on the poor quality of the food.

Asha snuck out with a new book when the others went to sleep. If the moon was bright enough and the lamp was on in the house, she could just make out the words. Her husband and his mother were heavy sleepers. She'd gotten braver as the months had passed.

She'd made it through the first two chapters of Harper Lee's *To Kill a Mockingbird* when his voice sliced through the air.

"What are you doing out here, wife?"

She snapped the book shut.

"You don't have to hide from me."

She took a deep breath. "I was reading."

He chuckled, turning on the large aluminum flashlight. She squinted as the bright flash hit her eyes. "You read a lot, don't you?"

Her back straightened so fast her spine ached. He knew.

"It's all right. I've seen you. Is it the nun who gives you the books?"

"She lets me borrow them. I'll come inside now."

"Why don't you stay out here?"

She smiled gratefully. "Thank you."

He held out the flashlight. "Take the torch so you won't hurt your eyes. I can't have a blind wife now, can I?"

She nodded, a pinch of guilt eating away at her. Why had she never felt any affection for this man? Perhaps she'd misjudged him, basing her selfish feelings on his mother and her own lack of choices.

He turned off the light and held it out to her, the long metal handle gleaming against the night. Asha reached for it just as he swung back. Its forward motion so swift her eyes didn't recognize the torch coming at her, but her open palm seared with pain as the heavy lens crashed against it.

Shocked and confused, she gasped against the pain. The burning intensity in her palm stole all her senses. She had crouched lower, covering her injured hand, when the heavy torch collided against her head. Before she could regain her breath, the object hit her face again. Warm liquid oozed from her nose. A wounded cry escaped her body, echoing around them.

"Shut up." His voice wasn't controlled like she was used to. He was crying, not sadly, but with a crazy rage she'd never heard. He dropped to his knees and pulled her hair with such force her head flung back. "Everyone is laughing at me. You disgrace me every chance you get. This is your fault. If I had chosen another girl, I'd have money now, but instead I only have you. You are useless." He kicked the book next to her. "What good is this going to do us? Is it going to bring money into our house?"

A pounding ache hit her temples. She considered screaming but knew it would do no good. No one was going to help her. She thought of answering him, but she had no voice and no words. She had nothing.

He stood. Then he kicked her once in the ribs. A cry of an injured animal rose from somewhere deep within her.

"Clean up and come inside." His voice was calm again as if his act of violence had provided a release.

Asha pulled her legs against her stomach. She laid there for a while, whimpering, praying, begging—for what, she didn't know. The taste of metal filled her mouth. A tiny white sliver gleamed brightly on the ground next to her. She gently pressed her tongue against her teeth until she found the vacant spot in her mouth.

Footsteps approached her, and her body went rigid with fear. The boy crouched down beside her. He was crying, too, but his tears, unlike his brother's, only contained sympathy and grief.

"Please, *bhabhi*, please get up. He'll come back if you don't go inside."

Somehow, with the boy's help, she was able to make the walk to the riverbank, clean her face, and lay beside her husband.

"I will kill you if you ever disrespect me again," he said.

She had no doubt he would.

* * * *

The next afternoon, Sarah arrived bringing a tin of English biscuits on the premise of discussing Mukash's schoolwork.

"Why is she here?" Asha asked Mukash after dragging him into a quiet corner.

"She asked me how you were, *bhabhi*."

"You shouldn't have told her the truth, brother."

The boy swallowed, his face contorting with frustration. "She's a nun. I can't lie to a nun. It's a sin."

Despite the bruise on her face, her aching hand, and the pain in her heart, his purity made her smile. She hugged him tightly. "She can't help. She'll only make it worse for me and herself."

"Have faith. Sister Sarah is a smart woman."

Hope was reserved for the innocent, Asha decided.

Hand in hand, they entered the villa. She took her place on the floor and tried covering her face with her sari, but judging from Sarah's wince, hiding the damage was futile. Her mother-in-law spoke decent English. There were no struggles in communication, at least not overtly.

"Sister, I know Mukash isn't a good student. Nevertheless, my late husband made me promise to pay his tuitions. It was his dying wish."

"I understand, Niti. I actually think he's improving in some areas. We'll work with him. I just wanted to bring by these books." Sarah turned toward Asha. "Hello, Asha, I haven't seen you in so long. How is married life?"

"Fine, Sister. Thank you for asking," Asha replied.

Her mother-in-law twitched, no doubt embarrassed the nun should see the physical evidence of the abuse sustained by her son's hands. "The goat hit her in the face," she explained. "She's not good with the animals."

Remarkably, the goat held a heavy metal flashlight.

"Actually, we need a new maid at the school. Do you think you might want to spare her?" The word *spare* had many meanings in that sentence.

"Her place is here working the farm," Niti responded, her voice morphing into a more curt tone.

"Well, as you said, she's not good at it. I was thinking this might be an acceptable solution. Asha could walk to school with Mukash in the mornings. It would give you an extra income. As you know, the school pays decent wages. The jobs are hard to come by, and Asha's familiar with the building. Her mother was one of our best employees." Sarah took a long sip of her tea, looking as calm as a breezeless day, but Asha saw her slim fingers shake when she put the teacup down.

Apparently, Mukash had told Sarah about more than just her face. The offer of employment after Aditi had caused their finances to plummet would appeal to her mother-in-law. The woman could smell money as if it was curry.

"Who will feed the animals here? And wash the clothes and cook? Who will prepare my son's breakfast? I am old. I can only do so much."

"Mother, I can do the laundry and cooking when I come home," Asha offered.

"We can feed the animals and take care of them in the mornings before school. If we do it together, it doesn't take long," Mukash added. Asha felt the alliance of the three of them, Sarah, her, and Mukash, conspiring together against Niti. A hint of guilt passed through her, but then her mouth began throbbing, stifling any remnants of remorse.

"My son will have to agree," Niti finally replied.

Sarah clasped Niti's hand. "I'd be happy to talk to him. After all, I know how hard he works. And we both know this union didn't bring you the wealth your family deserves."

Niti crossed her arms and nodded her head. "It did not. Not at all. I must have done something terrible in a previous life to deserve this fate."

Mukash was right. Sarah was a pious woman, but she was capable of scheming like a villain.

Aditi didn't agree at first, but he eventually wore down with his mother's insistence.

"Let the girl do something useful for us," she suggested.

"She is worthless in the house. Her parents have spoiled her," she berated.

"I could hire a maid of our own for what she'll make at the school. Any girl is better than her," she complained.

Asha appeared somber during the assaults. Secretly, it was the one time when she looked forward to the ritual of dinnertime denigration.

* * * *

On her first day of work, Sarah took Asha's hand and led her to the library. She locked the door and hugged her.

"How badly has he hurt you?"

"Just one time."

"Once is one time too many, child." She broke the hug, holding Asha at length. Asha hadn't felt the impact of being a married woman, her lost innocence, or her horrible reality until she looked at Sarah. Her composure crumpled, and she sobbed harder than she ever had. Sarah held her, whispering a mixture of prayers and promises.

"I should begin my work," Asha said, drying her tears.

"I agree." Sarah went to a large bookshelf and grabbed several textbooks. They hit the long worktable with a harsh thud. "This is where you left off. You'll have to work alone, but it shouldn't be difficult. I'll check over your assignments in the evenings and help you when you have trouble."

Asha regarded the mathematics and grammar texts Sarah laid before her. "I don't understand."

"When you're here, you are in school."

"Why?"

"You still have much to learn. You can't expect to read novels all day. An unfinished education is perhaps the worst cliffhanger of them all."

Asha chuckled at Sarah's attempt at humor, but the sound felt foreign to her. "My mother-in-law will expect me to bring home money."

"I have it all worked out. I'll be able to provide you payment from my personal funds."

"The other maids will suspect and gossip. It'll get back to her."

Sarah shook her head and gestured to the library's many shelves. "This library is in desperate need of reorganizing and cataloging. We will need someone with your qualifications for this type of work."

Asha looked around at the stacked shelves with their rows of pristine books, all lined up in perfect order.

"They won't know how long a job like this takes," Sarah added.

"The other teachers?"

"I've sworn them to silence and, trust me, there are perks to being a nun. People take vows made to nuns very seriously."

"Why are you doing this?"

Sarah hugged Asha once more. "Because there's very little I can do except for this. If I tried to take you away from him, there would be a scandal. The villagers might riot or shut down the school, demand my resignation, and everything we've done would be in jeopardy. But this I can do. You'll be away from her for most of the day. You'll be in a safe place, and perhaps the income you earn will insure against another attack. I can't give you much, but I can give you something to look forward to."

Asha's eyes filled with tears, but she wiped them before they could fall, determined to be strong for once. "Thank you, Sister."

* * * *

Asha, although not complacent, accepted her life. After all, there was very little she could control except when it came to her studies. If school was a race, Asha was running a marathon. She absorbed knowledge as quick as Sarah laid it in front of her. On their walks to and from the school, she'd tutor Mukash. They'd stop on the side of the road just long enough for Asha to spell some new words for him. He hadn't learned to read fluently, but he had started picking up enough so he wasn't so lost.

Her life was busy. Niti didn't dismiss her from any chores, and now she had much more to do, but she never complained. When she did feel sad, she only had to look at Mukash's sweet face to pull through again.

Aditi didn't hit her after that horrible night. He appeared contrite and distanced himself, especially when he noticed her missing tooth. In response, or perhaps retaliation, she smiled as much as possible in his presence.

Unfortunately, the trick didn't work when they went to bed, and he would often tell her to lay on her back. It was during those times, she was most grateful for all the books she'd read and the imagination the Gods had graced her with. Her imagination was not only a gift, but it became her protection mechanism. She trained her mind to conjure the masterful images Twain, Austen, Dumas, and Dickens painted when her husband's weight almost crushed her. He'd roll off her, and she'd fall asleep face down on the mat, trying to drown out his snoring while muffling her own cries.

For over a year, she lived in that life, content in her carefully constructed world. Even as a Choice Less, she could find joy in the pages of a book or Sarah's teachings or Mukash's smile.

Only there came a day when she could no longer drown him out.

Sleeping on her stomach wasn't possible.

* * * *

"It will be a boy," Aditi said proudly.

"It better be," her mother-in-law added.

Asha hated the baby in her belly. It was a thief, stealing away the last shred of her innocence. Her life would change once it came, taking away what little freedom she had. No more pretend work. No more school. No more grand plans of escape that her imagination created each night. She'd be tethered to this life forever.

Sarah told her she was carrying a miracle. The nun prayed over her belly and gave her books about pregnancy. Asha didn't feel like her worthless soul and weak body were capable of miracles. The baby wasn't a blessing. It was a curse.

In her third month, everything changed with one simple conversation. They shared the evening meal with Niti's gripes, Aditi's grumbles, Mukash's exuberance, and Asha's silence. As usual, Niti commanded the conversation.

"There is a woman in the city who can tell if the baby's a boy or girl."

Asha's ears perked up, and her hand went straight to her waist, rubbing it to comfort the soul inside her.

"She takes a pendant and places it over the stomach. If it goes up and down, it's a boy, but if it's left to right, a girl."

Asha wanted to ask why they would care, but she already knew the answer. The signs were there, but she'd been so selfish she'd never once considered the innocent child in her belly.

"It's better to know these things in advance. Easier," Niti continued as if she was talking about one of their animals giving birth to a sick offspring. The analogy held no similarity. When an animal gave birth, it didn't matter the gender of the baby. In fact, females were more appreciated since they would increase the stock. Asha's breath hitched, and a wave of nausea overcame her. She bit it back, not daring to get up when they were discussing her baby.

Her baby.

"I won't trust my child's life to a charlatan," Aditi said. Asha sighed gratefully. Aditi caressed her cheek. "Besides, I know it's a boy."

Just as he made the self-assured statement, Asha accepted her fated life was much too cruel to hand her a son. She was carrying a girl baby—an unwanted girl just like herself. A fierce need to protect overcame her, and something else…a love she'd never expected.

She wanted the baby.

She set about to convince her family that any child, regardless of gender, was a blessing. She tried to appeal to Niti first. "Another girl can help us with all this housework."

The woman's reply wasn't favorable. "And she will break us, too. We'll have to sell our lands to pay for dowry. Are you really this stupid? Do you not understand how a son brings wealth while a daughter steals it?" The older woman, in a gesture of camaraderie, placed her hand on Asha's shoulder. Asha forced herself not to move. "Don't worry, *beta*. It's not good for you to fret right now. You will have a strong son. One day he will command a great dowry and restore wealth to this house."

She appealed to her husband next when they were alone in the dark of night. He was breathing in a way that told her he hadn't fallen asleep yet. "Aditi, did you know the man determines the baby's sex? If I'm carrying a girl child, it's because your body told mine it's what you wanted. It's meant to be, husband."

His fingers gripped her neck with such strength all breath escaped her. "Stop talking nonsense. If we have a girl, it is your fault and only yours." His fingers pressed farther. She tried to pry them loose but his grip was too strong.

"Say it!" he screamed.

She shook her head, unable to breathe, let alone say anything. He released her but held her arms back, his nails digging into her skin. "Promise me you are having a boy."

She rasped and choked until she could sputter the words. "It will be a boy. I promise." It was ridiculous for him to think she could determine the gender of their baby, but in that moment, she would have pledged she was having an elephant if it appeased him.

She wore a yellow scarf to hide the finger marks on her neck from Sarah. They served as a silent reminder that she had no ally in her husband.

She prayed a great deal, for what she wasn't sure. Should she pray she was carrying a boy? Why? So he grew up cruel and merciless like her husband? Should she pray the girl would survive? And if she did, she'd have a horrible life. The abuse would only increase, its vicious aim targeting an innocent child, all because of her gender.

Asha walked around the house like a shadow, every kick in her belly signaling the inevitable. Her chores suffered because her feet swelled just like her waist. Her hair started falling out, and she had trouble keeping food down. Mukash took over as much as he could, but it didn't go unnoticed by her mother-in-law.

Asha sat hunched over a rock with a bucket of soapy water and a pile of dirty clothes. She washed each garment, slapping it against the rock, grateful she could be alone in her grief. She used the back of her wrist to wipe the sweat from her brow. Her whole body had become a cracked vessel for liquid—she was either sweating or vomiting or crying or urinating.

"You're washing it wrong, *beta*," Niti said, sitting beside her. Asha cast her mother-in-law a suspicious glance, not because of the criticism, that she was used to, but for the gentle tone of her voice, which she was not. Niti crouched next to her, taking the yellow scarf from Asha's hand.

"You have to eat more. You are carrying my grandson after all."

"Or granddaughter."

The older woman winced. "If you keep saying those things, it will be a girl."

"It's already been determined. Our wishes won't change it."

Niti turned to the girl, touching her hair in a motherly gesture. Asha squeezed her eyes tightly, hoping for the new wave of nausea to pass.

"Do you think this is an easy life? For a woman?"

Asha knew there were women in the village that did enjoy a wonderful life, but right now, she could not think of any examples. She only saw the misery. "It's a very difficult life. We work all day. We are not respected. We grow old before our time. We have no choices." Asha, surprised by her own candidness braced for Niti's backlash, but it didn't come.

"Then why would you want to subject your daughter to this suffering?" Niti asked. "We are doing the child a blessing. She will not bear any pain. I will see to it myself."

"How?" As soon as she asked the question, Asha regretted it. She didn't want to know.

Niti gave her a toothless grin, perhaps meant to comfort, but it did nothing to relieve her. The older woman dipped the bright yellow scarf into the water once more. She pulled out the saturated material. The sun shone through, highlighting the floral pattern. Niti folded it several times until it was a thick wet square.

"You take the cloth and place it on the baby's face."

Asha immediately reached for her throat, struggling to keep her lunch down. "You'll suffocate her." Then Asha realized that was indeed the woman's intention.

"It won't take much time. It's like going to sleep, *beta*."

"No…no," was all Asha could say, panic clinging to every cell in her body, like the water clung to the cloth.

Niti threw the wet cloth at her. It slapped her head, the lukewarm water coating her face.

"You think we don't have to make sacrifices in this life? You think I didn't have to? These things are required of us. They are our penance in life."

Asha waited until Niti was back in the house. She took the wet cloth in her shaking hand. She placed it over her face and tried to breathe. It felt heavy, uncomfortable, and after a few seconds, unbearable.

She rubbed her belly in slow circles. "I will die before I let anyone hurt you," she vowed in a steadfast whisper.

Asha steadied herself to let go of her pride and seek help from the one person who could save her baby.

* * * *

"They'll kill the baby if it's a female. Sarah, I don't want my baby to die. Please help me protect it."

"Dear God in heaven," Sarah said, making the sign of the cross. She put a hand on each of Asha's arms. "I will figure this out. Leave it to me. You just do one thing, honey."

"What, Sister?"

"Pray."

Asha did two things. First, she prayed as she'd never prayed before. Second, she ripped up the ugly yellow scarf and tossed the shredded material into the river. As she watched the waters carry the remnants downstream she stood taller than she had in a long time.

Chapter 19

"Wow, who is he and where has he been up until now?" Geet asked, shoulder bumping Shyla.

Shyla followed her co-worker's gaze. Her mouth parted at the sight of Nick Dorsey in running pants and a NYU hooded sweatshirt. Even in those simple clothes, he made a dramatic entrance.

The girls stood in the kitchen, looking out the window to the eating area. Most patrons didn't realize the tiny window's existence. Its purpose was to see if customers came in, but very few of them looked back.

Geet continued with her guessing game. "I bet he's a movie star or maybe a model."

"Why do you care?"

"If he's famous, mommy and papa will want his photo for our wall. Do you see the scar on his face? How can a disfigurement be so…so hot? I wonder if its makeup." She peered closer, pushing Shyla out of the way. "He's definitely a model. I would guess an underwear model. What do you think, Shyla?"

Shyla walked to the sink, her nerves on edge at the sight of Nick invading her little world. Geet was right. The man wasn't just handsome. He was striking with the kind of presence that caused even the most composed women to become giddy, not that Geet needed much assistance there. Shyla washed her hands in the sink, wringing out her nervousness in the process.

"That's Mr. Fifteen C, Bleecker Street, Geet."

Geet's jaw dropped. "OMGS. You're kidding."

"OMGS?"

"Oh my Gods…plural." They both shared a laugh before Geet's expression turned skeptical. "That's Mr. turkey tom on whole wheat? Shit, why didn't I do those deliveries? What have you been keeping from me?"

"His name is Nick Dorsey."

"Why is he here?"

Shyla gave a non-committal shrug, even though she had an answer to Geet's query. He was here for her. They both quieted as Nick made his way toward the cash register. Even from her limited sight line, Shyla could see Adesh's welcoming smile. "May I help you?"

"Is Shyla working?"

Adesh's pleasant expression turned sour. "She's on a delivery."

"I'm right here," Shyla said, opening the door from the kitchen.

"I meant to say I'm sending her on a delivery."

Nick's face reflected annoyance, but once he turned his attention to Shyla, he smiled softly. "Can we talk?"

"She can't," Adesh snapped. "She's working."

"Yes, I can. I'm taking my break now," Shyla said, surprised her voice didn't waver.

Adesh's harsh stare was chockfull of judgment and criticism. "You never take a break."

Shyla shrugged, handing him the brown paper bag with the delivery order. "Then I'm overdue. I'm taking one today."

"Who's going to take this to Washington Street?" Adesh demanded.

"You can take it," Geet said, coming out of the kitchen. "It's slow. I can watch the store, and mommy will be back soon."

Adesh shook his head at his sister as if she'd betrayed him by conspiring with the enemy. He sighed heavily, snatching the bag. If the door was capable of slamming, it would have, but its slow track prevented such dramatic gestures.

They all watched him go, a little lost by the theatrics of the moment. Shyla asked Nick to give her a minute. Geet followed her back to the kitchen. "Thank you," Shyla whispered, squeezing the other girl's hand.

"No need to thank me, but I'll definitely expect an explanation…with details. My brother's so pissed off right now." She rubbed her hands together. "Serves him right. He's such a dick sometimes."

Shyla tried to cup her mouth, but the giggle escaped just the same. "Geet, don't talk about him that way."

"Enough about him. I'm more interested in you. All this time, I pegged you for this innocent girl, but then this underwear model comes looking for you, and I wonder if you lead a secret double life."

"Next you'll be accusing me of stealing the state secrets of a small country."

"Huh?"

"Nothing."

Shyla grabbed two juice boxes from the fridge before leading Nick to a far table, one she knew was out of the sightline of the kitchen window and away from Geet's prying eyes.

Nick slid into the booth across from her. He laced his fingers together and looked around the small deli, taking in the brilliant photographs of the Rajasthan castles lining the wall. "I'm sorry to bother you at work."

"It's okay. You didn't get me in trouble."

She slid the small cardboard box to him.

"I missed these."

"I had a feeling you really liked them."

He punched the top with his straw. "You ever notice we drink them differently?"

"How so?"

"You hold it in your little hands so daintily and sip slowly. I just crush the box until it comes out of the straw."

"Is daintily a real word?"

He brushed back his hair. "I'll confirm later and get back to you. Anyway, I think it says a lot about us as people."

"You think?"

"Oh yeah, it speaks volumes about our personalities. For instance, you're graceful and patient, whereas I'm impetuous, impulsive, and sometimes a complete asshole."

"You gathered all that from the way we drink juice boxes?"

"Amazing, isn't it?"

"Nick—"

"I miss you."

"Is that why you're here?"

His eyes darted the room once more. "Nah, I wanted to see where my sandwiches came from." The mischievous glint in his eyes matched his wicked smile.

"You've never been here?"

"No, I got a flyer in the mail. It had the magic words—fast, sandwich, and delivery. That's all I needed to know."

Shyla arched her brows and crossed her arms, waiting for him to continue, but he didn't. "You've seen this shop from the street, though. At least you have for the past week."

"Shit, you saw me?"

"Unlike Max Montero, you are not a master of covert operations. I will admit I didn't realize it was you at first. You're lucky I didn't douse you with pepper spray."

Nick chuckled. "I would have deserved it." His knee knocked against hers. She would have thought it an accident if the movement hadn't been so lengthy. "Sometimes my masculine tendencies lean toward stupidity. You've been on your own for so long and in my life for a short time, but I worried about you getting home safely."

"That was sweet—strange and a bit stalker-like, but sweet."

Nick glanced at his watch. "How long do you get for your break?"

"I don't know. This is my first one, and I never asked."

"Everyone here seems extremely friendly. I bet you love it." The sarcasm in his tone, coupled with the nervous drumming of his fingers on the table, chipped her attempt at cool passivity.

She wanted to take his hand, but she held back. She'd missed him terribly. It wasn't just his laugh, his charisma, his seducing masculinity, or all the special things associated with Nick Dorsey, but also the way he made her feel about herself as if she was special, interesting, even tempting.

"I'm sorry Adesh was rude to you."

"I can deal with it. I'm having a more difficult time that he was rude to *you*."

"It's just his personality. I don't let him boss me."

"You don't have to make excuses for him. I recognize a dueling challenge when I see it."

"I don't follow."

Nick cocked his head and arched a brow at her. "You don't? It's obvious he has a massive crush on you, and therefore he hates me and the idea of you with me."

"I've told him I'm not interested."

"Well that's the thing about unrequited love, sweetheart. It only requires one participant."

"Is there a reason you're so interested in Adesh?"

He licked his bottom lip. "I'm making an observation. And just to be clear, my interest solely revolves around you. Although, I may be the best person to sympathize with his plight. I'm certain we will never be on friendly terms."

"Why are you here?"

He moved his hand toward her, a slow inch at a time. She set hers down, and he covered it, caressing the back of her hand. Shyla's heart let out a silent plea, asking her to jump into his arms. But her brain cautioned her to stay seated.

"I read your pages. It was hard to read."

"That bad, huh?" Shyla casted her eyes down in disappointment.

He tilted her chin gently. "Oh no, they were very good. I mean the subject matter was difficult. I'm identifying with your character. She's led a harsh life."

"So you liked them?" she asked, holding her breath.

"Yes. I made some minor changes. Just suggestions really, but I enjoyed what you wrote. I am confused about how this is a love story, though."

"It is."

"When does the male hero come in? It's certainly not the fucker she married."

"It's not that kind of love story. It's the love between a mother and child."

"I gotcha, makes sense."

"I think my break is over."

"Shyla, I want to help you finish the book. I think I need to."

In some ways, what he said made her very happy, but in others, it saddened her. Was his intention to finish the book or be with her? "You want to finish the story?"

Nick took his free hand and ran it over his hair. He drew a deep breath. "No, not just that. I've been thinking about what you said. About forgiving myself. I'll be honest, I'm not there yet, but I'm trying."

"I really hope you can, Nick."

"Shyla, when you came into my life, I thought I didn't deserve you."

"That's ridiculous." Her voice was quivered sharpness, and she regretted how it gave away the full breadth of her emotions.

Nick tightened his hold on her hand. "In a way, the fact you were going home justified letting you inside my world. I rationalized a temporary reprieve in my extremely scheduled life was acceptable. That even a man like me could justify bliss when it came with brevity."

"And now?"

"The more I know you, the more I want to know you—you are a craving that refuses to be quenched." He tilted his head, mouthing the words again as if they came from someone else's mouth.

She swallowed, sipping the remainder of her drink. "Yeah, I don't have the pretty words like you do, but I feel the same."

"Let me explain something to you, sweetheart. Something I rarely talk about outside of group. I figured it would be easy to quit my addiction, but the journey is…grueling. I question if I can ever become that man again. The people I might hurt if I choose a path of destruction for my life. Addiction runs in my family. My mother was hooked on liquor and abusive men. My grandfather was a gambler. I've maintained a routine that's gotten me through each day. I wasn't prepared for you to come into my life and knock me on my ass."

Shyla gazed at their enjoined hands. She wanted to interrupt him. To scream at him to take back his words since she didn't see him as someone who would hurt her. There was nothing malicious about the compassionate, giving man who sat across from her. She bit her tongue, though, because it was apparent Nick needed to say this and to have her listen.

"In other ways, I think you are the best thing that's happened to me in a long time...maybe longer than long. Maybe ever." He hesitated until she caressed her thumb against his wrist. "I'm sorry for the things I said to you. You're here for three more months. I want to resume what we had or maybe start over. I want that time with you, if you'll let me have it."

"It's yours, Nick."

Chapter 20

Nick opened the door to the girl who managed to usher sunshine into his life. The sad, hesitant expression on her face surprised him, but the sexy innocence of the white dress with its thin straps caught him completely off guard. As did her hair, loose for once, tumbling down in soft waves over her shoulders. No, the dress wasn't what aroused him. It was the girl who graced it.

"What's wrong, Goddess?" he asked, taking her hand and leading her inside. He shut the door and leaned against it, pulling her closer to him.

"I wasn't going to come."

His heart beat a rapid pace in his chest with her simple sentence. He cleared his throat in an effort to make his voice even. "Why not?"

"I didn't think you wanted me to."

"And what would give you such a foolish idea?"

"You."

"Me?"

"You texted me today and said not to bring food. We didn't talk about other plans last night so I wasn't sure exactly what you meant."

Nick placed a hand against each of her cheeks and lowered his head so they were at eye level. "That's why you're upset?" She bit her lower lip, as if she was embarrassed by her feelings. Although Nick hated her discomfort, he sort of loved she was as fucked up for him as he was for her.

"Listen to me," he said, rubbing her arms. "I didn't mean not to bring yourself over. I want you here every night. I thought that was clear, but let me convince you, anyway. A day without you is a day in the dark."

She smiled slightly, and he kissed her dimple as soon as it appeared. He tried to think of some other words, some sappy sonnet worthy of what he felt for her, but he couldn't. His mind blocked any coherent contemplation when he glanced at the hint of cleavage peaking through the neckline of her dress. Fortunately, his body was quite capable of communication. He pulled her into a deep kiss, lifting her off the ground and embracing her so tightly she gasped.

He moved to set her down and utter some apology, but she tugged at his hair, a simple act that made him completely weak. He put her down, but just long enough to discard her dress. He undid the top buttons of his shirt, throwing it over his head in a one-armed frenzy. He took a moment to nourish his eyes with her soft, sleek body—warm skin, large heaving breasts calling out to him, and voluptuous curves that caused his hands to twitch. She was a Goddess, his Goddess, and tonight he planned to worship her.

Her face shifted downward, her arms crossing to cover the very beauty he sought.

"Would you deny a peasant an opportunity to view a work of art?"

"Umm…no"?"

"Then don't." Nick moved her arms away.

He slid his hands down her side, the warmth of her skin on his fingertips. He lingered over her hips, trying to memorize their graceful slope. His moved forward, a hungry predator ready to feast. She moved back with his every step, her sexy mouth curved into an inviting smile, until she squeaked when he picked her up. At first, she seemed surprised, but her nails dug into his shoulders, her thighs tightened over his waist. He caressed her legs from ankle to hip and back again. The fourth time, he moved his fingers underneath the silky fabric of her panties, tracing the outline.

She moaned into his mouth, commanding his dick to show respect with a full salute.

"You have to put me down," she said.

"Why?" he asked, brushing his lips against her neck.

"Because you can't open a condom in this position."

He laughed. "Watch me." Her legs shifted, but he held her in place. "A little help, Goddess."

"What do you want me to do?"

"Reach into my back pocket."

For once, Nick was prepared. He'd been aching for her all day, and although taking her against the wall had never occurred to him, he did have the foresight to place protection in his back pocket.

Nick lowered her so she could reach. She leaned forward against him, reaching into the left pocket first. It wasn't in there, but Nick didn't correct her. Only a foolish man would tell a girl to stop groping his ass.

"It's not here."

"That's because it's in the other pocket, but you can look for it as long as you want."

She giggled, slapping his ass before grasping the condom. She held it against his mouth. "Hold this for a minute," she said. He bit the packet between his teeth, nipping her finger playfully in the process. She managed to unzip his pants. She slid her hands over his length from root to tip while he continued to work ankle to hip. She'd never been this bold before, always allowing him to lead, but he loved this new side of her. They just looked at each other, each slowly exploring the other's body while their eyes remained locked.

"Condom. Now," he said, as the gold foiled package fell from his lips. Luckily, the space between them created the perfect basket to catch it. She picked it up and ripped it open between her teeth.

Her expression was full of emotion. Nick saw both fear and frailty, but even more so, there was aggressive ferocity in her eyes. "I've never put it on before."

"Just slide it down, baby."

Nick sighed with relief in being freed from his undergarments, which suddenly seemed to have shrunk around his massive erection. She rolled the latex barrier. Her fingers traveled down once more as if to check for leaks.

Her legs were like a vise grip, her arms held him tightly, and with the wall pinning her, he had no trouble freeing a hand. His traced her slit with his finger before penetrating her. He slid his fingers inside Shyla's tight folds. Her legs shook with his touch.

His pinched the soft, sweet-smelling skin of her neck with his teeth. The bite wasn't deep enough to leave a mark, but contained just the right sharpness to make her moan and remember his presence there. He contemplated the moment for a split second...how desperately he wanted to both pleasure and possess every delicious inch of her. She tilted her head back, encouraging his access. She placed his cock between her legs, tightening her legs around him, her body begging him for relief. Relief he also longed for.

He didn't thrust as much as he propelled. Their breathy sighs giving away to savage grunts. Nick grasped a fistful of her hair, uttering Shyla's name like a vigilant prayer against her ear. When she said his, he almost lost it, but he held on waiting for her finish. Her fingernails dug into his shoulder with her climax. He followed her there. He didn't let her go when they'd finished. Instead, he looked into her eyes again, their heavy breaths filling the space between them.

* * * *

Shyla leaned on him a few minutes after they parted. Partially, to continue the intimacy, but mostly because she didn't trust herself to walk on wobbly legs. He steadied his hands on her hips until she stood on her own. And then he headed to the bathroom to wash up and discard the condom.

"Why didn't you want me to bring anything?" she asked when he came out.

"I made us dinner tonight."

She sniffed the air and winced with the pungent aroma. He did the same, his happy expression turning anxious.

"Shit," he said, pulling on his jeans and running to the kitchen.

Shyla reached for her dress, but decided to put on his white oxford shirt instead. She loved it when Nick wore long sleeved button-down shirts. He looked like an old-time actor. Surprisingly, he hadn't broken any buttons the way he had ripped it off his body. It came a few inches above her knee. She hugged it around her, inhaling his scent before folding her dress.

She reached the kitchen in time to hear Nick's slew of obscenities. He fanned the air around him with a dishtowel. He opened the small window in the kitchen. A smoky pot sat in the sink, its contents charred beyond repair.

"I thought you didn't cook."

"I don't. Isn't the evidence obvious," he said, throwing a spatula in after the pan and running cold water.

"I'm sorry."

"You should be. It's your fault." A naughty grin played upon his face as he snapped the dishtowel against her bottom.

"My fault?" she asked, pointing a finger at her chest.

"You're too damn distracting, beautiful girl."

"What were you making me?"

He walked toward her until his body was against hers. The fact he was shirtless almost made her suggest they go hungry.

"A feast worthy of a Goddess."

"Oh really?"

"Yes, one that will nourish her so she'd have the stamina required for this evening's vigorous activities. A meal worthy of royalty, albeit created by a peasant."

She peered over at the blackened orange substance in the pot and back at him. "It looks like macaroni and cheese."

He laughed. "It was. I got veggie burgers, too, and salad. They're still in the fridge."

"I love macaroni and cheese. I'm sorry it got ruined."

"It's not. I have enough to make another batch, and I didn't start on the burgers yet. I wanted to make something from scratch. At least one thing for you."

There was something so sweet about his need to please her she turned her head for a moment in a lame attempt to relax the ear-spanning smile on her face. Nick washed his hands in the sink. He grabbed fresh ingredients. She scraped the burnt pasta and took his place at the sink. She scrubbed the pot, occasionally taking sidelong glances at his naked muscular back and the intricate inked lines adorning it. Her eyes lowered. A man's butt had never been of any interest to her, but Nick's muscular bum in low-slung jeans gave her moment to pause and her heart to accelerate.

"Are you checking me out?"

Did he have eyes in the back of his head? "Just making sure you don't burn our food again."

"I got this."

He checked a recipe, boiling the pasta and creating a cheese sauce from scratch. She had to admit it was an impressive undertaking for someone who used his kitchen to store cereal.

"Have you ever had a veggie burger?" she asked him.

"No, but I like to try new things. Besides, I bought hamburgers in case it was gross."

He came up behind her. His powerful arms encircled her as she leaned against his strong chest. He turned the stainless steel lever, causing the water to steam.

"I don't know if I can get all of this out." She'd been scrubbing so hard her arms hurt.

"Let me," he said, taking the pad, their hands brushing. He continued to kiss her neck, occasionally running his tongue over her ear.

"I think you're distracting me."

"I'm helping you."

The steam billowed out of the faucet, causing her skin to flush…or maybe it was the way he kissed her. There was something hungry in his affection—something that made each moment with him intensely beautiful. She wanted to freeze time and stay rooted next to him without any space between.

"You look cute in my shirt," he said.

You look cute out of it.

"All done," he said, holding up the shiny pot, now magically clean. He playfully slapped her behind. "Now get out of my way."

"Give me something to do."

He gently massaged her shoulders. "I want you to relax. Pour yourself a glass of wine and pick out a record. This will just take a few minutes."

Shyla took two long-stemmed glasses from his cupboard and poured them each a generous glass of chilled chardonnay. She sipped, closing her eyes at the taste of the refreshing blend of citrus and grape.

She walked into the living room and chose "Pretty Girl" by Eric Clapton.

"Good choice," Nick said from the kitchen. "Can't go wrong with Clapton."

"Thank you."

He hummed along to the music. She glanced at the other records on his shelf. She knew most of them now. They'd even gone to a flea market one day in search of more. Nick had downloaded every song she said she liked to her phone.

She wondered if she should shower, but his scent still lingered on her skin, and she didn't want to take off his shirt. She had clothes here now. The way that had happened was sudden and unplanned, like everything else about their relationship.

He'd offered the use of his washer and dryer because he didn't want her wasting money using the facilities on campus. She ran late for class the next day, so she left the clean, folded clothes in the blue plastic basket on top of his dryer. When she came to his house in the evening, the blue basket sat in the same spot but was devoid of clothes. Nick explained, with an adorably impish grin, how he'd put her items in his dresser. Of course, all of these little things meant something, but right now, she didn't want to decipher them. She just wanted to enjoy their time. But when she truly considered it, they'd become entwined in a way she had never expected. In fact, it was difficult for her to remember the sad, lonely person she was before him.

She took a seat at his dining table, glancing at the papers there. It was the latest draft of their book. She shoved it aside, deciding to procrastinate for another night. This wasn't a night to think of the sullied past or the uncertain future. Tonight, they would live in the present.

She shifted her eyes to the other papers there, full of legal language and Nick's neat penmanship scrawled in the margins.

"Is this your publishing contract, Nick?"

"Yeah, I decided it was a good time to renegotiate since I've decided to write another Montero book. I'm going to my agent's house for brunch tomorrow so I figured I'd get a jump on it."

Shyla scanned the pages. "It looks complicated."

"Not really. Oh, I'm going to give her our partial on *The Choice Less*, too."

She bit her lower lip and squeezed her eyes closed. "Can you wait until we're done with it?"

"If you wish."

She sighed. "Thank you."

"I get it. I used to be superstitious, too. I never told anyone what I was writing until it was done."

"What does Right of First Refusal mean?" she asked, pointing at the section written in both bold and italics.

"It's a loyalty clause. It means if I write anymore Max Montero books, this publisher gets the first rights. They pretty much own the character."

"What if they don't want the book?"

"It hasn't been a problem so far. They sell very well, but if they don't want it then I can take it somewhere else. It protects both of us, and I'm sure it's non-negotiable. Not that I mind. I like this publisher. My agent, Carrie, worked out a good deal for me."

"Are you close to her? You said you're going to her house tomorrow."

"We're old friends. It's more of a social visit than work."

"How did you become friends?'

"You really want to know?"

"I wouldn't ask if I didn't want to know."

"Well, sometimes girls use that tactic to fish for information they don't really want, but you're not like other women I've been with so I can't apply the same theories to you."

He came to the table, two plates in his hand. Shyla gathered the papers and placed them on his desk.

"We worked late a lot, editing my book. One night we ordered Italian food and a bottle of Chianti. One bottle led to three. I slept with her."

Shyla took a long gulp of wine to choke down the emotions of his statement. "Oh."

"We both realized it was a mistake the next day. I wasn't thinking too clearly, and she wasn't interested in me. It made it very awkward for a while, but we worked through it and emerged friends."

"Really?"

"Yes, in fact, I was best man at her wedding. It would make sense we're close. After all, we have a lot in common."

"Like what?"

"We both find Indian chicks very hot. She married one. Her wife, Tara, is Indian."

"She married a woman?"

Nick pushed his pasta on the plate. "Is that strange to you?" There was no negative connotation in his question, only curiosity.

"I've lived in New York for a while now. I understand there are many kinds of relationships."

"It's more than a relationship. They're a family. I'm honored to be their friend."

Shyla quirked an eyebrow, waiting for him to continue.

"The only way to know your real friends is to measure from the bottom up."

"What do you mean exactly?"

"Like I told you, I fooled everyone about my addiction, especially me. I played the part of young successful author very well. I had a ton of friends, except they weren't really my friends. When I was in the hospital contemplating how my life turned out and the self-loathing son of a bitch I was, it was Carrie who came to visit me every day. She brought me get-well cards from Maya."

"Maya?"

"Maya is their daughter."

"They have a daughter?"

"She's Tara's daughter from a previous marriage, but Carrie adopted her. I dropped out of their lives for a while until I could get my own back on track, but they are very important to me. Anyway, Maya didn't know why I was in the hospital, only that I was sick." He surveyed Shyla closely as if waiting for her to comment, but she kept quiet.

He swallowed before speaking again. His voice sounded far away, wrapped up in some memory. "There's something magical about a get-well card drawn by a kid. She made them like a story. Each one had a sentence about a dog named Shakespeare and a crude crayon drawing on colorful construction paper. The poor kid spelled Shakespeare different each time, and the dog changed breeds, size, and fur color as well."

Shyla laughed, covering her mouth with a napkin.

"Maybe it's silly, but I told myself I had to make it through detox because I had to find out what happened to Shakespeare. The kid is crafty. She ended each story with a cliffhanger. And between the visits from Carrie and the cliffhanger cards from Maya, I made it through each day."

"It's not silly at all. She sounds like a smart little girl."

"She is. I want you to meet all of them. I think you'd like them."

"Maybe."

They were both quiet for a moment, the sounds of metal against porcelain accompanied by the riff of Clapton's guitar filling the room.

"This is really good," she said, pointing her fork to the pasta.

He shrugged. "It's a little rubbery."

"Thank you for making it."

He nodded, pushing aside his plate, his veggie burger almost untouched. "I'm going to make myself a hamburger. Would you like anything?"

"Didn't care for the veggie burger?"

"You can't say I didn't try."

"Shall we watch a movie tonight?"

"Sure, it's your turn to pick. What are you in the mood for?"

"I want to try something different tonight."

"Different?" he asked, coming out of the kitchen.

"Yes, it's like you say, 'It's always good to try.'"

Chapter 21

Nick's dirty mind considered the possibility of a skin flick, but he knew her too well to lend credence to the idea. He hadn't expected a Bollywood movie, though. She found one of her favorites on Netflix.

She leaned against his chest as he tried to concentrate on the subtitles.

"It's kind of multi-genre, huh?" he asked her.

"What do you mean?"

"It's definitely a romance, but there's plenty of action with the fighting scenes."

"Hmm…I suppose."

"Plus, it's a musical."

She turned her head to peer at him. "Music and dance are staples of Bollywood."

"Why is that?"

"Because all happy endings start with a song and dance."

He laughed, kissing her head, grateful she was sharing her culture with him.

"We should go to Jackson Heights one day. We can visit Little India. Have you been there?"

"Once with Geet."

"I think it'll be fun. Would you like to go together?"

"I would."

The heroine in the film was a pretty girl, but she didn't hold a candle to Shyla. Still, he sat up when the girl did a sexy hip-shaking dance, which appeared to combine classical, hip-hop, and salsa all in one.

When the credits rolled, she turned to him. "Did you enjoy it?"

"I did actually."

"What was your favorite part?"

"The fight scenes."

"Oh, don't be coy, Nick. You like the dancing, too, or at least when the girl danced. I was watching you watch her."

"It was okay," he said, nonchalantly.

"Just okay?"

He shrugged. "It was sexy as sin."

"I can do that."

His rubbed his jaw to keep it from falling. "Really?"

"Yes."

"Then what are you waiting for. Show me."

"Show you?"

"Dance for me, please." He jerked his head toward the television. "I want to see you do that, baby."

"I don't know. I'm out of practice."

"You're being very cruel. Why bring it up? All it's going to do is torture me now."

She bit her lower lip, blinking her eyes.

"Perfect, just add a sexy gesture to salt the wound."

She took the remote from the couch, hit the rewind button until they came to the point with the loudest song, and paused it. She turned to him, one hand on her hip, the other shaking a finger at him in warning. "No laughing."

"I doubt I'll be laughing."

She unfastened the last few buttons on the bottom of his shirt she still wore and pulled it into a tight knot against her waist, her lacey black panties fully exposed. Nick gazed in awe as her hands worked with lightening speed, twisting her loose strands into a tight bun. She placed a foot on his naked chest. He grasped it, but she shook her head. "I'm just stretching."

"Good idea. It's very important. In fact, I insist you stretch for a long time." He moved his fingers up her bare leg. Just as he was about to pull her against him, she shifted, doing the same thing with her other leg. Nick debated if he could make it through the dance number. "That's right, Goddess, keep stretching. I don't want you to pull a muscle." That wasn't true. There was a muscle he wouldn't mind if she pulled, but it belonged to him.

She surveyed the space between the coffee table and television.

"Need me to move anything for you?"

"No, I think there's enough room. Can you press play?"

He did before sitting back, transfixed on the woman before him, all beauty and shyness as she waited for the music to start. At first, her movements were small, almost demure and controlled. As the drums beat louder, she became bolder. She thrust her breasts, rolled her hips, and then she went in for the kill. She pulled at the bun she'd created, inducing all her glorious soft curls to tumble in beautiful waves across her back.

Nick could no longer be in her audience. The temptation of her stimulated every cell in his body. He needed to participate, not with the dancing, but hell, he just had to touch her.

He stood behind her, resting his hands on her hips as she grinded against him.

"This is my favorite part," he said.

She leaned her head back against his chest. "I thought so."

"Where did you learn this?"

"Watching Bollywood films."

"I think we should watch more. They're highly educational."

She turned and embraced him. "Not tonight. Tonight let's work off that meal."

"You're speaking my language."

* * * *

Lying under the cloud-like, down comforter, Shyla watched the raindrops splash the skylight above them. The whole sky would occasionally flash with a strike of lightning. Johnny Nash played on the record player, singing about the rain being gone along with all the obstacles. Nick had left a dim light on in the hallway as was his habit since the first night when she banged her shin into the coffee table. He did a lot of little things like that for her, without her needing to ask.

"It's a bad storm."

"I like storms. I sleep the best after a bad one." She traced the lines of his palm.

"What are you doing?"

"I'm feeling your love line."

"You're reading my palm?"

"I already did."

"Do you really believe in that stuff?"

"Palmistry has been around for a long time. We are born with these lines, and everyone is different. I can't believe there is no reason behind that. Surely, they say something about us—something about our destiny. Plus, I don't think the man that figures out personality traits from the way people consume juice boxes should judge."

He chuckled, propping himself on his elbow. "Touché."

"Your lines are interesting Nick Dorsey."

"What does it say? This love line of mine."

"It's deep and solid. That means you're very passionate and sentimental. I didn't need to read your palm to know that, though."

He took her hand in his. "Show me what your lines mean."

She took his index finger and ran them over every line of her palm. "This is the lifeline, the heart line, the head line, and the fate line."

"What does your love line say?"

"It's broken in the middle. It means I'll have heartache."

"I see, and your lifeline?"

"Yours is long. You'll live a long life with plenty of vitality."

"I'm asking about you."

She placed his finger across the line on her hand. "See, it's also broken."

"Does that mean a short life?" he asked, tracing the area with his thumb.

"Actually, it doesn't. It means there will be sudden changes for me."

"Shyla, we talked about this a while ago, but you didn't give me many details. I want to know. When you go back home will your father arrange your marriage?"

She stiffened, not expecting the question. He waited patiently for her to answer.

"Possibly."

"Won't it be strange? Marrying someone you don't know?"

"There are many happy arranged marriages, Nick. I'm sure it'll be fine."

"You're sure you'll be fine?" His voice grew louder. "That's not convincing."

"It's in the future. Right now, I don't think about it."

"How about we think about it for just a minute?"

"Why bother?"

"What about us?"

"What do you mean? We both knew this was a temporary situation."

He fell back on his side of the bed, letting go of her hand. She moved her body against his. "Nick, are we really going to waste time fighting about this? I'm on a student visa. I have to go back when I graduate."

"You know I worry about you when you walk home from work alone. What the hell am I going to do when you're across the world from me?" The admission shocked her into silence. He took her hand again. His finger traced the curved broken line she'd shown him. "How much of this is me? How much of this life line do I get?"

"It doesn't work like that. I will cherish this time I spent with you. It's been the best time of my life. But we aren't meant to be."

"Why—because our palms don't align? Because we have different backgrounds? Tell me why."

"Because I'm going back. You're making me feel guilty for something I cannot change."

She moved to separate from him, but he grabbed her and held her against his chest. She cursed the tears running down her face. She wanted to hide them and runaway.

He held her face in his hands and gently kissed them away. "Hey, don't cry. I'm just having a difficult time with this."

Another sharp crack of lightning struck, illuminating his face. His sad expression broke her heart, but she had to keep her resolve. She ran her fingers down his chiseled jaw line, trying to memorize his features through touch.

"I wish we would have met when I first came here. I regret we lost so much time."

He twisted a strand of her hair and kissed the side of her mouth. "I don't."

She chewed on her lower lip, confused by his response. "Why not?"

"I wouldn't have treated you the way you deserved if we had met back then. It's not the past I regret, baby. It's our future."

Chapter 22

The Choice Less

Asha woke in the middle of the night to stomach cramps. Her first thought was indigestion, but then the fear set in. She was in labor. An early labor. It wasn't supposed to happen this way. She was going to sneak out in two weeks, and Sarah was going to save them...both of them.

She stood, trying to be as quiet as she could. She slid on her sandals and walked out of the house. Staring at the sky, she sent up a silent prayer to the Gods. All the Gods she knew of from Krishna, Ganesha, Rama to Jesus and even Allah. She begged them to let the baby stay safe in her womb. She fell to the ground as another cramp seized her, confirming her prayers would not be answered.

"*Bhabhi?*" Mukash whispered.

She turned to him, a sigh of relief mixing with newfound dread. He didn't know her plans. She loved Mukash, but in the end, she didn't think it right to have him deceive his family.

"It is time," she said.

"I'll get Aditi."

"No," she said, gripping the boy's shoulders. "Please don't. I have to get to Sarah. I need your help."

Mukash studied her for a moment. In his eyes, she saw a clear understanding of the predicament. He knew. He understood far more than anyone ever credited him.

"I will help you. Lean on me."

She did lean on him both physically and emotionally. They walked like two shadows in the night.

The trail had never seemed so long, but she tried to concentrate on anything but the pain and fear. If the baby came too early, it wouldn't survive. If she was caught and the baby was a girl, she'd be killed only a few breaths old. If she didn't make it to her destination, perhaps they both would die.

That last conclusion didn't seem like such a horrible idea. The thought itself was a sin to her, but a part of her welcomed it. She changed her prayers. *If the baby dies, let me go with her*, she begged. *Let us be together even if it's not in this life.*

"We need to go through the jungle or someone may see us," Mukash said.

A new fear manifested in Asha. The jungle frightened her—an area she didn't dare travel during the day much less the night. There were wild animals and insects the size of her fist. The tall vines and strange trees tangled together, carving a difficult path. But Mukash was right. In this case, the most dangerous route was also the safest.

The boy brought the metal torch light with him. She held back her vomit when she noticed the dark stain on its tip. Blood. Her blood from so long ago. She almost tripped on some branches, but he caught her. Her face felt sweaty, and she couldn't breathe. She rubbed her stomach, repeating the silent mantra to her baby. *I will protect you. No one will hurt you. I love you.*

Water gushed between her legs. She leaned against a Banyan tree for support. She could walk no more.

"*Bhabhi?*"

"I cannot stand," she said, fear coursing through every vein.

"I can carry you."

She choked out a sound between a cry and laugh. "I'm too heavy for you." She slid down the Banyan tree, its rough wood scratching into her back.

"What do I do?" he asked, tears in his eyes.

She cupped his chin. "Get Sister Sarah. Tell her the baby's coming now. She'll know what to do."

"I won't leave you, *bhabhi*."

"It's the only way. Please hurry," she begged.

He handed her the torch.

"No, you take it. You'll need it to find your way. Go, Mukash. Godspeed." The boy simply nodded, wiping his tears.

Asha listened for the sounds of his feet on the earth until they were too far to reach her. She turned to her side and wretched, but nothing came out. She leaned her head back and closed her eyes. Liquid flowed from between her legs, but it wasn't water this time. The thick substance oozed slowly, sticky against her thighs.

Blood.

She lifted up her sari and rolled down her underpants. She spread her legs. Every movement drained her. She was fighting the exhaustion and losing the battle. Insects feasted on her skin, but she didn't have the energy to swat them away. She was sixteen years old, in labor, and all alone.

Except she wasn't alone.

It sounded like a man's bitter laugh, but the devilish high-pitched squeal didn't come from any human.

Her skin prickled. She wiped the sweat from her forehead and felt around the ground for any potential weapon, but came up empty. Her mind tried to think of how long Mukash was gone, to calculate time and distance, but even the simplest thoughts were difficult. The yapping grew closer.

She touched her womb and concentrated on the story of Ganesha. She whispered in between the contractions, telling her baby about the elephant-headed boy who went around the universe. It distracted her from the pains, which grew sharper with every breath. Her body shook with chills, even though it was a hot night.

She closed her eyes and clenched her fists, concentrating on taking deep breaths. She tried to dream of a happy child, one who would have many choices and excel in all ways her mother couldn't.

When she opened her eyes, she had a visitor.

Even in the dark, the animal's pupils glittered with a fiery evil.

"No," she screamed at the predator as if a conversation were possible.

The hyena circled her slowly, snarling occasionally. He howled, calling his friends to feast. She smelled his strong, rancid scent. The scent of death. The prayer she'd asked for had come in the form of a nightmare.

Some hidden strength flooded through her. She felt around again, struggling to grope farther, ignoring the wrenching pain. Her movements were small. She instinctively knew if the animal noticed, he would attack. She couldn't stand, much less run from it.

Her hand found purchase on a rock at the far side of the tree, buried halfway into the earth. Her fingers dug into the ground, breaking her fingernails. Finally, she was able to dig it free. She grasped its weight. It wasn't bigger than her hand, but jagged and heavy. She clasped it tightly, waiting for the animal to draw closer. There would be only one opportunity.

She was weak, and a moment ago, she had resigned herself to death, but now a new will for survival coursed through her veins. She couldn't see him except for the mouthful of sharp teeth and the glittering eyes that peered at her, but she could feel him. The rancor of the beast's breath and the rustle of sticks signaled he drew closer. The heinous dog stood a few meters from her. Its mouth drew a sinister smile before it pounced.

It pounced!

The stone left her hand with such accuracy and speed she wondered if another power guided it. The animal yelped as the object struck. It backed off but didn't run away as she'd hoped. There were no more stones.

No more chances.

No more choices.

"We will meet in the next life," she said, rubbing her womb. "I love you."

She closed her eyes one last time.

The passing of time was immeasurable. It didn't move fast or slow. It didn't exist in any real capacity for Asha. It was her, her child, and the demon who wanted to claim them. It was the fate of the little girl in the wooden box—an unwanted girl who should never have existed and the child that grew within that girl. Maybe it was best the tyranny ended this way before it could go on for the next generation. She had scraped to live, and now she had to come to terms with death. The last remaining shred of hope was for the animal to be merciful and take them quickly, but she doubted the outcome would be swift.

When hyena cries filled her eardrums, she snapped her eyes open to see Mukash smash the flashlight over the wicked creature's head. Then the boy encircled the predator's neck with his forearm. Mukash looked like a man then... a hero like Hercules. His muscles should have been no match for a Hyena, but somehow he found the strength. The Hyena escaped his grasp, but this time it did run off.

"I'm here, child. Look at me, Asha," Sarah said, wiping the girl's brow.

"The baby?"

"The baby's crowning. We don't have much time."

Sarah moved Asha's knees apart while Mukash shined the light between her legs. The little boy held Asha's frightened gaze, but then bowed his head, singing the words, asking the Gods to end all sorrows, shortcomings, and pain.

"Hare Krishna, Hare Krishna, Krishna Krishna, Hare Hare... Hare Rama, Hare Rama, Rama Rama, Hare Hare."

Sarah recited scripture while she worked, and their blended voices resonated with harmony.

"Push," Sarah commanded.

"Don't scream, *bhabhi*, they'll hear," Mukash warned. She wasn't sure if he was talking about the hyenas, who still growled from some distance, or the villagers.

Asha accepted the cloth Sarah handed her, biting down on it to release her agony and keep her silent.

Although she remained silent, her whole body screamed in agony—a gut-wrenching wail. Then she heard it audibly, a loud and demanding cry. Only it wasn't her.

She looked at Sarah. The sun was rising, giving light to the darkness. Sarah's expression was somewhere between a smile and frown. The three most dreaded words in Asha's vocabulary formed on her lips. "It's a girl."

Her fate was sealed.

The tears mingled with her sweat. Sarah did her best to clean the baby with a few bottles of water. She wrapped the newborn in a blanket before handing her to Asha. Asha held her daughter for what felt like seconds. She kissed her on the forehead.

"I'm sorry, child," Sarah said, wiping Asha's face.

"She's too small. She won't survive," Asha whispered.

Sarah tilted Asha's chin. "Listen to those lungs. She is strong just like her mother."

Mukash squeezed Asha's hand. "We have to go. The sun is rising. I have to get her back."

Sarah brushed her hair back. "It's light out. I cannot take both of you."

"Let me say good-bye," Asha said, gazing at the infant who miraculously quieted in her arms.

"We will get you out, too," Sarah said.

An epiphany had come to Asha. Even if they survived, what possible life could she give this little girl? And would she suffer the same fate as the other women in her line? Asha made one decision in her daughter's life—break the cycle.

"No, Sarah."

"Asha—"

"I said no. Take my baby far from here. Make sure she has a good life. Do this for me Sarah."

Sarah opened her mouth to argue but snapped it shut again when Asha shook her head. "Promise me."

"All right, honey."

"You know what to do?" Sarah asked Mukash, her voice quivering.

They spoke quietly, but Asha didn't pay attention. She was too busy memorizing every feature of her daughter. She took inventory of the ten tiny fingers and toes, the mop of thick black hair, the heart-shaped birthmark on her right arm. Birthmarks were a sign of luck. She hoped that would hold true for her child. She didn't want to let her baby go, but when Sarah said the child needed medical attention, Asha relinquished her daughter, whispering some final words against the baby's forehead.

"I don't have anything else to give you, but I promise you will not be a Choice Less."

Asha leaned on Mukash for support during the trek home. In many ways, it seemed a much longer journey. Her sari covered in blood, her face stained with dirty sweat, and her heart broken. As soon as she entered the house, they were waiting for her. She had no explanation.

As it turned out, she didn't need to speak. It was Mukash who spun the lie with such conviction that no one questioned him. Asha had gone for a walk and gotten lost in the jungle. He'd woken early and searched for her. The baby was born dead. And then the hyena came and took the lifeless body off to the thick growth of the jungle.

Aditi's stare was harsh, his eyes full of disdain. "Was it a boy?"

"She doesn't remember, brother. It happened quickly," Mukash said.

Aditi clasped her shoulders, shaking her. "Did you see? Was it a boy?" he demanded.

"You're hurting her!" Mukash screamed.

"Quiet," his mother chided. She approached Asha until their faces almost touched. "Answer my son."

Asha looked between the two of them.

She took a deep breath and straightened, even though it was painful. Her voice held no apology. No remorse. No compassion.

"It was a boy."

Her mother-in-law slapped her. In her weak state, she fell to the ground. Her husband cried out, a primitive wailing howl, similar to the sound the hyena made. Her mother-in-law's face flooded with tears. She touched her son's shoulder, but he shook off her hand. Aditi ran from the house, a crazed man in search of his son's remains. Mukash had taken care of that, too. He'd scraped Sarah's footprints from the dirt and managed to change the evidence to support the story.

She didn't understand why she'd lied at first. Later, she realized she wanted them to suffer with her. To mourn the loss of the baby as she would. To be angry with her. Maybe even to kill her. But of all the reasons, one rose to the top every time.

She craved revenge.

Chapter 23

The Choice Less

When she was healthy enough to return to work, Sarah took her into her arms.

"Where is my baby?" Asha asked before she even greeted Sarah.

"She's safe."

"I want to see her."

"I'm sorry, Asha. That's not possible."

"My life is incomplete."

"You rescued her."

"I don't know that. I will never know that, will I?"

Sarah stood and walked the room. "Our fate isn't in our own hands. You are young, much too young for what you've gone through, but God will not give you more than you can endure. You did an extraordinary thing."

"I did nothing."

"Yes you did, sweet girl. You made a choice where none existed."

"And now what do I do?"

Sarah placed a textbook in front of Asha. "You continue with your studies. You work toward bettering yourself."

She swept the book off the table until it landed on the floor with a thump. "No."

"No?"

"I don't want to do this anymore. I'll work with the other maids from now on and earn my pay."

"Asha, you have an opportunity. I see something exemplary in you."

She laughed, a bitter cynical sound that made Sarah wince. "Sarah, you see what you want to. What opportunity? The reality is I'm a poor village girl and nothing more. Let me ask you a question, Sister. If a fruit rots on the tree because no one is there to pick it, is it really a waste?"

"I try not to seek solutions to unanswerable questions, dear. But I believe a waste is a waste whether we recognize it or not."

"Let me riddle another for you—if you teach a girl about the world, about the math, science, and literature of it all, but she never uses her education, is she truly intelligent?"

"Of that I have no doubt."

"I think your wrong, Sarah. I wish you'd never taught me all of these things."

"Why would you say that?"

"Because in ignorance there is blindness, and in blindness there is comfort. I would accept the tragedy of my life more willingly if I were ignorant to it. It wouldn't hurt so much."

* * * *

She'd managed to make excuses for six months when her husband asked her to lie back. She told him she was bleeding, too fragile, too ill. He blamed her, so he accepted those excuses. He was disgusted with her for losing their son. He started beating her regularly. She wouldn't give him the satisfaction of crying. He beat her even harder for that.

She prayed she wouldn't get pregnant again. She couldn't go through it, and she knew, without a doubt, she wouldn't be able to save a second baby. Her thoughts became dark and bleak. Any joy evaporated like the rains after a drying sun. She was an emotionless creature who no longer had any fight. At night, she'd walk to the riverbank where Nalini had first found her. She'd dip her feet in the water and look into the horizon. The world was a big place, and she was a small person.

"Why did you lie? You should not have told him it was a boy," Mukash admonished her one night. "He wouldn't beat you if he believed it was a girl baby."

"Let him beat me. It's the only time I feel anything anymore." The words soured in her mouth. When had she given up?

The boy shook his head in disapproval. He stood to leave her.

"Please, don't go," she said, taking his hand. "Stay with me."

The boy sat back down and took her hand in his. "You have to have faith, *bhabhi*. Life will get better for you."

She nodded to appease him and offered a small smile. It was all she could manage.

"I hated this house after my father died. He was a good man. Not like Aditi. I prayed to God to bring him back. Instead, God brought you, and with you came laughter and love. Don't leave me now."

She soaked in his words. She always felt it was Mukash who saved her time and again, but the reality of what he said, the fact they had saved each other, cracked through the seed of bitterness she'd built. She stroked his hair and kissed his forehead. "I'm sorry, little brother. You're right and you're wrong. I needed you much more than you needed me. Not only because of how you saved me and my baby. You showed me something I never knew existed."

"What did I show you?"

"That the world has good men in it."

The boy's chest puffed with pride, and he embraced her. She wiped his tears with her sari and made funny faces at him until he laughed. "I haven't helped you much with your studies. But now, you're probably much more advanced than me."

He scratched his head, a skeptic look on his face. "I don't think so."

"Tell me what you are learning, my brave hero."

Mukash chatted on eagerly.

She started helping him again, tutoring him while they did chores. She never sought refuge in the pages of a book anymore, but she did manage to find tiny rays of sunshine in an otherwise dismal life.

One of which was the goat, who had become her friend. Maybe her misery had garnered the stubborn animal's sympathy. Asha sat with him while knotting a garland made of marigolds, one she'd wear in her hair to the Holi festival. It used to be her favorite holiday, but now she no longer looked forward to the season of change. Change was never good without choice.

The goat snatched a marigold from her hand and chewed, working its jaw slowly. Then he opened his mouth as if he expected another.

"You're a naughty goat." She held up the strand of flowers. "Just for that, you can wear it." She placed the garland around the animal's neck. "You look prettier this way, and maybe it will soften your foul mood."

"Silly girl, what are you doing?" Her mother-in-law's voice caused Asha's back to go ramrod straight. "It's all right, daughter. Don't be frightened." The old woman took a seat on the vacant stool next to her.

Asha went to remove the garland, but the cane the older woman now carried smacked her in the hand. "Leave it."

They sat in silence. Asha truly believe her mother-in-law had a devil inside her. The old woman smiled whenever Aditi hit her. In fact, she encouraged her son, and in many ways, her words provided the ammunition for the weapons that were his hands. The worst was when she berated Mukash, though. She called her younger son stupid and fat. Those words hurt Asha the most because Mukash believed them, even when she tried to convince him of the brave, handsome hero he was.

"Tell me why you did that?"

"What mother?"

"Why put the garland around the goat?"

"I thought it would look nice."

"It does," she said, chuckling. Asha forced herself to laugh along.

"You've been very sad, daughter."

"We all have."

"There is no anguish which rivals a mother's loss for her son."

"Yes," Asha replied, clenching her fists so her hands wouldn't shake.

"It's time for you to try again. My son may accept your excuses, but I recognize them for the lies they are. No woman bleeds as much as you claim to."

Asha swallowed, wiping away the trickle of sweat forming on her brow. "I— I—"

"I didn't come out in the hot sun to judge you, daughter." She tapped the goat with her cane. "I hear the gossip. People say you have a relationship with the nun. She treats you like a daughter."

Asha had no idea where this was headed, but the last thing she wanted was to bring more trouble to Sarah. "I was her student once. Nothing more."

"I know she came to your house when your mother died."

"She was concerned."

"It's all right, daughter. I understand she takes an interest in you, but I pray you don't become misguided by her intentions. She does it not to help you but to feel better about herself. Just as a woman decorates herself with jewels, she can also decorate her mind. But all decorations are false. In the end, we have little power and persuasion in this world. You put the garland on the goat, but do you think it benefits the goat?"

The old woman hobbled over to the animal. She removed the necklace of flowers and threw it in Asha's lap.

"Do you know the difference between the goat and you, my dear girl?"

Asha shook her head.

"The goat knows it's a goat."

* * * *

A few weeks passed since the disturbing conversation with her mother-in-law. She'd continued on, but what happened that morning frightened her enough to turn to Sarah once more.

"Tell me," Sarah said as soon as she set eyes on Asha.

"Aditi is going on a pilgrimage to pray we have a son. He told me when he gets back that I need to give myself willingly or he will take what's his," Asha said, shuddering through the words. "If I refuse him, he will overpower me. I can't Sarah. I can't do this again. I will die this time. I will gladly take all the beatings in the world if it means I will never carry another baby."

"I could help you escape," Sarah said, barely above a whisper.

"They'll know it was you. He'll look for me, and he'll have the villagers on his side. They'll shut down the school. He'll beat Mukash for information. All your good intentions will only result in destruction." Asha saw that line of fate clearly. Her only escape would be death. She'd contemplated taking her own life, but as soon as the thought entered, she shook it away. At her core, she was a spiritual girl, and her faith, although dampened, would never allow her to walk that path.

"What do we do?" Sarah asked.

From the way Sarah titled her head toward the ceiling, she confirmed the question was not directed at Asha. Asha answered it anyway. "We pray I don't get pregnant again."

Sarah was quiet for a long time, but her mouth moved, and her fingers clutched the cross around her neck. "We can do more. Wash up."

"Where are we going?"

"To a doctor in the city." She combed through the girl's hair with her fingers. "Asha, what we're going to do goes against every fiber of my beliefs, but there is a point where right and wrong intersect. We are in that space now."

On the ride back, Asha studied the packet of white pills in her hand.

"You'll have to hide them," Sarah instructed.

"I will. Thank you, Sister."

"Will you do something for me?"

"Anything."

"Resume your education."

"Why is it so important to you?"

Sarah took a deep breath. "My mother always wanted to be a school teacher, but her life took a different road. She married my father, and they had eight children. We were very poor. Each night, she'd take us girls to the sitting room and have us read from the three books we owned." Sarah smiled softly as if recalling some faraway faded memory. "The Bible, Charles Dickens's *A Tale of Two Cities*, and Louisa May Alcott's *Little Women*. Those are still my three favorite books. Anyway, she made all of us study, but especially the girls. My father said she would do better to teach us how to clean and cook than waste our time with books. I'll never forget my mother's response to him. It's the reason why your education and the work I do is so important to me."

"What did she say?"

"She said educating a woman is the worthiest of endeavors. When you do that, you raise up all the generations before her and give fresh hope to those who follow."

"But what use is it to me?"

"I don't have an answer for you, child. God's plans for us aren't always clear. This much I do know. You think you don't have choices, but this is something you can do. You can free your mind even if your body is jailed. That is a choice you can make and an opportunity to own yourself."

Chapter 24

Nick walked with his hand clasped around Shyla's through the few streets that made up Little India. The vibrant colors and smell of fresh spices indulged all his senses.

"These are called *samosas*," Shyla explained, pointing to a street vendor. "They are pastries stuffed with spiced potatoes, onions, peas, and lentils."

"Sort of like a hot pocket?"

"I suppose. Would you like to try one?"

"Sure."

He went to remove his wallet, but she held up her hand. "It's my treat."

She ordered in a mixture of Hindi and English. The clerk and her made small talk as Nick watched with awe. Her accent seemed more pronounced today surrounded with similar accents, although there were definite differences in cadence and speech. The clerk, a heavyset man with a wry grin, pointed to Nick and said something before laughing heartily. Shyla handed Nick the triangular fried pastry still hot and wrapped with tin foil.

"Is he laughing at me?" Nick asked her, an amused smile on his face.

"It's not a big deal," Shyla said.

"What did he say? C'mon, I want in on the joke, especially if I'm the butt of it."

"I ordered a spicy one for me and a mild for you. He said if it's for him, then you will want the extra mild. We make it special for the whites."

Nick arched a brow. "Oh, I see…for the whites."

"And then he said"—she held up air quotes for his benefit—"white men can't do Indian spice."

Nick wondered for a moment if the statement had some deeper meaning. The store clerk continued to stare at them, his chin propped on his hands, a mocking smile on his face. "You understand everything we're saying, don't you?"

The man tilted his head from side to side in a motion that neither confirmed nor denied Nick's question.

"I like spicy food, just so you know," Nick said, narrowing his eyes at the vendor. Shyla giggled, and Nick pulled her closer to him. "Et tu, beautiful?"

She patted his chest. "You're not used to this kind of spice. It's different. Mine is made with chili peppers."

"I can handle it."

The clerk snorted with derisive laughter.

"What? Is that a challenge?" Nick asked the man.

The man pointed to Shyla's *samosa*. "If you eat it, I will give you a sweet for free."

"Challenge accepted."

"Nick, you're being silly. You can't—" Before she could finish the sentence, he grabbed her wrist, brought the pastry to his mouth, and took a huge bite.

He chewed fast at first, but after a few seconds his jaw didn't want to move. Shyla gaped at him, her eyes wide and her mouth forming a perfect *O*. He could taste all the spices now. There must have been at least one hundred of them…a hundred degrees of spice melting his tongue.

"Nick, are you okay?" she asked, putting her hand on his chest as if feeling for a heartbeat.

He gulped down the food and wiped his forehead. "Yes," he said, his voice raspy from the burn. The clerk's loud chuckle reinforced his determination. He took a deep breath, which was a mistake because the air hitting his tongue only dispersed the five-alarm fire in his mouth.

"I'll get you some bread," Shyla said. Bread? He needed a fire hose to douse the flames.

"I'll take the sweet now," Nick said, holding out his hand to the shop clerk.

"I ran out. Come back in an hour, and I'll have a package for you," the man replied.

Nick tried not to show his discomfort, but he knew he was failing, especially when the man's grin resembled that of a Cheshire cat's. Shyla took a plastic bag of pita and placed another dollar on the counter. She clasped Nick's hand and led him away.

As soon as they were out of earshot, she started laughing.

"Oh, thanks," Nick said, bumping her hip and taking her iced coffee.

"Hey, that's mine," she said, trying to grab it from him. He placed his other hand on her head and held her back. She tried in vain to capture the cup.

He sipped it down until the full cup only contained ice. Then he opened the lid and swallowed the ice. "Sweetheart, I need this more than you. I'm about to self-combust."

"Your own fault."

"How can you eat that stuff?"

She shrugged, a seductive smile on her pretty mouth. "I like my food like my men…hot."

Damn, he loved her flirty side. "Let's sit," he suggested, pointing toward a bench.

His gaze trailed over her. She wore a green cotton top with white embroidery indicative of the Indian style, faded jeans, sunglasses holding her hair back, and golden sandals. Nick marveled at how beautiful this girl could look in anything she wore, but today she seemed downright radiant.

He put down the bags he carried with their purchases. Little India was mostly shopping, not something Nick enjoyed, but Shyla found some spice mixtures, tea, and incense there. Nick picked up a carved wooden flute for Maya, who'd expressed an interest in music lately. Although he suspected the girl would squeal at the gift, he grimaced at how pissed off her mother's would be when she practiced on it for hours.

Shyla held up her wrist, moving the silver bangles there. They glinted against the sunlight. "You shouldn't have bought these for me. It's too expensive."

Nick gave her a quizzical look because the baubles had cost very little. He'd taken the jewelry out of her hand and purchased them before she could object. He'd wanted to buy her something far more expensive with real silver or gold, but she'd given him such a hard time over the cheap jewelry, he figured it was best to hold off.

"It was nothing. Are you having a good time?"

"Yes, thank you for today."

"I'm enjoying it, too." He placed his arm around her and kissed her head.

She fed him pieces of bread, and although the fire in his mouth was sufficiently quenched, he didn't stop her.

"Did you read the pages I wrote?" he asked. He'd written the chapter from the notes she'd left on the recorder, but they hadn't really talked about it.

She looked down at her hands. "They were perfect."

"It's getting somewhat farfetched."

"How so?"

He sighed. "Well, a young girl in labor holding off a wild animal? Or a twelve-year-old boy wrestling a Hyena? Or a nun doling out birth control? Or a baby surviving birth in a jungle?"

Shyla shrugged. "People often confuse improbable and impossible."

"You make a point." He tucked a strand of hair behind her ear and kissed her forehead. "The story is good, Shyla. It's emotionally compelling." He'd struggled with those chapters. She had, too. On the recorder, her usual composed voice had cracked several times dotted with abrupt pauses where she'd turned off the device.

"You really think so?"

"I do."

She traced the area where his tattoo was.

"Shyla, does it bother you we're so different? That we come from such dissimilar backgrounds, religion, and ethnicities?"

She shook her head. "I don't think of it that way. Emotion is the same no matter what language you write it in. In the end, we are not so much the sum of our experiences but the journey of our souls. And you can't measure that."

"You're quite philosophical today."

"I should write fortune cookies."

"Seriously, though, you put a lot of credence into this palm thing right? And the stars aligning and all that?" He regretted bringing up the topic again when she frowned.

"I never said our palms didn't match, Nick. I think all paths lead to one place or another. It all comes down to who you are in your life and how you treat people." She ran her fingertips down his jaw. "I have no doubt that both of us are in the good column."

He clasped her wrist and kissed the underside. "You're in the great column. C'mon, I owe you another iced coffee." He jerked his head toward the crowded street. "Should we go?"

"Shyla, is that you?" A voice called as soon as Nick stood.

It was the bubbly girl Shyla worked with. Nick smiled at her and the woman who appeared to be her mother. He did his best not to scowl at Adesh who followed behind them.

The giddy girl enveloped Shyla as if they hadn't seen each other in years. "What are you doing here?"

"Just shopping. You remember Nick?"

"Hi, Mr. 15C Bleecker Street," the girl said, reaching out her hand. "I'm Geet."

"Hello, Geet," he replied, clasping her hand.

Shyla made the other introductions.

"Are you shopping?" Mrs. Dhillon asked.

"A little," Shyla answered.

"So how long have you been friends?" Mrs. Dhillon prodded, staring pointedly at Nick for the answer. Clearly, the lady didn't approve. Nick opened his mouth to reply, but Shyla answered first.

"For a few months. Actually, Nick is my boyfriend."

He smiled, squeezing her hand. "Yes, I am."

They made awkward small talk for a few minutes, avoiding any cultural clashes with observations about the climate.

"I'm picking up my wedding sari. You have to come with us to the shop. I want you to see it," Geet said, holding Shyla's hand.

Shyla turned to Nick.

"It's okay, go on. I'll wait here." Nick had no interest in going to a dress shop unless Shyla planned to try on some outfits for him.

"Are you sure?" she asked.

"I'll keep him company," Adesh said, clapping Nick on the back.

"Great," Nick said through gritted teeth.

Funny how things remained the same regardless of culture. The men were left holding all the bags while the women headed for the sari shop. Nick leaned against the brick façade of a building.

"You notice how people stare at the two of you here?" Adesh said as soon as they were alone. "More specifically, they stare at you."

Nick had noticed. There were other mixed couples like them, but they all received a few lingering, sometimes disapproving, glances, especially from the older shoppers. Shyla didn't seem to care, which lessened the awkwardness for Nick. "I figured they were looking because I'm so devastatingly handsome."

Adesh's surprised look was priceless. "What?"

"Relax, it's a joke, man."

He narrowed his eyes, his jaw tightening. "You're going to ruin her reputation. These things get around. She will have difficulty finding marriage prospects once the rumors start."

Her marriage prospects were not something Nick cared to think about. "It's nice how concerned you are, but our relationship is none of your business."

The other man continued as if Nick hadn't said anything. "In my opinion, I think it's very wrong what you are doing. She's an innocent girl, and you're this rich sophisticated New Yorker. Don't you feel you're taking advantage of her on some level?"

"Just so we're clear, no one asked for your opinion—not her, and certainly not me. We're both adults. It's you who is taking advantage by claiming she isn't intelligent enough to make her own decisions." They were quiet for a minute, each man taking in the other's harsh words, the tension thick with animosity. Finally, Nick couldn't take it anymore. "Why don't we talk about your real issue?"

"What issue?"

"You're jealous of me. I can't blame you. She is an amazing girl, but allow me to deflate any illusions you might be harboring. She. Is. Mine."

Adesh laughed. "For now."

The two words were very simple, but they piercced his heart with the precision of an arrow. "If it was up to me, she wouldn't work with you, but I don't tell her what to do. I respect her decisions, even if I disagree with them."

"What is your point?"

"Back the fuck off." Nick countered between clenched teeth, elongating each word.

"Sure man, I'll do that."

"Good."

"I get it. You were in the mood for something exotic in your life, and she was there." Adesh looked over at Nick. "It's apparent she was delivering more than sandwiches all this time."

Nick's fist clenched, blood rushed through his body, his anger reaching a boiling point. But he saw the families and small children walking around them. He rationalized the ramifications of what he was about to do and how it would affect Shyla. Nick saw the look in the other man's eyes, the challenge of his statement, and the possibility he wanted a physical reaction. He unclenched his hand and straightened, drawing himself to his full height, and used his words instead of fists to drive home the message. "If you ever speak about her in that way again, I will not be responsible for my actions. She loves your family. She speaks very highly of you, and I would hate to put her through any distress by harming you, but I won't let you insult my girl. And make no mistake about it, she is *my* girl."

Nick smirked, bearing all his teeth, his stance one of power. Adesh's eyes widened as he shrank back. Mimicking Adesh's earlier gesture, Nick clapped him on the back, with much more force than necessary.

"Good talk," he said, before walking across the street to search for Shyla.

Chapter 25

Shyla sat on the counter as they both listened to the popping sounds of microwave popcorn.

"What are we watching? It's your turn to pick," she said, a visible pout on her sultry lips.

He smirked, tucking a strand of her hair behind her ear. "Why do you say it like that? I stuck it out through Chronicles of Boring for you."

"How could you not like Chronicles of Narnia? *The Lion, The Witch, and the Wardrobe* was my favorite book as a child."

"It's definitely a children's story," he muttered.

"And so is Indiana Jones, or as you like to call it, 'the greatest movie ever made.'"

He chuckled at her use of air quotes. "Shyla, don't misquote me. I said it's the greatest franchise ever made. Except for the fourth one." He lowered his voice just above a whisper. "We don't talk about the fourth one."

"Please, can we take a break from it? I need one after the second movie."

"What? You didn't like Temple of Doom? That's not even a sequel, baby, it's an equal."

"I suspended my disbelief so much, I believe it's orbiting Jupiter right now."

"Oh yeah, because Chronicles of Narnia was completely based in reality."

She swung her legs back and forth. Nick stilled them. He secured them around his waist. "What do you have against Indiana Jones? He wears a fedora and carries a whip. What's more badass than that?"

She wrapped her arms around him. "I have issues with how my culture was portrayed."

"Oh yeah? Like what?"

"Well, first of all, Kali is the Goddess of empowerment. She's a warrior, but she's not evil. And most Hindus are vegetarians. We don't believe in eating animals, let alone…human sacrifice."

The beep of the microwave interrupted them. Nick took out the popcorn and threw it in a bowl. "There was definitely artistic license used, but there are always traces of truth in all fiction. The movie is based on a real group."

"It is?"

"They were a group of bandits who traveled across India and claimed to be the children of Kali. They were called Thugees—the original thugs."

She titled her head, surprised once again about his knowledge. "How do you know that?"

Nick shrugged, throwing a piece of popcorn into her mouth. "I'm a writer. I know a little about a lot of things. Anyway, I think Kali is interesting without any fiction. A warrior goddess who becomes drunk on the blood of her victims. The only thing that calms her from destroying the whole universe is her husband. I kind of love the role reversal."

"You know the story?" Shyla said with surprise.

"I saw you roll your eyes during the movie. I did some research."

She nodded, both touched and impressed by Nick's desire to understand her culture. Somehow, she couldn't put that into words so she went on with her diatribe of criticisms. "That's not the only issue in the movie. We certainly do not eat monkey brains."

"Chilled monkey brains," Nick corrected.

"Chilled monkey brains which resembled Jell-O. Ridiculous," she said, crossing her arms.

"You just said you don't eat it so how would you know what they look like?" He threw a piece of popcorn in her open mouth. "More salt?"

She chewed slowly. "Just a pinch. I'm no reptile specialist, but I'm fairly certain when a snake is cut open, little snakes don't come out of it."

Nick snorted. "You're right."

She flushed, watching the muscles in his arms flex as he reached into a cabinet. He turned toward her, his lips curled in a smug smile. "It's apparent you're not an expert. I mean, it's common knowledge when a serpent is cut open, little serpents spill out." He placed his hands on his hips, shaking his head. "I know you're not a biology major, but I question if NYU is slipping on their high standards."

She laughed, a sound that came out frequently around him. "Be serious."

"I am. I got your game, sister. You're trying to get me to denounce Indy. Well it won't happen."

She sighed. "I'm just trying to convince you to pick something else for your movie choice."

"C'mon, tell the truth."

"What truth?"

"You were freaked out the whole time. You clutched my chest like the damn white Queen was offering you Turkish delight."

"So you *were* paying attention during my movie."

Nick opened the fridge, "Juice box or wine tonight?

"Wine, please."

"Yeah, you probably need it to calm your nerves for tonight's movie."

She pointed to her chest. "Are you implying I was frightened?" She straightened up, her stubborn personality refusing to yield admission to his claim.

"It was a statement, not an implication." Nick handed her a glass of white and uncapped a beer for himself.

"I was not. Also, by the way, I don't think a heart continues to beat when you rip it out of a man's chest."

She took a sip from the glass, relishing the sweet taste. He licked his own lips before leaning in to kiss her deeply, his tongue mingling with hers. "Have you ripped out many men's hearts, Goddess?"

"No," she murmured, wrapping her legs around him.

"Don't worry, I have the perfect movie for us," Nick whispered.

* * * *

Seventy minutes later, Nick glanced at Shyla on the couch. The girl bit her bottom lip while clutching the pillow as if it was a life raft. He actually felt guilty, even though he'd chosen the tamest slasher flick he could find.

"Are you scared, baby?"

She managed an offended expression, but it didn't fool him.

"No, this is a dumb movie," she said, waving her hand in dismissal.

He smirked, arching a brow. "C'mon, you can admit it. I won't judge."

She shouldn't have revealed she'd never seen a horror flick or try to pretend his previous selection hadn't frightened her, especially when it was his night to pick a movie. Of course, he'd had an ulterior motive, figuring she'd cling to him, but Shyla was as stubborn as they came, and instead, the damn pillow had seen more action than he did.

"I'm not scared, I'm bored."

"Oh, I see. That's your bored look? Because you look more frightened than the actors."

"It is." She feigned an exaggerated yawn.

"Okay, give me the pillow then."

"Why?" she asked, her voice suddenly anxious.

"I want to rest my head."

"Rest it on the arm of the couch."

"No, that's not comfortable. Give it," he said, grabbing it from her.

She gripped it tighter against her chest. "I'm using it."

"For what? It's not going to save you." He scooted closer to her. "Baby, we can turn it off if you want. I thought you wanted a break from the Indiana Jones trilogy."

"Trilogy? You said there were four movies."

Nick shook his head slowly. "I also said we don't talk about the fourth one."

"I just don't understand, Nick."

"Understand what?"

"If everyone who goes to this lake dies, then why do they keep going?"

Nick chuckled. "There would be no plot if they didn't."

"How does he keep surviving? He's been shot and stabbed a thousand times."

"You know, I was freaked out the first time I watched this, too."

"You were?" she asked with surprise.

"Sure. I think I was five or maybe six years old. I almost shit my pants."

She threw the pillow at him.

"Finally," he said, setting it on the far end of the couch and laying his head down. "Now, no more talking. You're distracting me from this fine cinematic experience. By the way, there are like fifty of these movies."

Once the credits rolled, Nick got up.

"Where are you going?"

"To take a shower."

"I'll go with you," she said, standing up and closing the gap between them.

"You know what, why don't you get started, and I'll clean this up."

"I'll help you," she said, grabbing a glass.

He took it from her. "I've got this. Go."

She stood her ground, looking unsure. He kissed her forehead. "Unless you don't want to be alone right now."

"Why wouldn't I?"

He quirked his eyebrows, a mischievous grin on his face. "Because you're afraid of a certain masked man?"

"As if I would ever give credence to something so unrealistic. Teenagers having sex while a lunatic is running around?"

"Actually, I think that's probably the most realistic part of the movie."

She crossed her arms, a defiant smirk on her lips. "Don't underestimate me. I know your game, Nick."

"What game?"

"You want me to play the panicky girl, rushing into your arms." She placed the back of her hand on her forehead. "Oh Nick, I'm so terrified, I don't know what I'll do. Please hold me tighter. Please keep me safe."

Yeah, she totally nailed it.

"All right, if you're not scared, then just get in the shower by yourself." She straightened her shoulders. "I will do just that."

* * * *

Twenty minutes later, she crept into the living room, dressed in her panties and a white tank top. Nick was nowhere in sight. Even though he'd left the lone lamp on like he always did, it seemed creepier now than ever before. The furniture made large shadows on the walls, and the wooden floor creaked with each step.

"Nick?" she called out.

No answer.

"Nick, where are you?" she asked with more urgency.

No answer.

She walked toward the kitchen to get a glass of water. The television turned on, white fuzz covering the screen.

"Very funny," she muttered, turning it off and searching for him. He had to be playing with the remote.

She swung her head when a dull thud sounded from the closet, followed by a knock. She tried to ignore it but the sound grew louder, echoing through the space.

She chided herself for falling victim to his obvious prank. She headed toward the bookcase to choose a book, but the sounds didn't yield. Each time, they grew more sinister, more commanding. Did he think he was the only one who could play this game? She took a deep breath and padded toward the large walk-in closet.

She pulled open the door. Clothes swung with their hangers, but only darkness lay beyond the dim glow of light from the living room. A frustrated gasp escaped her as she went to shut the door, embarrassed for being so silly, until…a hand reached out, clasping her wrist, pulling her back inside.

She shrieked and stumbled to the far side of the closet.

"It's okay, Shyla, it's just me. I'm sorry, baby."

"Why did you do that?" she cried.

"It was just a joke, sweetheart."

"Turn on the light."

"Shyla—"

"Turn on the light right now!" she screamed.

He turned on the light switch inside the closet. She crouched in the far corner, her back to him, pretending to shiver.

He placed his hand on her back. "Hey, you're okay, sweetheart. I didn't think you'd have this kind of reaction. Please, forgive me." The worry in his voice almost made her change her mind…almost.

She turned around, her arms raised in attack. Nick fell on his ass.

"Fuck," he shouted.

She'd put on his goalie mask.

"Shit, where the hell did you find that?" he asked, holding a hand over his chest.

"From the bookshelf." She held up her arms, trying to achieve a villain's laugh. "Come here, baby. Let me hold you."

"Funny. Take off the mask, smartass."

"Sure," she said. She lifted it off, and he gasped again as she bared her teeth…vampire teeth from a Halloween party. She clinked them together. "I want to suck your blood, Nick."

"That's a good look for you… sexy."

She took out the teeth, crawling over him. "You deserved it. Turning on the television and then hiding in here."

"I didn't turn on the television."

"Yes you did. I turned it off."

"With the remote?"

"Yes."

"If the remote was out there and I was in here, how could I turn it on?" He tried to hide his impish grin, but his mouth wouldn't cooperate.

She smacked his chest. "Just admit it. There's no shame in being afraid." She leaned her ear against his chest. "I can hear it beating."

"That has nothing to do with being scared and everything to do with the fact that I can see your tits though your shirt."

"Just confess. I got you. It won't make you any less manly in my eyes," she said.

"I will admit only one thing."

"What's that?"

He playfully slapped her ass. "You're gonna get it, naughty girl."

"You'll have to catch me first," she said, springing away from him before he could grab her. She bounded out of the closet.

He ran after her, through the loft, her laughter intermingling with his predatory roars. She ran around the couch. He jumped over it. She ran to the far side of the dining table. He held the opposite flank. She tried to slide past him, but he grasped her waist. He picked her up and flung her over his shoulder. Gasping, she wriggled in his arms, but his hold was too firm.

"You can't escape me. I'll always catch you." He threw her on the bed.

"Maybe I wanted you to."

"Time for your punishment."

"How will you punish me?"

"First, I will utilize the strongest truth technique known to man, one so devious that not even the CIA will use it, but I am a desperate man on a determined mission."

"What technique?"

He flexed his fingers above her. "Tickle torture."

His fingers wiggled against her sides until she laughed so hard she couldn't breathe. She tried to pry his wrists away. They didn't budge. "Stop!"

His touch transformed from tickle to caress. She tried to regain her breath, but his feral glance at her heaving breasts made it difficult. She ran her fingers down the chiseled lines of his face. He hadn't shaved today. The full beard made him mysterious, yet alluring. The clean-shaven face created a boyishly handsome façade that made her knees weaken. But this…this in-between stubble was something new, and her whole body quivered in response.

His expression turned sensual with her touch. His eyes grew dark with lust. He kissed her neck and jaw line, his fingers running through her damp hair. He took off his shirt. She ran her hands down his chest and over his washboard abs. She unfastened his jeans. He hooked a finger on each side of the waistband of her panties, rolled them down, and tossed them on the floor.

It didn't take long until there wasn't a stitch of clothing between them. He kissed her ankles and worked up to her thighs. When he reached her mound, he spread her legs. She propped herself on her elbows, watching as his head moved between her thighs, his tongue exploring her. He teased her at first, tracing the area and stopping just before she came undone. His stubble tickled her thighs as his tongue drove in again. His fingers gripped her hips, keeping her from squirming against his exquisite technique.

"I love the way you taste," he whispered.

"I love the way you lick," she murmured.

He laughed, his warm breath washing over her skin. She moaned intensely as he deepened the connection. The sounds emanating from her were foreign …unruly, sexually-charged noises driven by her arousal and instigated by his talented tongue.

She didn't climb to her climax as much as soared. Every inch of her body shook with such ecstasy she didn't even grasp when he moved inside of her, and then she couldn't notice much else.

She tried to vocalize what she needed. "Condom?"

"I have it on." He guided her hand toward his shaft so she could feel it.

She nodded, grateful that he always remembered these things, and at the same time, she wondered how he could make her forget…about everything that troubled her. His lips sought out hers. His thrusts were fluent and demanding. His harsh grunts intermingled with her softer moans until they sounded like one.

He paused, gazing at her before rolling them over.

She was on top of him and unsure of the angle.

He took her hands, placing them on his chest and nodded at her. "I want you to fuck me."

She moved self-consciously at first, but each time he groaned, she became braver. Shyla wasn't sure what was more stimulating… the fact she was in control or that he relinquished it to her so willingly. His hands grasped her hips. She moved faster when aided by him. He let out a new sound. One she'd never heard from him.

"You growled."

"Yes," he said, making the simple word sound like it was the longest word in the dictionary.

"Do it again."

He lifted himself up and wrapped his arms around her. "Make me," he said in partial plea and command.

Shyla pulsed faster, digging her fingers into his shoulders for leverage. She wanted to own this climax…to hold the power to her pleasure and direct his. Her breasts against his hard chest, she bit his neck.

"You trying to mark me?" he asked, his voice raspy. Her answer was to do it again, tasting the sweet salt of his skin. He groaned in response. Their bodies became slicker with each thrust. Her nails raked his back. His hands wrenched her hair, causing her to shudder. His mouth was demanding as it sought hers. She tasted her own name as he spoke it. It was delicious.

The tingles coursed through her as she clung to him. Wrapped up in each other, neither spoke for a while, the sound of their breaths and heartbeats creating a language of their own.

She eased off him, then kissed his shoulder where she'd bitten into his flesh before he headed to the bathroom.

When he came back a few minutes later, he slid next to her, pulled the covers around them, and then her body against his.

"I like being on top," she said, enjoying the relaxing way his fingers stroked through her hair.

"Apparently." He kissed the top of head. "I love fucking you. I know that's not romantic, but it's the damn truth."

The sentiment stirred a new passion in her, a sense of sexuality she'd never experienced before. "It's perfect. I feel the same."

Their breathing slowed. She closed her eyes, but sleep wouldn't come. Nick was awake, too. In the cloak of night, her thoughts became as loose and naked as her body.

"After my mother died, I used to hide in wardrobes, usually with a book and a flashlight. I secretly hoped the wardrobe would open into another world like Narnia. Do you think that's crazy?"

"No Goddess, I do not."

"I was fifteen."

"Okay, maybe it's a little strange."

She popped her head up, laughing at his dry sense of humor. He cupped her face, his thumb running across her cheek. "I'm just kidding. It's not weird, not to me."

"Really?"

"You're talking to a man who still has an imaginary friend."

"True. We're not so different…you and I."

"No, we aren't."

She laid her head back on his solid chest. She didn't expect the question he whispered. "Were you seeking adventure or escape?"

"Both," she answered, shutting her eyes.

"Because you lost your mother?"

"I was lonely. I missed her."

He moved down on the bed so they were face to face. "Are you still lonely?"

She shook her head.

"Me neither."

"This is going to be a strange request."

"What do you want, Goddess? Just ask for it."

She pressed her forehead against his. "I know we just had sex, and it was amazing but…"

He quirked an eyebrow. "Ready so soon?"

"Actually, I want you to kiss me for a while. Will you do that for me? Just kiss me?"

"You want to make out after we just had sex?"

She squeezed her eyes shut, embarrassed by the stupidity of her own idea until she felt his lips on her neck.

"I'll kiss you as long as you let me."

"Then it will be a very long time."

Chapter 26

Shyla glanced at the clock. She closed her eyes again, scooting closer to Nick. Even in his sleep, he tightened his hold on her, his lips brushing her shoulder. Chapped lips just like hers.

She'd always slept on her stomach, her head buried into the pillow, but not with Nick. He'd spooned her that first night, and ever since, she couldn't imagine sleeping any other way.

She popped open her eyes a few minutes later, finally registering the time. She shot upright, breaking their connection. "Shucks."

"What's wrong?" he asked, his voice thick and drowsy.

"I'm late," she said, flopping over him to get to her clothes.

He sat up, rubbing the sleep from his eyes. "We forgot to set the alarm."

"No kidding," she said, jumping into her jeans.

"Baby, you can be late once. Hell, I was late to class all the time."

"Not today. I have an exam."

When he stood, she almost forgot what she was doing at the sight of his naked body, the sunshine pouring over him like a spotlight. Her gaze lingered on his taut muscles, pausing at his fully erect appendage. She blinked, mentally slapping herself out of the trance.

"Really, Nick?"

He followed her gaze, looking down at himself, a smile laced with carnal pride playing on his chapped lips. "Hey, this is your fault. It's not like I can control what you do to me."

She threw his boxers at him. "Put those on," she said, rushing to find a clean shirt.

"Yes, ma'am. Wow, you're bossy today."

"You're indecent, Mr. Dorsey, and it's rather distracting."

"I am but a weak man, incapable of decency in the presence of such exquisite beauty…even when she is kind of being bitchy."

Shyla laughed while running into the bathroom. She splashed some cold water on her face. She scoured the marble vanity, searching for a hair clip, a rubber band, a scarf, anything to tie back her wild hair. He came up behind her and kissed her neck.

"Nick, stop it."

"I just came to bring you this," he said, holding out the silver clip she'd worn yesterday. "You left it on the nightstand."

She sighed with relief, reaching a hand back to smooth his disheveled hair. "Thank you." The consummate gentleman, he squeezed the toothpaste on her toothbrush first. They brushed their teeth together, the act so simple, yet it felt exceptionally special.

"Do you have any lip balm?" he asked.

"No, I was hoping you had some."

"I'm a guy. I don't have those things. Aren't girls suppose to carry that stuff around with them?"

"Not me. But we can use the coconut oil you got for the rice recipe."

"I'm not going to put coconut oil on my lips."

She shrugged. "Suit yourself, but it works."

She rushed through her preparations, but lingered on their kiss. "So you won't put it on your own lips but kiss it off mine?"

"Yeah, it's much better this way. By the way, I made you coffee," he said, tucking a stray strand behind her ear.

"I don't have time."

"It's to go, sweetheart," he said, handing her a stainless steel tumbler.

"Thank you."

"And a granola bar. You can eat it in the cab. Good luck on your test. I'm sure you'll do well."

She glanced at the clock again. "I can spare a few minutes."

He lifted her onto the countertop. She pushed him back. "We don't have enough time for that, though."

"You're right. What I have in mind will take much longer than a few minutes."

She glanced at the opposite counter with all the ingredients she'd set up the night before. "I was going to get up early and make you pancakes."

"Damn, why didn't I set the alarm?"

She snapped her fingers. "How about pancakes for dinner? I don't work tonight, so I can come early. My last class ends at three."

"Shit, what's today?" he asked with a frown.

"The seventeenth."

"I can't. I have a charity dinner tonight."

She tried to school her face so her disappointment wouldn't show. Had she really become so attached to him a simple night apart had such a profound effect?

He titled her chin, carefully kissing the corners of her mouth. "Come with me."

"What?"

"I hate these things. Their black-tie, pretentious people faking their intellect, fancy food, and fine wine."

"Why do you want me to go if it's so awful?"

"Didn't I mention the wine?"

She pursed her lips. "I don't know."

"Come on, Shyla. I promise we can leave early. Besides, you'll be saving me from a boring evening, and it is for charity. That's the only reason I go."

"Which charity?"

"They provide after-school programs for disadvantaged youths. Now, as a future teacher, how can you not support such a worthy cause?" He gave her the boyish grin, which always weakened her resolve. "Will you do me the honor of accompanying me, Miss Metha?"

"Okay," she said, kissing him again.

* * * *

Shyla spent the whole day cursing the word "okay." Why had she agreed to this? She wanted to go with him, but he had said words that frightened her—black tie. Shyla suffered from the damning statement women had uttered since the first cavewoman fashioned a dress from animal skin and bones. *I have nothing to wear.*

Even worse, she had no time to go shopping. Not that she even knew what to purchase for such an occasion. She had some money saved, but how much would such an outfit cost? She had no idea.

She walked home from class. The day was warm and breezy, but fear gripped her. She didn't want to embarrass Nick by wearing the wrong thing or doing the wrong thing. She wanted him to be proud of her.

Shyla had no formal dresses. Elaine would lend her something, but Elaine was much taller and built differently than her. Shyla sat on her bed in the dorms and looked at her phone, contemplating cancelling on him. A kicking knock sounded at the door. "Are you there Shyla? Open up."

"Did you forget your key again?" Shyla asked, opening the door.

"My hands are full." Elaine walked in with several boxes in her arms with flourishing script on them. "I'm carrying my net worth in garments over here."

Shyla took a few of the boxes from her and set them on Elaine's bed. "You did a lot of shopping today."

Elaine giggled, shaking her head. "I wish. These were at the front desk addressed to you."

"For me?"

"Judging from the names, whoever bought these has very good taste. There's a card." Shyla took the envelope from Elaine and opened it. Nick's slanted handwriting greeted her.

"You better read it out loud," Elaine said.

She cleared her throat.

"Shyla, I would never be so pretentious as to tell a woman what to wear, but I wasn't sure if you owned an evening dress. If you like this then the credit is all mine, but if you don't, please feel free to blame the saleslady at Sax since she chose it. Actually, she based the decision on two things—my wild hand gestures trying to reconstruct your hourglass figure and some very simple instructions.

"I told her not to find a dress that would look good on the girl—a paper sack could do that. I asked her to find a dress that was in desperate need of a beautiful girl to fill it. I hope this fits the bill. Pick you up at seven. Yours, Nick"

"Wow! So flipping romantic," Elaine said.

Shyla nodded, her emotions unable to decide if she wanted to squeal with joy or cry with gratitude. "He is wonderful."

"Well, what are you waiting for, girl? Try it on."

The saleslady at Saks had clearly thought of everything. The pretty boxes contained all the items she needed —stockings and garter belt, a bra that would provide support and be discreet beneath the low cut dress, matching panties, and a pair of high heels, which caused Elaine to salivate.

The dress commanded all of Shyla's attention, though. Its simple lines and complicated design were breathtaking. The ankle-length gown had a deep slit up the side and a low back. The front sloped into a plunging V-neck that revealed her cleavage. The black chiffon material shimmered under the light as Shyla twirled.

"It's perfect," Elaine said, bouncing around Shyla.

"Almost. It's loose in the bust," Shyla said, pointing to where the material drooped.

"Yeah, a bit. Guess the salesgirl got that part wrong."

"Nope, this is definitely Nick. He thinks my breasts are much bigger than they really are. Maybe he has depth-perception problems and needs glasses."

Elaine burst out laughing as if Shyla had made joke. Shyla realized she had. It felt good to laugh with her. They were roommates and fit somewhere on the friend scale, but their conversations were usually stiff.

Elaine assessed the gown, tapping a finger against her lip. "I can fix this."

"How?"

"Good ol' needle and thread."

Fifteen minutes later, the gown looked as if it was tailored just for her.

"How did you learn how to do this?"

"My mother taught me."

"Thank you." She embraced the other girl.

"Hey, you're going to crush the gown. Now, anything else you need help with?"

Shyla stared at the shoes Elaine had so carefully rested on her desk. "I'm afraid of the shoes. I've never worn high heels, and those are like the Himalayas of high heels."

"Let's practice."

Shyla felt silly as she walked the stretch of their small room in high heels, a pair of linen shorts, and NYU T-shirt, but Elaine said she might rip the dress if she wore it. The third time she fell on her knees, Elaine stood up, her purple ponytail bouncing as she shook her head.

"It's no use, Elaine, I'm going to break the shoes."

"Oh sweetie, these are Jimmy Choos. They're built to last." She held her hand out to help Shyla up. "It's your knees and ankles I'm more worried about." She gasped suddenly. "I have an idea."

If Shyla felt silly before, she was now entering ridiculous mode. Elaine had added what she referred to as a necessary safety accessory to Shyla's ensemble—knee pads. Elaine turned on her iPod and attached it to the speakers.

"You're kidding," Shyla said when Justin Timberlake's "SexyBack" came on.

"This is inspirational. This song exudes sexiness. I mean, Justin brought it back just for us."

"Where did it go?"

"Don't know, but the way he moves, I'm sure it's here to stay. Now, c'mon girl, work it."

Shyla walked again, and Elaine joined her.

"What are you doing?"

"I can't let you have all the fun. Not when Justin's singing."

The girls met in the middle of the room, their hands clasping as they danced with provocative bravado.

"You should hop in the shower now."

Shyla nodded, carefully taking off each shoe.

When she came out, Elaine had an assortment of makeup on the desk and held up her hair straightener. "I borrowed some of this from Marni. She's similar in skin tone to you. Dry your hair quick so I can straighten it."

Shyla looked at the device, a bit hesitant.

Elaine sighed. "Relax, this is the second most important electronic device a woman can own. Trust me."

"What's the first?"

Surprisingly, Elaine blushed. "One I will never let you borrow."

Shyla blinked in confusion until clarity came, and then she burst into laughter.

Elaine worked on her hair until each strand glistened with shine and felt like silk. Elaine applied the foundation and blush like a professional, instructing Shyla how to play up her features. When it came to the eyes though, Shyla shook her head, taking the pencil from Elaine. "I can do this on my own."

"Are you sure?"

"I know how to use kohl."

"I would go darker on them."

"Elaine, Indian women invented the smoky eye. I've got this."

A few minutes later, Elaine let out a low whistle, obviously impressed by Shyla's handiwork. "Yeah, you definitely know what you're doing when it comes to eyes. Maybe you can help me when I need to get dolled up."

"I'd love to." Shyla studied herself in the mirror, shocked at the reflection peering back. "Thanks, Elaine. This was really nice of you." She was almost sad their afternoon of bonding was at an end.

"No problem, just call me your personal fairy god-sister."

"You mean fairy godmother."

"Shyla, we're the same age. I ain't no one's mama."

Shyla laughed at the joke, which kick-started a flurry of butterflies in her belly. The nerves mingled and flirted with her excitement at the thought of being on Nick's arm. Elaine frowned as she peered down at her phone. "I would stay and wait with you, but Greg and I are going to the movies."

"It's okay. Nick will be here any minute." She embraced Elaine.

"He sounds like a great guy."

"He is. I'm very lucky."

"So is he." She held Shyla back and smiled in approval. "You look hot."

"It's because of you. You didn't bring sexy back. You made it happen."

"I had a great canvas to work with."

Chapter 27

Nick watched as she walked down the steps of her building, mentally making a note to send the salesgirl at Saks a thank-you card. Shyla always looked beautiful, but tonight she glowed.

"Good evening, Goddess," he said, bowing slightly.

"I take it you like it?"

"Very much," he responded, a man lost in the trance of a beautiful woman.

"Thank—" Before she could finish the sentence, her footing faltered, and she tumbled.

He moved swiftly, catching her in his arms. "Are you okay?"

"That has to be the most ungraceful entrance ever."

He chuckled, helping her up. "It was perfect. C'mon my lady, our chariot waits."

She gasped. "You got a limo?"

"I wanted to make this as special as possible."

The driver held open the door for her. As soon as they were seated, Nick pulled her onto his lap. "You know the best part of having a limo?"

"What?"

"This," he said, pushing a button. A screen moved up between them and the driver. "Sweet privacy."

She frowned, taking in his tuxedo.

"What's wrong?"

"I got make-up on you," she said, pointing to a spot where the crisp white shirt gave way to a crimson matching her lipstick.

"I'm sure a little club soda will take care of it."

"I'm sorry."

"No need to be coy with me. I'm on to your little game."

"What game?"

"You wanted to mark me, didn't you?"

"Very funny. Although, you do look ravishing in this tux."

"Ravishing?"

"Yes, too bad we can't have sex just yet."

"Why?" He almost laughed at his own disappointment.

She adjusted his tie. "Because I've already ruined your shirt. If I fully unleash my desires, you'll be showing up in rags."

He chuckled. "I love it when you're naughty."

* * * *

Shyla sucked in a deep breath, wondering if she had stepped into a fairy tale. The ballroom at the hotel was breathtaking. The black and white marble floors gleamed against the pale blue walls with their intricate moldings. White, twinkling lights roped around tables decorated with tulle, each with a centerpiece of pink roses. A ten-piece band played a modern rock song. Waiters with white-gloved hands carried trays full of bubbling champagne and intricate hors d'oeuvre.

Nick led Shyla toward two beautiful women, one taller with red hair in an elegant up-do, and the other shorter with dark hair and tan skin in a glittering purple dress. "Shyla, this is my agent and friend, Carrie. And this is her wife, Tara. Ladies, this is my girlfriend, Shyla."

Shyla bit back her nerves, unprepared to meet them. Her handshake was weak and shaken, but neither woman seemed to notice. Nick kissed each of them on the cheek.

"What? I'm not your friend, Nick?" Tara joked, punching Nick's arm.

"I heard you were still mad at me, so I wasn't sure what the appropriate description might be in this case."

Tara smacked him on the chest playfully. "As it turns out, I don't mind dogs as much as I thought."

"Thank God. How's Maya?"

Tara frowned. "She seems to be enjoying the flute. Thank you for that, by the way."

"Sorry," Nick said, a boyish smile on his face.

"At least he didn't get her the drums," Carrie offered.

Nick rubbed his chin thoughtfully. "The drums... Now there's an idea."

"Nick!" they both said in unison.

Shyla laughed along, trying to swallow back her nerves.

"I have to go use the restroom," Nick said, pointing to his shirt.

"Probably a good idea," Tara said. She plucked Nick's shirt, staring at the stain there. "I would say you fell into some Estee Lauder Mocha Rose Pink. A very nice shade, although I don't think it's your color, babe." She turned to Shyla. "Am I right?"

"I think so. How did you know?"

"Tara's a makeup artist. She does Broadway shows and movies," Carrie explained, looking at the other woman with pride.

"Can you keep Shyla company?" Nick asked them.

"Actually, after you get cleaned up, I think we should talk to a few people about the return of Max Montero," Carrie said.

"Seriously?"

"Just a few minutes. It's a good networking opportunity. Do you mind if I borrow him?" Carrie asked apologetically.

"Not at all," Shyla replied.

"I'll keep Shyla company," Tara offered. "After all, us Indian girls have to stick together. Love your dress by the way," she said, taking Shyla's arm and leading her farther into the ballroom.

"I think I need a touch up, too," Shyla said.

Tara showed her to the washroom. Amazingly, the woman had every kind of vial and tube in her purse to put Shyla back together again.

"I swear you're a doppelganger for Katrina Kaif," Tara said while powdering her face.

Shyla struggled not to snort at the comparison to the beautiful Bollywood actress. "Thank you."

Tara brushed a little blush on Shyla's cheeks. "With these high cheekbones and pretty lips, I bet you could get work in Bollywood."

"It's never been a goal of mine. I've always wanted to be a teacher."

Tara smiled, nodding her head in encouragement. "Wonderful. The world needs teachers. We all have so much to learn."

Shyla, glad to have an opportunity to bond with the woman who seemed so cosmopolitan yet down to earth, returned the smile.

Tara grabbed two flutes of champagne as they made their way to their table. "Nick gives very generously to this charity so there's usually a ton of people who want his time."

Taking the seat next to Tara, she sipped the champagne, hoping the liquid courage would work quickly.

"I didn't know that," Shyla said, watching as Nick shook hands and traded smiles with other guests. He looked so handsome in his black, fitted tux with his mane of sandy brown hair neatly brushed back. Shyla couldn't wait until she could mess it all up again.

Nick was extremely charming, and tonight he looked truly happy. Shyla was proud of him, although she felt a twinge of jealousy when woman approached him and had no shame in pressing their bodies against his. Although, to Nick's credit, he did back away, maintaining a polite distance each time. Most people were still standing, conversing with each other. Tara had explained it was the cocktail hour, a time for people to meet and greet.

"I didn't think to ask him, but should I call him Keegan while we're here?" Shyla asked.

Tara laughed. "No, everyone here knows who he is. I suppose if a reader really wanted the information, they could find out Keegan Moon is Nick Dorsey, too."

"Oh, good. I don't think I would remember."

Tara laughed. "Yeah, he looks like a Nick."

Shyla wasn't sure he resembled any other man she'd met, but she nodded along. "Were you born here?" she asked Tara.

"Yes, in Long Island actually."

"First generation?"

"No, my grandparents came here in the late sixties. We're originally from Mumbai."

"I've been there. It's huge," Shyla said.

"My extended family lives there. I've visited a few times. Carrie and I plan to take our daughter, Maya, when she's older."

"Is it difficult being in a mixed relationship for you?"

Tara shrugged. "We've had so many difficulties it's hard to narrow down. I kind of went for the trifecta of a hard life." She winked at Shyla. "After all, I'm a woman, a lesbian, and a cultural anomaly."

"But those things weren't your choice."

Tara nodded. "I like you. You're refreshing in a caffeine-free kind of way."

"Is that a compliment?"

"Definitely. You're right. It wasn't my choice, but I do choose to live freely now, and not to sound cliché, but truth has consequences."

"Did your parents accept you?" Shyla immediately regretted the question. "I'm sorry. It's inappropriate of me to ask you something so private."

"It's okay, sister, you can ask whatever you want. After all, aren't all Indians family?" Tara's words instantly put Shyla at ease. "I realized I was a lesbian at a young age. My mother tried convincing me I wasn't. She said lesbians don't like lipstick and dressing up. My mother's great debate worked for a while. Believe it or not, I even did the whole arranged marriage thing."

"Really?"

"Yes, but I was just living a lie. I divorced him a few years into our marriage."

"Does he see Maya?"

"He died when she was one."

"I'm sorry."

"Actually, he didn't die. He's just dead to me. He revoked his parental rights when I told him I was gay. He actually believed I'd pass the trait onto our daughter, like an airborne illness."

"That's awful."

"I still think it had more to do with not wanting to pay child support than anything else, but I'm glad he's not in her life. Maya doesn't need poisonous thoughts around her. I met Carrie in college, and we loved each other then, but neither of us could admit it. We rekindled our relationship a year after my divorce. She adopted Maya legally, and I sort of adopted Nick figuratively. I'm still arguing I got shorted in the deal."

Tara's forthrightness was unexpected, but Shyla found herself hanging onto every word. "Do you have pictures of your daughter?"

Tara immediately pulled out her phone. Tara, in fact, had entire albums dedicated to Maya. Shyla listened intently while she narrated the settings of the photos and told her funny stories about the gorgeous little girl.

"Have your parents accepted your marriage?" Shyla asked.

"It's taken a long time, but they recognize who I am now. They love Carrie, too. They see how happy we are and how strong our family is. They even had a wedding reception for us. It's interesting how my strict Indian parents have accepted us, whereas her parents have not. I think it goes to show you can never really judge how a family will react."

"Why do Carrie's parents have a hard time with it?"

"Most likely because she didn't come out for a long time. You see, my parents always knew. They wanted me to hide it, disguise who I was. But when it came down to it, they realized we were all in hiding and no one was happy. Carrie denied her feelings for a long time so her parents didn't know. And then to come out, tell them she was in love with a Hindu woman who had a child…well, it was just too over the top for them."

"What happened for her to admit she was gay?"

Tara fanned herself. "It was me, darling. I told her as much as I love closets, I won't live in one."

Both women laughed.

Shyla took another sip of the champagne. "A few months ago, I wouldn't have understood such a concept."

"What's that, babe?"

"Falling for someone when you didn't want to."

Tara placed her arm around Shyla's shoulders, turning her head in Nick's direction. "But now you do because of the handsome guy right there?"

Shucks.

Had she really just revealed her emotions to a stranger? Shyla struggled to avoid the feelings, but the obvious was unavoidable. It seeped through, growing stronger with each moment they spent together. She'd completely fallen for him on every level. Her heart sunk as she crammed the thoughts down. She couldn't deal with them now.

"Yes."

"He's been through a lot. When Carrie first introduced us, I immediately decided I didn't like him. You see, I knew they'd had a rendezvous, and my jealous nature believed he might be after my woman. I realized their relationship is more sibling rivalry than anything else. He's been a very good friend to us. Maya calls him Uncle Nick."

"He says the same about you." She turned to Tara. "I know about his past."

"Oh good, no need to skirt around the past. You know, when I found out, I swear I was so shocked my make-up cracked...and that never happens."

"It is hard to believe."

"Yes, I'm surprised he told you. At his core, Nick is a very private person. It really says something that he's been so honest with you."

Shyla shifted, feeling the ironic weight of the heavy statement. After all, she hadn't been as forthcoming. She shifted those thoughts to the recesses of her mind as she focused on Tara. "Is it difficult raising a child here?"

"Sure, but the good news is things are changing faster than you can bat an eyelash...even a fake one with too much glue. Plus, we live in a very metropolitan, modern environment. We're raising our daughter to appreciate both our cultures. Sometimes kids at school make fun of her because of us, but she's a smart girl, and she has a good heart. She knows her moms love each other and, more importantly, they love her. When you raise a child in truth and love, it becomes easier to ignore the hate."

"That's beautiful."

"I can't believe how much I've just spewed. You're dangerously easy to talk to. Probably a great trait for a teacher."

"Or maybe I'm just nosy. Thank you for sharing so much with me."

"Of course, but enough about me. Tell me your story."

"What story?" Shyla asked, suddenly nervous.

"How did you and Nick meet? In all the years I've known him, would you believe I've never seen him with a girlfriend? I'm curious."

"I was his sandwich delivery girl."

"Oh sweetheart, I'm sure you're much more than that."

"We started dating about a year after I began delivering to his house. We're working on a book together. Just an idea I had. He's been very generous in helping me."

"Sounds interesting. Does Carrie know?"

"No, but I hope you'll both read it when it's finished. Nick says it's a bit unrealistic, but I think if you give it a chance, it'll make sense. I would really love for you to read it."

"I look forward to it. What's it about?"

"Just a girl growing up in rural India and her life."

Tara's eyes widened. "Sounds like the kind of book I'd like to read, but definitely not one I'd expect Nick to write."

"He's doing it as a favor to me."

"Well, hurry up and finish it so we can read it."

A high-pitched laugh interrupted them, piercing through their conversation. "Hello, Tara," a tall redhead in a sparkly silver dress said, taking the seat next to them. A shorter dark-haired man sat with her. "We're at the same table."

"Wonderful," Tara muttered. "Karma, this is Shyla."

"Nice to meet you," Karma said, extending her hand in such a way that Shyla wasn't sure if she wanted a kiss on the back or a handshake. She shook it awkwardly.

"This is my date, Steven," Karma said, gesturing to the man.

"It's nice to meet you," Shyla greeted, shaking his hand.

She turned to the woman. "Your name is Karma?"

"Her real name is Carla, but she didn't get callbacks as often," Tara said.

"You're an actress?" Shyla asked.

Her smile appeared more sinister than friendly. "You don't recognize me? I'm on a fairly popular television show. Tara used to be our makeup artist until we decided to go in a different direction."

"You mean when the show got cancelled, right?" Tara asked.

Karma narrowed her eyes, obviously unhappy Tara provided that tidbit of information. "So are you both dateless tonight?" Karma asked.

Tara sighed. "Sweetheart, we are about as dateless as you are tactful."

Karma raised her eyebrows as if she was contemplating whether the remark was meant as an insult. Shyla muffled her laugh.

"You know Carrie is my wife," Tara said.

Karma snapped her fingers. "Right, I always seem to forget you prefer carpet over wood."

Tara's smile didn't falter. "Shyla is Nick's date."

Karma choked on her champagne. Luckily, Steven clapped her on the back. "Nick Dorsey?" she asked.

"The very one," Tara replied.

"I don't think I've ever seen him bring a date to this thing. Now, he does usually leave with a girl, but that's a different thing entirely."

Shyla shifted, uncomfortable she was being discussed so openly as if she wasn't there. Not to mention, the girl's snide remarks about Nick's sexual habits were disconcerting. It was a fact Shyla had come to grips with, except now coming face to face with it, her grip didn't seem so sure.

"Looks like he was just waiting for the right girl, Karma," Tara said, narrowing her eyes at the other woman. "Chin up, darling, everyone is capable of change. For instance, I've never seen you without glossy lipstick, but I'm still hoping the day will come."

Karma rolled her eyes at Tara before shifting her gaze toward Shyla. "So, I hear an accent. What do you do, Sheila, something in IT?"

"It's Shyla, and I'm studying to be a teacher."

"You're pulling my leg, right?"

"No."

"Are you planning to teach in New York?" Steven asked. Shyla smiled, grateful for the sincere question.

"I'm going back to India after I graduate. I'll be teaching there."

Tara looked surprised and a bit sad about Shyla's statement. Karma giggled a high-pitch laugh, but Steven seemed curious. "Why would you go back?"

"She wants to teach the next generation of software gurus, Steven," Karma said.

"No, I won't be teaching students who have a future. I'll be teaching the ones without hope. Probably in a rural area."

"Wow, you're like a modern day Sister Teresa," Karma said. "She was Hindu too, right?"

"And that's why our schools are failing," Tara interjected. "It's *Mother* Teresa, and by her name, you should be able to decipher that she was a Catholic."

Shyla found herself getting more nervous. She knew cattiness was a quality in women, but she'd never experienced it like this. Tara must have sensed her unease because she asked Shyla if she wanted to walk around. "Oh don't go, we're having fun," Karma said. "You're so quiet. I'm surprised because Nick doesn't usually like the silent type."

She had no doubt the insinuations Karma was making. The band started up a new tune, one Shyla loved and, if for no other reason than to shift the conversation, she commented on it. "I love this song."

"Me, too," Steven said.

"I have an idea. Why don't the two of you dance together?" Karma suggested.

"Thank you, but I'm fine," Shyla answered quickly.

"Why not? I have an open mind. I don't mind lending you my date. After all, you both love this song so much. What's it called again?"

"Bittersweet Symphony" by The Verve," Steven said. He took the champagne glass from Karma. "I think you should take it easy on these. You're making her uncomfortable."

"You're making everyone uncomfortable," Tara groaned.

Shyla felt Nick's presence before his hand clasped her shoulder. "Hi Karma, Steven," Nick said. "I see you've met Shyla."

"Yeah, she was just telling me how much she loved this song, and I think she should dance with Steven. So, are you guys going or what?"

"Karma, are you actually suggesting my date dance with yours?" Nick asked, his annoyance evident.

"What's the problem?" The redhead peered at her watch. "Are we in a time machine? Is it a quarter past the millennium or the bicentennial? FYI, women's suffrage ended a long time ago."

Shyla craned her neck toward Nick, wanting for a brief moment for him to rescue her. He opened his mouth, but Karma's shrill voice cut right through whatever he was going to say.

"Oh my God, are you seriously asking him for permission? I had no idea Nick demanded such obedience. No wonder it didn't work out between us."

Shyla didn't acknowledge the other girl. Nick's face transformed under the light of a glittering chandelier. A vein on the side of his neck pulsed, and his jaw clenched in a way that hurt her teeth in sympathy for his. Shyla snapped her attention back to Karma. In that instant, she saw her, really saw her. A girl, who despite her beauty and accomplishments, lacked self-confidence. Sometimes the sphere of the tongue is sharper than the blade of the knife. Luckily, Shyla was practiced in that weapon.

"I wasn't asking him for permission," Shyla said.

Karma tilted her head, a smug smile on her unnaturally generous lips. "Then what's up with the whole submissive stare you just gave him?"

"I was giving him first right of refusal."

Everyone was quiet for a moment, the tension at the table flickering like the candle in the centerpiece. Tara laughed first, and Nick followed, putting out any potential flames.

"That's one option I plan to aggressively exercise," he said.

Shyla offered the redhead a generous smile. "FYI Karma, women's suffrage refers to the right to vote. By stating you thought it ended, you, in turn, incorrectly conveyed a woman's right to vote ended. I don't think that's what you meant. Also, the bicentennial in this country happened in 1976, a time when Margaret Thatcher was the prime minister of the UK, Golda Meir ruled Israel, Shirley Chisholm was the first African American woman elected into the house of representative in the US, and only two short years later, Sally Ride was accepted into NASA. There was a woman ruling a country on every continent and one in space. Although, there are still struggles for women, I think we've come a long way, but it's important for a woman to be ladylike as well as independent. I prefer to think of myself as both."

Karma's lips curled into a sneer. Tara applauded. Steven bowed his head, hiding a grin. Nick pulled out her chair and led her toward the dance area.

"Have fun, you two," Tara said.

"Well, if the teacher thing doesn't work out, you should plan a career in political activism," Nick said.

"Sometimes I get carried away."

"I loved it. If you ever need a soapbox, I'll be happy to carry it for you."

"She was very mean spirited."

"You know what they say about Karma, don't you?" Nick asked, taking her into his arms.

"What?"

"She's a bitch."

Shyla laughed, feeling more relaxed again. "What kind of history do you have with her?"

"A very short one. And definitely a lesson I never want to repeat." He rested his hand on the small of her back and pulled her closer. "I have too many mistakes in my past to count. Sometimes they come back to haunt me. I really wanted you to enjoy tonight. I'm sorry."

"I am having a good time. Although, I have to admit I have no idea what I'm doing."

"I don't know. You held your own with her. And you saved me from being a total asshole, which she deserved. Although my ego is a bit bruised, my reputation thanks you."

"It was my pleasure, but I meant I don't know what I'm doing with the dancing."

Her heel scraped against Nick's shin as if to bludgeon the point.

"Ouch."

"Sorry, did I hurt you?"

"No," he said taking a deep breath. "I don't understand. You had some crazy sexy moves when you danced for me the other night."

Shyla shrugged, watching her feet. "It's in my blood to dance Bollywood, but I've never slow danced."

"I'm honored to be your first."

She tried to follow his steps, moving in sync, but her heel still managed to hit his shin.

"The salesgirl at Saks must hate me because I swear your heels are made of switchblades," he muttered.

She backed up, cupping her hand to her mouth. "It's not the shoe. It's user error. We should stop before you need stitches."

"We're going to dance even if it kills me, and it may do just that. Take off your shoes."

She blinked, replaying his request in her head.

"Trust me."

She took off her heels and held them by the straps. He placed his hands on her waist. "Put your arms around me and your feet on mine."

She slid her feet on top of his. "You can't be serious."

"Why not?"

"There's no way you can dance with me clinging to you like this."

He kissed her cheek. "Watch me."

"I feel like a hypocrite."

"Why?"

"I just gave a speech about women's independence, and here I am not even standing on my own two feet."

She expected Nick to laugh, but his expression was serious. "We all need someone to lean on from time to time. It's my honor to be that person for you…anytime you need it."

He spun her around effortlessly to that song and the next two. She finally felt comfortable with the movements and the rhythm they created together. In his arms, all of her fears, big and small, diminished.

Things became much easier afterward. The dinner was extravagant. Nick had even taken the courtesy of requesting a vegetarian meal for her. He whispered in her ear about all the delicious things he wanted to do to her. She found herself either blushing with his flirtations or laughing at

Tara's jokes. Shyla decided she really enjoyed Carrie and Tara's company. The two women balanced each other. Even Karma settled down, although she alternated between sulking or glaring. The glare became heavier with Nick's gestures toward Shyla, no matter how small.

"I can't believe they put us at the same table. Someone here really wanted high drama to put Nick and me in the same place as Karma. Sorry you got caught in the crosshairs, but I can't believe how well you held your own with her," Tara said.

"No bother. I'm no stranger to bullies. I'm really happy we had a chance to meet, Tara."

"Me too, sweetie. Don't be a stranger. Carrie and I would love to have you and Nick over for dinner one night."

"I have exams coming up so it might be difficult as far as timing. I'm going back soon, but thank you for the offer."

Carrie and Tara left after dinner, stating they had to relieve the babysitter. Each woman embraced Shyla.

"There's someone I have to talk to. Will you excuse me for a second?" Nick asked Shyla.

Shyla nodded. "Of course." When he shifted his gaze to Karma who was now on the dance floor with Steven, she reassured him. "Nick, mean girls are not exclusive to this country. I'll be fine."

"I don't mind being your bodyguard."

"Funny, I thought I was the one protecting you."

He took the underside of her wrist and kissed it. "Okay, simmer down, Jason Voorhees. I'll be back."

* * * *

Nick made his way to the other end of the room, but Carrie cornered him.

"Hey, you didn't think I could leave without getting you to spill."

"Spill what?"

"What's going on? I thought maybe she was just a date, but after observing you all night, I can see it is much more. She's lovely, Nick."

He nodded, looking past Carrie at the girl who owned his heart. "Shyla means a great deal to me."

"How long has it been going on?"

"Only a few months, but she's special, Carrie."

Carrie asked a question Nick wasn't expecting. "Why is she special to you?"

The answer came easily to him. It rolled off his tongue like a sentimental soliloquy in the rampant pace of runoff sentences, his smile growing bolder with each sentiment. "She's crazy smart, she makes me laugh, she gets my jokes, and she's got this uncanny ability to call my bullshit and not care how I'll react to it. I never realized what a turn-on that is. She doesn't swear, which I know is a weird thing for me to mention, but it speaks about who she is. It's an innocence she carries in everything she does. She cares about people. Although, I sometimes think her judgment naturally slopes toward finding the good in others. To be honest, it scares the hell out of me because I just want to protect her. At the same time, she also has an ability to read people, especially me. And there are many more things I could mention, but then you'd have to pay your babysitter overtime. It's easy for me to see all her wonderful. But what I never expected or accounted for was to see a better me through her."

Carrie's mouth gaped. "Wow."

"Well, you asked. That's just my random spontaneous thoughts off the cuff."

Carrie sighed in that way women did when they were happy, but she knew him well. Her curiosity wasn't easily satisfied. "You didn't mention how beautiful she is."

Nick arched his brow. "Isn't it obvious?"

"Of course it is. I only bring it up because I find the fact you omitted any physical characteristics very interesting. It's unlike you." She did her impression of Dr. Ruth, which Nick always joked sounded more like Sigmund Freud. "What can one decipher from that?"

"Watch it, Carrie. You decided not to pursue psychology remember?"

"Oh, I still read a great many texts on the subject, and by text, I do mean books not messages."

"You make me sound very shallow."

"You are very shallow, Nick." She smiled, patting his chest. "Or maybe I should say you were. Does she know?"

"Know what, Carrie?"

"Holy shit, Dorsey, do you know?"

Nick was quiet a moment, waiting for her to continue, but she didn't say a damn word. "Are we playing charades? What are you saying?"

"You love her."

Nick shoved his hands in his pocket, not because he was nervous, but he could have kissed Carrie for putting in such succinct language what he had struggled with for weeks. Leave it to a writer to use far too many adjectives when only a verb was required.

"I love her very much."

"Tara told me she's leaving after she graduates."

"Before you intercepted me, I was going to catch Grace Madsen to get some advice."

"Ah, I gotcha. I hope it works out, Nick. You deserve it."

"Thank you. Give Maya a kiss for me."

"Will do," she said, embracing him.

Nick didn't know Grace Madsen very well, but the few times they'd met, she'd left an impression on him. The woman secreted personality like sweat. He approached the tall, almost willowy woman dressed in a gown adorned with peacock feathers. Grace, an eccentric intellectual with a charitable pocketbook and a vulgar, unapologetic mouth, waved him over.

"Joseph, would you mind if I had a word with your wife?" Nick asked the distinguished silver-haired man who held her hand.

It was Grace who replied. "My dear Mr. Dorsey, is it chivalry to ask a man for permission to speak to his wife in private, or is it antifeminist?"

He kissed her hand, bowing slightly. "I'm sorry, Mrs. Madsen, the answer to your question is far above my pay grade. I promise my intentions are humble and my query is sincere."

Before William Madsen, Wall Street entrepreneur and financial capitalist, could respond, his wife took the liberty, "Excuse me, darling."

She offered her arm to Nick.

"Where should we go?"

"Outside, dear boy. I'm dying for a smoke. And I'm a real bitch when I'm nicotine free for more than an hour."

As they approached the large glass doors, a waiter said, "I'm sorry, ma'am, you can't take the drink with you if you're going to the patio."

"Damn, I almost made an escape," she said, handing her drink to the server. She tsked at him. "I don't know what's worst, the fact you deliberately take my libation or that you referred to me as ma'am."

They stepped out into the crisp but comfortable air.

"You know the best thing about marrying a rich man, Nick?"

"I wouldn't have the slightest idea."

"You can pretty much say what you think. People will still hate you, but they'll do it behind your back. And what's behind me, I have neither the strength or desire to acknowledge."

"I suppose it is a benefit. Although, your particular brand of honesty is a breath of fresh air, even if your habit is quite the opposite."

Grace leaned against the banister, her silhouette imitating a fine feathered quill in both the shape and texture of her gown. She tapped a long slim cigarette against her palm. Nick took her gold plated lighter and held it for her.

She took a deep puff. "There are very few young men who balance gallantry with such grace."

"Thank you, Mrs. Madsen."

"Call me Grace, dear." She used her cigarette like a pointing device, gesturing with hand movements, which were somehow very feminine despite how grand they were. "I enjoy smoking, especially when I drink, but now it seems I can never do the two at once. It's a shame really, like having sex without the benefit of foreplay."

Nick chuckled. "Definitely a tragedy…the example more so than the act."

She lifted up her cigarette, staring at it. "Funny how something that was once considered social now makes you a social pariah."

"There are many ways to be a pariah these days. Take it from someone who knows. In fact, I'm in a much lower subgroup of the pariah species than you."

"I heard. How are you doing, Nick? Off the smack or whatever the kids are calling it these days?"

"Clean and sober."

"Good for you."

"I'm sorry to take up your time."

"Pfft, a man as handsome as yourself seeks an audience with me? It's time well spent. As a bonus, it'll increase my stock value as far as Joseph is concerned, so for that alone, I thank you." She winked as if they were conspirators. "A little intrigue makes for an interesting marriage."

"I hope he doesn't misunderstand."

"Nick, I'm twice your age."

"You don't look it."

She smiled appreciatively. "Thank you. I always hope my merciless fishing expeditions hook a compliment, but one never knows. The truth is Joseph has been jealous of you for years." Nick scratched his head, waiting for an explanation. Thankfully, Grace didn't disappoint. "I've spent many nights with Max Montero." She flicked the long line of ash that accumulated on her cigarette. "I find the character extremely…stimulating."

"I'm glad you enjoy the books."

"Every girl loves an alpha…at least in short spurts." Nick had no idea how to reply, and shifted from foot to foot, feeling uncomfortable with the way the conversation was going. He wasn't sure if Grace was coming onto him or the character he'd created. His question was simple, but he didn't want to seem rude by jumping into it. Thankfully, Grace moved on. "So, tell me what I can do for you."

"Before you married Joseph, you were an immigration attorney correct?"

"In a previous life, but don't hold it against me."

"Are you still familiar with the laws?"

"Darling, it wasn't so long ago, and I retain partnership in the firm, so I keep up." Her schooled expression turned excited. "Is this for a book you're writing?"

"It's a personal matter, actually."

"Ah, anything to do with the exquisite girl I saw you dancing with?"

"It has everything to do with her."

"Well, in that case, you have half a cigarette left before I start billing you."

"I'll make it quick then."

She smacked him on the back. "Just kidding, lawyer humor. Take your time, honey. There is no greater story than a love story."

"I was wondering how difficult it might be to turn a student visa into a more permanent situation."

"When does she graduate?"

"In a few weeks."

Grace frowned. "She only has sixty days from graduation to leave the county. I'm afraid there's not enough time for her to apply for any type of extension or permanent residency."

Nick sighed, unprepared for the blow she had laid. "Are there any options?"

"There are always options. The law has plenty of loopholes. How far are you willing to leap?"

"Skyscrapers, Grace."

"What is she getting her degree in? Engineering? Something with computers?"

"Elementary education."

"Oh dear," Grace exclaimed, expelling a plume of smoke. "How unfortunate. Not due to the major, which I consider an honorable endeavor, but it limits your choices."

"I don't follow."

"If she had some type of business credentials unique and in demand to this country, it would be possible for her to get a work visa. A business could hire and sponsor her. In fact, I can think of a few off the top of my head that are searching for qualified candidates. Unfortunately, no school district has the kind of funds for such an investment."

Nick tried not to let his disappointment show. "Any other suggestions?"

"Just one more." She paused and inhaled her last bit of her cigarette for dramatic effect. "Marry her."

Nick choked. It had nothing to do with the screen of smoke he was inhaling courtesy of Grace Madsen. "You're saying I should marry her?"

"Oh no, you asked me for options, and I'm giving them to you. I'm saying you *could* marry her. And as long as immigration deems it a real marriage and not a perpetrated fraud, they would let her stay."

"I see."

"Sorry I couldn't be of more help."

"You have been. I appreciate your time."

"You make a very cute couple, Nick. You paint the kind of image that belongs on wedding toppers and new age cereal commercials. Best of luck to you."

* * * *

Shyla glanced over at the glass doors where Nick was talking to a tall woman in a colorful dress.

"Hi," Karma said, taking the seat next to her, previously occupied by Nick. "I think we got off on the wrong foot before."

Shyla struggled not to sigh or roll her eyes. "Thank you for apologizing."

"I wasn't apologizing. I just meant you might have misunderstood my intentions."

Shyla laughed at the gall of this girl. "I don't think so."

"I want to offer you some advice." Shyla was thinking of a polite way to pass, but Karma continued, her words slurring together in a pattern with no pauses, making it difficult to decipher when one ended and another began. "It's cute how Nick's run out of hometown girls so he had to outsource his latest conquest. But I should warn you about him. He'll hurt you."

"I'll ignore the racist remark and your attempts to play the part of mean girl, even though it's a commendable performance."

"Tell me, Shyla, did he put you in a book? I'm in number four. I think he described me as the fiery girl who breathed new life into Max Montero. You see, honey, when it comes to women, we're all characters for Nick Dorsey to play with and manipulate. Just be careful."

Shyla's skin prickled; her heels ached. Not the ones she wore, but her Achilles heel. Karma had found it and plunged the poison dart.

* * * *

Nick looked at her as she gazed at the skylight above his bed. "What's wrong?"

"Nothing."

"You've been quiet since we left." He propped his head on his elbow and kissed her. Her lips gave away what her voice did not. She was pissed. "Tell me."

"I liked Tara and Carrie very much."

"They liked you, too. Are you avoiding my question?"

"I'm making a statement."

"Answer the question."

"What makes you think I'm upset?"

"Well, there's your demeanor, sharp and cold. It injures me far more than your heels could have. Also, there is the fact we haven't had sex."

"Is sex a barometer for you?"

"Yep, it sure is, and that's not me being chauvinistic. It's me reading you. You enjoy our strenuous activities too much, and you've never rejected me, so the only explanation is that your disinterest is a manifestation of your distress. What is it?"

"Did you put Karma in one of your books?"

The question surprised him. "Yes." Shyla frowned as if she was hoping he'd deny it. He didn't mean to laugh, but her question was ridiculous to him.

"Maybe it seems silly to you, but I thought it was special when you based the character on me, but you put all your girls in books, don't you?"

Nick sighed, frustrated by the complications of the evening. "You are special, but not because I put you in a book. The OCD waitress in the café made it in there, too. I'm not fucking her. I'm a writer. If you're around me, your personality is fair game."

"Thanks for explaining it," she said, shifting away from him, clearly not happy at all.

"Look at me, please."

She didn't turn to him but laid flat on her back instead. Her disappointed expression caused many curses in his head. "You are different because of the way I feel for you."

"How many women have you been with?"

Nick sighed. "We gonna do this right now?"

"Do what?"

"Have an argument over something I cannot change?"

"I'm not trying to argue with you. Maybe I don't have a right to ask, especially since I have no claims when it comes to you, but my mind isn't always rational."

"You can ask me anything, and I'll be honest with you, but you might not want to hear the answer."

"You're right. I'm feeling fragile right now. Just ignore me. Goodnight."

They lay in silence, each lost in their own thoughts, both tired from their long day. He clasped her hand, joining their fingers. He tilted her chin until she looked at him. In the dark of night, he made his confessions.

"I've been with so many women I've lost count. I was a jackass on many levels and a very selfish man. My recovery has helped me acknowledge the sad, cold truths of my past. It's been hard work, and I still struggle with it. I was celibate from the day I woke up in the hospital until I met you. It took me a long time to accept who I was and become free from my addictions…all my addictions. Recently, you've helped me with some of that. My past isn't pretty, but I've told you about those dark times. My present wasn't much better. I was alive but not living. I have never felt the way I do right now. Not once in my life for any other girl. I honestly didn't think I was capable of what you bring out in me."

A small tear fell from her eye. Nick wiped it away.

"I feel the same way. Sometimes, I wonder if it would be better if I hadn't met you, so I wouldn't have a pain in my heart when it's over. Then I think about all the things we've done and the way you make me feel. I love that you try to protect me, but it's the fact that you also let me lean against you when I need it, and most importantly lift me up."

She leaned her head against his chest. He stroked her hair. "We should talk about the future, Shyla."

"There is nothing to talk about."

"I think there is."

She placed a hand on each side of his face. "Not tonight, okay? I just want to be in your arms."

"Shyla—"

She put her dainty hand over his mouth. "Nick, I had an amazing time, even if I got a little jealous."

"You don't think I was jealous?"

"Of what?"

"Maybe you didn't see the way men looked at you, but I sure as hell noticed. There was an inner battle going on."

"What battle?"

"Between me and my inner caveman."

"Is he the one that growls?"

"Yeah, and he beats his chest and has a hard time not reverting back to monosyllabic words."

"I know that guy. He's sexy."

"You're sexy, but we're not done talking, are we?"

"I don't want to end on a sour note. Let's be thankful for the days we have left and not dwell on what lies beyond the horizon."

She was right. Nick had a lot of thoughts to digest and analyze. This was not the right moment to have this conversation. "Fine."

She took his hand and traced the lines of his palm. "I graduate in two weeks."

Nick defined that day as bittersweet because no matter how happy he was for her, it also meant the end of them.

"I know the date very well. Are you excited?"

"It's hard to believe that this phase of my life is ending."

"Is your father coming?"

She shook her head. "It's too far and expensive. I won't have anyone there."

"You'll have me, Shyla." *You'll always have me.*

"Really?" she asked, sitting up in bed. "You'll come?"

"I wouldn't miss it. I'll be clapping so loud you'll hear me over the 'Pomp and Circumstance.'"

Chapter 28

She regarded herself in the mirror, a thick layer of steam coating the reflection, but she could just make out the grim expression on her face. She looked at the pajamas she'd brought into the bathroom, not quite ready or willing to put them on. Instead, she picked up the white oxford shirt he'd discarded in a wicker hamper labeled *dry cleaning*. She pressed it against her nose and inhaled his scent.

Her mind became a cacophony of treacherous, tangled thoughts. So she inhaled deeper, trying to focus on the scent and not the man it belonged to. Could she recreate it? There were so many elements to a person's scent, and Nick was more complicated than most. But she knew his smell so well. She had all the ingredients. The bar soap, shampoo, and conditioner were household names, available in any country. Nick had a tendency to be loyal to his brands. The detergent and dryer sheets might be more difficult. Their labels boasted locally made, eco-friendly ingredients. Then there was his shaving cream and aftershave, items she never imagined shopping for. Of course, she couldn't forget his expensive cologne in a dark square bottle. That wasn't all, though. There was his minty baking soda toothpaste, a paste not gel, and his spearmint-flavored mouthwash.

The amount of ingredients for the recipe would make it complicated, but she could be a chemist, mixing them in the right proportions until she achieved the desired result. And maybe in the darkness of night when she was all alone, she could place a few drops on her pillow and inhale deeply. She sniffed the fabric again. Then gave up on the idea of her experiment immediately. There was a deep, underlying masculine scent she would never find in any jar, bottle or box, no matter how hard she searched—one that was unique to him.

The tears streaked down her face once more. She slapped at them. She refused to cry in front of him. It would only hurt him. She had worn a yellow sundress today with a paisley pattern. It had a vintage look with its tight bodice and flared skirt, which swooshed when she walked. He had told her she looked lovely, like a tonic of sunshine. They had a picnic in the park, coffee in a café, a movie in an old-fashioned theatre where he'd put his arm around her, his fingertips brushing against her skin as they watched Audrey Hepburn and Gregory Peck enjoy a *Roman Holiday*. It wasn't his typical choice. He liked old movies, but the kind that involved birds pecking at humans or flies caught in transformers. He thought this might be more romantic, though. And it was.

It was the most romantic day she'd ever had. He had held her hand while they walked home and whispered sweet somethings in her ear. She wouldn't refer to them as sweet nothings because they all meant something.

They'd arrived home late. He had unzipped her dress, and it had fallen with dramatic flourish. He let out a sound between a whistle and a growl. His hands caressed her curves and edges, following one path while his lips opted for another direction. Across her back they went and down her spine. She shivered, remembering them pressing into her shoulder and neck. She wanted him with every cell of her body. But the pit of her belly ached, and her emotions threatened to surface, so she had told him she was tired. She wanted to take a shower and go to bed. The lust in his dark eyes shut off with a blink, replaced with immediate concern. He'd held a hand to her forehead and asked her what hurt. What he could do to make it better. How could she explain it was her heart? She couldn't, so she claimed it was her head instead.

She folded his shirt, the small stain of her lipstick still visible on his lapel. She would be a stain on his life and he on hers—indelible, unshakable, a permanent reminder love could blossom between the least likely people. She could scrub herself raw and never be able to wash away his memory, so she would embrace it. Maybe she'd succeed in making a passable Nick Dorsey scent potion, but she couldn't recreate the feel of his flesh over hers, the warmth of his smile, the various forms of his kisses. Oh, how she loved all those forms! From the demanding, mouth-crushing, breath-taking ones to the gentle, exploratory presses of his mouth, hinting heavily of his desire.

She hated herself for the situation she'd created. She looked down at her palm and traced the lines etched there, regretting all the paths she could not change.

She put on her pajamas, flannel adorned with pink polka dots, an unflattering outfit with the sexual appeal of cotton candy. She crept to the bed and hid under the covers.

The bed dipped when he sat. "Here," he said, two white pills on his palm.

She shook her head in objection. "I'm fine."

"Shyla, don't be stubborn. This is part of my sure-fired remedy to cure you."

She took the medicine he offered, swallowing it back along with the lump in her throat. "What remedy?"

"Take two aspirin and fuck me in the morning."

She laughed despite all her fears. He could always make her laugh. He placed the book she was reading on the nightstand beside the water before he retreated to take his shower. She regarded the nightstand, which had somehow evolved into her nightstand. There was an old-fashioned alarm clock there, each tick mocking her, bringing them closer to the end of this journey.

He slid into bed beside her, fresh from his shower, dressed in nothing but low-slung boxers. Every ounce of him chiseled, cut artistry.

She closed her eyes, trying to fade the image of him, although she could feel it in the curve of his body as he put his arms around her. How could people be so comfortable embracing they could do it in sleep? She hadn't known it was possible until him.

She hated her deceit and the petty jealousy she felt, but not about his past. She'd accepted that, but about the future women that would come after her. About the lives they would lead separate and apart from each other.

"Do you want to talk about it?" he asked, caressing her hair.

"I'm nervous about tomorrow," she lied.

"You just walk on stage and grab your diploma. Try not to trip and fall into any other guy that's not me."

"I'll remember that."

"We should go to sleep. You have a big day tomorrow."

She swallowed. "I think we should stop writing the book."

He shot up, his face searching hers. "Why?"

"We shouldn't let it hinder the rest of our time together. I'm not enjoying it anymore."

"Shyla, we have to finish it. We're so close to the end. Everyone gets into a slump, but I promise, you'll feel differently once it's finished."

"Why is it important to you?"

"You're important to me." Her brain silenced the thud of her heart. He twirled a strand of her hair. "Every story deserves an ending."

She gave him a weak smile, nodding. "Maybe."

"Not maybe."

"Okay."

"How's your headache?"

Her smile widened. "I think I'm ready for the second part of your remedy."

He chuckled. "Really? Because we don't have to."

She sat up and straddled him. Her hair dropped in a curtain around his face as she kissed him. He was reluctant, searching her face for reassurance. She answered him with more kisses, growing hungrier until he grasped her hair and pulled her closer.

"I hate these pajamas," Nick said, peeling off her top.

"Yeah, they aren't sexy."

"That's not why. The material is rough, whereas your skin is soft like silk. I just want your skin."

He flipped her on her back. He pulled down her panties.

His fingers grazed up her legs as he crawled back toward her. "Touch me," he said, lowering his boxers.

Her hands were unsteady, unsure as she grasped him. He placed his fingers over hers, moving them against the hardness of his erection. He traced her lips with the tip. She grew bolder, pressing her mouth around him and taking him deeper.

He cupped the back of her head, but he didn't push her. His breath hitched, encouraging and exciting her. He whispered her name in the dark, a silent plea for satisfaction. She pushed forward taking more of him, sliding her tongue around his shaft. She choked. She pushed past it, determined to pleasure him despite the volatile sounds her throat made.

He moved away from her then. He laid her head on the pillow and rolled to his side of the nightstand.

"Why did you stop me?" she asked, disappointed she couldn't finish what he started.

"I didn't. Your body stopped you. I just happened to be listening."

"Nick—"

"Shyla, I don't enjoy your discomfort."

He opened and shut the drawer. He rolled the condom on. He clasped her breast, slowly squeezing it, making her nipples harden. His tongue licked her left nipple while his thumb flicked over her right. He slowly sucked while she clutched his hair. And when she couldn't stand it anymore, he reversed course.

He shifted her to her side. "You have a beautiful back, do you know that?"

She wasn't sure how to answer, especially since she never gave much thought to her back. As if to emphasize the point, he traced her spine with his tongue.

"It makes watching you go almost as hot as watching you come…almost."

She gasped as he penetrated her. His thrusts were slow, allowing her to get used to the new position. His hands caressed her front. They travelled lower until they reached her mound. His thumb circled her nub. Her mouth searched for his until their lips found each other. He drew farther out and pushed into her with a new force, leveraging his legs against hers, their bodies working in tandem.

Their voices intermingled with the plains of passion, a symphony where they were the conductors building to that crescendo.

"I love to worship this body," he whispered in her ear, his fingers digging into her hips as she let go.

When it was over, he kissed her shoulder, his warm breath washing over her skin, relaxing her and causing new sensations at the same time. She watched as he walked to the bathroom to discard the condom. The dim lamp provided just enough light to illuminate his muscular form.

When he once again slid beside her, his arms wrapped around her. She turned around, leaned her chin against his chest, and stared at the outline of his face against the darkness.

"Do you know one of the many things I love about your body?" she asked between kissing his chest. Although he could not see, she was sure he felt her playful smile as it pressed against his skin.

"What?"

She traced his lips with her tongue. "That beautiful muscle you possess. When it flexes, it causes two tiny dimples on your cheeks. It robs me of all coherent thought."

"You like my smile?"

"I love your smile, Nick, but I was talking about your arse."

His hearty laughed echoed through the room.

* * * *

Dressed in his T-shirt, she carefully propped herself against the hard wooden headboard with one of his yellow legal pads and an ink pen. He slept soundly, his arm across her lap. She tried not to shift because she didn't want to wake him or cause him to move. He always gravitated toward her, even in his subconscious.

Nick preferred legal pads for writing and silver cross pens. "For those occasions when your thoughts come so fast, you need to freeze them," he had said.

Tonight her thoughts flew through the air, scattered as if they were frail leaves, hurdling without direction at the mercy of turbulent wind. She was unsure if this was the right ending, but every story had to conclude. And it was time to end…both stories. She wrote the words to the last chapter in her own writing, her fingers clasping the pen so hard her knuckles ached. It wasn't a modern or comfortable way to write, but she wanted the cramps in her hands and the stiffness of her fingers—anything to distract her from the pounding ache in her heart.

Chapter 29

The Choice Less

Asha was a childless mother and a disgraceful wife. She hadn't borne him a son. He blamed her questionable origins as the source of why she was incapable of performing the duties of a woman. Her family concurred she was barren. She deceived them for a long time, carefully swallowing the white pills in the dark of night without the aid of water, and then hiding them inside the rip in the mattress. She was successful in her sham.

Until that warm night she walked to the river after the recent rains. She heard his loud, crunching steps against the soft earth before she saw him. Her body immediately trembled. Aditi never came to the river.

"Asha, dear wife, why do you always come here?"

She kept her back to him, not wanting to show the fear on her face. "It's peaceful."

His hand grasped her shoulder, his fingers digging roughly into her skin. "Look what my mother found today." She turned her head, but she didn't have to look to know what he was holding.

"What are they, wife?"

"Medicine."

"What ailments are you suffering from?"

She swallowed, her head hung low as her eyes searched for weapons. There was nothing, not even a rock.

"I'm waiting for your answer, sweet wife."

"Vitamins. They give me energy."

"Liar." The accusation hung in the air, like a lead weight.

"Husband, please—"

She didn't get a chance to finish the statement. He kicked her in the back. She tried to scream but no sound came out. He clutched the back of her head in his heavy hand and pushed her face into the water.

Her mouth filled as she struggled against him. Her head pounded with pressure. Just as the pressure gave way to lightness, he pulled her out. His voice screamed words laced with rage. His face contorted into that of a monster's. She couldn't understand the statements he screamed at her.

"You deceived me. Everyone is laughing, saying I'm infertile. Why did you do this?" His expression twisted with anguish. His eyes were wild. "Answer me, bitch."

For some odd reason only one phrase came to mind. And if she was capable of speech, she would have vocalized it. *It was a girl and she was beautiful and she was ours!* Her head plunged into the water again before she could even make sense of her thoughts.

"You don't provide a dowry and now not even a son. You are a useless woman, one that should have died a long time ago on this very river. I will correct the mistake today."

"No, please." She flailed her arms, trying to find purchase on any object to keep her grip, but he was too strong.

He pushed her head in again. Her lungs burned as if they were on fire. She forgot about holding her breath as the water filled her nostrils. She forgot about searching for a weapon or pleading for her life. She forgot about not swallowing the water into her lungs. She forgot she had lungs. She forgot about surviving.

He grasped a fistful of her hair and pulled her out so quickly she couldn't remember to spit out a lungful of water. He pushed his face into hers. "I gave you everything. Why did you shame my family this way?"

She shook her head, unsure of the questions, and even more so of the answers.

He spit in her face.

He plunged her into the water once more. This time she didn't fight.

Her mind traveled to the lit corners of her safe places where her imagination could go freely, even if her body could not. Unlike the times before, she didn't head to the Mississippi River to help a slave get his freedom. Or to Meryton in Hertfordshire near London to chat with Elizabeth Bennet. She didn't journey to New England and later New York with Jo March. Instead, she traveled to a place she'd never been…one where a little girl with a huge dimpled smile held her hand and called her "Ma."

She went home.

Chapter 30

NYU's commencement was at Yankee Stadium. The air didn't smell like hot dogs and beer today, but of excitement and hope. There were no foul-mouthed fans waving foam fingers. Today, there was a sea of violet caps and gowns. The ceremony was long, the keynote address given by a famous actor and activist. It brought back memories of Nick's past when he took the very same stage five years earlier as a jaded, cocky kid who believed the world owed him something. He'd learned the truth through hard lessons.

He clapped loudly for her. In his heart, he'd dreaded this day for so long, but now he only felt hope. He thought about just asking her—spontaneously laying it out. Perhaps a wiser man would have hinted at such a huge step, tested the waters so to speak, but Nick wasn't feeling particularly rational, especially not when it came to her. He wanted her to remember their engagement in a romantic sigh-worthy way. *Out of left field, taken by surprise*, and *heart-pounding* were phrases he hoped would capture the moment. Nick wasn't particularly old fashioned, but he had concluded that a man shouldn't propose to the woman he loved in a half-hearted way or without the benefit of a ring. His heart was completely full, and thanks to the fine jeweler's of Tiffany & Company, he had a ring as well.

No, a proposal would not be sincere without a ring, a grand gesture, and a heartfelt speech. So he had plotted the moment, carefully constructed like a major plot twist. He wouldn't ask her today, though. Today was her day and hers alone. He would not steal even a second. The day he asked her to be his wife was their day, and it deserved its own mark on the calendar.

He waited for her outside the stadium. The streets flooded with a sea of violet until the waves receded and there was just him. A tiny hint of panic set in, although he dismissed it quickly. He was being ridiculous. Even though he had convinced himself she was fine, he still breathed a sigh of relief when his cell rang with her number.

"Where are you?"

"Nick, I'm so sorry. A friend of my family's came for my graduation. It was a surprise. He's only in town for the night."

Him?

"I know you made plans for us, but he wants to take me to dinner. Do you mind?"

There was something in her pattern of speech that felt rehearsed, as if she was nervous to veer from her sentences. "Do you want me to join you?"

"Actually, we're already on our way to the restaurant. Nick, I'm so sorry. I wasn't expecting him to show up."

Nick could take a hint. He wasn't wanted. But something about this seemed suspicious. Then again, her family probably leaned toward the conservative side, so it made sense she wouldn't want to combine her two worlds. That was his biggest fear about proposing in the first place, and the one setback he'd prepared for.

"Will you come over tonight?"

"It's been a long day, and I'd like to get a good night's sleep. Can we do something tomorrow? I promise I'll make it up to you."

Nick let go of his pestering contemplation. He'd read too many mystery novels. Shyla had never given him a reason not to trust her.

"Sure, sweetheart. I just wanted to be the first one to congratulate you."

"It meant so much to me that you were there today, more than you'll ever know."

"I wouldn't have missed it. I'll see you tomorrow. Come over at eight."

"So late? I don't work anymore. I can make it earlier."

Nick would have loved to spend the day with her, but he had many things to set up. There was no way their night wouldn't be perfect.

"Come at eight. I have some errands."

"Okay, I'll see you then."

He tried to cancel their reservations at the five-star Indian restaurant in the vicinity, but their phone was busy. He walked to the exit to hop on the train back to midtown. He tried to keep his head occupied with his grand plans for tomorrow and not focus on the disappointment of her cancellation. He realized he was fairly close to the location in question and, as it happened, he was starving, so he walked in. They seated him in a back booth with plenty of privacy per his request. He studied the menu, wishing Shyla was there to help him order. In the end, he went for a fusion dish that featured a more Americanized version of a classic Indian plate.

Nick wasn't used to eating alone and, as a result, he hurried through his entrée and paid the bill quickly. On the street, he paused to admire a shiny Aston Martin parked at the curb. What his gramps would have called "a highfalutin' machine."

The driver got out and opened the door, looking almost mechanical in his movements. He wore a cap and suit, and Nick had an urge to greet him with, "'Ello, governor." He laughed, wondering if maybe he should rent a car tomorrow and take Shyla on a drive through the city at night. Maybe even a motorcycle. He hadn't been on one since the accident, but the thought excited him. There was nothing like the power and freedom of riding a bike. His mind jerked back to the present when he heard her familiar laugh. The man who accompanied her was older with reddish hair and a stiff build.

"Thank you, Rich," he said to the driver in a noticeably British accent.

"Where to now, sir?"

"The lady and I would like to go to the lounge."

The rich bastard gestured for Shyla to get into the car first. She smiled graciously at him before entering the vehicle. If she had looked to her left, she would have seen Nick. But her eyes never veered.

Nick's first reaction was…what the fuck? By the time he regained his composure, the Aston Martin was speeding along the street.

He knew the answers to his questions as soon as they entered his mind. This was all kinds of wrong. Shyla had never mentioned a family friend. And she came from a middle class Indian family in a village. It didn't add up that her parents would be friends with a white, extremely wealthy British man, although some part of him realized he passed judgment where he shouldn't. Because if he really analyzed their relationship, their backgrounds were vastly different, and yet they had become friends… best friends, actually. But there was also the fact the man had said they were going to The Lounge, which Nick knew was a chic martini bar on the East side. She had been nervous during their brief conversation. All of these thoughts rushed toward him as the D Train hurtled through the tunnels deep underground the city.

He crammed them all down before he made a mistake and pushed her away. He'd ask her, but not tonight. Maybe tomorrow.

Should he ask before or after he proposed?

Will you marry me? Who was that guy? What's going on? Nope, there wasn't any natural rhythm to those questions. The whole thing pissed him off, so when he got home, he went for a jog around the city. He almost veered into her neighborhood, but he stopped himself. He wasn't this petty, jealous man who showed up at his girlfriend's house demanding answers to ludicrous questions.

He told himself everything was fine. Today would not influence tomorrow. And tomorrow would be the beginning of a new chapter for them...unless she said no.

Then it would be the end of them.

Chapter 31

She smiled brightly at him the next night when he opened the door. He wore a charcoal gray suit and a navy pinstriped tie.

"You look so handsome. Are we going out? I didn't know we were dressing up."

"No, we're staying in…sort of. Don't worry, you look perfect as always." She wore dark jeans and a simple white tank top, but damn she looked sexy just the same.

He took her messenger bag and set it inside before taking her arm and leading her to the stairwell.

"I thought you said we were staying in."

He punched the up button. "We're going to the roof."

He'd never taken her there. She'd asked him once how far into the city you could see. The building was on the shorter side, so it wasn't too far, but he figured the privacy and open space would be the right backdrop for what he had in mind.

He led her to the flat roof of the Bleecker Street building and mentally patted himself on the back when she gasped.

Her eyes darted from one corner to the next. He stood, hands in his pockets, watching her.

When Carrie and Tara found out what he was doing, they both wanted to be involved. Actually, they'd insisted. Nick complained they were taking things too far, but when he saw Shyla react with such awe, he silently thanked them.

Tall shrubs planted in large stone urns stood along the parameter of the square space, each decorated with a string of white lights. Baskets of white tulips, hydrangeas, and peonies stood at attention, their petals glowing against the moonlight. Flickering candles danced on top of a table built for two.

"I can't believe you did all this."

"I had help."

"It's beautiful."

"Let's sit," he said, taking her hand and leading her to the table.

"I'm starving. Did you make this?" she asked, staring at the vegetarian lasagna on her plate.

"I got it from the Italian place around the corner, but I did take it out of their containers and arranged the food on my own plates. That has to count for something."

"It does. This is lovely. I hope this wasn't what you were planning for yesterday. I'm really sorry."

He poured her a glass of wine. Each of her wrists gleamed with the glint of silver—one adorned with the cheap bangles he'd bought her and the other a watch.

"It was for tonight. Is this new?" he asked, taking her wrist.

"A graduation gift."

"From your friend?" The word friend came out much sharper than he'd intended.

"Yes. Is something wrong?"

"How was your dinner?"

"It was nice."

"Can you extrapolate?"

She gave him a confused smile. "Extrapolate?"

"Just wondering how he became your family friend. I saw you last night. Ironically, we were at the same restaurant. I watched you leave with him. The explanation you gave was mysterious. He's older than you, but not by much. He's very rich, and you went to a bar afterwards. I trust you. I'm not the kind of man who shines suspicion where it doesn't belong, and you're not the kind of girl who would hurt me in that way, but I also need more information from you. I'm trying my best not to become a monosyllabic caveman, but I have to tell you, I'm losing the battle. So yeah, please extrapolate."

She took a deep breath. "I suppose I shouldn't have said he's a family friend. He's *my* friend, Nick. The Charles Breckenridge organization sponsors schools in third world countries."

Nick digested the information and repeated the name. "I know that name."

"His family owns hotels all around the world."

"I see."

"I wasn't expecting him, but I'm glad he came. He's the reason I'm here after all."

"He is?"

"He gave me the scholarship."

"You mean his organization did."

"No, he personally did. He's done a great deal for me. But I swear to you he is just a friend. There is nothing sinister between us. I was selfish yesterday because I really didn't want to spend the time with him. I wanted to reserve it all for you, but it would have been rude. We did go to a bar, but all we did was talk. Do you believe me?" She didn't ask the question with any sarcasm, only sincerity.

Nick did believe her. She wasn't lying to him, but there was something in her demeanor that suggested she wasn't telling him the whole story either.

She stood up and walked over to him. He pulled her down on his lap.

"He gave you the money out of his own pocket, Shyla?"

"He's my benefactor." She leaned her head against his chest. "Can we stop talking about Mr. Breckenridge? I want to enjoy this."

He kissed her hair. "Even the suggestion of another man with you, no matter how misguided, drives me crazy."

"If the situation was reversed, I'd be asking you the same questions, although I would have done it last night…maybe making a scene."

Nick laughed. "I thought about it, but the fucking Aston Martin was down the street already."

She brushed her fingers through his hair. "I can't believe you did all this…for me."

"There's no one else in the world I would do it for."

She took a deep breath and placed her hand over Nicks. "I want to memorize everything. It's such a beautiful night. You can see the stars so clearly."

He followed her gaze. "There's something about looking at the sky and seeing all that darkness dotted with gold. You realize your purpose. That everything which happens has a pattern, a place." He kissed her temple. "And every person you meet shapes you."

"I see it, too."

"I have some things to say to you. I rehearsed them, but I don't think they'll come out the way I planned."

"Just say them."

"I knew my life was grim, but I was satisfied in it. It's as if I'd forgotten what the sun felt like. I'd get little glimpses of it whenever I ordered a sandwich. No one can eat that many sandwiches, by the way."

She looked at him quizzically. "I don't understand."

"Sometimes I'd order the food and give it to the homeless guy around the corner."

"Why?"

"Because I craved the few minutes of sunshine. I loved your smile. Hell, I even loved your stupid weather reports. And then you asked to come into my world. As each day passed, I felt like I was living again… or maybe alive for the first time."

She caressed his cheek, her fingers shaking against his skin. "You've done that for me, too. You made me smile…really smile and laugh, too."

"I don't want to let you go." He kissed her forehead. He gently eased her up and then stood up himself. He took her hand before kneeling down.

"Nick?"

"We don't have to end this. I love you, Shyla. I love you with all my heart. Will you marry—"

"Stand up, Nick." Her voice wavered but her tone was cold.

"I'm not done."

He looked up at her face and the tears there. He swallowed the lump in his own throat. Because he was in fact…done.

"I can't marry you."

He stood, taking her shoulders. "I know it's fast, but this is the natural path we are on. I wouldn't have asked you this soon, but we are against a clock, and I've thought of nothing else since you came into my life except how to keep you there."

"I have to go back to India."

"Not if we get married. I've done some research."

"You don't understand. I want to go back."

"Shyla, let's talk about this."

"I don't love you." The words would have stabbed him except the gesture that followed pissed him off too much. Her face shifted down, and she twisted a strand of her hair before tucking it behind her ear. Her tell.

"You're lying to me…or maybe to yourself. You love me."

She shook her head, backing away. She wiped away a tear. "I'm so sorry, Nick. I thought we were on the same page."

"Same page? What fucking chapter are you on? I don't think we're reading the same book," he said, his voice low and jaw clenched. She winced in response.

"We were passing into each other's lives, but we were never meant to set anchor. We made some memories, and I will always be grateful."

"Grateful?"

"I don't know what else to say." She wept openly now, but it just made things worse because he wanted to shake the truth from her.

"Is it because of Charles Breckenridge?"

"No! He has nothing to do with this."

Nick's laugh was bitter. "I think he does. People don't have personal benefactors. We're not living in a Dickens's novel for Christ sake."

"I have one."

"How exactly do you benefit your benefactor?"

She narrowed her eyes, her fists clenching at her side. "Do you have a question for me?"

"I believe I'm asking it." He held up her wrist, glaring at the diamond-encrusted watch. "How do you earn a watch like this?"

He felt her hard, cold slap before he even realized she'd pulled back her arm.

Her eyes widened, her expression completely furious. She hit her tiny fists against his chest. "Do not speak to me that way again."

She turned, her shoes clicking against the cement squares of the roof.

"Shyla, wait."

"Leave me alone, Nick," she said in a voice somewhere between fury, disappointment, and grief.

She slammed the door to the roof. He wanted to run after her. To apologize for the things he suggested. But at the same time, he couldn't look past his own hurt and anger.

He wasn't so self-assured he hadn't accounted for the possibility of her rejection, but he never expected her to deny she loved him. It was evident in her kiss and caress. In the things she did for him. In the way they made love and the little talks they had. Even in the way they goofed around. Now all he felt was emptiness. He kicked over a planter. It crashed against the brick wall and crumbled into pieces of broken clay, dirt, and petals.

He leaned against the wall. The sky opened and, without warning, pelted him with rain.

"Really?" he screamed at the sky.

He didn't go inside, though. The rain was good. It hid his tears. He hated crying. He avoided it.

The tears brought with them all the pain of the other three times he'd cried.

The night Jenny died.

The day of his grandfather's funeral after he delivered a heartfelt eulogy to a room full of die-hard card sharks.

The day his mother dropped him off at Gramp's trailer. She had told him she needed a break. More importantly, Peter needed a break. Grandpa took one look at Nick, and his hands shook. He took his daughter into the house. Nick sat on the stoop, but he heard them just the same.

"It's just for a little while," she said. The same thing she always said. "A little while" varied with his mother. Sometimes it was a few days, a week, or three months.

"Don't come back this time," Gramps replied.

"Dad—"

"Do not come back for him unless you get some help and leave that son of a bitch. You've put him through enough. You're no good…not to yourself and not to him."

Why did Gramps have to make her feel bad about herself?

"Peter is the only good thing in my life."

"Dammit, are you really this screwed up? That boy out there, who is the sweetest kid I know, is the only good thing in your life. Why don't you be a mother to him for once?"

"His dad ran out on us. I'm doing the best I can."

"This is the best you got? Really?"

"You keep him," she said. "You're right. He does better with you."

"That's not what I'm saying."

"I don't need a lecture, Dad. I'm done. You want him? You keep him."

It was grandpa's fault—the mean bully. She wouldn't have said those things if he'd been nicer. She stepped out of the trailer, mussed Nick's hair once, and told him to be a good boy before she got into Peter's rusted Buick.

Gramps came and sat beside Nick. "Nicky, I have to talk to you." The old man said some stuff, but Nick wasn't paying attention. All he saw was the Buick's taillights disappearing down the dirt road. He stood and chased after the car, ignoring his grandfather's shouts. She had to drive slowly. The path was uneven and the tires on the car completely bald. Even so, she managed to get two blocks, refusing to acknowledge him even though she looked in her rearview mirror several times. Finally, she stopped when he screamed after her. She reached over and rolled down the passenger window. Nick leaned on it because his legs no longer had the energy to hold him upright.

His mother's face was sunken and pale. Her hair was long and ratty, absent from the benefit of a good brush. Despite that, she was still beautiful to him. He saw his reflection through the mirrored lenses of her sunglasses—a skinny eight year old with trembling lips, a big black shiner adorning his left eye. It was an overcast day. She didn't wear the sunglasses to protect her from any harsh rays, rather to hide her own matching black eye.

"What is it, Nicolas?" she demanded with a heavy sigh.

"I want to go home," he said.

"You shouldn't have gotten in his way."

"He was hitting you."

"And he would have whether you were there or not." She gestured to his face. "Now look, we're no better off for it. Peter's not good with kids, honey. This is the best thing for everyone."

"You're not coming back, are you? You pick him. You always pick him." And because he was no physical match for the bastard, he kicked the man's car over and over until his foot hurt.

"Cut it out," she said. Her face softened slightly. "When you're older, you'll understand."

Nick knew without a shred of doubt that he would never understand her decision. A million years could go by, and he'd still be as upset and confused as he was right then.

"Be good for Grandpa."

"Mom...please."

"Step away."

"No, I won't."

"Step the fuck away from the car," she barked. Nick didn't even flinch anymore. He recognized the signs. Her hands gripped the wheel tightly, yet still trembled. She needed a fix. She hadn't had a drink today. She wouldn't risk a DUI with Peter's car. He took a step back.

"Don't look at me with those puppy-dog eyes. And stop crying. You aren't a baby. You'll be just fine. You always are."

He watched as the car took off, its tires kicking dirt onto his shins.

He didn't go back to Gramp's place. He ran. Just like he did every morning since that day. He ran through the streets, trying to exhaust his body to the point where he could only feel the physical pain and nothing else. When he couldn't run anymore, he climbed the water tower. His legs dangled off the edge, and he peered down, wondering if he hurt himself enough if she'd come back.

His grandfather called for him. "I've been looking for you for three hours, Nicky."

"Go away. I hate you."

Gramps didn't go away, though. He climbed the long ladder of the water tower. Nick silently watched the old man who had arthritis in his hands and a morbid fear of heights shakily climb every rung until he got to the top. Gramps took slow, deliberate steps until he reached Nick.

He was breathless when he put his arm around the boy. They were both silent for a long time.

"Why did you climb up here? You could have hurt yourself," Nick said.

"I would do anything for you, son."

"She hates me."

"She doesn't. She loves you, but she's confused right now."

"She told me once that I was an accident."

Gramps took a deep breath. He leaned back on his palms and pointed at the dark sky. Nick hadn't realized how late it had become.

"Have you ever looked at the sky and said there are way too many stars up there?"

Nick crossed his arms. "No."

"That's because when you look at all of those twinkling heavenly lights, you just know."

"Know what?" Nick asked, mimicking Gramp's position.

"Every star is connected, and they draw off each other's energy."

"What does that have to do with anything?"

Gramps didn't answer for a while. He lay on his back and looked up. Nick did the same. "What's true in heaven is also true on earth, Nicky."

"I don't get it."

"Everything and everyone serves a purpose. There are no accidents, kiddo."

"What's my purpose?"

"I have no idea. Probably, you don't know either, at least not yet. But I do know this—you have one."

Chapter 32

Nick figured a day was sufficient time to get his emotions under control and for Shyla to forgive him.

When she opened the door, he cursed himself in a million ways. Her eyes were puffy, an aura of grimness surrounding her. But it was her sad attempt at a smile which wrenched his heart completely.

"Someone was leaving when I walked in. That's how I got past the front door." He said the phrases for no other reason than to fill the air between them. He was in danger of losing himself to the grimness, too, and right now he just wanted to pull her out. To give her a symbolic hand. To deliver a strong hug, one that would protect her. To provide a kiss full of passion and purpose. To love her.

"Come in."

Nick had never been in Shyla's dorm room. It was small, and every object was in doubles, one side of the room mirroring the other. Two twin beds, two dressers, and two nightstands. Everything was the same except one side had hot pink bed sheets, movie posters, and picture frames, while the other—undoubtedly Shyla's side—contained gray sheets and walls empty of any identifying mementos.

"Have you started packing?"

"Not yet, but I booked my flight. I leave in four days."

They stood awkwardly. Nick struggled not to beg her to stay.

"I'm sorry for what I said to you. I was upset and confused. It's not an excuse. I just want you to know that if I could take it back I would. Will you forgive me?" he asked.

"Yes."

He expelled the breath he'd been holding since he stepped onto Bleecker Street that morning.

"Will you forgive me?" she asked him barely above a whisper.

Nick struggled to maintain a smile. "For breaking my heart? I doubt it." Her face shifted downward. He tilted her chin. "But I'll try."

"Why did you come if you can't forgive me?"

He walked to the far side of the room, needing the space from her. Nothing he said sounded quite right. He didn't trust his feelings. They were more powerful than him. He glanced at the collection of porcelain teddy bears on Elaine's side of the room. They were each doing ridiculous human things like riding a bike or juggling. "I finally read the last chapter." It wasn't the reason he'd come, but he couldn't express the real reasons…not yet.

"What did you think?"

"Worst ending ever."

"Why do you say that?"

"We've been with this character through all of the horrible things she's endured. We've rooted for her, cheered her on, and felt her sorrow. We can't just leave her dead or whatever at the riverbank."

"It's the right ending, and she's not dead."

"It's hard to grasp that the way you wrote it."

"It's open ended. The reader can decide."

Nick spun around and faced her. "The reader doesn't want to fucking decide. It's your job—no, your obligation—to provide satisfaction." He slumped onto her bed. "I hate it. We have to change it. I haven't interfered in the story at all. It's your story, but this ending is god-awful. As a writer and, more importantly, a reader, I can't let it exist."

She walked over to him. He pulled her into his lap. It was an automatic gesture, one that had turned into habit, like how she crossed her arms when angry or how he cracked his knuckles before writing.

"I don't think it's that ending your upset about, Nick," she whispered against his ear. The barricade damming up all his emotions broke apart. He nuzzled her neck and held her close. It must have been the same for Shyla because she started weeping. They stayed in that position for a long time. She stroked his hair. He rubbed her lower back. They didn't speak, but somehow they communicated a million sentiments in that time. She was hurting as much as he was. He felt the loss of her in every cell of his body. He leaned back and curled his arms around her. Her sobs finally stopped.

"Why, Shyla?" He didn't need to clarify the question.

"My purpose is to be a teacher, Nick. I've always known that on some level. There are many unwanted girls in my country. But things are changing. It's not a third world problem. It's everyone's problem."

"It's selfish of me, but I can't understand why you would sacrifice the life you could have here…with me."

"It's not selfish. I've thought about it a great deal, but I made this choice a long time ago before I met you." She sighed, brushing her fingertips through his hair.

"You can't save the world from its problems."

"I can be part of the change. I've had many experiences that told me this was the right choice, but one in particular stands out for me. Maybe if I explained it to you, you'd understand."

"I'm listening."

"I lived in Mumbai for a while before coming here. It's where I finished my education." She chuckled, her face recalling some memory. "I think just living there prepared me for New York. It's a huge city. I lived in a very nice place, but I saw so much poverty, things I'd never seen in the village. In particular, there was this homeless family that lived on the street across from me. A mother and her two young sons, dressed in nothing but rags. One boy was missing his right arm, and you could see their ribs poking through their skin, but they never complained. They always had smiles on their faces. I watched them beg for money. Most people ignored them. I gave them money every day. I decided to do more so I went to a shop and purchased new clothes and food for them. The mother thanked me, and the boys were so excited. In my ignorance, I decided I'd done something good, Nick. Like I made a difference."

"You did, baby."

"No, I didn't, Nick. When I came the next day, they were dressed in their old clothes again. I asked their mother where the new items were. She told me that no one would give them money if they were dressed so nicely. She said I would bankrupt them with my generosity. I was angry with her. I accused her of being a bad mother."

Nick's eyes widened. He knew such brutalities existed, but to hear her talk of them in such a real way angered him, too. "She was a bad mother."

Shyla shook her head. "Yes and no. You see, I'd observed them for a long time. I saw she loved her boys and she was…she was their world. She held them when they were sick. She made them laugh when they were sad. She gave up her own food to make sure they had a meal. The mentality was ingrained because it's what her mother and her mother before her did. There was a hopelessness so profound it was tangible. That family stayed in my head for a long time. But what if she had an education? What if she knew her family didn't have to live this way? Giving food, shelter, and clothing is one thing, but it's like putting a bandage over a broken bone. Shifting the mind is much more difficult, especially when you're working to undo generations of beliefs. But in order for there to be real change, that's what needs to happen. It was that day I vowed to be part of that change."

He rubbed her back in slow circles, digesting her words. "I resent how good you are. I want you to be selfish like me. We'd get along much better that way."

She laughed. "There is nothing selfish about you, Nick. I refute your statement. I am not as good as you think I am, and you are a much better man than you give yourself credit for."

"Maybe."

"Do you believe me about Charles? I swear we are only friends."

"I believe you, and I'm sorry for my accusations on that front, too."

She lifted her head, her fingers playing with his hair. "Nick, do you regret us?"

"Never, Goddess. How could I?"

"Because you're angry with me. I understand because I'm angry with myself, too."

"I read this story once about this artist—a sculptor. I don't remember the name of it, but I remember the story because it stuck with me."

"What happened?"

"He was famous and rich. He went blind in an accident, and he could no longer work. He became a bitter man and hated the world. The Gods looked down at him and decided to send him a muse. She was an angel—compassionate, beautiful, and smart. She kick-started his creativity, which I guess is what muses are supposed to do."

"And he made a masterpiece?"

"You'd think that. His new work was criticized. People hated it. He blamed the muse and shunned her. He swore at the Gods for bringing her into his life."

"That's sounds like a worse ending than our book."

Nick chuckled. "Yeah, but it had an important message. You see, he misunderstood why the Gods had sent him such an important gift. She wasn't there to inspire his work."

"Then why?"

"To inspire his heart and mend his soul. The problem was he didn't learn the lesson until it was too late." He kissed Shyla's head. "At least I didn't make the same mistake."

"Did he find her again…the muse?"

"No…the Gods took her away. He died alone and heartbroken."

"That's awful."

"See what I mean about crappy endings?"

Shyla grinned at him. "Yes, I do."

"You could have at least admitted you loved me."

"Would it change anything?"

"No, but I would know I wasn't alone. That we aren't an illusion of my own creation."

She took a deep breath and sat up on the narrow bed, straddling him. She took his hand in hers and ran his thumb across the line of her palm. "You asked me how much of my lifeline was yours once. I honestly don't know that answer. None of us does. But this is my love line." She looked at him, her lower lip trembling. "This one belongs to you and only you, Nick Dorsey."

He crushed his mouth against hers. Nick kissed Shyla in many ways, sometimes with calm slow seduction and other times with fast-paced frenzied sexual exuberance, but tonight they came together differently. Tonight there was a hunger and longing in each exchange.

He unbuttoned her shirt, his fingers working deftly, relying on the sensation of touch to guide him. She moaned against his mouth. He flung the material across the room.

"Your roommate?"

"She won't be home tonight. You'll stay with me."

Although she hadn't asked a question, he still affirmed the answer. He nodded, unbuttoning her jeans. She worked on his belt. Their lips constantly searching out one another. They undressed quickly, their hands familiar with the other's garments until each shred of clothing was on the floor. He placed her beneath him, trying not to fall out of the narrow bed.

He fell against her, a string of expletives echoing his frustration.

"What is it?" she asked.

"I don't have a condom."

"What?"

He kissed her neck, following a path to her lips. "I can pull out."

She did a slight nod before shaking her head. Something flickered across her features—a look of panic. "No, please don't."

"Please don't pull out?"

"No, I mean…we should have a condom. It's important."

She pushed against his chest. Nick rolled over to his side, his groan evident. "Shyla, you don't have to say please. I would never force you."

"I know."

"I can go get some."

She looked so disappointed he cupped her face and pressed a kiss against her forehead. Suddenly, she snapped her fingers. "Elaine might have condoms."

"Fuck, then what are we doing in bed. We have to find them."

She found them quickly. She ran in from the bathroom and deposited a handful on his chest. He laughed as he looked at all the gold foil packages. "You seem to have a great deal of confidence in my abilities."

"I think you're up for the challenge." She ripped open a packet between her teeth.

They didn't use all the packets, but far more than Nick thought possible. When they were both exhausted, she lay on top of his chest, and he stroked her back.

He asked her to describe her life pre Nick, pre-America, and to give him a glimpse of the future. He wanted to imagine her accurately. She spoke barely above a whisper, giving him the details he craved.

"I wake up later than I do here. Around nine. I will first make my tea. You'd like masala tea—it's rich and spicy. But before I do that, I'll have to turn on the geyser."

"What's a geyser?"

"It heats the water."

"Really?"

"Yes. It's not as modern but it is far better than boiling water."

"I suppose."

She went on, telling him about the cobblestone walks and the children playing in the streets. The monsoon rains and gigantic birds. How elders, respected and admired, were referred to as uncle or auntie even if they were unrelated. She filled in rich details for him that made it easier to picture her in that setting. But nothing would ever make it easier to let her go.

Then he told her about Gramps and the water tower. "For whatever reason, that was a defining moment in my life."

She clasped her hand over his, merging their fingers. "I understand it."

"You do?"

She kissed his scar. "He overcame all his fears because of his love and concern for you. Because you meant that much to him."

"Yeah, that was it."

"It's what you did for me, Nick."

"What do you mean?"

"Well…figuratively, anyway. You didn't want to feel with your heart because it had been hurt so many times, but you did. You climbed the water tower for me, Nick."

Chapter 33

Shyla leaned against Elaine's bed and Nick against Shyla's, their legs entangled. He sipped the coffee, trying and failing not to grimace.

"I would have made it for you on the French Press, but Elaine packed her microwave so I can't heat the water. I know the coffee's subpar."

"This is great," he said, tipping back the paper cup and gulping down the lukewarm, flavored water.

She kicked his foot. "You don't fool me, coffee snob."

He chuckled, holding his hand against his chest. "Me? A snob? I prefer the term connoisseur."

"We can go out."

"Thank God. This is crap." He grinned when she laughed. "But I think we should go to my place so we can rewrite that ending. I meant it when I said I hated it."

Her smiled tightened, creating an uneasy feeling in Nick. There was a sixth sense that everyone had, but seldom used. His gramps called it poker prowess, the instinct that a cheat was taking place. It had existed for Nick when he was eight, and he could tell from Peter's demeanor if he was just drunk enough to hit him or too drunk to do any damage. It existed now. Something was awry.

"Not every ending can be a happy one," she said.

"True, but it can be satisfying, and this isn't. Not in the least."

Shyla opened her mouth to respond, but the sound of the door opening drew both their attentions.

"Oh hi," Elaine said, her head shifting between the two of them.

Nick helped Shyla up and put his arm around her. She blushed slightly. God, she was so innocent.

"Elaine, this is Nick Dorsey."

"Ah, mystery man with good taste," Elaine said, shaking his hand.

"It's nice to meet you, Elaine. I've heard a lot about you."

"Wish I could say the same, but this girl is very tight-lipped," Elaine replied, bumping Shyla's shoulder.

"We were thinking of going out for lunch. Would you like to join us?" Shyla asked her.

Elaine shook her head, her face falling into a frown. "I don't think I'll be very good company today."

"What's wrong?" Shyla asked.

"You're going to think I'm stupid," Elaine said, feigning a weak smile.

"I promise I won't," Shyla said.

"Do you want me to leave?" Nick asked, feeling like an intruder between the two girls.

"Oh no, it's not like that," Elaine said, waving a dismissive hand. "It just…I just found out my favorite author is not going to be writing anymore books. I know that seems dumb, but I've sort of fallen in love with his character. You know every year you get a book or two that chronicles this guy's crazy life, and it just brings you a little joy. You look forward to it. Now, I won't have that anymore. Damn…I sound like Annie Wilkes from *Misery*."

"Annie Wilkes?" Shyla asked.

Nick smiled because he immediately understood Elaine's reference to the Stephen King novel. "Not at all. In fact, I was just explaining this to Shyla."

"You were?"

"Yeah, I was telling her that a character belongs to the reader as much as the writer. That it's an injustice when you are left without a satisfying conclusion."

"Exactly," Elaine said, bobbing her head with excitement.

Nick turned to Shyla, wanting to utter the famous and annoying "I told you so" statement. "See, your roommate totally gets it, sweetheart."

Shyla returned Nick's smile, crossing her arms. "Elaine, why don't you tell Nick what author you're referring to."

Elaine looked between the two of them. "Keegan Moon. Have you heard of him? He writes the Max Montero novels."

Nick's smile fell, and Shyla started laughing. "Ironic, don't you think?" Shyla asked, elbowing him.

"What?" Elaine said.

This conversation had definitely backfired on him. He should have kept his mouth shut. "Elaine, there will be more books. Or at least one more for sure."

Elaine shook her head. "I don't think so. I have it on good authority there won't."

"Trust me, there will."

"How do you know?" she asked.

He turned to Shyla who raised an eyebrow at him. "Because I'm Keegan Moon."

"What?" Elaine gasped, taking a step back and looking at him with great doubt as if Nick had told her he was Robinson Crusoe.

"It's true," Shyla offered. "Keegan Moon is his pseudonym."

Elaine was quiet for a minute.

"Elaine, are you okay?" Shyla asked.

Elaine smacked Nick on the chest so hard he took a step back. Damn, the girl was freakishly strong. A high-pitched shriek that hurt Nick's ears emanated from her. Thankfully, she punched Shyla more gently. "You've been dating fucking Keegan Moon, and you didn't tell me?"

Yes, they were both dating and fucking, thank you very much.

"First of all, ouch," Shyla said, rubbing her shoulder. "Secondly, yes I have."

"Holy shit, you have to sign my books," Elaine said, running over to her bed. She pulled out a basket full of books. "I'm your biggest fan ever."

"Okay, now you really do sound like Annie Wilkes," Nick said, feeling a little uncomfortable with the attention.

"Shyla, can you go down the hall to Marni's room?"

"Why?"

"She borrowed books four and five. I want him to sign the whole collection. Oh God, I will kill her if she bent the pages."

Shucks.

This was going to take all day, and he had no intention of wasting the time he had left with the girl he loved to autograph books. He turned to Shyla while Elaine was organizing her pile and searching for the perfect pen.

"Really?" Nick asked, lowering his voice.

"You can make her day," she whispered. "And trust me, she is a huge fan."

"I don't doubt that."

"Will you be okay?"

Nick laughed. "Of course, it's not like she's going to chop off my foot or anything." He leaned closer to Shyla, rubbing the back of his neck. "Is she?"

Clearly, Elaine possessed exemplary hearing because she answered. "Not now that you've told me there is another book."

Nick and Shyla gaped at her until Elaine burst out laughing. That laugh was almost villainous in nature.

Elaine narrowed her eyes. "Unless you tell me you're killing him off in the next book. You're not, are you?"

"Ah, it wasn't the plan," he replied, adjusting his collar.

She clapped her hands. "Excellent."

Nick's hand cramped as he took in the signing station set up on the desk.

"Can you make it out to your number one fan, Elaine?"

"Sure," Nick said, taking a seat at the desk.

"I can't believe Max Montero is in my dorm room."

"Um…just so we're clear, my name is Nick Dorsey. My penname is Keegan Moon, and the character is Max Montero."

"I know that. I'm your biggest fan, remember?"

"Of course." How could he forget?

"Shit, you look like how you describe him."

"Write what you know," Shyla said, squeezing his shoulder. "I'll be right back."

"Don't be too long," Nick replied. "I mean it." He heard Shyla's laughter even after she closed the door.

"Nick Dorsey… That name sounds familiar, too," Elaine said once Shyla left.

"Yes, I just introduced myself, remember?"

"No, but from somewhere else." Realization came over her features. "Hey you wrote a book under your real name, right?"

"Yes. *Irish Hold'em.*"

"Shyla loved that book. I remember her reading it last year."

"I think you're mistaken. I gave her a copy in February. She read it this year."

Elaine shook her head. "No, I'm sure it was quite a while ago. She must have read it like ten times. She lent it to me. I'm sorry. I just couldn't get into it."

Nick tried to dismiss what she said, but his heart pricked, and his gut screamed. "Are you sure of the timeline?"

"Yep," she said, opening a drawer. "I think you mean she bought the hardcover in February. See, she has it in paperback, too."

Elaine handed him the two books, the one he'd given Shyla and the other, a dog-eared copy, signaling the pages had been turned quite often. He flipped through it as if the book could provide answers. His body tensed as Elaine chattered on. If Shyla lied about this, how many other things were a lie? She'd played him, bluffing him like the bad hand he was.

"Excuse me, Elaine."

"Where are you going? I thought you were going to sign the books. I have so many questions for you, and we should take some pictures."

"A rain check," he said, heading toward the door. He had to leave.

All of the unease hit him at once. Every doubt and fear he had about their relationship surfaced at the same time, even the ones he'd reconciled in his mind. Unfortunately, his racing heart didn't give a fuck what his mind thought. She was lying that night when he tried to propose. She was lying about Charles Breckenridge. She was dishonest with him from that first day, creating an illusion, one a former junkie would cling to.

Gramp's advice came back to him. *You're smart enough to know that there is a sucker at every table, but I hope you'll be wise enough to realize that sometimes it's you.*

He reached the street just as Shyla called to him. "Nick, where are you going?" He turned to her, and she must have read his expression because she took a step back. She looked guilty.

"What's wrong?"

"You knew who I was when you came to my door. That I was an author." The expression on her face confirmed it. "Nick…"

"Why did you do it? Was it about money? Prestige?" She kept shaking her head, increasing his frustration. "Why? Fucking tell me why?"

"I told you I wasn't interested in that."

"Then you used me to further your own agenda, right? The plight of the Choice Less? Why me?"

She shook her head again. "You don't understand."

"Make me understand."

"There is more truth than fiction between us, I promise you. I…I wasn't trying to hurt you."

"Don't. Don't keep up the charade." He took a deep breath. "Just answer one question, and for God's sake, don't lie to me. Did you invite yourself into my house and my life because you were interested in me or because you wanted to write a book?"

She closed her eyes, her lower lip trembling. "Both."

He let go of her and turned.

"Wait! Don't go like this. You love me. Don't end us this way."

He turned back. "Love you? I don't even fucking *know* you."

She bowed her head, her shoulders lowered. She took his hand and squeezed it. "Maybe it's better if you hate me, but the story we wrote is good. Will you still give the book to Carrie?"

In that question, he accepted the rouse she'd played and his stupidity for believing they were something more. "You're wasting your talent.

You should stay in New York and become an actress. I swear I've never seen a better performance."

He walked away from her, justified in his anger. Happy to hold onto its security. Happy to hate her because, God knows, he loved her, too.

Chapter 34

Nick spent the next four days battling his own demons. Recovery was a precarious place, but he was determined not to go back to the person he was. She'd broken his heart, but he wasn't a weak man. He talked to his sponsor. He doubled up on meetings. He ran as if he was training for a marathon. Finally, he just escaped to Brooklyn.

He studied her last text message for the hundredth time. *I'm leaving at ten pm. I need to see you. I have to explain.*

He hit the delete button and brought up her pictures, ready to delete them as well. He got through the first two but paused at the third one, number *3* of *62*. Her hair was flying in wisps around her on the ship bound for Ellis Island. She looked strong, almost resilient, yet there was something fragile about her expression. How had she managed to trick him?

"Who is she, Uncle Nick?" Maya asked, peering behind his shoulder.

"No one," he said, his finger hovering above the delete button. The precocious child grabbed the phone from him. "She looks like Princess Jasmine."

"You think so?"

She nodded, holding the phone up as if Nick hadn't memorized every pixel of the photo. "Is she why you're sad?"

"How can I be sad when you're around, kid?" he asked, mussing the little girl's hair.

"I have to take Shakespeare for a walk. Will you come?"

"Sure."

The girl jumped up with great excitement, her smile revealing the slightest dimple on her right cheek. They walked the small puppy to the park.

"We should work on Shakespeare's story, Uncle Nick. Will you help me?"

He laughed because it seemed like the irony of his life was coming full circle. Another girl was asking for his assistance in writing a book.

"You're a good writer, Maya, and a great illustrator. You don't need my help."

Maya pouted as they stopped to let the dog do his business.

"Illustrator?" she asked, the word coming out like "ill traitor."

"Drawer. You're a great drawer."

"My moms say that, too."

"They're smart women. Hey, you have to keep writing the stories because I can't wait for the next installation of Shakespeare's adventures."

"Can you do the yucky part?" she asked him, pointing to the remnants the dog left.

"No wonder you asked me along," Nick said, taking the plastic bag from her.

It was a full day, but Nick had spent most of it checking his watch, counting down the minutes. *It'll be easier not to think of her when she's far away.*

"I finally got Maya to bed," Carrie said.

"Yeah, it's more difficult when someone gives her candy an hour before bedtime," Tara said, a mock look of indignation aimed at Nick.

"Hey, I'm the cool uncle. I have a reputation to protect."

Carrie opened a bottle of wine and poured three glasses. "I should be going," Nick said.

"It's early. Besides, I think you should talk about it," Tara said, passing him the glass of wine.

"There is nothing to talk about. It didn't work out. She wasn't the girl I thought she was. I know that you are both concerned I will rely on my old methods to get me through this, but I assure you, I won't."

"We know that," Carrie said. She placed her hand over his. "But you are hurting something deep. We're here for you."

"What happened, Nick?" Tara, the blunter half of the couple asked him. "It was very clear to me the night of the benefit she cared for you."

He almost choked on the wine. "She used me."

"For what?" Carrie asked.

"To write the book."

"That doesn't sound right," Tara said.

"I have trouble with it, too, but she lied to me. The deception speaks for itself. Even if her feelings changed, our relationship was based on deceit and dishonesty. How can I trust all of the other things that happened between us? Really, it doesn't matter anyway because even if I could forgive her, she's leaving." He checked his watch. "In about sixty-two minutes."

"What was the book about?" Carrie asked.

"It doesn't matter."

"She told me it was about a girl growing up in rural India," Tara offered.

Nick sighed, deciding to give them some insights. "It has some dark themes…about the trials of a young girl. Her lack of choices, even when it came down to keeping her baby."

"I wanted to read it before but that makes me even more intrigued," Tara said.

Nick tried not to react with annoyance. "Why?"

"Because of Maya. She was adopted from India," Tara said barely above a whisper.

"What?" he asked. "I had no idea."

"Keep your voice down. She doesn't know either," Carrie explained. "We've discussed it. We'll tell her, but right now, she's dealing with so much we want to wait until she is older."

Nick nodded, his fingers clasping tightly around the wine flute, his disgust with Maya's father surfacing. He'd met Tara through Carrie, but he'd heard the stories. He couldn't understand how any man could reject his child.

"Why did you adopt, Tara?" he asked, not only because he was naturally curious but also he wanted to desperately change the topic of conversation. How did he end up being best friends with two girls? They were no good at helping him through this misery with their insistence on talking out feelings and crap.

"My husband and I couldn't have children. The adoption was my idea. I wanted a girl from India. He never really approved of it, and I think that's part of the reason he found it so easy to be absent from her life."

"Don't make any excuses for him, Tara. He's pathetic, and really he's the one who lost out because you have an amazing daughter. But it's better this way because she has two kickass moms."

The two women smiled at each other. "It's funny how life works out," Tara said.

"What do you mean?"

She took a deep breath. "I don't think we would have gotten Maya if it was Carrie and I that showed up that day in the hospital."

"A hospital?"

"She was a preemie and had some health issues. I remember thinking it would be an easy process, but there was this nun there, and she asked us a million questions. You could tell she loved Maya and—"

Nick's wine glass broke in his hand. That feeling of unease grew to depths he didn't think were possible.

"What was her name?"

"Are you all right?" Carrie asked, standing to pick up the mess.

He swallowed. "Fine," he said, keeping his eyes locked on Tara's. "What was the nun's name, Tara?"

Tara looked confused. "What's going on, Nick?"

"Please try to remember. It's important."

"She introduced herself as Sister Mountain. She was a French-Canadian nun living in India. I can't remember her first name, but I always thought that was interesting."

Nick swallowed, the blood draining from his face. Shyla's words echoed in his head. *My name means daughter of the mountain.*

"Sister Sarah Mountain, right?"

Tara's body stiffened. "How did you know?" Then she clapped her hand over her mouth.

Oh dear God, how did he miss it? All the signs became obvious at once. Maya had a heart-shaped birthmark on her right arm. Maya had dimples.

He stood up, glass falling from his lap. "I have to go."

"Where are you going?" Carrie asked. "What's going on?"

"I have to find Shyla."

Tara gasped, realization washing over her. "Nick, it can't be... I mean, that's impossible."

"Is it impossible or just improbable?" Nick asked, wishing Tara could answer him.

"I don't understand," Carrie said. "What am I missing?"

"I'll explain later," Tara said. She took Nick's hand. "I think you need answers, Nick. We all do. Go."

He looked around at the shards of glass. "I'm sorry."

"It's an omen," Tara said. "It means good luck. Go."

Nick hopped into a cab. As it made its way through traffic, he took out his phone and gaped at her photo once more. It was like seeing it for the first time. There had always been this depth to her, and in this picture, he saw it more clearly than ever. She was...stoic. His mind's image of the young girl he'd written about and the real image of the girl he'd fallen in love with merged into one.

Her words came back to him with haunting clarity. *There is more truth than fiction between us.* He leaned forward, cursing at the traffic. "Whatever it says on that meter, I'll pay you triple if you can get me there in twenty minutes or less."

Chapter 35

She'd gone to Nick's apartment once more and waited for him far longer than she should have. The confusion and guilt hammered away at her. She hadn't eaten or slept in four days. But it was too late now. She cursed the long lines and getting to the airport late. At least her flight was delayed. She waited to check in, trying to make herself so small she'd disappear.

The counter lady had a perky smile that soured her mood further.

"Oh dear, you're running very late to check in for an international flight."

"I know."

"You'll have to hurry to the gate. It'll be a sprint, young lady."

"Okay."

"Better start stretching now," she said, jabbing at her keyboard with skilled dexterity. Shyla lifted her huge suitcase on the machine. Surprised by its weight, she rubbed her shoulders. That suitcase represented her four years here, but it mostly contained mementos from the past five months. All of Nick's books were in there. Everything he'd written. She'd packed the French press, the few T-shirts of his she had, the outfit he'd bought her, and a few records they'd found on one of their scavenger expeditions. As heavy as it was, it was insignificant to the massive heartache in her chest.

"Shyla!"

She darted her head, searching for the owner of that deep voice. "Nick?"

He was out of breath, his hair sticking up in every direction. "Thank God, I found you. I need to talk to you."

"Almost done," the clerk said, her smile turning suspicious as she glanced at Nick just beyond the roped barricade of the line.

"I'm checking in," Shyla said to him, pointing to the clerk as if it wasn't obvious. The other passengers in the long winding queue looked back and forth between them.

His hand clasped the plastic straps that separated them. "Don't check in."

"I have to," she said.

"She has to," the clerk responded. "She'll miss her flight."

"Miss it," Nick said.

"Excuse me, but some of us have planes to catch," a sour-faced women said to Nick. "You're holding up the line, young man."

Nick didn't look away from Shyla when he answered the interrupting woman. "Lady, I'll hold up the world right now."

"My visa is expiring. I'll be deported or arrested," Shyla said. "It's too late."

"If you make me follow you around the world, I will, but it's not too late. I did the math. You have another six weeks on that visa. There's another flight in nine hours. I'm just asking for the next nine hours. You owe me that."

Everyone was looking at them now. She turned to the attendant who was punching the keyboard energetically. "He's right," the attendant confirmed.

She turned to him. "Nick, I have to go home. I'll write you."

"I don't want a damn letter. I need to talk to you." He swallowed and closed his eyes. "Asha."

Her back stiffened. She leaned against the counter for support before her knees gave out completely.

"Your passport says Shyla?" the attendant said, arching her manicured brow.

"It's a nickname," she responded nervously. She took her passport before the woman could stamp it. "I'm not going to be on this flight."

She rolled her suitcase through the throng of passengers. Some sighed or muttered under their breaths. One woman elbowed her husband and said something about romance not being dead.

Nick followed her, grabbing her suitcase and lifting it over the roped barricade as if it contained feathers.

He met her at the end of the line…or rather the beginning of it.

"I don't think you should draw so much attention to me right before I board an international flight," she whispered.

He took her arm and led her toward the exit. "I had no choice."

He placed her bag inside a waiting cab and ushered her inside before she could even respond.

"You know?" she asked.

"You're Maya's real mother?"

She nodded. The affirmation provided both relief and tension.

"How much of it is true?"

She clasped her hands together so they wouldn't shake. "All of it."

Chapter 36

She sat at the table where they had started so long ago with her simple request to share his space and his company. His movements were those of a cautious man, both restrained and distant. Somehow, the few feet seemed as wide as the Pacific, or perhaps The Indian Ocean was a better analogy.

"Asha Mistry?" he asked in a low voice.

"It's Shyla now. Asha did die at the riverbank that day."

Nick was quiet for a long time, his posture completely rigid. His hand gripped the neck of a wine bottle so hard his knuckles turned white. A gamut of emotions flickered over his face. Hurt, surprise, betrayal and then the anger came as he sucked in a deep breath between clenched teeth. Except this anger wasn't directed at her.

"He did all of those things to you?" He stood and walked the length of the room in frantic circles to the point of making her dizzy. "He hit you, he hurt you, oh my God, he raped you...many times." Each word seemed to represent a new revelation for Nick.

"I never said no."

"Did you have a choice?"

She shook her head.

"He almost killed you."

He hadn't looked well at the airport, but now he had transformed into a deeper state of unwell as the minutes ticked by. His sparkling blue eyes were flat. The tilt of his mouth formed a tight line. His skin was overly pale and the dark circles under his eyes more pronounced.

"I survived. I had a great deal of help, but I'm here. I'm not afraid of him anymore, Nick."

"This is difficult for me. I'm trying to reconcile the character you created...the one I wrote about was really you." His voice strained into a soft whisper. "I...I can't believe all those fucked up things really happened to you. I don't want to believe it."

"Yes, that's my fault. I've been telling the truth and lying to you, too. You said you didn't know me the other day, but the truth is you know everything about me. All of the ugly things I've never been able to share with anyone else." She smiled at him, trying to comfort him because he looked as if he was in pain. And she realized he was. "I've been talking about myself this whole time…in third person, no less. Your biggest pet peeve." He didn't laugh.

"There is nothing ugly about you, but you're wrong. I don't know everything."

"I tried to explain it to you that day, but I was so ashamed of what I'd done and the complications I'd created. I didn't want you to hate me. And I didn't want to fall in love with you either. But both of those things happened, didn't they?"

"I need to know everything."

"I don't even know where to start."

"Start at the last chapter. The real last chapter, and then tell me what happened after that."

She lifted her head, her eyes bloodshot and her lips quivering. "And then?"

"Then we'll figure out what happens next…together."

She nodded slowly, her shoulder lifting slightly. "Okay."

There were no legal pads for taking notes or recorders. There was just him and her. She took in a deep breath, wondering if the air had left the room. He poured two glasses of wine. He stood back, offering her a sad smile. "Would you prefer juice?"

The silly question relaxed her. "The wine is good. Leave the bottle at the table, please."

"I planned to."

Chapter 37

The Choice Less—the real last chapter

Asha thought she was dead, except death couldn't be this painful. Her skull felt as if it had been ripped open, her back throbbed, and her skin burned like someone held a torch to it. She couldn't even breathe, but her ears worked. She heard the boy's cries and felt him squeezing her hand.

She blinked her eyes awake and kept blinking until Mukash came into focus.

Sister Sarah wiped her forehead. "Mukash found you and brought you here." The nun's lips quivered. "We almost lost you."

She tried to respond, but her throat wouldn't cooperate.

"Don't talk. There's a tube to help you breathe. Mukash, you should go home. Your family will be looking for you."

A newfound fear gripped her. She tried to remove the tube, but Sarah stopped her. "Calm down, child. You're safe. They think you're dead."

Sarah looked at Mukash with admiration. "Don't make me leave," he pled. "I've been waiting three days for her to get up. They won't even realize I'm gone."

"Mukash is a very brilliant boy," Sarah said. It was a fact Asha already knew.

Mukash smiled proudly. "After I brought you here, I took your sari and ripped pieces from it and laid them down in the water with some strands of your hair. Everyone assumed you'd drowned. Aditi thinks he killed you so he called the search off quickly. He's scared they will find evidence against him."

"Come back tomorrow after school, Mukash," Sarah said, tousling the boy's head. He nodded, kissing Asha on the cheek before leaving.

Asha reached for the tube again, this time not letting Sarah push her hands away. Her voice came out raspy, the words inaudible. "Where am I?"

Sarah embraced her. "We're in a city hospital far from the village. The people here have been paid well not to reveal your identity."

Her body shivered, tears streaming down her face.

"Dear girl, don't waste your energy crying. You have nothing to fear now."

It took a few minutes to find her voice between the painful swallows. "I'm not crying because I'm afraid," she choked.

"Then why?"

She spoke the words, knowing the woman who loved her so much, who had sacrificed and put herself in danger for her, would be incredibly hurt by them, but she didn't care anymore. "I'm crying because I wanted to die. You should have honored my wishes."

* * * *

She stayed in the hospital for a week, recuperating and getting stronger.

"Why did you want to die, child?" Sarah asked her, sitting on the edge of the hospital bed.

"I still do. Present tense, Sister."

"Enough. I won't stand for this. It's a sin."

Asha laughed. "A sin? What about the other sins? I've had everything taken away from me in this life. I've been tortured in every way a person can be. What good is any of it? I have nothing left to fight for."

"There has to be something."

Asha was quiet so long the sun dipped and the room grew dark. Sarah remained patient, praying silently while waiting for the answer. Asha hated herself even more for making Sarah cry. For hurting Mukash. But she was a weak girl who had forgotten how to live.

"I want my daughter back," she whispered with quiet conviction.

Sarah turned on the harsh bedside light, causing both women to adjust their eyes. The nun shook her head. "She's with people who love her."

"Who better to raise her than her own flesh and blood? You asked me what I would live for, and the answer is her. It wasn't my choice to give her up. My sacrifice wasn't a choice."

"If you had an opportunity to get her back, would you regain your will?"

Hope flooded through Asha. Even in her unconsciousness, she'd held steadfast to the memory of the little girl holding her hand. "Yes."

"Rest now. I need to tend to some things."

Sarah came back a few hours later. She looked tired. Her usually clear features were sunken and her posture slumped. She'd lost so much weight her skin sagged. Asha chided herself for not noticing sooner. "Sarah, are you all right?"

"Fine," she said, waving her hand in dismissal. "You'll be fine too, honey. I've arranged for you to leave on a train later tonight."

Asha sat up in the bed. "You'll take me to my baby?"

"Not yet. She's very far. It'll take some time to organize the details, but we need to get you away from here. There's a chance someone from the village might see you."

"Where will I go?"

"A very good friend is going to help us. You're going to meet him in Mumbai."

"Mumbai?" It sounded like Mars to Asha. "It's so far, and it's a huge city."

"All the better to get lost in. You'll be safe there. You must listen to everything Charles tells you."

"I have to say good-bye to Mukash." As she thought of it, she suddenly wondered how she was going to leave the boy. "Can he come?"

"Absolutely not. What's more, he wouldn't want to. You know he loves the farm."

Asha nodded, wiping her tears.

"He wants this for you, honey. He can take care of himself."

Sarah was right. His family mostly ignored him now, his mother's attentions solely focused on her eldest son.

* * * *

Asha arrived in Mumbai on a rainy Tuesday. Charles Breckenridge sent a servant to pick her up. She had read stories about the city, but the sights and sounds of the crowded streets invaded her senses. But it was the smell, a pungent aroma of opulence and decay, she'd never forget.

Charles was a cold man. He spoke in clipped tones as he showed her around his luxurious flat in the center of the city.

"I'm still moving in myself," he said, opening doors as he walked briskly thought the rooms. "You will stay here. I have hired tutors for you."

"Why, sir?"

"There are huge gaps in your education we need to fill. Don't call me sir. Call me Charles. You are not my maid, nor my employee."

"Sir, I mean Charles, I don't understand."

"You want to see your daughter, don't you?"

"Yes."

"As it turns out, she's in America."

Asha cupped her hand to her mouth. Her little girl was living across the world from her? She would have paused to take in his shocking statement, but Charles kept talking as if he hadn't said anything remarkable. She sped up her steps to keep up to him.

"As someone who has no family or ties in the States, the easiest way to get you into the country is through a student visa. My legal counsel advises this is a battle best fought on Yankee soil. You'll have more sway as a legal resident. You'll also have an airtight identity. It's important you get used to your new name." She started to bow to him, the sign of respect, but he stopped her. "Use your words." His voice registered annoyance.

"Thank you." It was such a simple sentiment, but she didn't know how else to express her deep gratitude.

"I daresay, you should prepare yourself. You require a great deal of work. This won't be easy. If this is something you truly want, I'd suggest you learn how to absorb information like a sponge because we barely have a six month time frame until the next round of standardized testing comes."

Each question was difficult for her. She'd never spoken openly to a man, let alone a white, rich man. Charles Breckenridge had no patience for her coyness. "Don't look down when you address me. If you have a question, you look me in the eyes."

She lifted her head, feeling the weight of it—a lifetime of subservience manifesting itself in the simple gesture. "What will happen when I get to America?"

"You'll go to college. I'll finance you and give you a monthly stipend. I suppose that is the easy part, but you will have to work with diligence and efficiency."

"How will this help me get my daughter back?"

"There are ways to dispute if the adoption was legitimate. Understand this, girl, Sarah did some illegal things to give your daughter a good life. We will have to expose those things to get her back."

Asha's heart wrenched at placing Sister Sarah in jeopardy. "What will happen to Sarah?"

"That's not your concern, but I assure you it won't matter. Timing is everything, as they say." His stern face yielded to a softer, sad expression.

He showed her the library and her bedroom. The marble floors, four-poster bed, and shelves lined with books looked like a sheik's private quarters. She'd never slept so high up from the ground. What if she fell from the bed?

Charles led her to an office. "And this is where you'll be studying. I will oversee your education personally, but I'm not a teacher. You will have the best tutors money can buy. I should know. I'm footing the bill." He walked her back to a large dining room. Charles rang a bell on the polished wood table. "Now then, let's have some tea."

He regarded her with horror when she attempted to sit on the floor in the corner of the room. "Oh dear God, this is going to be more difficult than I predicted." He shook his head. "Either you sit at the table with me, or you don't sit at all."

She swallowed, trying to keep her composure and hide the anger quaking inside her. She did as he asked…but on her terms. She stood while drinking her tea, keeping her back ramrod straight the whole time. For some reason, this amused Charles.

"You are quite something."

"What do you mean…sir…Charles?"

"You're subservient and rebellious at the same time. What an interesting combination."

Charles was wise enough to realize Asha needed to overcome some serious psychological issues, but he was also smart enough to appreciate he wasn't the man for the job. He hired a therapist along with the tutors. He also paid for expensive plastic surgery and cosmetic dentists so she would have no reminders of her vicious past…at least not physical ones. In many ways, though, it was Charles's unrelenting attitude that helped Asha the most. Even when he angered her, which was often, she gained more confidence with each exchange.

She both feared and admired Charles, although he seemed to hold disdain for her. She missed Sarah and Mukash, so she threw herself into her studies, craving the distraction, determined to meet her goals. Some days, she would work for sixteen hours, pausing only to eat and sleep. A mutual respect grew between Charles and her, although Asha would never describe their relationship as friendly. It took a whole month for her to look him in the eye. And another month after that for her to hold a conversation without his prodding. And yet another month for her to freely express her opinions and debate him.

She marched toward the dining table. "Why are you making me go shopping with Sita?" she asked on the first day of the fourth month.

Charles sighed, pinching the bridge of his nose, his irritation evident. "You need new clothes, and as I recall, the last time I told you to buy some, you used the money to purchase items for homeless children instead." She shifted her head down in guilt, but his next statement prickled her skin. "You look like a poor village girl."

"I *am* a poor village girl." She jutted her chin, an act of pride and defiance.

"I am charged with the task of turning you into a strong, educated woman—you can be both. In fact, you must be both. You need to leave the house more and get comfortable in groups. Sita is your age, and she's well educated. You have to learn social skills."

"I am polite."

"I agree, but you are polite in a way which makes you appear feeble and inferior. I guarantee you won't last a Mumbai minute in New York City with that attitude."

"I am social, too."

He laughed, folding his newspaper. "Playing with guttersnipes is not what I had in mind."

"You are a mean man, Charles."

"Good God, she has an opinion. I'm delighted to see, despite your many limitations, you are at least observant."

She balled her fists, finally finding the courage to ask the one question she desperately needed the answer to. "Why are you doing this for me? You don't seem to like me very much."

He sighed, narrowing his grey eyes. "Correction, I don't like you at all. You've been a proverbial thorn in my side for eighteen years."

"I don't understand."

He took a seat at the dining table and called for tea. "I suppose there is no harm in telling you. Sit."

Asha sat across from him, her eyes darting around the room nervously. She'd had many conversations with him, but never one so personal.

"I will wait until you can look at me. I thought we were past this."

She folded her arms.

"Don't expect me to feel sorry for you, Asha. Pity, much like charity, begins at home."

"I don't want your pity or your charity."

"I admire your disgust for the prior, but you absolutely do need the latter."

"You have my gratitude, but you will need to earn my friendship."

He chuckled, a rare sound for him. "What makes you think I want it?"

"You're lonely and sad. It's made you cruel."

He nodded and was quiet for a long time. Asha wondered if perhaps he forgot what he was going to say.

"I do admire you, Asha. You've been through a great deal. Your strength is tangible."

"That's hard to believe coming from you."

"Do you think I'm artificial in my compassion?"

"I don't think you're all that compassionate to begin with…artificial or otherwise."

Charles chuckled again. "I deserve that. I am sorry." The statement was simple, but Asha felt the weight of it. Charles was not a man who apologized with pretense.

"Thank you." For the first time since she'd arrived, she smiled.

"You don't remember me, do you? I once complimented your English."

"I remember you, but I wasn't sure if it was appropriate to mention it. I've changed a great deal from the little girl you met." The image of him kissing Sarah all those years ago swept through her mind once again.

"We've all changed, dear. I first came to India as a young lad with equal quantities of optimism and stupidity. I was here to look after my family's hotels and the charity my father founded, which funded schools in third world countries. That's where I met Sarah."

Asha wondered how someone as kindhearted as Sarah would ever be friends with this man, but his harsh features softened as he spoke. Tenderness came into his eyes as he talked about Sarah. "I don't know what's stranger…that I was in a love triangle with God, or the fact I won."

"You loved Sarah?"

"No…I love Sarah. You may be able to plug up a dam, but the water still rages behind it. She loves me, too. She was going to leave the convent to marry me. We had it all planned."

"What happened?"

Asha had never seen the great Charles Breckenridge look so unsure of himself, so she repeated the question.

"A baby in a box washed up on a riverbank. Sarah said God spoke to her and told her she should take care of this child."

Asha's heart pounded in her chest as she digested his statement.

"I never realized the sacrifices she made for me. I was unkind to her. Charles, I know I can't contact her, but I have to tell her how much I love her." Asha had once sworn she would make Charles Breckenridge pay for Sarah's tears. She now realized she'd already done that a long time ago.

"No worries, love. You'll get your opportunity. She's coming here."

Asha smiled, relief flooding her. "She's leaving the convent then? She is coming to be with you?"

"Not in the way I intended."

"What do you mean?"

The circles under his eyes deepened as he took a deep breath. He appeared to have aged since he'd started the story. "She's dying. She has cancer."

Asha froze, her heart wrenching with his statement. "Surely something can be done for her. You have so much money."

His voice strained. "Don't you think I insisted on the best medical care? I even flew out my personal doctor to view her test results. There is no hope. She's coming here because she wants to spend her last days with her family. For Sarah, that's you and me." His voice cracked, the cold façade of Charles Breckenridge disappeared before Asha's eyes, and she saw the real man, the one who loved Sarah so much he'd waited for her all these years. He'd even taken care of the girl who was the cause of his misery. "We are her family, and therefore we are tied to each other. I want to hate you, but I cannot."

He took out a neatly pressed handkerchief. He moved to wipe his own eyes, but paused. Instead, he wiped her tears.

She hugged him, the tears coming so hard that a simple handkerchief wasn't enough. Charles acted surprised at first, as if he'd never been embraced, which was a possibility. He hugged her back. They cried for a long time, both grieving for the woman they loved.

* * * *

Sarah came to Mumbai, much like Asha, on a rainy Tuesday afternoon.

She'd lost a few stone. Her hair had fallen out, and her skin sagged on her bones like loose clothing. Charles insisted on carrying her into the house. In fact, he took the brunt of responsibilities when it came to Sarah's care, even though he'd hired additional staff for that purpose. He did everything to make her last days comfortable. He'd even had his gardener plant all her favorite flowers so she could gaze upon them from her bedroom window. Asha and Charles took turns watching over her. At night, Asha read to Sarah from her three favorite books.

"Asha, put the book away," Sarah said one evening. "Let's have a chat."

Asha closed the novel. "I have to say some things to you too, Sister. Are you sure you're well enough?"

Sarah chuckled, which turned into a serious cough. Asha held the plastic bucket for her and rubbed her back. "I'm not well enough, but I don't think waiting is wise."

Asha set the bucket down. "All right, as you wish."

"Charles tells me you received an excellent score on the standardized test."

"Yes, it's good enough for New York University. Charles says it's a top school."

"It is. I'm incredibly proud of you."

Asha tried to smile, but her heart wouldn't let her. Instead, she placed her head in her hands to hide her weeping from Sarah.

"Now now, none of that. I've had a good life."

"It's not just that, Sarah."

"Then why, dear?"

"I am so ashamed. I don't deserve all of the things you've done for me. I've never appreciated them."

Sarah shifted to a seated position. Asha tried to help her, but she waved the girl away. "Don't ever say that...don't think it." Sarah's green eyes grew wistful as she took Asha's hand. "They say love at first sight is a ridiculous notion, but I know it to be a true phenomenon."

"Because of Charles?" Asha asked.

"No, child, because of you. The moment I saw you, I knew my purpose and so did Nalini."

Asha swallowed back the lump in her throat, willing herself to speak the words she'd been holding since Sarah's arrival. "I used to think the Gods hated me. The river, the box, the knife were meant to kill me just as my real parents intended. I always felt like an imposter—an unwanted girl. I realize now how blessed I am because I was given not one, but two mothers."

Sarah's smile was strong despite her illness. "You're right my sweet, brave girl. You are my daughter, too. Now it's your turn to make a choice as a mother. What will you do when you get to New York?"

"Charles has some contacts there—barristers."

"They call them attorneys in the states, honey. You must learn the terminology."

"Yes, attorneys."

"I want you to think about this and pray on it. Your daughter has a life and parents who love her. She'll be three when you get there. You'll have to decide if you want to take her from the life she lives now and drag her through a court case that could take years."

"You think it's selfish?"

"Only you can answer your question, dear one. I have no doubt you'll make the right decision on her best interests. That's what a mother does. That's what your mother and I tried to do for you, even though we disagreed sometimes."

"I understand, Sister."

"Will you do something else for me?"

"Anything."

"I want you to enjoy yourself. To be carefree for once, but I also want you to get your education and come back here to continue my work."

Asha's shoulders stiffened with panic. "You want me to be a nun? I'm Hindu."

Sarah laughed. "No, dear heart, you don't have to be a nun to do good work. Many girls here need guidance. Who better to teach them than you?"

"Mother, I will make you proud."

"Daughter, you *do* make me proud."

Chapter 38

The first rays of sun peeked through the clouds. The empty wine bottle sat between them. Nick had listened to her with his full attention. Now, Shyla stood to stretch her legs. Her body confirmed she'd sat there for hours replaying the most intimate details of her life to him, but in her mind the time sped by with no rational measurement. He hadn't said a single word, his face revealing sorrow and sympathy, but he never interrupted her...not once.

"Sarah died a month after I got here."

"I'm sorry."

She clasped her hands together. "That's the whole story, Nick. How I went from unwanted girl to the luckiest girl on earth, from child bride to college student, from victim to survivor. You know it all."

"It's unbelievable, and yet I should have guessed at some point. There were clues something was off, but I didn't want to acknowledge it."

"How could you have? I deceived you. I'll never be able to apologize enough."

"I didn't put it together because the girl who could go through such traumatic events didn't seem like the same girl who asked to share my space that first night." He sucked in a deep breath. "You were so...brave."

"I was trying to protect my child. It's what a mother does."

"Not all mothers do that."

She understood he referred to his own. Her heart wrenched for him. "I would have been another statistic if it wasn't for the people in my life. It's because of Nalini, Sarah, Mukash, and Charles that I'm here. But it was you, Nick, who taught me how to laugh and what it means to be alive."

"Why didn't you file for custody of Maya?"

"I did as Sarah asked. I watched Maya from a careful distance. When I first saw she was being raised by two women, I was shocked...maybe even disturbed. It didn't take long for me to realize what a happy childhood she had and how much her mothers love her." Shyla smiled, recalling the memories. "She takes dance classes, American and Indian. She goes to temple and church. Recently, she got this cute dog with floppy ears. She walks him every day with her mothers."

"I bought her that dog."

"I should have guessed." Shyla nodded, a weak smile on her lips. "I couldn't take her away from everything she knew and all the people who loved her. It was the hardest decision of my life, but at least I had a choice in it, and for that, I am grateful. I realized, just like me, Maya is also blessed to have two mothers."

"Do you want to see her?"

She bit her lower lip. "At one point I did, but I don't want to confuse her. Maybe someday...but not now."

"Why did you ask me to help you?"

"I stayed here because of my promise to Sarah to get a proper education. I threw myself into school. But I still watched Maya whenever I could. I was waiting for any sign of distress in her life, but none ever came. I saw you one day at the park. You were teaching her how to fly a kite."

"I remember that day."

"I wondered what your relationship was to my daughter and their mothers, but I put it out of my mind. And then a few years later, you started ordering sandwiches from the deli."

"I see."

She wrung her hands together. "I don't think you do. I believe things happen for a reason. I decided this was some kind of sign. You had a connection to Maya and now to me. It was a stretch, but I grasped onto it. I looked you up that night by your real name. The one on your sandwich order. I swear I didn't know about the Keegan Moon novels."

"I believe you. Your reaction was too priceless when I told you."

"I saw the other book, though. The one about your grandfather, and I purchased it. Although I wasn't honest about not having heard of it, I did tell you the truth when I said I loved it. I kept thinking about your book and rereading it. I'd accepted that I wouldn't get involved in Maya's life. Still, I thought there had to be some way to leave her the legacy of her heritage. My time here was growing short. I didn't want her to wonder about me. About her origins as I so often do about mine. I wanted her to have the truth...the good, bad, and ugly of it all. But how could I do that? She's so young. She wouldn't understand. Naturally, Carrie and Tara would be hesitant to let me into their lives."

"So you used me for that purpose?"

"No, it wasn't like that. I got the idea to write a book for my daughter based on yours long before I asked to share your space. I wanted it to be honest and real."

"It is. You didn't sugarcoat anything. It's a gruesome account."

"Her birth certificate shows the village name. There are clues she could trace back if she ever wanted to know the truth. I didn't want her to go in search of it. I never wanted her to meet… her father. Also, I know better than anyone how she might feel when she found out. I wanted to answer all those questions for her, no matter how horrific the answers were. I tried doing it myself, but it came out like rubbish each time. When you asked me what my dreams were, I blurted it out, not even thinking of the consequences."

"Why didn't you just tell me the truth? I would have found out once Carrie and Tara read the book."

"I didn't think it all through. Showing it to Carrie was your idea, not mine. I just wanted to write my memoirs to my daughter. In the end, I felt if Carrie and Tara read the story, they would be more receptive. I should have told you, Nick, but I wanted to keep the two things separate. You never looked at me with pity, and I never wanted you to. I thought we could be a fling, a sweet memory we could each hold onto. I wanted to know what it meant to be with a kind man. One who made me feel like an equal and treated me compassionately. It was too easy to fall in love with you. I couldn't stand for you to hate me for my dishonesty. I considered telling you so many times, but the deeper we got, the more difficult it became."

"You do love me then?"

She held herself back from touching him, but she could not hold back the cracking of her voice. "With everything I am, Nick Dorsey."

"Will you be in danger when you go back?" he asked, his jaw clenching.

"From Aditi? No, I'll be teaching far away from my village. Charles is building a school for me to run. It's a school for mistreated girls."

"What happened to them?" Nick didn't say her family, and for that she was grateful. Except for her little brother, they weren't her family.

"They think I'm dead. Charles pays for village gossip. My mother-in-law is going mad, some form of dementia. Aditi married again. His new wife cannot bear him a son either. I worry for Mukash, but Charles tells me he has taken over more duties at the farm and manages to make a small profit. He's saved my life more than once. I can never repay the debt I owe him."

"It's *our* debt," Nick said. He stood and walked around the room. "His bravery is the stuff of legend."

She dropped her head in her hands, her shoulders shaking. "I love you, Nick. I wish to God I could change what happened between us. Make it right. I wanted to bring you happiness, not misery. You told me I was your muse, but you…you are my joy."

His shadow fell against her. Nick's fingers threaded though her hair. She lifted her head to meet his eyes. He took her arms, pulling her out of the chair and against his chest in a tight embrace. "How can I be mad at you, Goddess? The Gods brought us together because we needed each other. Maybe we never planned for the path to lead us to this place, but I'm glad we're here…together." He tilted her chin and kissed her forehead. "It's difficult for me to digest it all. You've had so much pain in your life." He wiped the tear from her cheek. "But please believe me when I say I will never regard you with pity…only awe. When I look at you, I don't see a broken girl. I see a hero. I see a Goddess. I see a goddamn miracle." His voice choked on the last sentence, a single tear falling from his eye, which she wiped away. She leaned against him, closing her eyes. The beat of his heart comforted her despite its rapid melody.

She released a deep breath, one so long she may have been holding it since the airport. "Nine hours wasn't enough time. There will never be enough time for us, will there?"

"I don't want nine hours anymore, sweetheart. I want the next ninety-nine years…longer if possible."

She blinked her eyes in confusion and swallowed the large lump in her throat. "I have to go back. It's the promise I made to Sarah and my personal vow. I love you with all that I am, but I cannot stay here."

He placed a hand on each side of her face and drew her in for a deep kiss. He was smiling, the first real smile she'd seen since he picked her up. "Anything in this vow about me not being able to come with you?"

Shyla's mouth gaped as his words sunk in. She didn't trust the emotions rushing through her. "I can't ask you to do that. You love living here. This is your home."

"You're going to fight a difficult battle. You'll need help. Didn't Kali's husband support her in battle and make her strong?"

"Yes."

"That's what I will do for you."

She allowed herself a smile. For the first time, her heart filling with the possibilities that their story didn't have to end at all. "You don't even like Indian food."

He laughed, picking her up and spinning her around. "I'll learn. I told you I had so much to teach you, but it's you who has taught me about compassion and hope and what it means to love somebody. I don't want to stop learning. My home is where you are." He cleared his throat. "We're going to try this again." Nick grasped her by the shoulders and guided her to the middle of the room.

He walked around her in slow circles.

"What are you doing, Nick?" she asked, turning as he rounded her.

He fell in front of her feet after the third rotation. "Shyla, I would go around the universe for you. You are my world, after all. I would climb the highest water tower, cross every ocean and continent, and remove every obstacle in my path—in our path—to be with you. I don't deserve you, but luckily, I'm selfish enough that I don't care. I love you. Will you marry me?"

Chapter 39

Nick and Shyla—The real last chapter

Nick never imagined being married, but then he'd never imagined a girl like her would step into his life. Their wedding, like all weddings in India, was a celebrated event. Despite Nick and Shyla's objections, Charles Breckenridge insisted on paying for the festivities, stating Shyla was the closest thing to a daughter he'd ever have.

The guest list was small since there were only a few special friends they wanted in attendance. Carrie, Tara, and Maya were there. Elaine and her boyfriend had taken the long trip as well. Then there were the people they both loved who were there in spirit—Nalini, Sarah, and his grandpa. His only regret was that his bride wanted her little brother there. But after much debate with Charles, they'd all agreed that, although he knew she was alive, it would be too great a risk to invite Mukash.

The day was a joyous one. The guests commented they had never seen a husband look upon his bride with such reverence. Of course, the bride was stunning in the traditional red marriage sari, every inch of her adorned with jewels and decoration. Her hands were adorned with the traditional henna, but the design was unique. She'd chosen a tree, the lines on her fingers darkened to represent the branches, her new initials hanging from those branches like leaves.

A scarf tied her sari to his suit, symbolizing their eternal bond. They walked the seven steps to signify the beginning of their journey through life together. Each step represented a sacred vow to each other.

First step: To respect and honor the other
Second step: To share in each other's joy and sorrow
Third step: To trust and be loyal always
Fourth step: To always strive for knowledge
Fifth step: To confirm their vow of family duties and spiritual growth

Sixth step: To follow principles of righteousness

Seventh step: To nurture the unbreakable bonds of friendship and love

When it was over, Nick smiled at his wife. "Will you marry me again, Goddess?"

"I would marry you a thousand times."

"Once more is enough. We need to get on with it. Our bridal bed awaits."

Shyla made her way over to Maya and crouched next to the girl. He choked back the wave of emotion at the sight. They had discussed it with Carrie and Tara. Together, they had agreed one day they would tell Maya the truth, but that day was far into the future. For now, Shyla did have a place in Maya's life as Aunt Shyla, the woman who married cool Uncle Nick.

"You look like a princess," Maya said.

"So do you, sweetie," Shyla said, straightening Maya's white flower girl dress.

"I'm excited for this part."

"Me, too."

The child led them as they walked across the hall of the posh hotel to the second ballroom. Nick took his place at the end of the aisle. Maya threw petals down a white runner, Carrie and Tara following her. When the music changed, he only had eyes for one girl. Charles led his bride to him and placed their hands together. A Catholic priest performed the ceremony.

Those who knew them well understood. If it was one thing they both believed in, it was that all paths led to the same place, and the sun shined on every one of those roads.

Epilogue

Havoc was used to bloodshed. He was in the bloodshed business after all, and business was booming. He lived like a king in a country that knew how to treat royalty. Still, the American aroused his curiosity, a trait Havoc considered a hindrance in his line of work.

Clients used his firm because they didn't want to get their hands dirty and insisted upon discretion. The American, unlike other customers, wanted dirty hands. In fact, he craved it. In reality, he had reduced the army of highly trained men into nothing more than well-paid translators and gophers. Havoc watched as the tall white man with hair the color of a lion's mane deliver another round of bone-crushing strikes to the villager. The target's face had the consistency of fresh pulp.

The American had rejected all of the preferred weapons—the gun, the knife, the poison, opting to use his own body. He wouldn't even allow Havoc's men to hold back the target, demanding a fair fight. This wasn't one man wanting to rid himself of another for money or power or problems. Havoc had seen enough men die to recognize the fists of revenge.

Normally such theatrics would have irked Havoc, but he admired the American. His own fists twitched to deliver a few blows as well. The target in this case was a man rumored to have killed his first wife, although it never had been proven. The man's second wife had given birth three times, yet they had no children. There was only one explanation for such a discrepancy. People considered Havoc a cold, blood-thirsty man, and the reputation served him well, especially in his line of work, but all personas had threads of falsehood. There were three people Havoc loved—his wife, his mother, and his daughter. He cherished them above all others. If anyone ever hurt them, he'd react the same way as the American, like a skilled but feral animal.

"Flashlight," the American said, holding out his hand.

Havoc's associate handed over the heavy, long-handled torch he'd requested.

The white man shined it in front of the villager's face.

"Please let me go. I haven't done anything."

Havoc stepped forward to translate the Hindi to English, but the American held up his hand. "I understand what he's saying," the American growled, before crouching at eye-level. He whispered in the other man's ear.

The target's eyes widened as a single, fat tear fell down his cheek, causing him to wince as the salt lodged into his wounds. The American had said the phrase in Hindi in a low voice, but Havoc wore a device designed to pick up such sounds.

"This is for Asha, you bastard."

And then he delivered the last damaging blow using a weapon after all. Although Havoc found the flashlight impractical, he still admired the man's ability to swing it with such grace.

The American stood and strode over to Havoc. He wiped the blood from his face and looked at it with disdain. It wasn't his own after all. He seemed dissatisfied, but not that the deed was done. No, the man was disappointed the target hadn't presented much of a fight. Havoc handed him a clean shirt. The American's body was a myriad of scars and ink, which made him look more menacing.

"Is your blood thirst quenched, sir?" Havoc asked.

"I could kill him a thousand times and it wouldn't be enough," the American answered.

"I understand." Havoc did. He'd witnessed many men die, most by his own hand. The American, although skilled in combat, was not a fighter by trade. His hands were too clean. His eyes too clear. His manners too intact. In fact, when Havoc had met him in the dense jungle, he'd spied his client with his hands pressed against the trunk of the large Banyan tree, his head bowed as he wept openly. He figured the man had a change of heart, but when he pulled himself straighter and turned to Havoc, the rage radiated from him into the dense air of the jungle.

"I trust our business is concluded?" the American asked, his face coolly composed as if he hadn't just killed a man with his bare hands.

"Yes sir, just as you've asked. The hyenas will be released from the cages.

The American shined the bloody flashlight on the three steal cages they'd trapped the animals in. "Are they hungry?"

"Blood thirsty. They will leave no trace, sir."

"Excellent," he said, patting Havoc on the back. "What about the rest?"

"We've confirmed the target's mother is in a sanitarium. She will be there the rest of her life. She feels her deceased daughter-in-law has cursed her family and the girl's ghost haunts her." Havoc paused, pondering if he should add the last tidbit of information, but in the end, he decided not to edit. *"The daughter-in-law's spirit comes to her in the form of a goat."*

The American stared at him before he shook with laughter. The strange response heightened Havoc's curiosity.

"Something funny?"

"I couldn't have imagined it any better," the American replied. *"What about the boy?"*

"He is a man now, and we will do as you instructed. My man will approach him in a few days with the fake inheritance left to his deceased sister-in-law by her biological parents."

"Will there be any legal problems?"

"No, sir. As her only living relative, he will easily get the money. It is a large sum and will make him the wealthiest man in the village…in most villages, in fact."

"I will wire the rest of your fee tonight."

The American turned to leave the jungle. Havoc wasn't an impetuous man, but he could not silence his questions any longer.

"Mr. Montero, sir."

The American paused, slowly turning back. *"Yes."*

"Our firm has been asked to do many things, but nothing like this. Why does a rich and powerful man like yourself care about the tribulations of a small village? Why would you want one brother severely punished and the other generously rewarded?"

The American considered his answer for a moment. *"I assure you there are reasons, but that is not my story to tell. Good day."* He nodded toward the other men, all of whom looked upon him with respect. *"Gentlemen."*

Nick deleted each word with a harsh keystroke. He picked up the newspaper Charles had sent them a week ago. It had been handled many times since then, the newsprint smudged with her salted tears and the paper itself crumbled by his own hand. He had watched her read it. She'd held back her building emotion until she had fully translated it for him. Then he had taken her in his arms, and she released years of pent up anxiety and fury.

The truth of Aditi's fate was not as dramatic as Nick's version, but it was just nonetheless. The story spoke about the village man attacked in the jungle by wild animals. Shyla wanted to go to her brother, but Nick didn't think it was wise for her to travel, especially in her condition. So he had gone today in her stead as much to confirm Aditi was dead as to thank Mukash for taking care of the woman he loved. The other man refused to accept the envelope full of cash, but Nick insisted, shoving it in his hand. A wife, whose shoulders appeared permanently stooped, had survived Aditi. The farm was on the verge of bankruptcy thanks to Aditi's foolish dealings. The money would at least help in that regard. Neither he nor Mukash voiced it, but the relief in the air was evident nonetheless.

He had visited the school and all the other places he'd written about. Shyla's descriptions provided an easy roadmap for him to follow. He had even stopped at the sanatorium to inquire about her ex-mother-in-laws health. She was plagued with nightmares about her first daughter-in-law who ironically took the form of a goat. The rugged truth was richer than any fiction he could conjure.

His own thirst for revenge couldn't be sated. How badly he had wanted to climb that last water tower for her and end Aditi. But in the end, her kindness and warmth had calmed his lusty desire for vengeance. After he returned today, he had found himself still yearning for catharsis and had written one last Montero chapter. One last time to release the emotional restraints that dammed his regret the man had not expired by Nick's own hands.

He closed his eyes, taking a deep breath and backspacing the last fucking word out of existence. Now, he could go to her, his mind free of rancor and revenge. His soul cleansed, his heart pure, and belonging only to her. Just as hers belonged to him. Everything about his life had started to change when they broke bread together that cold February night so long ago. They came from two different worlds, but they recognized each other's hurt. Hurt translated the same in any language. His world shifted in every way, tilting toward the sun.

He stood and looked around the classroom before turning off the light. On the whiteboard behind him, she'd already written the next day's lessons. His classroom was directly across the hall. He taught the more advanced students English literature. They had two hundred girls at this school. Each one had suffered great atrocities in her life. But one of the most important lessons his wife had taught him was that the human spirit had an amazing capacity to heal and grow.

Shyla had gone from victim to survivor, and now she was an advocate. The girl was a natural-born leader in a battle that required many warriors. She gave lectures, ran a school for unwanted girls, and next year her novel, *The Choice Less*, would see publication. He couldn't be prouder.

He did still write every night and ran every morning, but these days he wasn't running away or chasing something. No sir, these days he was happy in his present. Max Montero would see no more books...at least none that were published. He did finish the last book, though, and even managed to give the character a happy Elaine-approved ending. A new heroine emerged from those pages. Natasha was a kick-ass kind of girl, capable of bringing a man to his knees while having him enjoy every increment of his rapid descent.

He locked up the room and headed for their small cottage behind the school. He wrote in the school building at night so he wouldn't disturb her sleep. Nick regarded the simple house with great pride. It was reminiscent of something from a Hemingway novel. A floor-to-ceiling wall of books spanned the length of the living room. Nick made a mental note to talk to Shyla about securing them to the wall— safety first. He adjusted the frame with his grandfather's cards and then the photo on the wall of Maya surrounded by her family—her mothers, Uncle Nick, and Aunt Shyla.

He headed toward the bedroom. His wife lay asleep on the bed with the night table lamp on and a book perched open on her protruding belly. Nick stripped down to his boxers and slid next to her. He wasn't planning on waking her, but she moved toward him, placing her hand on his chest. He kissed her temple and worked his way down to her lips. "Hello, Goddess," he greeted.

"Hello, husband."

"It's late," he said.

"I was trying to wait up for you."

"I thought you were attempting to teach our baby how to read already," he said, punctuating each word with a kiss. He removed the book.

She laughed before her expression turned serious with worry. "How is Mukash?"

"He's fine, baby. He'll come here to visit soon."

She exhaled a deep breath. "Thank you for going."

"I'd go to the ends of the earth for you."

"I believe you already did."

He chuckled, pressing the underside of her wrist to her lips. "How are you feeling?"

"Great."

His lips made a path down to her belly. "Morning sickness today?'

"No," she said, tousling his hair. "I think that phase is over, thank God."

"Good. Did I miss anything? Any kicking?" he asked, hoping he hadn't.

"The doctor says it's still early."

Nick pressed his ear against her stomach. He couldn't wait to be a father. They had decided they didn't want to know the gender, not that it mattered. In India, it was illegal for doctors to reveal the sex of the baby. The government had passed the law because there were too many female-targeted abortions. It was just as his wife had once told him: changing a mindset was the true battle, one that required education, faith, and hope.

"Nick, what are you doing?" she finally asked him.

"Just listening."

She giggled, tugging his hair. "My belly is not a conch shell. Come here."

He sat up and held her in his arms, kissing her head. "What else did the doctor say? I hate that I missed it."

"There will be many more appointments." She took a deep breath and turned to him, biting her lower lip.

"What is it?" he asked, his hand immediately going to her waist again, his heart rate suddenly increasing. "Is everything all right?"

"Yes, yes, baby, it is."

"Then what?"

Shyla swallowed, placing a hand on each side of his face. "The doctor heard two heartbeats on the sonogram."

"Two?"

Irrational fear seized him. "What does that mean? Our baby has two hearts?"

She laughed again, shaking her head. "Twins."

His mouth opened and snapped shut several times as he absorbed her one-word statement, which ironically doubled everything they had planned.

"Say something, Nick."

"Twins," he repeated.

"Say something else."

"Shucks."

"Nick!"

Nick swallowed, his heart filled with pride and love for this girl—woman—who had shown him the true definition of family.

"That's the best news I've ever heard, Goddess."

Meet the Author

M.K. Schiller is a hopeless romantic in a hopelessly pragmatic world. In the dark of night, she sits by the warm glow of her computer monitor, reading or writing, usually with some tasty Italian…the food that is!

She started imagining stories in her head at a very young age. In fact, she got so good at it that friends asked her to create plots featuring them as the heroine and the object of their affection as the hero.

She hopes you enjoy her stories and find The Happily Ever After in every endeavor. M.K. Schiller loves hearing from readers. Find her on Facebook, follow her on Twitter @MKSchiller, and visit her website at www.mkschillerauthor.com.

Be sure not to miss Forget Me Not by Crystal Bright, coming February 2016!

Forget Me Not

Roses are red, violets are blue.

Only one woman could make NFL star Gideon Wells walk away from the Super Bowl: His Mama, "Queen" Elizabeth, the beautiful, strong black woman who adopted him and his two white brothers when they were just kids. So when Elizabeth develops a pressing health issue, Gideon doesn't hesitate to come home and run the flower shop she loves almost as much as her boys. But there's an unexpected complication in Queen Elizabeth's shop: and that complication looks really good in a gardener's apron and pruning gloves.

This mama's boy has a naughty side too.

Janelle Gold has always thought of herself as a geek, more into books than sports, preferring brains over brawn. So a gorgeous jock like Gideon Wells is not exactly the type she usually goes for. But there's something about the hot quarterback that makes Janelle think sometimes opposites do attract, and it's not just his dedication to his family, or the fact that he can hold his own in the flower shop. There's just something irresistible about a man who stops to smell the roses.

If you enjoyed Unwanted Girl by M.K. Schilling, you'll love The Bollywood Bride by Sonali Dev. Available Now!

The Bollywood Bride

"A fresh new voice."
—Susan Elizabeth Phillips, *New York Times* bestselling author

Ria Parkar is Bollywood's favorite Ice Princess—beautiful, poised, and scandal-proof—until one impulsive act threatens to expose her destructive past. Traveling home to Chicago for her cousin's wedding offers a chance to diffuse the coming media storm and find solace in family, food, and outsized celebrations that are like one of her vibrant movies come to life. But it also means confronting Vikram Jathar.

Ria and Vikram spent childhood summers together, a world away from Ria's exclusive boarding school in Mumbai. Their friendship grew seamlessly into love—until Ria made a shattering decision. As far as Vikram is concerned, Ria sold her soul for stardom and it's taken him years to rebuild his life. But beneath his pent-up anger, their bond remains unchanged. And now, among those who know her best, Ria may find the courage to face the secrets she's been guarding for everyone else's benefit—and a chance to stop acting and start living.

Rich with details of modern Indian-American life, here is a warm, sexy, and witty story of love, family, and the difficult choices that arise in the name of both.

Prologue

How do you explain losing your words to someone? When it's the words that are gone, what would you even use? If Ria could, she would have told them it was like trying to cook without ingredients, paint without color, laugh without air. But there was nothing to tell them with.

They'd given her paper and a pen. As though it was her voice that was lost and not her words. They'd given her other things...

A ruler on her knuckles. Talk.

Hours in the punishment room. Talk. Pills that made her sleep all day. Talk. Baba's tears. Please, beta, why won't you talk?

If she could've done it, if she could have touched with her tongue all the things the monster had broken inside her when it broke her bones, if she could've spoken them without screaming so loud they burst Baba's eardrums, his tears would have done it. But the thing that took your words in the first place could hardly be what brought them back.

In the end what brought her words back was not being asked.

And him.

The day he arrived at the foreign house, he had grabbed her hand and dragged her off the couch where she wept, unable to stop. Out the door and into the sunshine, he pulled her along as they ran and ran, hand in hand.

"It's a magic tree," he shouted, the way people shouted when they ran as fast as they could. "It's like a castle, with bridges and towers and a moat."

She sped up, racing him as though she ran across grass in her bare feet every day.

It wasn't a castle at all. Just the biggest, tallest tree she'd ever seen.

"I'll race you to the top," he said, his hand still in hers.

She snatched it away and flew. Up on the bridge. Branch to branch to branch, rough bark scraping her soles, smooth leaves slapping her cheeks, higher and higher. Her feet clasping, her hands grasping until there was no higher to go. Until sunshine and wind kissed her face and she was all the way at the top of the world where there was no one else but her, and a boy she'd never seen before today on the branch below.

"Wow! Can you teach me to climb like that?" he said, beaming at her with eyes exactly like the kaleidoscope Baba had given her back before her words went. Blue and silver, stars and sparkles. Remnants of bangles and beads, opening and closing and pulling her in. But it was the wonder in his eyes that changed everything.

No one had ever looked at Ria that way—no tentativeness, no pity, no fear. None of the things she sought out in eyes. Nothing that jumped out and demanded words and stole them. Nothing but a spotless invitation letting her in, and it let her out.

Standing up there on the frailest branch at the top of the tree, looking down at the face that would change her life, Ria's tears stopped. After a week of leaking down her cheeks incessantly, they dried up just like that. For the first time since Baba had thrust her at the flight attendant and broken into a run without turning around to wave good-bye, her tears were gone.

"Who are you?" The words slipped out, her first after a year of silence.

"Vikram." He said his name like it was a badge of honor. "Vikram Jathar. You want to be friends?"

Chapter 1

Ria would have given anything to be left alone, but she knew being left alone was not in a Bollywood star's job description. Not even if you were universally acknowledged as a freakish recluse and rather aptly nicknamed The Ice Princess.

Did ice princesses battle beaded fabric? And lose?

Ria tugged at the dress pulled halfway over her head and strug- gled to free herself. But the stubborn thing grabbed her breasts in a vicious grip and tied her up in a knot of hair, arms, and pure frus- tration. Somewhere to her left her phone continued its relentless ringing.

Folding over with the skill of a contortionist, she squeezed down her breasts—a photographer had called them "magnificent" today—maybe the blasted things had swelled with pride. She put all her strength into the next tug. The dress flew off, throwing Ria back on her substantially less magnificent behind. Thank God for the rug that pooled beneath her. Standing up, she used her foot to straighten the flaming orange silk that jarred against the white minimalism of her bedroom, mimicking her mood perfectly, and grabbed her cell phone off the nightstand.

"Yes, DJ?" she said in a voice so cool no one would ever know that she'd just been sparring with her clothes. If only acting in front of the camera were as easy as acting in real life.

"Isn't that your sleazeball agent?" Her cousin's beloved all- American drawl instantly melted Ria's irritation. Her tensed-up muscles relaxed. Then just as suddenly they went into a panicked spasm.

"Nikhil? It's two in the morning! What's wrong?"

"Ria, sweetie, everything's okay. Calm down. Jeez." Nikhil's bratty smirk—the one he had perfected on her growing up— flashed in Ria's mind. "Shit, is it really two in Mumbai? Sorry, I'm not used to Malawi time yet." Nikhil and his girlfriend had just moved to Lilongwe for a medical mission. "You sound wide-awake. Are you at a shoot? Or did someone finally drag you to a party?"

Ria rolled her eyes and pulled her slip back in place. "Yeah. I decided it was time to come out of my shell." Nikhil knew better than anyone else how dearly she valued said shell. She carried the dress into her closet and hung it in its color-appropriate spot and grabbed her oldest pair of shorts off a meticulous stack, adjusting it so its meticulousness stayed undisturbed.

"Good, because there's somewhere you need to be." Excite- ment simmered in Nikhil's voice like the soda cans he liked to shake before he popped them open. Ria's heartbeat sped up. "Jen and I picked a date," he said, and the tiniest shadow of tentative- ness crept into his voice.

Ria squeezed the phone between her ear and her shoulder and pulled on the shorts, her hands suddenly clammy.

"They're giving us time off next month. After that we won't be able to get away for another year. So we're getting married in two weeks. And there's no way we're doing it without you."

She grabbed the phone off her shoulder and clutched it to her racing heart for a second before bringing it back to her ear.

"It's time to come home, Ria."

Home.

The word caught in her throat. Exactly the way her breath had when she'd ridden her bike full speed into a low-hanging branch and hit her head so hard she hadn't been able to scream or cry or breathe until she hit the ground. And then her lungs had filled so fast she thought they'd explode.

Home.

For ten years she hadn't let herself think the word out loud.

Nikhil cleared his throat. "Ria?"

She had to say something. But her breath was still trapped in her lungs. There was no way she could go back to Chicago. It had been ten years since she'd been home. Ten years since she'd pushed it away to where not even her dreams could touch it.

Nikhil sighed. "Listen, sweetie, will you at least think about it?"

She needed air. She crossed the room, the marble floor cold be- neath her bare feet, and pushed past the French doors onto the balcony. The sweltering Mumbai night slammed into her as she left the air-conditioning. She sucked in a huge humid lungful and let it out. "Nikhil, I'm in the middle of a shooting schedule." A lie. She'd sworn never to lie to him again.

He let out another sigh, heavy with disappointment. "It's okay, Ria. I understand."

Of course he understood. Every decision she'd ever made he'd stood by her like a rock, no questions asked. And here she was ready to miss his wedding. His wedding!

Wrapping an arm across her belly, she leaned into the railing. The rough-hewn sandstone scraped her elbows. Fourteen floors below, silver moonlight danced over the bay, the restless waves all turbulence under the steady rhythm. "Actually, you know what? I might be able to throw one of those diva tantrums and move things around. Give me a day to figure it out?"

"Oh, thank God!" he said with such relief that shame flooded through Ria. "You have no idea how badly I need you there. Jen's going nuts with the traditional Indian wedding thing. She wants the vows around the fire, the henna ceremony, all sorts of dances and dinners. I swear she's making some of those rituals up. She's even talking about me arriving at the wedding on a damn horse!" His voice squeaked on the word and Ria couldn't help but smile.

Jen was fire to Nikhil's earth. Despite his whining, love colored his voice.

"You poor baby. Deep breaths." Ria attempted one herself.

"And Aie's not helping at all. She's doing everything she can to encourage Jen."

Of course Nikhil's mother would support Jen explicitly. Ria knew only too well how fiercely her aunt loved. Uma Atya was the only mother Ria had ever known. All she wanted to do right now was crawl into one of her jasmine-scented hugs and block every- thing else out the way she had done as a child. "A horse isn't that bad, Nikhil. In my last film, the groom used an elephant—it's the latest craze."

"Yikes!" Nikhil said. "Have Aie or Jen watched that one yet?"

"It isn't out yet. But if you give them a hard time, I'm sending them a DVD."

"Traitor," he mumbled, laughing. Then he got serious again. "Ria, Just come home. Everything will be all right. Trust me."

And with that impossible promise he was gone, leaving Ria lean- ing over the railing, suspended over the world, memories squeezing out of her heart with the force of seedlings breaking through con- crete at the first sign of a crack. And idiot that she was, instead of pushing them back, she clutched at them the way a starving street urchin snatches at food.

She was going home.

To him.

Viky.

No, just Vikram. Not Viky. Not anymore. Only she had ever called him that. He'd been her Viky since she was eight years old. Been as much her home as the redbrick Georgian that had changed her life once. He would never let anyone call him that again, not after what she had done to him.

The bay gleamed onyx in the moonlight. In a few hours the sun would paint the waves the palest gray-blue—an entire ocean the exact color of his eyes.

Great, now she was acting like one of those lovesick drama queens she played in her films. Next she'd be grudging them their absurd hope and their contrived happy endings.

No, she couldn't go back.

But how could she not? Nikhil wasn't just her cousin, he was her brother in every way that mattered. Maybe Vikram would choose not to come. But that was just as ridiculous. Vikram couldn't miss Nikhil's wedding any more than she could. Nikhil and his par- ents, Uma and Vijay—Ria's aunt and uncle—were as much Vikram's family as they were hers. Not to mention the fact that Vikram had never backed away from anything in his life. Except her.

She, on the other hand, had backing away down to an art.

The phone buzzed in her hand. A text from her agent. Trust DJ to be up at two in the morning texting her. Usually she had no trouble indulging his compulsive excitement about a new script, but right now she couldn't think about work, not before she slipped back into Ice Princess mode. The press couldn't have come up with a better nickname for her. It was perfect. Hard and cold and unbreachable. And she needed it now more than ever.

Instead of reading the text she reached behind her, gathered the heavy curtain of hair that hung down to her waist, and slung it over one shoulder in a loose twist. The movement hurt. But the fa- miliar soreness in her muscles anchored her in the present, which is where she needed to be. This was her life. Two hours at the gym before a twelve-hour shooting schedule. Focusing on her body was the only way to keep the mess that was her mind buried deep, the numbing exhaustion the only way to put her to bed every night. Except tonight, there would be no sleep.

She leaned into the railing and stretched her back, arching up, then down like a cat. Rickshaws whirred in the distance, cars honked. Even at this hour, there was no silence in the city, no peace. Billboards and streetlights threw a twilight glow over the tightly clustered buildings and sparkled off the water like stars shooting out of an inverted sky. An intense urge to flip it the right side up overwhelmed her. She thrust her body over the railing and twisted around, letting her hair spill into the night.

The cell phone slipped from her hand and landed on something hard with a crack. She straightened up, frowning, and glanced around to find it. But it was gone.

Bloody hell. Her entire world, all her contacts, it was all in that phone. For a split second she considered not searching for it at all. It had disappeared and maybe she could disappear too. Go back home as though the past ten years had never happened.

But then the fluorescent screen flashed at her from the outer ledge of the swirling balusters and nipped her flight of fancy in the bud. There was no escape. She had to retrieve it. In one easy move- ment she pulled herself onto the railing and swung herself over it.

Her legs were too long for her body. They had always made her feel awkward and gangly. But now they made her lithe, almost graceful, as she landed on the wide cantilevered overhang. She picked up the phone and shoved it into her pocket. Her low-slung shorts slid even lower down her hips. A gust of wind caught her hair and lifted it into a flapping cape behind her. She faced the ocean. The old heady freedom of being so far away from the earth wrapped itself around her. She threw out her arms and let the un-restrained beauty of the sparkling night sink into every pore.

Suddenly a spark shone too strong, too bright, and broke through her trance. Then another. Then another. Blinking, Ria followed the flashes to the rooftop terrace of the neighboring building.

A hooded figure shrouded in black leaned over the concrete wall and reached into the meager space separating the two build- ings. A giant bazooka-like contraption projected from his hands and he had it aimed straight at her.

A lens.

The realization slammed into Ria, the force of it turning every cell in her body to lead and locking her in place, as the rapid flashes went off incessantly.

Suddenly they stopped. He moved the camera aside, looked di- rectly at her, and made a bouncing, diving action with one hand.

He was signaling her to jump.

www.ingramcontent.com/pod-product-compliance
Lightning Source LLC
Chambersburg PA
CBHW021341250626
47155CB00002B/728